DATE DUE		
	RECEIVED		
	JUN 2 5 1999		
	By		

Like a
Diamond

Also by Malcolm Macdonald

Like a Diamond

Malcolm Macdonald

St. Martin's Press
New York

For Corrina and Myles
stars who shone in a dark year

ISBN 0-312-20557-0

First published in Great Britain by Judy Piatkus (Publishers) Ltd.
●
First U.S. Edition: May 1999

10 9 8 7 6 5 4 3 2 1

F
MAC

ADH-5489

Contents

Part One

Love, at first sight

1 Gemma looked at Martha. Martha looked at Gemma. Which of them would yield first? Really it was Martha's turn to answer the bell, because Gemma had taken the breakfast up to Mr and Mrs Walker, the butler and housekeeper, only ten minutes earlier. And although Gemma was younger than Martha by five years, they were equal in status, both being parlourmaids.

The bell rang again.

"Let me spare those weary *old* bones of yours, *Miss* Unwin," Gemma said as she rose and went toward the door of the servants' hall.

"I'll save you this." Martha grinned in petty triumph as she cancelled the flag that showed the origin of the ringing — the housekeeper's parlour. (Quite unnecessarily, as it happened, for, until the de Vivians arrived to take up their new residence later that same day, no other interior bell was likely to ring.)

"You are too kind!" Gemma gave a grouchy half curtsey and flounced out.

"They'll want more hot water, my lover." Miss Eddy, the cook, handed her a cloam jug in a knitted cosy as she passed through the kitchen on her way to the servants' stair. Silver for the master and mistress; cloam for the upper servants; pewter for the scullery and stables. In some households on board wages the butler and housekeeper would have indulged themselves with silver service until the master and mistress arrived, but not the Walkers. They ran the household just as if the master and mistress were away for the day.

All the same, Gemma thought, as she started on the long climb to the housekeeper's parlour, it was a mercy that the de Vivians were arriving today, at long last.

When a household comes off board wages it suffers as many aches and pains as an old man or woman might feel on waking to a new day. It is bad enough when only a skeleton staff is kept on, but Mrs de Vivian had kept on the full complement from the days of the Deverils, the previous owners of Number One, Alma Terrace, Falmouth, and that made it far worse.

True, Mrs de Vivian had rented all their furniture three weeks back and moved it into the house at once, so that it might acquire the deep lavender-beeswax shine she expected to see her face in when she arrived; and she had moved all their bedding in a week ago, so that it could be thoroughly turned and aired in front of the fire before they had to sleep in them. But the Deverils had left back in February almost two months ago, and for most of that time there had been neither furniture to dust, nor carpets to hide the dust under; nor were there beds to make, nor baths to carry, nor clothes to sponge and press and mend ... nor all those myriad services to perform that exhaust the servant's body and quench the fires of combat. And servants thus liberated have time enough to exploit their knowledge of one another's strengths and weaknesses, the blind spots, the pet hates, the hopes and fears that drive them all beneath their usually well-disciplined exteriors.

As Gemma mounted the stair, Mrs Walker, the housekeeper, was saying to her husband, James, the butler, "One more week without a family to keep us busy, and there'd have been murder under this roof. More toast? Where *is* that girl?" She pressed the electric button again and heard the distant tinkle. "See? It *is* working. I said it was."

"I believe one more slice would not come amiss, my dear," he replied. "That's what these communists don't understand with all their talk of working-class solidarity. Take away our masters and mistresses and where's your solidarity, eh? Flown out by the window, that's where. There's only one thing unites us — repression by our middle-class masters, nothing else. We could do with some more hot water, too."

Gemma Penhallow, the younger of the two parlourmaids, stood in the doorway — a slender, good-looking girl of eighteen with light green eyes and pale ginger hair; though it was long and slightly frizzy, she kept it tied in two firmly disciplined buns, above and behind each ear.

"You took your time!" Mrs Walker snapped, holding up the empty water jug. "Arguing the toss with Martha about who should answer the bell, weren't you!" She saw the replacement jug in Gemma's hand and said, "Oh," in a softer tone.

"Shall I bring more toast?" Gemma swapped the jugs.

Mrs Walker nodded and managed the ghost of a smile as Gemma left. When they were alone again she said, "I begin to worry about that girl."

He cleared his throat and returned his attention to the two remaining slices of toast and marmalade. "Pray, why, my dear?" he asked casually.

"The de Vivians have a boy of around twenty — name of Peter. And, from one or two things Mrs de V was saying last week, I gather he's not the sort who collects stamps and butterflies. She as good as told me that one of their reasons for moving to Falmouth was to break all ties with his present set of cronies — young men of the world."

Her husband sniffed. "She's in for a rude awakening then, if she imagines the young bucks of Falmouth are all Sunday-school teachers."

"Quite. Still, that's their worry, not ours. Ours is that thing which rears its ugly head when young masters of that age and inclination live under the same roof as pretty young things like Gemma. *As we know only too well!*" she concluded pointedly.

He laughed drily and with little humour. *"He's* the one who's in for a rude awakening if he tries anything with Gemma. Especially since ... well, you know."

"I know," she replied ominously. "And *you* know. And that's the way it had better remain, Walker, dear. No one else here knows. None of the other servants knows why Ruby really left us. So — ignorance is bliss, eh? There's certainly no need for the de Vivians to hear of it."

"I'm not so sure we're the only two who know — apart from Gemma herself, of course. She may have told Martha. You know the way they chatter after lights-out up there."

"Not her." She shook her head emphatically. "She felt the shame of it more than anyone. More than the Deverils did. She's never so much as mentioned it, not even to me. And she has no reason to hold her ..."

"To you?" Walker frowned. "But why should she mention it to you? I mean, you were there. We both were."

"That's what I'm saying. I was involved from first to last. I even saw it coming. So she has no reason to be coy with me. I often thought she'd like to talk about it — such a loss. A *twin* sister!" She broke off as a new thought occurred to her. "By the by," she said, "I forgot to tell you — *Mister* de Vivian asked me to make sure no one speaks of twins in his wife's hearing. The young master had a twin once — Peter and Paul, they were —

and she never got over Paul's death, he said. Anyway — to get back to Gemma Penhallow — she's never once referred to the business about Ruby, from that day to this. Not to me. Not once. Not so much as a flicker of an eyelid when the topic of servant girls keeping their honour has come up. No!" She shook her head again. "I agree with you there — she has a hardness in her as would blunt the blade of any young master who tried his luck. There'll be none of *that* nonsense from our Gemma. But as for Master Peter ..."

"Where *is* she with that toast?" her husband asked irascibly as he licked remnants of the marmalade from his fingertips.

At that moment Gemma was standing over Bridget Condron, the little sixteen-year-old kitchen skivvy, who was hard at work scrubbing down the front steps. "Well?" she asked.

"Well what?" the girl responded pugnaciously.

"I told you to get another rack of toast from Miss Eddy, that's what. And take this down, while you're at it." She thrust the empty jug at the skivvy.

Bridget butted it aside with her shoulder. "And I'm after telling you I'm busy at these steps. Go fill it yourself. Have you no hands on them arms nor legs beneath them skirts?"

"I'm not going to argue with you, Condron," Gemma said. "I'm simply telling you — go and get that toast. At once."

"And I'm telling you no." Bridget went on calmly scrubbing the doorsteps. "Not unless cook says I may. You go ask Miss Eddy. She's the one I take my orders from — not you. And I just know what she'll tell you! She'll eat you a mile off."

"Hellew, hellew, hellew!" Henry Trewithen, the valet-footman, parodied an upper-class accent. "All the jolly jollies, eh!" He rubbed his hands enthusiastically. "Trouble on the lower decks? Muttering among the serfs?" He noticed a thread sticking out of his white gloves and picked it off fastidiously. "Can't have that."

"Piss off, yew!" Bridget cried, not even pausing in her toil. "*Some* of us has to work around here."

She was scrubbing so hard she did not see the shock her words — or that one word in particular — had given the two upper servants. A lesser man than Trewithen would have burst out laughing, but years of maintaining a poker face while waiting at a table where outrageous things were being said came to his aid. Besides, to laugh at so shocking an outburst with young Gemma there would have lost him all her regard. At the slightest suggestion of coarseness, in word or gesture, she turned into a veritable ice-maiden. He leaned over Bridget and, tipping her a wink where Gemma wouldn't see it, said severely — and in his normal Cornish accent, "If you ever use such coarse language again, maid, you'll be out of this house within the hour. Have you got that?"

"Yes, Mister Trewithen," she intoned in a tendentious singsong, half sighing the words.

"I wouldn't have you *touch* their toast now," Gemma said, salvaging what dignity she could from the girl's refusal to obey her. She stumped off through the house, down the long corridor to the kitchen.

"Take a tip, my lover," the footman said when she was safely out of earshot. "Never use a coarse expression or tell a coarse tale or make a coarse gesture when that one's around."

"Jaysus!" Bridget relaxed and mopped her brow. "What is she — a runaway nun or something?"

"She just will not tolerate coarseness, that's all. And somehow she makes the rest of us conform. When my sister called and took a dish o' tay with us, two weeks ago it was. Your day off, I believe? Anyway, she told a harmless little tale — leastways, the rest on us thought it harmless enough, but not Miss pure-as-the-driven-snow Gemma! She told my sister …"

"What tale? Go on — tell us. My arms think my head's a tyrant." The girl sat back on her heels and trained her large, searching eyes on him.

He chuckled. "Don't get your hopes up. I said 'twas a harmless wee tale about a little girl who wouldn't let a little boy into her bedroom. She was in the bed, see? And the boy asks why not. And she says 'cos she's got her nightdress on and her mammy told her never to let little boys into her bedroom when she's got her nightdress on. And then there's a short pause, see, and then she calls out, 'All right, you may come in now. I've tooken my nightdress off!' That's all. I said 'twas harmless enough, but Miss lawdy-daw Gemma didn't think so. She told my sister to apologize or be gone. Honest! Go and never come back. You could have cut the air and sold it to the silent monks. So you just mind your PS and QS when she's around, see?"

They were both laughing as a furious Gemma emerged from the kitchen with a full rack of toast. "Nice for some!" she said as she started back up the stairs to the housekeeper's parlour.

"Keep out of her way for a while, eh?" was his final advice to Bridget as he set off after Gemma.

He caught up with her on the first landing. "Don't be too hard on the kiddy, eh, Miss Penhallow?" he suggested as he followed her up the passageway. "She is Irish, after all."

"What's being Irish got to do with it?" Gemma snapped. "You're in my way."

He leaped aside like a dancer. "She's a fish out of water here, that's what I mean. God knows where she ought to be but ..."

"About time!" the butler barked at Gemma as he jerked open his door and saw the pair of them standing there. "Do we think we have time to stand around gossiping, eh! Is the silver all set out?"

"Yes, Mister Walker," Trewithen replied.

"And spread with Silvo?"

"Yes, Mister Walker."

"Well, cut along and start polishing. I'll be down as soon as I've shaved — which I would be already if *someone* had hurried up with the toast."

Trewithen stared at Gemma, daring her to admit that she had tried to palm the chore off on little Bridget; but Gemma just muttered something about the stove not wanting to draw, what with the wind being in the northeast. The butler didn't even bother to listen.

"God knows where she ought to be," Trewithen went on as if their previous conversation had suffered no interruption — a trick familiar to all in service — "but if we treat her right and don't try to iron out too much of her spirit all at once, we could make something useful of her, don't you think?"

Gemma pursed her lips but did not argue.

He pressed his point home. "Act of charity, eh? Never know when we'll be in need of help ourselves. Eh?" He bent forward and peered up at her, for she was trying to turn her face away. "Eh — come on now."

She relented and smiled at last. "Has anyone ever been able to stay angry with you for longer than ten seconds, Mister Trewithen?" she asked.

"Angry?" He spoke as if the word amazed him. "Were you angry with me, my lover? Why on earth should anyone get angry with me?"

"Well, I'm not," she said. "And to prove it, I'll give you a hand with the silver — if you have a spare pair of gloves."

"You shall have the best," he promised, leading the way to the butler's pantry, whose door he unlocked with a flourish; Trewithen did most things with a theatrical flourish. Sometimes Gemma wondered if he was entirely sane.

She put on her gloves and, picking up one of the smaller pieces, polished the Silvo off the cartouche. "So that's the de Vivian coat of arms," she murmured, gazing at the engraving. "A hussar about to chop a toy bridge in half. What's it mean?"

The valet put on a superior face. "I don't know about making something useful out of little Condron out there — we'd better start with *you,* my 'ansum. That is not a coat of arms, it's just the crest. And it's not a hussar about to chop a toy bridge in half. The proper heraldic description, in case you're interested, is: 'Issuing from a bridge of one arch, embattled, at each end a tower, a demi-hussar of the Eighteenth Regiment, in dexter a sabre, in sinister a pennant, flying to sinister, gules.' So there! And the motto, *Vive revictmus,* means 'Live like a man who knows he will survive.' See?"

She stared at him, open-mouthed in admiration. "How do you know these things, Mister Trewithen?" she asked.

"I don't, Miss Penhallow — or I didn't until last week. But the minute this silver arrived, I went down the library and looked it up." He glanced slyly at her. "As a matter of fact, you Penhallows have a crest, too — but I suppose you know that."

She laughed, not believing him for a moment.

"It's true," he assured her. " 'A goat, (passant,) azure ...'"

"A *what?*"

"A goat ..."

She shook her head and laughed. "I'm not going to believe that. You're *codding* me, as little Condron says. A goat, indeed!"

"Believe it or not," he went on mildly, "it's a fact. A goat means wisdom, by the way, so you needn't think it's an insult Your goat is 'hoofed and attired' — that means with horns — 'or.' So there you are!"

"Or what?"

"No, 'or' means golden in heraldry. 'Gules' is red."

"Ho ho!" She laughed and stuck her nose in the air. "So the Penhallows have real gold and the de Vivians only have red paint!" More soberly she added, "Mind you — the Penhallows did once have lands and title." Then, remembering her manners, she asked if the Trewithens had a crest, too.

He shook his head and pretended to weep. "The Trewarthens, yes, even the Trewarthas. But not us Trewithens. Boo hoo!"

They laughed and set about polishing the crested silver with some vigour.

After a while she glanced at him shyly, for he was some ten years her senior, and risked saying, "You're something of a dark horse, Mister Trewithen. Where did you learn all that about heraldry and suchlike?"

"A valet has many idle hours to fill, my lover. It's not like being a lady's maid. A maid has always got lace to take off, lace to blue, lace to goffer, lace to sew back on, velvet to revive … et cetera, et cetera. I only hope Mister de Vivian has more than astronomy books in his library. A good book is a powerful killer of time."

"Talking of lady's maids …" Gemma ventured.

"Yes?"

"Did you hear anything about Mrs de V having one? Is she going to bring one with her?"

He shook his head. "I don't think she is. She must have had one but I can't imagine any lady's maid being willing to leave Plymouth for the same position in Falmouth." He gave out a single laugh. "The Walkers would have a fit to hear me say it but it's the truth. The world has changed since they started in service. Servants interview masters and mistresses these days, not the other way round. Why d'you ask, anyway?"

"Well …" She licked her lips hesitantly. "I was wondering if I might have the makings of one. I've already begun learning …" She paused.

"Yes? Learning what?"

"You won't tell anyone? Swear it?"

"I swear it."

"The others would only laugh if they knew. They'd say I was giving myself airs."

"Why d'you think I wouldn't, then?"

"Well — learning all that about heraldry. You'd understand. The thing is, you know I go to my mother's in Penryn every Tuesday evening?"

"Yes."

"Well, I don't. At least, that's not all I do. I see she's all right, then I come back to the Drill Hall ..."

He laughed. "You! In the Territorials?"

"No!" She laughed at the idea and then, shouldering a long soup ladle like a musket, marked time, saying, "Left, left, left, right, left!" Then, dropping the horseplay, she explained, "The WEA holds classes there, too. And I've been ..."

"What's that, then — WEA?"

"The Workers' Educational Association. We meet in the committee rooms upstairs. I've been taking French classes there. The teacher is Miss Isco-Visco, who teaches French at the grammar school."

"That's a grand old English name," he commented.

"She's French. She says I'm quite good."

"Voulez-vous promenader avec moi ce soir?" he asked, making no attempt at a French accent.

She laughed and said, *"Promener.* Not *promenader."*

He shrugged ruefully. "And it's all in aid of becoming a real lady's maid, eh?"

She nodded. "Not to pretend I'm French, of course. But just so's I'm not left out among the others."

He had never met anyone, man or woman, so concerned about the opinion of those around her. But now he understood why she had so generously offered to help with the silver. "Maybe ..." He spoke as if thinking aloud. "Maybe I could suggest it — in passing, you know — to Mister Walker? If the topic were ever raised, I'm sure he'd ..."

"Oh!" She stared at him as if the idea had never crossed her mind. *"Would* you, Mister Trewithen? That would be so kind. Also ..." She bit her lip.

"Yes, Miss Penhallow?" Her terrier-like persistence both amused and impressed him.

"Well, Mrs de Vivian has a daughter, we hear. Miss Beatrice?"

He nodded. "Aged eighteen. Actually, there are three daughters ..."

"Yes, but Miss Beatrice is the only one still at home."

"And you think the two of them might share a lady's maid — in short, *two* reasons to advance your cause?"

"Well ..." She cleared her throat and braced herself to say, "Actually, I was thinking ... what with the de Vivians being so rich ... perhaps they'd need *two* lady's maids? One apiece."

"You and ... Martha?" he teased, knowing that Martha Unwin — a big-boned country girl who could just about read and write — would be quite unsuited to the post.

Gemma laughed. "No! I'm fond of Martha, of course, but — no. I was thinking of my cousin, Lucy Carminow. She was here at Christmas."

He nodded, having a vague memory of the girl. "Age?"

"Seventeen. She'll be eighteen come the fall. They live in Penryn, too. She's been to domestic school and she can ply a needle so's you'd think it was little fairy's work. So — if they wanted a lady's maid each — two girls who get on well together and who wouldn't argue about helping each other out ... well ... you see?" She broke off and grinned. "Do the Carminows have a coat-of-arms, too?"

"Crest." He corrected her. "I'll look it up tell you tomorrow."

Later that morning, when she and Martha were making up the beds with the by now well-aired bedding the de Vivians had sent on ahead, it suddenly struck her that Trewithen must have looked up the Penhallow crest entirely off his own bat — all that stuff about the goat 'attired' with the golden horns and so forth.

That was interesting, surely?

It showed he had some kind of interest in her, taking the trouble to look up her family crest. She wondered what sort of a husband he'd make. Not necessarily to her ...

Well, yes, to her.

He was quiet, reserved, abstemious, a diligent worker ... She was sure he'd saved a good share of his wages, meagre though they were. He never uttered a coarse word — at least, not in her presence — and just look at the way he'd pitched into the Condron creature for saying that disgusting cuss.

He was even-tempered, too. She'd seen him annoyed, of course, but never angry. And, as she'd told him, it was impossible to stay cross with him for more than a minute on end. Also he was interested in the world — always reading bits of this and snippets of that from improving books. Ambitious but not absurdly so. He'd never over-reach himself, put on airs, make himself seem ridiculous.

It was curious she'd never thought of him in a romantic light before now. Actually, even now it was hardly *romantic*. She distrusted romance. She wanted nothing to do with it. Romantic marriages always ended in disaster. One should choose a husband with all the care that went into life's other important decisions, like what household to work in, where to live, where to worship, and so forth.

She decided she must take a greater interest in him from now on, now that the possibility of choosing him as a husband had occurred to her.

2 Moving ought to be so simple. You get in touch with a firm whose daily business it is to pack up people's belongings and transport them safely from the old place to the new, and they send in a band of skilled men whose one aim is to make the whole process as smooth and painless as possible. And so your new life in your new surroundings settles easily and calmly into its old familiar ways.

It could have been like that for the de Vivians when, on that bright, breezy Tuesday afternoon in early April, 1910, they moved from Plymouth to Number One, Alma Terrace, Falmouth — a distance of some sixty miles. Indeed, as far as the physical movement of books, heirlooms, clothing, and bricabrac was concerned, the move passed off as conveniently as anyone could wish. The snag — the fly in the ointment — was in human form. To be precise, in the form of Peter de Vivian, the family's son and heir.

What made the events of that afternoon so very annoying was that Ada de Vivian had devoted *days* to the planning of the move, and, up until that moment, everything had gone so well.

For example, almost all their furniture in both the old house and the new was rented, right down to the last lace curtain; so it was merely a matter of sending one lot back to the repository in Plymouth and choosing a new lot from an equally well-stocked repository in Falmouth. Then, too, she had kept on the ten servants employed by the Deverils, the former owners of Number

One — that is to say, a butler, a footman-valet, a housekeeper, a cook, two parlourmaids, a kitchen maid, a gardener, an under-gardener who doubled as groom, and a boy; so there was none of that awkwardness which usually follows the assembly of a new household — the settling-down phase during which maids claim privileges never granted them in any previous position while butlers and housekeepers try to reassert powers that actually died out with old Queen Victoria.

Then, again, the de Vivians had rented the new furniture three weeks before moving in, to give the servants time to polish it, wax the drawer runners, camphor the wood, and do all those other things that a repository *ought* to do but never does. Finally, a week before the move, she had sent down a full set of bedclothes: feather beds and the big square pillows for herself and her husband, who still slept semi-upright in the old-fashioned manner; and oblong pillows and hard coir mattresses of a character-forming nature for Beatrice and Peter, her only two children still living at home; and, of course, linen sheets, woollen blankets, down quilts, and art-silk bedspreads for all. These were to be aired for three days in front of roaring fires in the bedrooms, which also warmed and dried the house to welcome them.

So, really and truly, all that she and her family needed to do was walk into their new home and start living. Every bag, box, trunk and tea chest was labelled, so the removal men and servants would know without being told where everything was to go. Unfortunately, just as Nature abhors a vacuum, so there is something in the human spirit that cannot abide simplicity. The de Vivians' wealth had made the house purchase a mere bagatelle; four thousand-odd pounds was hardly even pocket money to them. And the institutions of modern society — the railways, the removals firm, the furniture repositories, and the existence of an universal servant class, each grade well schooled in all its duties — had combined to make the move as easy as drifting down a broad, placid stream in a comfortable boat on a summer afternoon. But from the moment they boarded the westbound train at Plymouth, Ada de Vivian began to fret. A sense of foreboding possessed her and yet she could not say what caused it — she only knew that it had everything to do with young Peter.

Her husband, Terence, was happy enough. He had chosen Number One, Alma Terrace, for the high turret that embellished its northwest corner. During the past three weeks a small team of carpenters, engineers, and plumbers had erected a revolving dome upon it, large enough to house his new ten-inch reflector. He had *almost* discovered a new comet last year but some bounder in France had beaten him to it. He was sure that the smoke from all the factories, yards, and ships in Plymouth had hindered him; but the prevailing sou'westerlies over Alma Terrace blew clear off three thousand miles of ocean. He was now on tenterhooks, dreaming of the first cloudless night. As the train chugged over Brunel's bridge, high above the Tamar, he gazed back at the city's sprawl and down at the anchored fleet and bade them a silent goodbye without a twinge of regret. Even so, he might never have summoned the energy to move house if Ada had not insisted on it. She had lately detected a disturbing trend among their friends and acquaintances in Plymouth — one that had made it essential for her to get her two youngest children away as soon as possible.

The people in their circle had all been much of the same age — she was now forty-three while Terence was fifty-four — and most of their children had already fled the nest, leaving one or two fledglings about to try their wings. In the de Vivian's own case, for instance, there was Beatrice, who had just turned nineteen, and Peter, who would come of age in October. Beatrice really ought to be engaged by now; indeed, she ought already to be married. Florence, her eldest sister, had become engaged at sixteen, married at eighteen, and now, at twenty-four, had a family of three; and Charlotte, her elder sister, had married at twenty, after a three-year engagement, and now, at twenty-two, was about to be delivered of her first child. If Beatrice did not land a fiancé this Season, after the tragedy of last year, spinsterhood would be staring her in the face. Unfortunately, the prospect did not seem to ruffle her in the least. Anyone would think she actually *wanted* to be an old maid.

And Peter ought really to start thinking about the army or the law. His idea was that, having left school with no examinations to his credit (and distinctions in woodwork and metalwork were certainly not to his credit), he could now devote himself to sailing, golf, hunting, and ballroom dancing. Well, that had to be stamped on severely. Naturally, he promised it was only for a 'sabbatical year' but she wasn't swallowing that one.

In short, neither young person would take life seriously, and she blamed Plymouth for it — specifically, their circle of friends there. Wealth had gone to their heads. The de Vivians were an old landed family; in fact, they had come over with the Conqueror. But they were one of the few landed families with the good sense to sell up before the great agricultural depression of the last century had made land worthless. They had moved into merchant banking instead. Terence's father had gone one better. Back in the 1870s he had sold his share in the merchant bank to the rest of the family and put the proceeds into everyday banking, starting with three branches in Plymouth. By the Nineties there were de Vivian banks in every town in Devon and Cornwall.

But the de Vivians had always known how to get out of the game while they were still ahead. Terence, for instance, knew very well that in matters of business he was no equal to his father. So, when the old man died in 1904, he had sold out to Barclay's and retired a millionaire, (though one never said anything so vulgar, of course). He still sat on the board of Barclay's, for which he received a little honorarium of twenty thou' a year, but he knew, and every banking insider knew, that it was merely because the name of de Vivian still inspired confidence among the bank's West Country customers. A powerful telescope and a cloudless sky were all Terence asked of life nowadays. And meals on time, of course. And a smooth-running household that called upon him to make decisions as infrequently as possible.

By contrast, most of their friends in Plymouth — or former friends as she now hoped they were — had come from nowhere in a mere three generations. Or even two. Indeed, in several distressing instances, they had made their pile entirely in the present generation. Not for them the caution born of centuries, of watching fools and their money confirming the old adage as they passed from clogs to silk slippers and back again to clogs in three generations. The *nouveaux riches* of Plymouth had been conscientious enough to see their elder children well settled. Ada, who considered herself pretty free of any taint of snobbery, had had no quarrel with them in those days. Indeed, Florence's husband, William Shipman was almost exactly what his surname implied; one day he would inherit the city's leading shipping agency, founded in 1837. And Roger Pearce, Charlotte's husband, was the grandson of an humble ship's chandler in Devonport, though now Pearce & Co. was a big supplier and victualler to ships, with depots in Bristol and Cardiff as well as the head office in Plymouth. So, with two daughters married into 'trade,' no one could call Ada a snob. (It was *wholesale* trade, of course.) But when it came to settling the younger offspring, it seemed that the stamina of the Plymouth arrivistes had weakened and died — either that or the younger half of the younger generation had developed a stubborn mind and will of its own. The girls wanted votes and freedom while the boys wanted sailing and golf.

The idea of doing something honourable and useful with one's life hardly seemed to enter the minds of those younger sons who had been Peter's contemporaries — just as the prospect of securing a good marriage and making a home and family seemed to hold no allure for the girls in Beatrice's circle. Over their firmament one word stretched from horizon to horizon in an arc of rainbow colours — *amusement.* Ada had once overheard Peter saying to his cronies, "What's the point of having all those de Vivian ancestors slaving away, century after century, getting richer and richer, if no one is ever going to have good, simple, old-fashioned *fun* with the proceeds!"

Naturally, he would never have voiced such thoughts out loud at home, but if there was ever a single moment when Ada had decided it was time to leave cosmopolitan Plymouth and settle in old-world Falmouth, where loftier principles might still imbue the young, that was it.

And yet, now that the deed was done, the die cast, the boats burned, she could not help but fret. Her eye fell on Beatrice — dear, dreamy Beatrice, head buried as always in a novel — and she fretted. Her eye moved across to Peter, gazing superciliously out at the greening Cornish countryside, a smile twitching at his lips as he contemplated heaven alone knew what devilment in the unknown territory ahead, and she fretted.

She would have fretted a great deal more had she known what was about to happen, the moment they arrived at their new home.

3 Cornwall proclaims its independence of England at its very border. Carriages and cars from Plymouth cannot simply drive across some notional line upon a map; they must all converge on Saltash and cross the Tamar by ferry. Others must cross the same river higher up by bridge. It is as if the county were an island. Indeed, if the Cornish were to dig a mere five miles of canal, linking the headwaters of the river with the Atlantic at the very northern end of the county, they would make it one. The scheme has crossed the mind of many a true Cornishman down the years.

For travellers by rail the separation is made even more dramatic by Brunel's mighty bridge, which soars at a dizzying height over the deep chasm of the river and the chains of the car ferry. And the moment it reaches the Cornish shore the track curves sharply south to give the passengers one last, lingering look at England, as if to say, 'There! Now you really have left it all behind.'

Such, at least, were Peter's thoughts as he took his own last, lingering look at Plymouth, the city of all his twenty-one years (well, *nearly* twenty-one), the home of all his friends, and the arena of all his pleasures. He gazed until he could no longer see it from inside the compartment; then he rose and went out into the corridor, rising on tiptoe and craning his neck until the embankment and the greening hedgerow cut him off at last. The lump in his throat almost choked him.

"Penny for 'em?"

He glanced round to find that Beatrice, his younger sister, had joined him.

He pulled himself together swiftly. "Not really repeatable," he told her. "It's all very well for you. There are libraries and bookshops in every town. But what's there for *me* in Falmouth?" He spoke the name with a sneer.

"One of the best yacht clubs in the world?" she suggested.

He shrugged, unable to deny it.

She went on: "I don't know about golf but there are three good hunts around Falmouth and some pretty good country to hunt in, I should think."

"That remains to be seen." He waved a disgusted hand at the passing scenery. "Not if *this* is anything to go by. Look at it! And we're still within reach of the civilizing influence of England. Patchwork fields, tiny houses, muddy little lanes already overgrown — and it's only April yet …"

"What's wrong with it?" Beatrice protested. "I think it all looks extremely picturesque."

"What's *wrong* with it?" he echoed. "What's right? Can you imagine the sort of lives people lead in little backwaters like that? Probably the high point of their week is to stand in the grocer's and marvel at the bacon-slicing machine. I've a good mind to open the door and chuck myself out this minute."

"You could enroll at Plymouth art school. That would get you back to civilization during term time at least."

He shook his head despondently. "There's sure to be an art school in Truro. Or even Falmouth. If not, Pater would probably endow one just to make sure I'd stay at home. Besides, I object on the principle of the thing."

"What principle? I'd have leaped at the chance — but, of course, they wouldn't offer it to *me*. Lady art students carry a discount in the marriage market."

"I object to the principle that I should *do* something in life. Why should I? I'd only be depriving someone who *needs* the salary. Besides, aren't there enough busybodies in the world as it is? Up early and late. Parading their good intentions. Grabbing the world by the ear. Telling everyone they must reform. They miss the point."

"What is the point, then?"

"It's not the *world* that needs reforming, it's *them* themselves. I don't need anyone to reform me. If I've been smart enough to choose rich parents, why can't I just enjoy it? Why do I have to *do* something as well? What does Pater *do,* come to that?"

"He's retired — be fair. Shall we see if there's a buffet car somewhere on this train?"

"There isn't." He spoke with a morose kind of triumph. "They disconnected it at Plymouth. I suppose the cost of putting in troughs for the Cornish to eat out of isn't worth it. Oh God!" He mimed the tearing-out of his hair. "What am I going to *do*? It's going to be a daily diet of 'What regiment, Peter? What law office, Peter? What profession, Peter?' until I give in. You're lucky. All that's expected of you is to find a man, get him to the altar, and say, 'I will'!"

After a pause she curled her gloved fingers around the door handle and said, "Shall I jump first?"

He slipped an arm around her shoulders and gave her a brief hug of encouragement. "You really mean it, do you — this indifference to marriage?"

She looked at him in surprise. "How can you doubt it?"

"Well ..." His arm dropped. "I'm not the only one. Several of the chaps said it was a rattling good wheeze for getting a fellow interested in you — being jolly and warm and open and amusing and sympathetic and yet utterly indifferent to romance and all that sort of rot."

She laughed without a trace of humour. "It's not a 'wheeze.' Let me assure you."

"But it's like saying you don't like ... mangoes, or something."

"But I've never tasted mangoes."

"Exactly! You've never tasted marriage, either — that's my whole point."

She said nothing.

"Well?" he prompted. "You haven't, have you!"

"Florence has. Charlotte has." She named their elder sisters.

"And they don't advise it?" He was surprised.

Beatrice now wished she had not spoken.

"What's Flo got to complain about?" he asked. "Bill's going to inherit the biggest shipping agency in Plymouth. And living at Elburton Lodge, with its own park and boating lake ... forty servants ... three lovely children ... most women would give ..."

"Yes, yes!" Beatrice interrupted testily.

"And Lottie's sitting pretty, too, I should think. Roger may not be an Adonis but they say Pearce and Co. are the biggest ships' victuallers in the west ... what's up?"

Beatrice had her eyes tight closed and was pressing her knuckles to her forehead. "Really, Pete!" she said. "If you are going to live in idleness, you might while away the time by learning a little tact."

"Tact?" He was genuinely puzzled. "What on earth did I say that was tactless?"

"Oh, only that my two sisters have made such excellent matches, and live in grand houses, and have all the money and servants they could possibly need! D'you think I'm not aware of it? D'you think Mater and Pater don't din it into me every chance they get? I'll give them two weeks to settle in down in Falmouth and then they'll start on me again."

Peter shifted uncomfortably and transferred his gaze to the despised landscape. "See what you mean, old thing," he said. "Sorry and all that." After a pause he added, "D'you really not want to marry at all — or is it just the sort of people *they* want you to marry?"

"I don't know." She rubbed her eyes until he pulled her hands away, warning her she'd make them look inflamed. "I was walking along one of those little backstreets the other night, just off the western end of the Hoe — where the workhouse used to be. That very calm evening, remember? With the smoke going straight up from all the chimneys. Not a cloud in the sky and a frost as soon as the sun went down. The lamplighters were just going round and people were lighting the gas in their little parlours and drawing the curtains. You got this wonderful feeling of the day's toil ending and all sorts of secret lives beginning ..."

"Poky little lives," he sneered, "in poky little rooms where they have to think twice before they throw another lump of coal on the fire. You'd die of boredom after half an hour of it, Bea."

"I wouldn't, you know," she replied calmly. "If we'd ever had a good-looking coachman, I'd have run away with him by now. Honestly. I'd love to be poor. Well ... not exactly poor but just ordinary middle class — where you have to count every penny. Either that or I'd like to be an explorer. Or go with an explorer on his expeditions. Across the Gobi Desert or up the Congo or to the North Pole ... wherever."

Peter laughed at the disparity between these two dreams, which his sister had put forward as if they were close alternatives. "Anything else while you're at it?" he asked.

"Well ..." She hesitated.

"Let me guess. A circus lady — part of the high-wire act?"

"Yes!" she replied, as if that particular variant of her ambition had not actually occurred to her before.

"But that isn't what you were going to say."

She became wary again. "I think there's a certain fascination in wickedness, don't you?" she mused.

He eyed her askance and said, "Depends."

"I wouldn't mind marrying a rogue," she said. "A real rogue, I mean — not the sort of milk-and-water rascals you and your cronies were in Plymouth."

"What d'you mean?" he expostulated.

"Stealing policemen's helmets ... dressing up as labourers and digging holes in the street ... masquerading as an Indian maharajah and ..."

Peter laughed. "It fooled the admiral. If Terry's make-up hadn't started running, we'd have been given a grand tour of the entire fleet ..."

"But I mean a real rogue, not just a prankster. A jewel thief, say. Or a swindler. You remember that man who swindled our bank out of ten thou'?"

"A chap called May. Or Hay?"

"May. Charley May — remember the joke: It wasn't a case of Charley may so much as Charley *did!* He did us out of ten thou' and grandad said he was the most likeable rogue you could ever hope to meet. He'd charm the fishes up onto the banks, he said." A wistful look came into her eyes. "I wonder if he's married? He must be about due to come out of prison by now." Her voice acquired a harder edge as she added, "Of course, there are two things against him."

"What?"

"One — he got caught. And two — he didn't have a title. But a rogue with a title — hee hee! Just think how it would tear Mater and Pater in two! Their youngest daughter married to a lord! Lord Lovat, let's call him." She imitated her mother: " 'Have you met our daughter ... Lady Lovat, don't you know?' And all the time he'd be the world's greatest uncaught jewel thief and swindler! Of course, he'd only rob the rich — people like us, who can afford it ..."

"A sort of Robin Hood?" Peter was warming to the idea.

"Oh no! No giving to the poor — or not directly. Just the odd library or children's playground or public footbath — enough to get a thoroughly undeserved reputation for nobleness. Incidentally, why are they called *foot*baths — d'you know? I'm sure people bathe much more than their feet in them." But when Peter drew breath to reply, she waved him to silence. "Don't tell me. I'm sure it's euphemistic in some way. Most misnomers are. But if you want to do me the most enormous favour, brother darling, you'll make the acquaintance of a titled young man, *beastly* handsome, who's engaged in some kind of villainy." She smiled sweetly. "D'you think you might manage that for me?"

"I shall make it my very first commission as soon as we are settled in Falmouth," he promised.

"You'll have to do it before June, though."

"Why?"

She glanced heavenward. "Because of the Season! Mater and Pater are bound to take me up to try and marry me off ... why the grin?"

"It's just occurred to me that they might take me this year, too." His grin widened. "So, even if I don't find you a wicked lord down there in Falmouth — which, let's face it, is a pretty tall order — I'm almost certain to run across a whole pack of 'em in London."

"It's a bargain," she said. "Meanwhile, I'll support you in any little nefarious scheme you may be hatching, all right?"

He laughed. "Now that's what I *call* a bargain." Then, serious again, he said, "Actually, I think I might try to build my racing dinghy at long last."

She flapped a hand at him. "Oh, you and your woodwork!"

"Well, I shan't have the distractions that surrounded me in Plymouth."

Back in the compartment, separated by mahogany and thick plate glass, Ada said, "They seem to be taking it very well, my dear. Of course there's no reason why Beatrice shouldn't — since she formed no deep attachment of any kind in Plymouth. But I thought we were going to have to endure weeks of moping and surliness from Peter."

"He's maturing, dear," her husband replied. "Of course, he'd never admit it, but I think he was beginning to grow just a little tired of the frivolous sort of company he was keeping in Plymouth. I shouldn't be at all surprised if he didn't settle down quite quickly in Falmouth and turn his mind to more serious pursuits ... cultivate loftier ... you know." He smiled complacently and returned to his almanacs.

"Mmh." Ada wished she could entirely agree.

4 As the Greeks at Marathon must once have stared anxiously at the vastly outnumbering army of the Persians, as weary Saxons after Hastings must once have peered at the invading Normans, knowing them to be their new masters, so the four de Vivians and their ten servants eyed one another at their moment of meeting on that bright Tuesday afternoon in the early April of 1910.

Ada de Vivian had already met all ten of them, of course, and her husband had met the principals, at least; but the two younger de Vivians had not given them a second thought until then. In their privileged world, servants were always *there,* just as shops and libraries and railways were there. One hardly thought of railways in between the occasions when one actually needed them; and even then one put up with their service rather than actually enjoyed it.

This coolness was matched on the servants' side, too. To them, masters and mistresses — and their offspring — were more like institutions than actual people. Some were harsh and demanding, in the manner of the army, others more benevolent, in the manner of a church mission; but all were impersonal. Even the best came no closer to the warmth of humanity than a strict and remote father might come to his children. So, when ten servants lined up in welcome before Number One, Alma Terrace, and four de Vivians descended from the hackney that had brought them up from the station, expectations were low and wariness was high. And the wariest among them wore the widest smiles of all.

Ada had been trained in the ways of a hostess from her earliest nursery days. To recall a mere ten names and to fit them correctly to their faces was child's play to her. "Walker!" she exclaimed delightedly as she advanced to greet the butler.

A tiny smile twitched at the corners of his lips as he dipped his head in acknowledgement.

"Walker," de Vivian murmured.

The concessionary smile vanished and the second dip of the head was solemn — not so much man-to-man as manservant-to-man.

"And Mrs Walker," Ada said with equal delight though in a calmer manner. To the two of them she said, "These are Miss Beatrice and Master Peter."

Nods, curtseys, and cool smiles were exchanged among them, as was appropriate.

Then, like platoon commanders with a visiting bigwig, the butler and housekeeper took a pace forward and prepared to conduct the de Vivians down the rest of the line.

Ada, however, was keen to show that she knew them all already, partly because it was good for their *esprit,* but mainly to let them know she was not only alert and observant but also had an excellent memory. So she kept a pace or two ahead, leaving the Walkers to introduce each servant to her husband and the two young de Vivians.

"Miss Eddy." She smiled at the cook, who seemed surprised to have her name remembered. "We have often spoken since of the hotpot you made on our first visit. I hope you can live up to the high reputation you have now earned with our children."

Flustered and delighted, the cook curtseyed and said if not, it wouldn't be for want of trying.

"Trewithen," she said to the valet. "Your brother was to inquire about a serviceable pleasure boat for us."

"She's at anchor this very minute in Mylor harbour, ma'am. Up the Fal. You may inspect her at any convenient time."

"Good man!" She progressed onward to Martha. "Unwin, you're looking well, I'm glad to say. Were you able to get that mauve-coloured twist?"

Martha curtseyed, looked flummoxed, and wiped her hands nervously in her pinafore. She darted a glance at Gemma, next in line.

Gemma smiled, curtseyed, and said, "I found it, ma'am. I had some other messages to collect yesterday and found it on my way back."

"Good for you, Penhallow!" But Ada was puzzled. "Your search must have been diligent," she said. "Neither of the two largest haberdashers had any when I called on them last week."

Gemma smiled. "Mrs Geach, the greengrocer's wife, is famous for her coloured embroideries, ma'am. And Cook finds their vegetables excellent so we may acquire any thread we desire and of any colour, too." She smiled and curtseyed again.

"Excellent." Ada gave her a penetrating stare, as if there were much more she could say, but on some other occasion, and passed on.

Gemma turned toward the other three de Vivians, taking a particular interest in the two younger ones, whom she had not seen before. The father was talking to Trewithen ... something to do with the pleasure boat at Mylor. The son — Peter, it must be — had his head turned away, gazing at the hackney horse. The daughter, Beatrice, had the quivering nostrils and upper lip of one suppressing a yawn. Their eyes met. Beatrice swallowed heavily, blinked rapidly once or twice, and then smiled a guilty little smile.

Oh, yes, miss — we're going to get on all right, Gemma thought contentedly. It was odd how trivial little moments like that could tell you so much.

No sooner had that thought formed in her mind than Peter turned toward her and their eyes met ... and she felt suddenly weak at the knees. This rush of emotion was so unexpected, so unlike anything that had ever happened to her in all her eighteen years, that she dropped her guard completely. She was so agitated, she had no idea what sort of expression she was wearing; all she knew was that the impassive mask she had learned to wear ever since she had gone into service at fourteen slipped in that instant. Her face was a page on which anyone might read thoughts and feelings of which she herself was still barely conscious.

It's not happening, she assured herself desperately. *It's a mistake. An illusion. A dream.*

A soldier once told her about fainting on parade — how it happened to even the biggest and strongest among them. They were always 'put on a fizzer' for it, charged with 'idle breathing.' She began to breathe deeply to dispel her dizziness. Except that it wasn't exactly dizziness. She felt weak but not faint. Her heart was certainly not faint — it was hammering away like one of the steam piledrivers down in the docks.

As for him, his expression was unreadable to her — at least, since she had never set eyes on him before, she did not yet know how to read it. He was plainly agitated, too, but whether toward anger or ... or toward something she'd rather not name, she could not tell.

Beatrice, however, proved of some assistance in this. She was still looking at Gemma when that electrifying surprise hit her. She followed the maid's gaze to its object and then turned to Gemma once again; and now her features wore an expression that a child could have interpreted: shock, tinged with a degree of amusement.

The whole incident was over in less than five seconds but for Gemma they were the five longest and most portentous seconds of her life. The shock in Beatrice's eyes brought her to her senses. The hint of amusement made her angry. She wished there were some way of shouting out so that only the girl would hear — a mind-to-mind sort of shout: 'If you think you're witnessing the start of some weary, sordid little *affaire* between a young master and a maidservant, you've never been more wrong in your life! If only you knew! If only you knew!'

But, of course, Miss Beatrice never would know and she, Gemma, would never actually tell her just why she could be so certain of herself.

She averted her gaze, chose a single point of focus dead ahead of her — a single cotoneaster leaf in the border, as it happened — and stared at it hard. And now the familiar servant's mask was firmly back where it belonged. The soldier had told her that was how to avoid a 'fizzer' when an inspecting general stopped and pretended to be interested in your name and length of service.

The old mask might be back but her newly stirred heart was still going like that piledriver. She became quite annoyed with it for she felt certain *he* would notice. She knew all about young masters-of-the-house and the thoughts that young female servants put in their minds. He'd be looking out for any such sign, of course — the victim's weak points. In self-protection she began to cast him in the role of seducer-pursuer, the traditional backstairs Lothario. She had already forgotten his face; instead she invested him with the features of Roger Deveril, the son of the previous family at Number One, who had been just such a domestic Don Juan. To his great chagrin, Roger had taught her more about guarding her virtue than she might have learned at any dozen finishing schools for ladies.

So her second glimpse of Peter's actual face, rather than the convenient image of a man who had never been able to put the slightest dent in her armour, was just as powerful and disturbing to her as the first had been — even more so, indeed, since he was now standing right before her, blotting out the helpful cotoneaster leaf and making the entire border seem to shimmer and break up.

Gemma was the last of the 'upper' servants in that line — the servants who were due something more than a nod and a smile. Below her only Martin Hall, the head-gardener, was entitled, like her, to a brief conversational exchange.

"And how long have you been part of this household, Penhallow?" Beatrice asked.

"I ... I ..." It was no more than a whisper. Gemma meant to speak. Everything within her *felt* as if she were, indeed, speaking. But no sound emerged. Desperately she willed herself to turn her eyes from Peter's, but her eyes refused to obey.

"Hallo." His voice could not have been more neutral.

"Hallo," she whispered, now with just a hint of recovery in her tone.

And then he did the unthinkable.

He held out his hand to shake hers!

The movement was slow, trancelike, deliberate. At the time it seemed like a lifeline to her, a gesture that would rescue them both from a situation for which neither was prepared. If only she had paused for another second — a fraction of a second, even — she would have realized it was just about the most dangerous and idiotic thing either of them could have done. But by then their hands were clasped and electricity was flowing and there was no world outside them and that point of contact between them filled the universe.

A collective gasp — from servants startled out of their composure and masters shocked out of their complacent superiority — brought them to their senses.

"Peter!" his horrified mother cried; a rifle could not have cracked the air more sharply.

He was swift to recover his poise. "Why not?" he asked with a truculent smile. "Indeed, why not? We are all human, I believe. When Adam delved and Eve span, who was *then* the gentleman! Unwin!" He grabbed Martha's hand before she could realize his purpose and pumped it vigorously. "Glad to know you! Trewithen! The same to you, man!"

An amused valet met him halfway and gave a manly shake. He admired the young fellow's presence of mind.

"You are most vexing, sir!" de Vivian roared, putting a stop to his son's horseplay. "Stand behind me, now, where I shan't need to apologize for you twice — as, indeed" — he turned to Gemma — "I now must to this embarrassed young maid."

"Oh-please-sir!" Gemma found her voice at last and rattled the words out.

"No, no!" He silenced her with an imperious hand. "You are not to blame for my son's picayune manners. He thinks it the greatest jape to stand convention on its head. But let me assure you of this ... and this goes for all of you." He looked sternly up and down the line and went on to say something to the effect that if his son annoyed any of them, they were not to hesitate to tell Mr or Mrs Walker, or, indeed, to come directly to him or to Mrs de Vivian ...

Gemma heard no more than the gist of his words for, in looking away from her, he had liberated her eyes to turn where they would — directly back to the errant son, who, though now isolated behind his father's back, was still facing her. If at that moment he had smiled or winked, as Roger Deveril would certainly have done, her defences would have been rebuilt on the spot. But Peter neither smiled nor winked. Quite the opposite. His face was gray as ash. His lips were quite bloodless. And he stared at her balefully, as if *she* had harmed *him* in some way.

And that, indeed, was what he felt, despite his truculent response to his father's reprimand. For he had no more expected to be so stricken at the sight of her than she had at the sight of him. He had the same eye for a pretty face as any other healthy young man, and if that had been all there was to it, Gemma's good looks would have amused and delighted him. And, in the days and weeks to come, he would have tested her resistance in the old, time-worn (if not exactly time-honoured) ways and maybe have stolen a kiss or two. His hopes might have gone beyond that modest achievement but previous attempts along the same lines had starved them of much substance. Still, a kiss was a kiss.

But this ... this ... what could one call it? He was damned if he'd call it *love,* though it was sufficiently greater than every other tender emotion he'd ever felt to deserve the name; but one simply did not fall in *love* with servant girls. One would be the laughing stock of any group one might like to join. This 'instantaneous obsession,' for want of a better name, had shaken him to the foundations. He must either get her dismissed or ... or what? Leave the house himself. Somehow, though he had no previous experience of an emotion as powerful as this, he already knew it would possess him, would heap his days and nights, if he did not deal with it at once. He squared his shoulders and set his mind to his decision.

He had not heard a word of what his father said to the others, so the odd looks the remaining servants now gave him, some wary, others sympathetic, mystified him. Not that he spent much time thinking about it. His mind was still turning over schemes either to get rid of Gemma Penhallow or to join the navy himself.

5   The growler, laden with the de Vivians' trunks and boxes, arrived from the station just as the servants' line-up was dispersing. Trewithen and the outdoor lads spread canvas over the gravel and helped the driver unload. The de Vivians would no more have supervised the unpacking than they would have carried a parcel from a shop in their own hands. "They are all marked," Ada told Mrs Walker, waving a vague hand at the growing pile. "If you need to know anything, ask Miss Beatrice. I shall be in the lower garden." And, pausing only to take up the novel *Howards End*, which had arrived at her new home that very morning in her regular parcel from Hatchard's, she went out to sit by the gazebo. There she would read and relax and recover from the strain of their two-hour journey until one of the maids came out with the tea. "Mister de Vivian, dear," she said, "will you not take a book and join me?"

"Presently, dearest," he replied. "I should first like to see how those men have progressed with the observatory." The many glances he had shot toward the tower on the corner of the house showed what a sacrifice it had been to stay outdoors and smile at one potato face of a servant after another all ths while.

"A lost soul!" she murmured affectionately as she sauntered indoors in his wake.

"Not lost but gone before," Peter corrected her jovially. It was one of her sayings.

She rounded on him. "And as for you, young man, well, you've disgraced yourself — and us — quite enough for one day. I suggest you work off some of that devil inside you by helping the menservants carry our things upstairs and telling them what goes where. Beatrice, dear, will you join me?" she added, quite ignoring what she had just said to Mrs Walker.

"I'd like to see the house first, Mater, if it's all the same to you," the girl replied.

Ada shrugged. *"C'est pareil."* The use of French often indicated slight annoyance in her.

Meanwhile, Mrs Walker collared Gemma, almost literally, and took her up to the mistress's bedroom — ostensibly to help unpack but really to ask her what on earth had come over her out there. "I've never known you behave in that fashion," she said. "Did that young fellow make some ... er, gesture? Some sign? Because if he did ..." Her voice trailed off as she saw the girl shake her head.

"It was just idle breathing, Mrs Walker," she said.

"I beg your pardon?" The woman eyed her askance.

"Like what soldiers get on parade. They call it idle breathing, though a soldier told me it's really from standing too long back on your heels."

The housekeeper lofted her eyes to the ceiling and said, "I suppose you know what you're talking about. I'm blessed if I do. No, no! Don't try and explain. Just make sure nothing like it ever happens again, eh? You understand? I was mortified."

"Yes, Mrs Walker." Her contrition was as mechanical as the other's reprimand — just one more ritual that people in service had to undergo.

"You of all maids," Mrs Walker said heavily.

"I know." Gemma sighed and bit her lip. There was nothing mechanical about these gestures, though.

"History is *not* going to repeat itself, I trust?"

"It is not!" Gemma asserted with quiet vehemence. "I'd run away and live in a hole on Bodmin Moor before I'd let such a thing happen again in our family."

It was all the housekeeper hoped to hear. And so, for the next fifteen minutes they reverted to doing what they would have done if the embarrassing incident outside had not taken place at all — that is, they unpacked their new employers' clothes and admired or sneered at them with a frankness that would have astonished those same employers had they overheard.

Fortunately, they happened to be admiring a slightly old-fashioned but nonetheless splendid ballgown when Beatrice entered the room and took them by surprise. "I say, Mrs Walker," she cajoled, "d'you think you could spare me Penhallow for half an hour? Unwin is willing and good-hearted enough in her way and so forth, but ... you know?" She smiled disarmingly.

Mrs Walker did know. Her heart was heavy with the knowing. Mrs de Vivian had hinted on one of her earlier visits that she thought Gemma might train up very well as a lady's maid. And the girl, moreover, not being corrupted by city ways, would not be so demanding as the lady's maids in Plymouth. The London ones were even worse, with their claims for holidays and half-holidays and rooms of their own and magazine subscriptions and heaven knows what else. They were quite out of the question these days. And as for genuine French maids, well, one could just about afford such an extravagance for the Season, but not a day longer.

"Of course, Miss Beatrice," she replied. "Would you like me to help, too?"

Beatrice sniffed. "I hardly think there'd be room for *three* of us," she said.

The housekeeper, who felt a sort of proprietary tenderness for the house, did not take kindly to the criticism. "I imagine you'll wish the room would be even less large on a cold winter night, miss," she said.

Beatrice made no reply but led the way back along the landing. When they reached her room she stepped aside as if to let Gemma pass. But, when the girl drew level, she kept pace beside her and even walked a little out of the way, trying to force her toward the window. She wanted Gemma to see what was happening down in the garden. Unfortunately for this ruse, the maid was more interested in the clothes that lay sprawled across the bed, so Beatrice herself had to peer out of the window and exclaim, "Oh, look! Is that a man-of-war?"

Gemma glanced at the vessel, which was almost on the horizon, and said she thought it was more probably a liner. She did not add that battleships were more careful to suppress their smoke; she would have thought anyone who grew up in Plymouth would know that.

"Oh, it's *such* a pretty garden," Beatrice went on — and at last Gemma was tricked into glancing downward.

And then she understood what all this unsubtle manoeuvring was about: Peter was down there, standing in a rather napoleonic position, with his arms folded and his head down. No doubt, if they could have seen his face, his eyes would have been brooding darkly on the horizon. Buonaparte on Elba.

"I've never seen it, miss," she said. "Except from one of these windows, of course."

"What — never been out in the garden at all?"

"Not this garden. The Deverils would never have permitted that. Nor the Walkers while they were in charge. I've just been out on the terrace to serve tea, no farther."

"Well, well. We never prevented our servants in Plymouth from ..." Beatrice broke off and stared at the garden. "Mind you, I suppose it is a good deal smaller here. Anyway ..." She turned back to the task in hand — now that Gemma could not have failed to see Peter brooding away down there. "Let's finish the unpacking, eh?"

Gemma wondered how Miss Beatrice had got rid of Martha a few minutes earlier. Had it been done with a kindly excuse or a brusque word? People like her never understood how easy it was to poison the atmosphere among their servants; sometimes a frown at one followed by a smile at another was all it took. Fortunately, in this case, Martha was as afraid of being asked to act the lady's maid as Gemma was eager to volunteer for the post. Nonetheless, there were good and bad ways of making even such foregone decisions known.

"Had you a lady's maid before, miss?" Gemma ventured.

"I had a French maid for the London Season last year," Beatrice replied. "And I expect I shall again this time, too." She sighed. "Regardless of expense!" There was a heavy lilt of irony in her voice.

Servants' ears were attuned to such nuances, for masters and (especially) mistresses hardly ever spoke their minds fully and frankly. Was Miss B hinting that her parents begrudged the pittances paid to their servants? Gemma wondered. She said, "I should think that's just about the most enjoyable thing ever, miss — the London Season?"

"Oh!" Beatrice fanned her face. "It is wearying beyond description. After one week I was fit only for screaming. I should consider *three* balls to be more than enough for anyone — man or woman."

Gemma looked at her in dismay, suspecting for a moment that she was making an indelicate joke. But apparently not. The statement was quite artless.

Beatrice was saying: "As I said, I was ready to beg for mercy after the first week. There was a ball somewhere every single night, you know. And I don't just mean a ball — any old ball. These were festivities (so-called) that one absolutely had to attend. Oh." She took a dress from Gemma and laid it out on the bed — in pale watered silk with peach-coloured vertical stripes. "Needs a good clean, wouldn't you say. Could you take the cuffs and collars off." Neither sentence was a question. The next, however, was: "Have you ever accompanied a lady to London for the Season?"

"No, miss!" Gemma pretended to laugh at the very thought, though the possibility excited her.

"Well, you probably will this time. I have a feeling that my mother has already earmarked you as a possible lady's maid. D'you think you could do it?"

Gemma drew breath to reply but then hesitated, not wishing to seem too forward.

Beatrice, thinking she understood the cause, shook her head. "For her, not me. *I* must have a good *French* maid — a woman in her thirties who knows the ways of the world inside out. If I don't ensnare a husband this Season, people will start to say I'm on the shelf." She eyed Gemma shrewdly. "D'you know what happened to me last year? Has my sad story gone out ahead of me, then?"

Gemma shook her head uneasily. It was only natural that an eighteen-year-old mistress should feel a certain sisterhood with an eighteen-year-old maid; but this was exactly what Mrs Walker had warned her against. A servant should never yield to a mistress's apparent desire for intimacy. They could be chummy with you for years but when the gauntlet was down and the penny was on the drum and you really needed to rely on them, they'd abandon you faster than a hare would leave the slipper's hand on a coursing field.

"I shouldn't listen to such tattle, even if it had, miss," she replied. "Which I assure you it hasn't."

Beatrice drew a deep breath and a hard light entered her eyes as she spoke. Gemma guessed that she was not the first to hear the young woman's sentiments: "You know what the whole point of the London Season is? No? Well, it's to bring together eligible young spinsters and eligible, not-quite-so-young, bachelors. All in strictly controlled conditions, of course, so that they may exchange perhaps as many as a *dozen* whole words on such topics as the weather, the opera, the races and ... er, well, of course, there's always the weather to fall back on. As a result of which they magically divine that Fate intended them for each other from the very day they were born ... whereupon he gives her a ring set with precious stones and says that were they the most precious in all the world they could not be more precious than she, and she, of course, weeps tears of joy and vows in her heart that she will be the perfect wife and adore him for ever and never cross his will and ..." She broke off and swallowed heavily. Her angry, bantering tone had deserted her. "And then he goes and falls off his horse the following week and dies."

Her voice shook and she looked away. "I'm sorry," she said a few moments later. "Anyway, that's what happened to me." She smiled bravely and blinked several times. "I thought I'd got over it by now. Obviously not."

Gemma, whose eyes were somewhat watery, too, said, "Oh, miss, I am sorry." She did not pause in her work, though, and hoped the other noticed her diligence.

"The family thinks I have, so not a word about this. The odd thing is ..." Beatrice went and sat in the window seat, slumping heavily, as if the weight of these memories was suddenly insupportable. "It's strange." She made a 'church and steeple' of her hands and stared at it. "I didn't actually like the man. Frederick Conyers. They're a Devon family. I didn't dislike him either. My feelings were absolutely blank. But I'd been to about twenty balls by then and I'd danced with some of the most dashing young men in London — at least, all the other girls said they were dashing. And I had absolutely no feelings about them, either. So I talked it over with Mam'selle Garence, my

French maid, and she was wonderful. She said I'm a lucky girl. She said falling in love is not a joy for a woman. It's a tragedy. It's a prelude to disaster.''

"Yes!" Gemma said in a rapt whisper. She was no longer troubling to make herself look busy. "That's the truth!"

But Beatrice was so lost in her memories that she did not notice. She laughed. "You know there must be a moment when a mouse first smells the cheese in the mousetrap? Its nostrils twitch and its little heart begins to beat with anticipated pleasure? And maybe it even lives long enough to enjoy the first tiny nibble? Well, Garence said, that's what love is like for a woman. But a calm, clear-eyed marriage is like gaining the key to the larder where they keep the whole cheddar — the one they cut the little bit of bait from. So, when Freddy proposed, I said yes to him and I vowed to make him the most dutiful wife ever — quite genuinely — here in my heart. And then he goes and falls off a horse! So now — having steeled myself to the decision and done the actual deed — I've got to start all over again. Fortunately our engagement had not been officially announced, so I didn't have to go into a twelve-month of mourning. Just one in black and two in mauve. They're in that trunk there. I looked very fetching in black, actually. Perhaps I should be a missionary's wife. Oh!" She let out an exasperated sigh and, leaping to her feet, began pacing around the room. "I'm *bored.* Shall we go for a walk? You may chaperon me. Unwin can come back and finish this. You can show me Falmouth. Are you from here?"

"From Penryn, miss. Which is just a couple of miles up the creek, west of here. But of course I know the town — the respectable parts, anyway."

"Oh?" Beatrice's eyes sparkled. "And if I should wish to peek into one or two of the less respectable parts?"

Gemma's face froze. "All of us may *wish,* miss."

Her young mistress composed herself swiftly. "And if," she went on, now in a serious vein, "I should wish to do works of charity in the less respectable parts?"

"I'm sure Mrs de Vivian would herself accompany you, miss, or Mrs Walker. They would not expose an unmarried maid to such pollution."

Beatrice rose and threw up the window sash. She took off her ribbons and shook her hair free in the breeze that now eddied into the room. "Well, we shall see about all that," she said vaguely. "There's time enough."

Her mother looked up, waved, and returned to her reading. Peter was sprawling in a deck chair beside her, still brooding; at least, he did not look up.

"If I had a farthing for every minute of my life that I've spent standing at windows looking out at ... nothing," she said, "I could afford a house of my own with a hundred windows to stand at." She laughed but with little warmth. "If only something would *happen,* Penhallow. Don't you long for something to happen sometimes? Anything! If a German band came marching up the drive, for instance — wouldn't that be fun! Or if the king went driving by and his carriage wheel came off and we had to entertain him while it was attended to! What would *you* wish to happen like that? What would transform the day for you?"

Gemma thought rapidly. If the Walkers got a sudden inheritance and she was made acting housekeeper and proved so good at it ... no. If Trewithen got made butler somewhere and asked her to marry him and come along as housekeeper? It would be exactly the sort of marriage Garence, the worldly wise French maid, would approve of — and her reported remarks had allowed Gemma to think seriously of such a match for the first time. But no, again — she could never say such a thing to Miss B.

Aware that Beatrice was still waiting for an answer, she said the first thing that came into her head — and it was very much the sort of thing that any girl in her situation might have said: "I suppose, miss, that if some solicitor was to come to the door and tell me they'd found new evidence about the Penhallow lands which proved me to be the lawful owner ..." She laughed to show she knew it was no more than an idle dream.

But sensation-starved Beatrice was suddenly fascinated. "The Penhallow lands?" she echoed breathlessly. "Are they real?"

Gemma smiled indulgently and went to stand by her at the window. "See that castle, miss?" She pointed out St Mawes castle, on the farther shore of the Fal — the smaller of the two ancient castles that guard the entrance to Falmouth harbour. "Yes?"

"Run your eye up the line of the hills above it. D'you see one tree on its own, then three together?"

Since the trees in question were several miles distant, they appeared as no more than tiny blobs against the sky.

"I think so," Beatrice replied. "I'll take your word for it that they're trees. Is there a tiny dot of white among them?"

"Yes!" Gemma was amazed at the woman's eyesight. She herself could see the white dot because she already knew it was there; otherwise she was sure she'd not have noticed it unprompted. "That's Penhale Jakes, which was once the property of ..."

"What a strange name! Does it mean anything? I know 'pen' means a hill or headland. What does 'hale' mean?"

Gemma shrugged. "I'm no Cornish scholar, miss, but I was told once that Penhale means 'hill above an estuary' — which is plain enough to see without any dictionary."

Beatrice smiled. "And 'jakes'?"

"That's what this bed is if we don't start tidying things away soon — a *jakes*. That's modern Cornish, that is." She returned to the bed and suited her action to the words.

"And is it also true?" Beatrice came and joined her. "Is the estate a mess?"

Gemma spread her hands as if to say she had no idea. "I never saw the place close-to, miss. I only ever had it pointed out from this side of the Fal. The *inheritance* of it was a right old mess. I know that much."

"Do tell!" Beatrice attacked her clothes with a vigour that made Gemma wince, slapping their material and raising clouds of dust and lint.

The maid opened the door to create an outward draft and, taking the gown from her mistress, carried it to the window to complete the cleansing. "How did they gather so much dust and stuff?" she murmured.

"Oh!" Beatrice said contemptuously. "Hobson, my lady's maid in Plymouth, was the idlest creature who ever drew breath. But she came with such glowing testimonials from Lady Gregory that my mother could not throw her out. Not with our move here to Falmouth being so imminent. It wasn't worth upsetting Lady G. I shall never believe a glowing testimonial when I am mistress of my own household. They just mean that somebody wanted to get rid of somebody with the least possible fuss. Anyway — tell me about your messy hill above the estuary."

Gemma laid a dress out carefully, covering it with fresh tissue and camphor powder, before she folded it. "My great-grandfather," she said, "one William Penhallow, died by his own hand — or so they said — though we always claimed it was murder done up to look like suicide ..."

"Who were 'they' in this case?"

"The coroner's jury. Neighbours who bore a grudge against him, mostly. It seems he wasn't an easy man. Anyway, they said it was *felo-de-se*, as the official wording is, and so the whole of his estate was forfeit to the crown."

"Oh yes!" a horrified Beatrice exclaimed. "So it was in those days. When did all this happen?"

"In eighteen-and-seventy, miss, just two months before parliament passed the law that did away with forfeiture to the crown!"

"And you can still laugh!"

"Well ..." Gemma laughed again. "What else can you do? It's forty years ago, now. The land passed to the crown — to the Duchy of Cornwall, I believe — and they sold it on. The people who own it now have good legal title, I'm sure."

"But ... listen!" Exciting possibilities were crowding in on Beatrice from every corner of her mind. She paced about the room once more, tugging at her fingers and shooting out words like a machine-gun. "If it could be *proved* beyond all doubt that your grandfather was ..."

"Great-grandfather."

"All right. If your great-grandfather actually *was* murdered, if it could be proved beyond all doubt ... I mean, did your family suspect anybody? They must have done. Suppose one of them is still alive and confessed to it now — a deathbed confession — people do, you know — an act of repentance — so as not to be cast into the pit of Hell for all eternity — suppose that happened! Why, you'd be" — she laughed and clapped her hands — "you'd be *the* Miss Gemma Penhallow, the notable Cornish heiress! Or d'you have an elder sister?"

Gemma hesitated a moment before saying, "No, miss."

Beatrice noticed the hesitation but was too interested in her own daydreaming to remark upon it. "Think!" she gushed. "Dowagers would be sending their sons to entreat for your hand. We could go to balls together and compare notes after —

because the same gentlemen would be after my fortune, too, you know — and we could see what lies they told us. Oh, Gemma! Wouldn't it be *fun!*"

She grasped the maid's hands between hers and entreated her with bright eyes that flickered rapidly, staring now into one of Gemma's eyes, now into the other. Then, realizing where her enthusiasm had led her, she stared in horror at her hands, dropped Gemma's as if they were hot coals, and began babbling her apologies, begging the girl to forgive her and to overlook the gaffe. "It's almost as bad as what Peter did," she concluded.

"Oh, it's nothing like as bad as that," Gemma replied crossly, wishing the woman had not mentioned it at all.

Beatrice, quick to detect the nuance of panic in this dismissal, was equally swift to recover her composure. "Yes," she said firmly. "I shouldn't exaggerate. What he did was quite dreadful, I agree. It's different between two females, isn't it. Why did you let him? Why didn't you just snatch your hand away?"

Gemma returned to the now diminished heap of gowns and underclothing on the bed. "I'd rather not talk about it if it's all the same to you, miss," she said primly.

"Of course not," Beatrice said soothingly.

For a while she and the maid worked away in silence, reducing the unsorted pile still further. Then, apropos nothing in particular, Beatrice said, "I wonder if I'm really quite as incapable of falling in love as my experience last Season made it seem?"

Gemma made a noncommittal noise.

"Perhaps it happens, *bang* — like that! Out of the blue. Just when you least expect it. The very instant you meet the person … before you know his name or anything about him. You just *know* he's the right one. By magic. D'you believe in love-at-first-sight, Penhallow?"

Gemma did not raise her eyes to look at her. She repeated her earlier words: "I said I'd rather not talk about it, miss. If it's all the same to you."

She expected an angry outburst at this second rebuff but none came. She still did not look up. If she had, she would have seen her young mistress smiling: smiling at this confirmation of her suspicions that the topic of Peter's social gaffe and the topic of love-at-first-sight were — to Gemma Penhallow, at least — one and the same thing.

6 After ten minutes or so Ada could stand her son's brooding presence no longer. She closed her book on her thumb and said, " 'What can ail thee, wretched wight, Alone and palely loitering?' You put me off, standing there like a little Napoleon. Either come here and sit by me or go and practise your scowling farther down the garden."

Peter relaxed a little and even managed a wan smile, but he did not move from where he stood.

"What are you scowling about, anyway?" she asked.

"I'm not *scowling,*" he insisted tetchily.

"Just pretending, eh?" she countered. "You do it jolly well."

"Oh, what's the use!" He spun on his heel and stalked off toward the house.

She let him take several paces before she called out after him.

"What?" He turned and stared truculently at her.

She patted the deck chair at her side. "Come on," she said. "Come and tell me all about it."

He shambled back toward her. "All about what?" he asked as he sat in the chair she had indicated.

"Anything. You could start by explaining that extraordinary scene in front of the house just now. What on earth possessed you to do such a thing?"

"Possessed me!" he echoed, implying that it was the perfect word to describe what he had felt.

But she misinterpreted his tone and thought he was about to deny the whole thing. "Yes — what possessed you to grab the poor creature's hand like that? You saw how it embarrassed her, poor little thing."

Peter had, indeed, seen how it embarrassed Penhallow — but only after a much profounder emotion had shown itself for an instant in her eyes, an emotion that he, too, had felt in the same instant. Yet to call it an instant was absurd. A casual observer might have imagined it was all over in a flash; but a thought-reader would know that the 'instant' lingered within him still, playing itself over and over again in his mind, tormenting him with its sweetness.

Being almost twenty-one, he had, of course, already lost his heart to dozens of girls of every rank and station in life — enough to let him know that this time it was utterly different. Other girls had set his heart racing like this; their images had haunted his memory's eye like this — girls glimpsed in shops, seen from the carriage, danced and spoken with briefly at balls and tea-dances, smiled at across the theatre pit. Servant girls, girls in shops, schoolgirls, friends' sisters, titled young ladies — Cupid had taken aim through their eyes and his darts had pierced Peter's heart more times than he could remember. And each time he had told himself it was, at last, the real thing — quite different from all those other occasions. Now, however, it really was so.

And the difference, this time, was that he did *not* welcome it. On those previous occasions, when he had felt that indescribable squirt of pleasure in his veins, it had been like the cry of tally-ho or view-hulloo to the dedicated huntsman — a call that tightened the sinews, quickened the blood, and excited all his faculties to join in the chase. The chase itself was the thing, of course. Often he did not care if he won or lost; the thrills of the hunt and of the lively fantasies that spurred it on were enough. The fantasies he had enjoyed about some of those girls would have made Casanova blush.

So why was it not happening now with the Penhallow maid? Why was he not relishing plans to waylay her in corridors for a snatched kiss and a hasty fumbler's feast? What made such enjoyable sport suddenly seem unworthy ... despicable, even? Without a qualm he had once planned the seduction of a *titled* girl, no less. True, he had never made the slightest move to carry it out but he had relished every detail without provoking the smallest twinge of conscience. His parents — and even his friends — would have been aghast if he had so much as loosened one of the girl's buttons. The seduction of a simple servant girl, by contrast, would do no more than raise the odd eyebrow and provoke the occasional tut-tut. So why, when he tried to indulge that same fancy in connection with *this* servant girl, did he suddenly feel unworthy?

It was most annoying — even more so in that, by long habit, he could not help imagining what it would be like to slip an arm around her waist, to seek out her lips with his, to feel her firm young body pressed tight against him. It was enough to make any fellow scowl.

And to make him think.

His wiser half despaired at his folly in having anything to do with her, or even in contemplating such a thing. The other, more reckless and romantic half told him he must stop being such an idiot and start boxing clever. The mater and pater must not suspect that his exhibition back there on the drive was anything more than a silly, misguided prank. The very absurdity of it was on his side. No one would imagine that anything serious could come of it. However, the whole world knew that idle young bachelors in their wild-oats days could fall for pretty servant girls, make them extravagant promises, and generally get themselves and their families — and, indeed, the girls — into trouble. The usual cure was to find the girl another place, agreeable to her, and let her go. Above all, he mustn't allow such a tragedy to separate him from Penhallow.

'But yes!' shouted his wiser half. 'That's exactly what must happen. You must put as many miles as possible between yourself and her. Anything else would be sheer folly. There is no hope of a serious liaison there.'

His mother laid down her book, though she still marked her place with her thumb. She stared out to sea, or to the patches of it which could be seen among the budding branches of the trees lower down the garden. "I asked what possessed you?" she murmured absently.

"It was a stupid prank," he conceded, hoping his tone was casual enough.

"Very stupid," she agreed. "I feel you ought to offer the poor girl an apology — but only if we may be sure she would not give herself airs for weeks after. I shall speak to Mrs Walker about it and be guided by her. Perhaps it would be best to find some other situation for her?"

Her questioning tone and the nonchalant way she turned to examine his response warned Peter that he, and not the idea, was being tested. "Absolutely," he replied languidly. "Best thing all round." He stretched out, crossed his legs at the ankles, linked his fingers behind his head, gazed up at the sky, and suppressed a yawn.

"Although I have her in mind as a lady's-maid."

He knew she was still testing him. "Whatever you think," he agreed mildly.

Apparently satisfied, his mother turned to a more direct assault. "I just wish you'd do something *useful* with your life, darling. Why didn't you stay on at school?"

"They wouldn't let me grow a moustache." He fingered the tentative adornment nervously. Would it appeal to the Penhallow girl? He must find out her attitude to moustaches in general and his in particular — subtly, of course.

"That would hardly have been the end of the world," she countered. "You could have played lots of football. You know how keen Mister Marsh was for you to stay on. You'd have been captain of football and could have made life beastly for the colts. I thought that was what you always wanted."

He closed his eyes and instantly saw Penhallow's as they had been in that moment of truth between them. "One's ambitions change as one matures," he said loftily. What was her Christian name? He must find out.

"Ambitions?" she echoed in mildly shocked surprise. "You have ambitions?"

From her tone he could not tell whether she placed ambitions on a par with measles or with talent; either way it would unnerve her, he suspected. "D'you want to hear them?" he asked, making her be the one who pressed the admission out of him.

"Mmh," she replied warily.

"I have an idea for a single-handed racing dinghy — long, narrow, shell-built, very nippy. If we'd stayed in Plymouth, I'd have built her — if only to wipe the smiles off a couple of very superior faces around the yacht-club bar."

"Superior faces," his mother murmured, pulling her thumb out of her book at last and folding her hands across it in her lap.

"What about them?" he asked.

"I was just thinking ... what makes a face superior? That Penhallow girl — she has what I would call a superior face, don't you think?"

So the mater was still not satisfied! But she wasn't going to trap him that easily, even though, as it happened, he agreed with her. It was time for a little ridicule. "The tiara and diamond necklace helped a lot," he said.

She shot him a bewildered look.

"Well, Mater!" he scoffed. "Put almost any woman in a costly ballgown and jewels, and spend an hour or two on her hair and manicure, and the whole world would call her superior. It would work with Gertie Penhallow, I'm sure."

"Gemma, dear, not Gertie."

Hiding his triumph he continued: "Well, she *looks* like a Gertie to me. I say it'd work with *almost* any woman because all the jewels and silks in creation never did much for poor Lady Pemberton. You said yourself that you had to hold back from asking her to brush your coat for you."

"You weren't supposed to hear that. Anyway, you're wrong. One isolated example proves nothing. Superiority goes with true breeding. Look at the Arab thoroughbred and the diddicoy's nag. And there's breeding somewhere in Gemma Penhallow's pedigree. I'll stake my reputation on it."

When Peter made no reply she turned to him and prompted: "Mmh?"

"Shell-built," he said, "from the thinnest ply possible. And I'd use copal varnish, not boiled linseed oil. Racing yachts of the future are going to stand or fall by their choice of varnish, I'm sure." He chuckled. "You could say varnish is the opposite of pedigree, couldn't you!"

"I think I'll make her my lady's-maid. Mine or Beatrice's. For a trial period, anyway."

"Is there a spare room in the cellar, I wonder — a boiler room or something?"

"I'll consult Mrs Walker on that, too. It'd serve better than an apology, perhaps."

"Somewhere I could set up a workshop."

"Also, I could keep an eye on her better."

"And the heat of the boiler would help dry the varnish. If the air's the slightest bit damp, the stuff dries all milky-looking and rough. Is there?"

She heard him at last. "Is there what, dear?"

He rose to his feet. "Never mind. I'll wander in and look for myself. D'you want a rug or anything?"

"You could bring my shawl if Mrs Walker has .... no, on second thoughts, don't bother. Just ask Unwin to bring it out with the tea things. She may come in twenty minutes, tell her." When he was halfway to the house she called after him, "And tell your father and sister, too. He's not to get stuck into some celestial observation and she's not to go on a spree of trying on all her dresses."

She watched him until he went indoors. She opened her book at random, but did not look at it. Instead her gaze returned to the patches of sea among the branches. "Well, Paul, my darling," she murmured, "I wish you could tell me what's really going on inside your brother's mind. I'm sure you know. You know everything now. I'm sure you also know of a suitable young girl for him down here. You understand what we require — one who'll bring out his nobler qualities and make him set the Old Adam aside. Are you going to lead us to her? Or her to us? One way or the other, my dear, I beg you do it quickly."

Paul, Peter's twin brother, had died of appendicitis in 1904 at the age of twelve. She often spoke to him in times of travail and doubt — when she was alone, of course.

Peter returned at that moment, accompanied by a tall lady with an elaborately plumed hat and a short fur cape. She looked to be in her early thirties, a slender woman with an aristocratic bearing, easy and confident.

"I say, Mater ..." he began.

"My dear Mrs de Vivian," the lady interrupted. "I do apologize. I see I picked quite the wrong day to disturb you. I was sure you had arrived yesterday. I am Guinevere Roanoke, a friend of Margaret Corder's?" Her questioning tone as she advanced, holding out her hand, suggested that no further explanation was needed.

Nor, indeed, was it. The Corders were good friends of the de Vivians in Plymouth and Margaret had told Ada that she had written to this Mrs Roanoke about her new neighbours. "Why, you could not have called at a more opportune moment, Mrs Roanoke." Ada rose and shook her hand, holding it for perhaps a second longer than strict etiquette required. "You are very welcome."

"I was about to withdraw myself but your son said you would not mind."

"Not *mind?*" Ada turned on him angrily. "What a thing to say, Peter!" She favoured their visitor with a rolling of her eyes. "Young people these days! I am, of course, quite beside myself with delight, Mrs Roanoke. I had intended leaving cards with you tomorrow — and all the other ladies to whom my dear friends have written about our move to Falmouth. We are about to have tea. I hope you'll join us? Peter — cut along and tell the others, there's a dear." She pointed vaguely toward the gazebo and hoped that Mrs Walker had ordered its furniture to be scrubbed clean of moss and bird droppings.

The visitor said she'd be delighted. "As for leaving cards," she said, "we do more-or-less observe the customs down here but, being quite a small community, I suppose we are not *quite* so punctilious as we should be in London, say, or Plymouth. You're too kind. You're quite sure I'm not imposing?" She sat down even as she asked.

Ada was determined not to be trapped into repeating her effusive welcome; the woman had been reassured quite enough. Instead she said, "Dreadfully!" and was rewarded with a shocked glance from Mrs Roanoke. She laughed. "Of course you're not imposing! After all, it isn't as if the whole household were moving into occupation today. The house is already running at full steam ahead. That's the advantage of keeping the servants on. I'm sure you know them better than we do."

The teasing reply to her earlier question assured Guinevere Roanoke that this Mrs de Vivian was not going to be one of those stiff-and-starchy, we've-been-here-since-the-Conquest ladies, so she risked saying, "Candidly, Mrs de Vivian, I was rather hoping you'd dismiss the lot of them."

"Oh?" Now it was Ada's turn to show shocked surprise.

"So that I could snap them up, of course!"

The two ladies laughed. In the easy silence that followed, Guinevere sighed, "But," she said, "the only masters who dismiss servants these days are people returning from the Empire. They have no idea that good servants are like gold dust now. Poor Mrs Larkin, a widow from India, dismissed a maid last month just for sweeping dust under the carpet! She still hasn't found a suitable replacement — but she'll learn! The rest of us cling fast to them no matter what disasters they perpetrate — short of actual criminality or ..."

Her voice trailed off as a small party emerged from the house and began down the short path that led diagonally across the sloping lawn to the gazebo.

"Or what?" Ada prompted her.

"Or the other thing," she murmured, not taking her eyes off Peter, who, seized by a fit of inappropriate gallantry, was trying to lift the teapot off the tray the maid was carrying. And, since the maid was Gemma Penhallow, it looked as if Number One, Alma Terrace, was in for some interesting times — yet again.

When the introductions were over, the men hovered around to carry the teacups to Beatrice and their visitor. Beatrice meanwhile cut the cake and Gemma carried the slices round.

Peter looked at her hands and saw they were as delicate as any lady's.

"How is your family, Penhallow?" Guinevere asked pleasantly.

"Pretty fair, thank you, ma'am," she replied.

"*All* of them?"

Gemma behaved as if she had not heard.

Ada was about to reprimand the girl for her silence when she saw a glint of merriment in the visitor's eye, which made her think better of it.

A moment later she wished she had not — for her silence revealed that she now suspected that the question had been provocative and that the maid had good reason not to answer. Which, in turn, meant there was now a seed of doubt in Ada's mind about Penhallow's family and why Mrs Roanoke had felt it necessary to ask about *all* of them. Was there a black sheep among the Penhallows? Or a black ewe, perhaps? She must consult Mrs Walker.

Oh dear! There were so many things to consult the house-keeper about; she really ought to start writing them down.

"Does anybody ride to hounds?" Guinevere asked, peering at Beatrice.

"As long as they don't actually catch the poor little foxes," the girl replied. "I enjoy the riding part."

Guinevere, recognizing a young person's pose, responded with a vague smile. "Or sailing?" she asked.

Peter raised a finger. He wondered it did not tremble. Gemma was standing immobile at his side, waiting to be needed. All he could think of was how easy it would be to reach out, slip an arm around her waist, and pull her to him. The whole side of him that was nearest her felt warm and tingly.

"He's going to build his own little racing yacht in the cellar here," Ada said. "He uses a special varnish."

"How interesting." Guinevere peered at him intently.

For a moment Peter had the strangest feeling that he could picture her both as she would be when old and as she must have been as a young girl.

"My husband is looking for a good eighth man in his crew," she said.

The gentlemen took their seats.

"I must toddle down to the harbour and look the boats over," Peter said. "What's he got?"

"A Yarmouth yawl, built by Hastings of Yarmouth, in fact."

Peter whistled, bringing down further glances of disapproval from his parents.

"Yes, well," Guinevere said, "it obviously means something to you, young man. As for me, I don't know the sharp end from the blunt. I just sit on the yacht-club terrace and wave encouragingly whenever I suspect my husband of remembering I'm there at all."

"Does he sail her with a lugsail?" Peter asked.

She shrugged. "There are two sails, that's all I know. One in the front and one a little bit behind it."

"Ah, then he doesn't." Peter sounded satisfied that Roanoke knew what he was doing. "They row very easily when becalmed but they're pretty tender under sail. He'd want a crew that knew what it was doing." He hoped Gemma was impressed by all this.

"You sound just the man for him, Mister de Vivian. May I convey your interest?"

"Please do. And let me know when I may call."

She smiled. "Call tonight, if you wish. He dines at the yacht club on Tuesdays but if you call around seven, you should find him still at home. Come in tails and he'll probably take you with him. Good crewsmen are also hard to get down here, you know. So he won't begrudge the red carpet."

The implication that Peter should play the mercenary and sell himself dear did not please either of his parents. However, the Corders had warned them that the Roanokes were quite 'big' in Falmouth society so they suppressed their annoyance and smiled encouragingly at Peter, giving him leave to thank the woman and accept her suggestion.

Guinevere stayed just fifteen minutes, as etiquette demanded of those paying social calls At Home. She said she could find her own way out but Peter accompanied her to the front gate. As they passed from sight around the corner of the house she stumbled on the crazy paving and grabbed his arm for support.

What happened next unsettled him — and, perhaps, her. The stumble had been genuine; he did not doubt it. She half let go, even before she had fully regained her poise, as if the mere touch of him shocked her. But then she changed her mind and clung to him once more — all the way to the street, where her gig was waiting.

There was an odd look in her eye, too, at that moment when she half let go and then grasped him again. It was as if she could not make up her mind which was worse — to drop him as if he scalded her or to go on holding him, as if the contact pleased her. Although she chose the second of these alternatives, he did not think it was for the pleasure of it — rather that she was paralyzed by the fear of deciding upon either course. He surmised that she was not a woman given to such 'accidents.' Even less was she accustomed to taking advantage of them.

What she said about waving at her husband whenever he seemed to notice she was there *at all* was interesting, though.

On his way back to the gazebo he met Gemma, who had been dismissed from waiting on them. "Help me, Penhallow," he said. "Is there something I should know about that lady? Her behaviour is not entirely conventional."

She eyed him uncertainly but all she said was, "Lord, sir, I hardly know her well enough to answer that."

"But … people talk? People always talk about one another." He spoke just to have the chance to go on looking at her. His mother was right — there was a marked suggestion of superiority in her face. She would not easily blush nor become tonguetied, he suspected. Nor be easily cowed.

"As you say, there's talk about lots of people, sir," she replied. "It's best to speak as you find."

"Well, I find her …" He could not think of an appropriately anodyne word.

"Sir?" she prompted him.

It struck him that she might be trying to keep their conversation going, too — not exactly to prolong it but so as not to cut it short, either.

"She seemed a little bewildered," he said vaguely.

"Peter!" his mother called out, loading the one word with plenty of annoyance.

"But if," he said, stepping aside to let her pass,"there's anything you *do* know about her but couldn't tell *me* — directly, I mean — perhaps you might mention it to my sister for her to pass on? I'd be most grateful."

Gemma nodded gravely and continued on her way indoors.

It was fatally easy to read significance into glances and words that were quite innocent of any such thing, he reflected. For instance, the way her pale green eyes seemed to burn, and the devastating effect it had on him; it was hard not to believe she intended that effect, desired it, wished it on him.

"What was the girl saying to you?" his mother asked sharply as he rejoined them.

"Nothing. I was apologizing to her," he replied. Well, he told himself, it had been a *kind* of apology.

"Good," she said, though from her tone you wouldn't have believed she saw anything good about it at all. "We have been discussing Mrs Roanoke. Don't look so shocked. You're long enough in the tooth to take part in the occasional grown-up conversation by now. I wonder — did she say anything of significance to you on her way out?"

"Just that her husband had never won the Falmouth-to-Wolf-Rock and had set his heart on it this season, and had I ever been to Cowes? Yachting talk. I don't think she's as indifferent to the sport as she made it seem."

"Well ..." His mother was somewhat mollified. "We think there's quite a lot about Mrs Roanoke that is not quite what it may seem. We cannot cut her, of course, not if she's as important locally as the Corders say she is. But there's something NQOC about her."

"Oh, Mater!" he exclaimed. "Not Quite Our Class? A shade antediluvian, don't you think?"

"All we're saying is go slow, eh? Tell her no more about yourself or us than politeness demands and do not encourage any intimacies until we are a great deal better acquainted with her and her husband."

"Intimacies!" he said awkwardly.

"Yes!" She gave her son a penetrating stare. "I could wish that she were somewhat older and greyer."

7   Peter's mind was full of yachting talk as he made his way
    that evening to Wodehouse Terrace, where the Roanokes
lived. The half-mile walk gave him his first good view of the port
and town, for that afternoon's cab drive, from the station up to
Alma Terrace, had taken them through the newer suburbs on
the seaward side of the Pendennis peninsula. The port, naturally,
was built in the lee of that land, guarded by Pendennis castle
and facing north into the sheltered waters of the Fal estuary.
Combined with the estuary of the Penryn River, also to the
north, it offered reaches a couple of miles long in almost any
direction — good sailing in any weather except, perhaps, on a
breezeless evening like this. A score of yachts of various sizes
were lying becalmed out there at that moment.

The town had begun, some three centuries earlier, as a single
winding street at the foot of a long hill that formed the
southwestern margin of those same sheltered waters. The hill
was so steep that the town had quite literally grown *up* it — in
the form of three more streets running roughly parallel along its
precipitous slope. In fact, it was so steep that what looked like a
two-storey house on the downhill side of the topmost street was
built directly on top of another two-storey house on the uphill
side of the street below — making a single four-storey building
with two addresses in two different streets!

At the southern end of the town, where the hill began to dip
toward the sea, the slope became gentler and there you could
find one or two cross-streets running uphill, connecting the
three that ran along the slope; elsewhere only granite steps and
snaking footpaths led the way between them, among the higgledy-
piggledy buildings.

Wodehouse Terrace and its continuation into Clare Terrace
formed the topmost of these three later streets. Standing on the
very brow of the slope, it was built up only along its inland side;
thus every house commanded a superb panorama of the entire
estuary and of the St-Just-in-Roseland peninsula on its farther
shore. It had once been the most select of all the town's streets
— the 'Nob Hill' of Falmouth — but those laurels had recently

passed onward to Wood Lane and Alma Terrace. The Roanokes' house, easily distinguished as a grand, porticoed dwelling in the centre of a plain Georgian terrace, was the last to be lived in by one of the town's great merchant and trading families. Its neighbours, though by no means raffish, had certainly slipped a notch or two in the social scale since their heyday. One house had a brass doctor's plate on its gate — which was always the first sign that a street was passing into a genteel decline. With other houses the decay had gone further still. Little cards in window corners announced discreetly that there were 'Rooms to Let' en pension or that the house sought lodgers. One establishment, just three doors short of the Roanokes', proclaimed itself on a painted shingle as 'The Roseland View Teetotal Hôtel — Terms Daily, Weekly, or By Arrangement — Annexe for Respectable Single Business Ladies.'

At first Peter wondered how people as allegedly important as the Roanokes could remain in such a street, but then it occurred to him that the hint of social decay probably suited the wife very well — if she really was as NQOC as his mother had indicated. Here she would be the undoubted doyenne of the terrace, yet she was not so far from Wood Lane and Alma Terrace as to be outside their pale.

He glanced up at their house and was almost certain he saw her draw back from an upstairs window — a hasty movement, betraying a certain excitement. However, by the time one of her maids admitted him, she was downstairs in the drawing room, looking as if she had been there for ages.

"Hallo, Mister de Vivian!" Her voice had a tremor and her hand shook as she offered it to him. "Um … a … a glass of sherry, perhaps?" She nodded at her butler, who asked if Peter preferred sweet or dry.

He chose dry and seated himself — apparently in Roanoke's chair, for she drew breath sharply to say something, then thought better of it, and subsided with a wan, nervous smile.

It was, he noticed, characteristic of her. She would do something, or say something, almost on an impulse, then think better of it, *almost* take it back, and, finally, settle into an awkward silence.

They chatted inanely for some minutes until he was ready to scream. Then, when he dropped some remark about not having been in half the rooms at Alma Terrace yet, she suddenly asked if he'd like to see over her house. It was a strange invitation but what could he say other than yes?

Is this how it happens? he asked himself as he followed her upstairs. She had a lithe, willowy figure, which he could hardly help noticing, since her gown clung to it so closely. Did Gemma know what effect her intense green eyes had on him? Did Mrs Roanoke know what effect her lissome body would have on him — on *any* man — swaying like that and so close? Did women know anything of that sort?

"I hope we shan't disturb your husband," he said. "When people interrupt *me* while I'm dressing for dinner ... well!"

Well, what? he asked himself. *You can't leave it there!* "That's when I break collar-studs," he concluded lamely.

"Roanoke's late. He must be on his way up from the club now," she replied, throwing open a door. "This is the nursery."

To Peter it looked like any old bedroom for adults.

She followed his gaze and added, "Yes, quite! No little cots. No rocking horses."

Embarrassed by her bitterness he went to the window. The house commanded what must be the town's best view of its bay. Perhaps that was why the Roanokes stayed on here? A yachtsman laid up with a fever could enjoy his sport vicariously from any window in the house.

The same twenty sets of sails still hung slack down there. But ... what was that, just rowing round the point between the two river estuaries — a Yarmouth yawl?

He turned sharply and stared at her.

"My eyesight!" she started to say. Then, "Is it ...?"

"It's a Yarmouth yawl," he confirmed. "Sporting a red pennant at her masthead. What's that headland?"

"Trefusis Point. He's been becalmed there before."

"I see. So he's unlikely to ..."

"He didn't know you were coming. I mean, I haven't seen him since I suggested you should call by tonight. So he's not being ... you know."

"Oh, that thought hadn't even crossed my mind." He gazed back at the yawl. They were resting oars for a moment, so they must have been rowing for some time. "I suppose I'd better trot back home, then," he said.

"Mmh."

"I mean — Miss ... Whatsit — our cook — can probably rustle up ..."

"Miss Eddy. Actually, I was about to dine, if you'd care to ... er, pot luck, I'm afraid."

Pot luck? Had she not warned the cook of an extra place at table? She was so hesitant that he did not feel he could answer heartily, amiable though the invitation was. "D'you think that would be ..." He was going to say 'wise' but changed it to the more neutral "... acceptable?"

"It certainly would be acceptable to me," she replied more confidently. Now that the ice was breaking, she began to smile.

"In Plymouth, I know, it would cause one or two eyebrows to elevate. But not in Falmouth?"

"Oh!" She flapped her hand in exasperation. "One cannot let one's life by tyrannized over by tittle-tattle like that. Come on! You're dressed for dinner and so am I — and *he's* becalmed where he ought to know better." She took his arm and led him back downstairs; over her shoulder she told the butler to lay an extra place.

So she had not told them he was expected. Or the place allegedly laid for her husband had actually been his, Peter's. He had the impression that her suddenly sprightly behaviour was new to her, if not exactly foreign; it was as if she were trying it out for the first time — and discovering she could manage it quite well.

"I *could* send you down to the club with a note," she offered half-heartedly. She was going through the motions rather than making a serious suggestion.

Also, he thought, it was more for the servants' benefit than for his. "Or?" he asked.

"Or, *after* you've taken pot luck with me here, we could *both* go down to join him and his jolly crew for a nightcap?"

Honour was thus satisfied. Only a cad would now assume she had some ulterior motive for inviting him to stay to dine. The only question now was: did she *want* him to be a cad? He would have to test the waters rather delicately.

"I expect you're ravenous." She turned him toward the dining room door. She made 'ravenous' sound almost sinful.

"Not beyond the bounds of good manners," he assured her.

He sat at her right. A place was laid for her husband at the far end of the table. But hadn't she said he would dine at the club? Maybe it was to reproach the man for his neglect?

"I expect you've done this before," she said in a mildly teasing manner. "Dined *tête-à-tête* with a married lady."

"My mother is a married lady," he pointed out.

She laughed and patted his arm and told him he'd do; she seemed even more at ease now — probably because flirtatious and teasing talk around the dinner table was not only permitted, it was almost required.

"It's nothing to speak of," she remarked as she spread her napkin. "Just a little pâté, a bowl of soup, a lemon sole, some game pie, and I-don't-know-what for pudding. I do so dislike heavy meals in the evening."

Silently the footman and a maid served the pâté and fingers of toast.

"You may go," she told them. "We'll ring when we're ready for the soup."

If they were surprised at this risqué command, they did not show it.

"Servants!" she said when they were alone. "What are we to do with them — and yet how could we manage without!"

"Quite," he replied, no longer completely at his ease.

"After all, why shouldn't a grown man and woman dine alone together? Why does the world always *assume* the worst — as if we're all animals?"

"And yet," he reminded her with a gentle sigh, "when all's said and done, we *are* all animals!"

"Well, we can accept that without feeling obliged to prove it at every possible chance we get."

"Yes," he agreed smoothly. "We do have a *choice* in the matter. We are the ones who decide." *And I can hardly put it plainer than that!* he thought.

She understood him well enough but chose to change the subject. "I don't know if you heard my remark to your mother this afternoon," she said, "but I really would give my eye teeth to employ the servants the Deverils assembled for you at Alma Terrace. One in particular." She watched him closely as she added the name: "Gemma Penhallow."

He started. "Indeed!" he said. "I mean, indeed?"

"Oh yes. They're a most interesting family altogether, those Penhallows. I don't know if you've been told anything about them, yet? No, of course not — they're just *there*, aren't they — servants! Part of the scenery."

"That is *not* my attitude," he protested stiffly, though he realized with some regret that it wasn't far off. Or hadn't been so until now.

"Good," she murmured, and smiled as if he had passed some kind of unannounced test. "So you'd be interested to hear something of them?"

He nodded. What a strange woman she was! All nerves and hesitation one moment and bustling confidence the next.

"Thomas Penhallow, her father, is the foreman at Fox-Stanton's timber yard in Penryn. They're C of E folk. Highly respected and respectable." She hesitated. "You've probably guessed as much from Gemma's bearing?"

"She ..." He dried up.

"Yes?" she prompted.

He sighed. "Something ..." He relapsed again into silence.

"Something ... happened?" she guessed when the silence had gone on long enough.

"Yes!" He looked at her in amazement for her tone suggested she already knew whatever he might be going to say. She was so different from his mother, who never dreamed of prying into her children's lives; as long as they behaved with dignity and did not break the rules of good form, she had left all of them alone to grow up as best they could. But Mrs Roanoke, with her wide, fascinated eyes, which seemed to promise secrecy, tenderness, counsel ... everything he despaired of finding at home, was something quite outside his experience.

"You see!" she said. "We could not possibly have this conversation if the servants were hovering around, could we!"

He shook his head. "Something happened this afternoon," he said. "May I tell you?"

"Of course."

"In confidence?"

Her glance chided him for needing to ask such a thing. "My dear young man!"

"I was so unprepared. It has never happened before. We were doing the usual masters-meet-the-servants ritual, just moments after we arrived. The Walkers had them all in a row and we were working our way down the line ..."

"Your parents, your sister, and you?"

"Yes. And when we came to Gemma Penhallow — or, rather, when *I* came to her ..." He swallowed heavily.

"Mmh?"

"I ... *shook hands* with her!" He lifted his downcast eyes to hers, ready for anything — derision, anger, amusement, anything. But her face was a basilisk mask. A single lift of an eyebrow was all the response he saw.

"Yes," he repeated, not knowing how to make it sound more dreadful. "Actually shook hands!"

He laid down his spoon and stretched his hand across the table, as if he thought she might not otherwise understand. He did not advance it toward her but she reached out and took it nonetheless. She was wearing long-sleeved mittens of fine black silk. The combination of silken hand and naked fingers was disturbing to him.

"You mean," she said, "just as if she were a real *person!*" The words were mocking yet her tone was oddly wistful. She released his hand again.

It took him a moment to digest what she had said — what she had *really* said. Then he realized that, in those three words, Mrs Roanoke had cut through to the very heart of the business: *a real person.*

That was what Gemma had been to him from the instant he set eyes upon her — she had been a real person masquerading in a servant's dress.

"Yes!" he exclaimed, unable to keep the amazement out of his voice. "That's it exactly. Servants — almost by definition — aren't real people, are they! In the same way that children aren't real people — just sort of prototypes of people." As the excitement gripped him the ideas began to tumble out, so hard on each other's heels that the connection was lost. She hung on every word, just to keep up. "And yet," he went on, "I always used to resent that as a child. Not being treated as a real person. They still don't, of course, at home. I've often wanted to shout, 'Oy! Ask *me!* Seek my opinion, too! Don't just talk over my head like that — as if I'm not here!' And yet it's what we do all the time when there are servants in the room, isn't it. We talk and we ignore them completely." He closed his eyes briefly and shook his head. "They must have felt the same. God! I've never thought of them as having feelings before! Except for hot and cold and things like that. And *simple* pleasures — kicking footballs and playing fetch with dogs and so on. But feelings like *our* feelings ... never. Isn't that *awful?"*

After a pause she said, "And yet, you know, I've often wondered if they even *want* to be burdened with our secrets. Most of us are rather boring, don't you think?"

He frowned.

"Especially our complaining," she added. "We're all guilty of it. Sometimes I look into their eyes and I think, *I know, dear — you want to scream, don't you!* Sometimes I wish they would."

"What d'you complain about most?" he asked, mainly for something to say.

"Only two things," she replied. "My husband and my husband."

"Oh!" He stared in embarrassment at his empty plate.

She rang for the soup — and dismissed the servants again as soon as it was served.

"I shocked you," she continued when they were alone again.

"Rather!"

"I just thought one confidence deserved another."

An image of the nursery that was just another bedroom came into his mind; her voice had been just as bitter up there, too. "Don't feel you *have* to," he said. "I mean, it's not like repaying a loan."

"You just want to unburden yourself to me?" she asked coldly. "But you're not actually interested in me at all."

"I didn't say that!" he protested.

"So!" She pressed on relentlessly. "You *are* interested?"

He risked taking her hand, briefly, as she had taken his earlier. "Of course. I just didn't want you to say anything you might later regret. You don't know me at all. I might spread it everywhere."

"Is that a warning?"

"No!" He laughed. "But — suppose you told a secret to a dear friend last month, and now you repeat that same secret to me. And then, next week, you discover that several of your other friends also know it. Who are you going to blame — your dear friend of many years or this almost complete stranger?"

She conceded his argument with a dip of her head. "No need to ask how the de Vivians made their money! Caution's in your very blood."

He felt pleased that she compared him to his cleverer ancestors, who had always seemed much *too* clever and earnest to him.

She rang for the fish, which was served with a cool white wine from a decanter whose label simply read *Hock*. Again the servants withdrew.

"I shall tell you, nonetheless," she said. "I mean I can't leave it half spoken like that. My husband was an only child. He has six paternal aunts and uncles, all married, but not a single cousin on that side of the family at all. D'you understand what I'm saying? He is the only member of his generation. What does that suggest to you, Mister de Vivian?"

He cleared his throat awkwardly. Did she want him to state the obvious? "A certain lack of attention during advanced biology lessons in their youth?" he suggested.

She was not amused. "I, on the other hand, am the youngest of a family of eight and have more nephews and nieces than I can easily name. What does *that* suggest to you?"

"That they needed no biology lessons at all — advanced or otherwise? I don't mean to mock ..."

"But?"

"Well ... such explosions of procreation occur in every family. *And* such extinctions of this or that branch. No one is to *blame* for it, surely? It's not anyone's *fault.*"

"Until the dying branch starts blaming the prolific branch — or its one representative among them!"

"Ah!" He tried a sympathetic smile.

"And then — even worse — when he turns his back on you and says it's no longer worth trying!"

He swallowed heavily and concentrated on searching out fishbones. This was not how he imagined that light dalliances were supposed to begin.

"Bless you for listening, anyway!" she said. "May I call you Peter? And you may call me Guinevere — when we're alone together, at least."

After the fish, the footman and the maid served the game pie. The hock was replaced by a claret. They were alone again.

"How much d'you want to know about Gemma Penhallow?" Guinevere asked casually.

"What a question!" He gave an embarrassed laugh.

"Indeed, it's a perfectly reasonable question," she protested. "If you're a romantic spirit, you'll say, 'I desire to know nothing more, thanks,' and you'll keep her shrouded in mystery." She left the corollary unspoken.

"I suppose I'm a realist," he replied after a brief silence.

"Well, as I started to explain," she said, "the Penhallows are a most respected and respectable family — which made what happened to Gemma's sister all the more shocking."

"Her sister?"

"Ruby Penhallow. Their parents obviously had some obsession with precious stones. Gemma and Ruby were identical twins."

"They *were?*"

"Ah, yes, I don't know why I said that. She's probably still alive — though her parents speak of her as dead. And she *is* dead to them, I'm sure. They would simply stare right through her if she stood before them. For myself, I cannot imagine *ever* being able to cut a child out of my life like that. Not that I'm ever going to be given the chance, mind!" She smiled wanly. "I wonder how Gemma feels about it?" She looked at him sharply. "And I wonder if she'll ever tell *you?*"

"Ruby is the black sheep — or should one say black ewe — of the family, eh?"

She nodded. "It's a common enough story. Tell me — it would be interesting to know — how did Gemma respond to your social gaffe this afternoon?"

"No — finish the story first." He smiled. "Please?"

"It is part of the story, believe me. Did she turn tail and flee? Did her ears burn beetroot red?"

He thought awhile. "That's one of the most extraordinary things," he replied. "Just for a second I had the feeling that she understood perfectly why I was offering to shake her hand. I mean, I did it quite spontaneously, without thinking. Certainly without calculating. Just as I'd automatically shake hands with any young lady to whom I might be presented at a garden party, say. Anyway, I got the feeling she was taking my hand in exactly that spirit, too. And then, of course, what with people gasping and yelling for smelling salts all around us, we both realized our true situation and ... well, I don't know which of us was the more embarrassed."

Guinevere smiled as if that was precisely what she had expected to hear.

"So, what has that got to do with your story?" he asked.

"The other thing you might like to know about the Penhallows is that they were once landowners. Not in a big way. But they were proud, independent yeomen farmers, once." She leaned forward and peered out of the window. "No. It's too dark now. Did you notice a tall tree on the far skyline over there? No? Well, you have a look tomorrow. You won't miss it. The tallest tree on the whole Roseland peninsula — a wellingtonia, I think. And there's a little white speck to the left of it — which is actually a substantial farmhouse — set among three smaller trees. That's Penhale Jakes, the farm that was once owned by generations of Penhallows. There *is* such a thing as breeding, you see. It *does* show."

"And did it show in Ruby?" he asked.

"Ah!" She smiled. "You think that's facetious, but I'm sure it *did* show in her, too. I'm sure that young fiend Roger Deveril played on it — suggesting a quite impossible alliance of their two families in order to 'have his way with her' as the saying is. The idiot!"

"I had an identical twin brother once," Peter told her. "His name was Paul. Try to avoid talking about twins in my mother's hearing, by the way ..."

"He died?"

Peter nodded. "When we were fourteen. He got an attack of appendicitis and never recovered. My mother never truly recovered, either — from his death, I mean. She still swears he comes and visits her. He sits on her bed, she says. Tells her he's happy. She asks his advice on things, too."

"And he answers her?"

"So she says. It's not a thing one questions too closely. If Ruby *is* still alive, Gemma's lucky — because there's still the possibility of meeting her again. I think of Paul every day — though I don't for one moment believe he's 'out there' somewhere, able to get in touch."

"Well!" Guinevere sighed. "There is yet one more bond between you and her!"

8 The I-don't-know-what was a summer pudding. Halfway through the course, Guinevere went to the window and noticed that her husband's yawl was no longer visible down there in the estuary. She became agitated and clearly wished Peter to be gone by the time he returned; her earlier talk of dropping down to the club for a nightcap appeared to be forgotten. It seemed to him that she was already beginning to regret her confidences — as if she feared he might take advantage of the loneliness her confessions had revealed.

To reassure her, he tried bringing the conversation back to Gemma, which was a subject close to his heart, anyway. He knew it was impossible for someone of his rank to court a maidservant honourably — unless he was prepared to marry her and live outside Society. And that was out of the question, of course. In short, he knew the whole business was absurd.

But knowing is one thing and feeling is another. If the fairy godmother had offered to grant him a single wish at any earlier moment in the past seven years, he would have asked for Paul to be brought back to life; but now he would not even hesitate before wishing something for Gemma — for her to be made of equal rank to him. Better still — for the Penhallow lands somewhere over there in Roseland to be restored to her family, and extra acres if necessary — enough to make her more lady than farmer's daughter.

Idle fantasy apart, he wanted someone to tell him there *was* an honourable way for him to enjoy romantic thoughts about Gemma — not to court her, since that was clearly impossible, but just to dream about it. That someone had to be a guardian of Society's rules, a woman of some standing in the community, which made Guinevere Roanoke ideal for the purpose. Also, he thought, if he kept harping on about Gemma, it would reassure her that he had no caddish intentions toward *her,* especially now she had revealed she was potentially vulnerable to offers of a clandestine *affaire.*

But, having rattled the skeleton in the Penhallow cupboard, Guinevere was unwilling to talk about her in any more positive way. She remained terse and edgy until Peter told her he really ought to be getting back home as he didn't think his mother would be overjoyed to hear how the evening had turned out. She told him he ought by now to know the difference between outright lying and a simple failure to tell the complete truth — and to correct any false impression that others might gain from his careless use of words.

"Like saying 'they' instead of 'she'?" he suggested.

She laughed happily and told him he was a quick study. She also told him her doggy needed a walk, so she would accompany him to the end of the terrace. 'Doggy' proved to be a snuffly sealyham. She let it run freely ahead, like a lost handkerchief on a capricious breeze, while she took Peter's arm and slowed him down. "I hope I did a wise thing this evening," she said. "Telling you so much."

"About Gemma Penhallow ... or yourself?" he asked.

"You know I don't mean about Gemma Penhallow." She sighed. "Everyone has a breaking point, you know. Society tries to hold us in these bands of steel. And the church. And our own consciences. They all try to make us conform to *their* ideas. But we all have our breaking points."

She seemed to be tiptoeing her way toward another confession. He tried to introduce an impersonal note. "There were chaps at school who would cheerfully swipe up any loose coins or desirable property that other chaps left lying around. Quite decent chaps, too, most of them. They knew jolly well it was theft but they'd say it was the owners' fault for leaving the stuff about. I asked one of them once ..."

"Property!" she exclaimed, interrupting him.

"What about it?" he asked, puzzled.

"Oh ... nothing." After a brief silence she added, "Do you think a wife is her husband's *property?*"

He saw that he had not managed to deviate her train of thought by the smallest degree. If he said yes, she'd start probing his attitude toward theft. "Surely there is a mutual ownership of their affections?" he replied, choosing the words carefully. "He owns her love as she owns his. If you call that 'property,' then I suppose ..."

"And if it's all gone?"

"If the account is overdrawn, you mean?"

"Yes, that would be the de Vivian way of putting it!"

"Well, when any two partners overdraw their account, they jolly well have to roll up their sleeves and work to build up a bit of capital so as to ..."

"All right!" she snapped. "Forget I spoke."

"It's very hard for a fellow to know what you want ... er, Guinevere?" he said.

"Yes!" She chuckled, but with little humour. "I can certainly agree with you there, Peter!"

"You mean even you don't know?"

"I want *everything*," she said. "I want *more* — more than I have, anyway. But the very least I'll settle for is someone I can *talk* to." She sighed. "You've no idea what loneliness ..." She halted. "No. I'm not going to recruit you through pity." She brightened suddenly. "And, come to think of it, I don't need to. *You* want someone you can talk to as well — don't you! Can you unburden yourself to your sister about your feelings for the lovely Miss Penhallow?"

Miss Penhallow! It was a cunning promotion for it suggested that Gemma might, after all, be within range for him. "I couldn't breathe a syllable," he replied — which wasn't quite true. In an absolute extremity he could, indeed, confide in Beatrice, but it didn't sound as if Guinevere were talking about extremities of any kind.

"Then we may forge a pact, here and now," she went on. "That we may talk to each other. Really talk. We will set aside all Society's conventions as to what is fitting for a lovelorn young bachelor and a lonely, still youngish married lady to discuss, and we shall *talk!* Agreed?"

She held out her hand.

"Goodness!" he gasped. "Twelve hours ago I didn't even know you existed — nor you, me."

"Nor you and Gemma." She still held out her hand.

"That's true."

"Some decisions require no time at all."

He laughed. "I can't deny that!"

"And others have to be taken inside minutes — or else they drag on for months without any resolution."

He doffed his hat and shook her outstretched hand at last. Anyone watching would imagine they were taking formal leave of each other — which, indeed, they also did.

He hoped the first person he'd meet indoors would be Gemma. He wanted to let her know he'd heard Ruby's story and that she need have no fear that he would behave like that other young master. Not that he'd be able to get out the actual words but he'd find some indirect way to reassure her.

And Gemma was, as it happened, the first person he saw when he got home, but she did not see him. As he mounted the stairs he heard her voice chatting away in the most lively fashion, somewhere down the end of the corridor. In fact, as he drew nearer, he realized she was in Beatrice's room and that Bea was with her, putting in the occasional word. Cautiously he approached the door, which was a few inches ajar. He couldn't see Bea but there was Gemma, sitting on a stool at the foot of the bed, her nimble fingers making the needle and thread fly. His unseen sister said, "How d'you do it so quickly, Penhallow? Look at me! I'm only halfway still."

And Gemma replied, "I'll go slower if you want, Miss Beatrice."

And they both giggled.

They weren't talking, really, he thought — not a *real* conversation. They were doing that strange thing which females almost always do on settling down to some task together, regardless of class or station: saying things to make each other giggle, things they could say 'Yes!' to, and 'I *know!*' and 'Really?' and 'Never!' — all with whopping enthusiasm. He stopped listening and watched Gemma ply her needle instead.

How firm and sure her fingers were, and how easily she carried her skill! She neither hurried nor did she hesitate; she did not knit her brow (as he felt sure Bea was furrowing hers), nor lick her lips, nor hold her breath in concentration. She was calm and serene. The whole world seemed different when she was near. Time passed in a more exciting way and the very air seemed vibrant. *You are the girl I ought to marry,* he thought. *And devil take Society and what others might say!*

'Some decisions require no time at all'!

He wandered toward the spiral stairs that led to his father's observatory. He hoped to find the place empty so that he could really brood about Life-and-Everything up there in the dark, dwarfed by stars. Too late he realized his father was there, lying on his back, his right eye stabbed with celestial light and gleaming brighter even than the brass latticework of the instrument itself.

"Hallo, old chap," he said without looking up. "Will you be crewing for this Roanoke fellow, then?"

Peter had almost forgotten that arrangement. "Oh," he said vaguely, "he was out on the water. Some trouble with the ... I expect he got becalmed in the lee of Roseland. Anyway, he wasn't there. The rest of us went on with dinner."

"The 'rest' being ...?"

"Mrs R is quite sure he'll want me to crew for him. There's talk of a race from Falmouth to Cowes."

"Amazing!" his father sighed.

"It's not all that far."

"No — I mean what one can *see* here, compared with Plymouth and its eighty thousand chimneys and electrical lights ... stars I'd forgotten. My dear old friends!"

"Ah." Peter was only too glad that the talk had drifted away from the numbers around the Roanoke dinner-table. Seeking to push it even farther, he added, "I hope you're pleased, sir?"

"Yes and no," his father replied. "I'm pleased you'll have some occupation, of course, but I'd be obliged if you didn't get too close to the Roanokes. At least wait until we're more certain of them, eh?"

"In what way d'you mean, Pater? Close?"

"I know they're friends of friends and they come with certain recommendations, but there's something a bit *outré* about her. Harry Corder hinted *she* wasn't quite out of the top drawer. He said nothing against Roanoke himself, but it makes him questionable. A man is judged by the wife he chooses, after all."

"*Outré?*" Peter questioned the word.

"Something NQOC about her, don't you know."

"Pater! This is the twentieth century!"

"Scoff away, dear boy! These things are still important. The Roanokes were mere shopkeepers only two generations ago. There's something about that woman I don't trust — her especially. Did you see the way she walked?"

"I can't say I did," Peter replied guardedly. "How?"

"Tucking her feet into a straight line under her, *as if walking a tightrope*. You ought to read some of my books on psychology. People give themselves away, you know, entirely without meaning to. Our actions are metaphors for what we *are*. Guinevere Roanoke is walking some kind of tightrope. You'll see."

"I found her rather jolly." Peter sought for conventional praises that would let his father know he had no real opinion of (nor interest in) the lady.

But the old man, having said his say, had already lost interest. "You know," he went on, "it still gives me a little shiver when I realize that the light I am presently focusing on my retina left its star of origin several million years ago, when dinosaurs roamed the earth. That star could have exploded itself to bits before mankind began to walk upright, but I can still see it — because I am seeing it as it was all those millions of years ago. All that time! And the light travels at ... what? Can you remember?"

As if he could forget! It was probably the first fact he had ever learned — and he had learned 'a fact a day' (his father's favourite catch phrase) since then. "Six hundred and seventy million miles an hour," he said. "As long as there aren't too many potholes in the road."

He waited for his father to explode with indignation but all the old man said was, "I'm sure you think you're being very funny, Peter. In fact, 'potholes in the road' isn't a bad description of flaws that have recently been discovered in the structure of space-time. Take this fellow Einstein — grand old English name, what! ..."

For the next few minutes Peter said oh and ah and really and well-well while he peered down into the garden through one of the four small lancet windows that pierced the walls of the observatory dome. He had never understood his father's fascination with the stars. Once you had marvelled at their distance and filled yourself with wonder at the sheer number of them and humbled yourself into feeling terribly small and insignificant ... what were they? Random pinpricks of light in the sky. You couldn't even play children's games and join the dots to make bulls, bears, archers, fishes, and so on, because the Greeks or someone had done it for you ages ago.

His eyes were well accustomed to the dark by now and he could make out the light from Beatrice's window. It cast a bright trapezium across the lawn. It was a new phenomenon with electricity, he realized. Oil lamps on the table and gas lamps on the wall sent their feeble rays out horizontally through the windows; and the same was true of the tiny wall lamps they'd had with their own generator back in Plymouth. But these much more powerful lamps from the electric company, which hung high against the ceiling, cast their light *down* upon everything, like little bottled suns. It changed the night-time aspect of the entire world, indoors as well as out.

"A new phenomenon," he murmured.

"It certainly is," his father said. "I hope to observe it for myself at the very next transit of Mercury."

"Well, we must pray for a clear night, then." Peter made to go back downstairs.

"Why did you come up here?" his father asked.

"Oh …" He thought rapidly. "Nothing really. Just to tell you I hadn't managed a chat with Mister Roanoke. Why?"

"Ah." His father cleared his throat and stared rigidly into the telescope eyepiece. "I thought it might be to discuss … something else, don't ye know."

"Something else?"

"Yes — like that strange little scene out in front of the house this afternoon."

"Oh, that!" Peter laughed dismissively.

"It's no laughing matter, m'boy. You embarrassed the poor girl dreadfully."

"I know."

"Did you apologize?"

"Sort of. One doesn't want to give her airs above her station, you know."

"I don't think there's much danger of that, do you?"

The ambiguities in the question were too much for Peter. Either his father knew something about Gemma Penhallow or he was insulting her, suggesting she was too much of a ninny to give herself airs. "Mrs Roanoke says the Penhallows were once landed gentry," he said in Gemma's defence.

For the first time his father unglued his eye completely from the instrument. "Really?" He groaned theatrically and reached out a hand. "Help me up, there's a good fellow. Gentry, eh?"

"Yeomen, anyway. Freeholders. We could probably see their former lands from here. Over on the far side of the Fal. Through that telescope you could count the windowpanes, I'm sure."

"How interesting." The old man stretched his limbs, one by one, sighing with satisfaction. "I was saying to your mama, not an hour ago, that the girl has an amazing air of dignity and self-possession. I would not be surprised to learn of some great tragedy there, in her past." In a different vein he continued, "So tell me — what have you learned today? One should learn a fact a day, you know."

Where to begin!

"I learned ..." Peter spoke slowly, desperately editing his thoughts before he could blurt them out rashly "... oh, lots and lots of things."

"Ha! Name one!"

"I learned" — he was suddenly calm again — "that moments do not last."

His father just stared at him. "Are you feeling quite well?" he asked at length.

"You think that's too obvious a thing to learn?" Peter replied.

"Not at all." His father was thoughtful. "Quite the contrary, in fact. It's very profound. It's what I was trying to tell you just now. The light of those distant stars — or, rather, the moment in which they emitted that packet of light has existed for millions of years. The actual *moment* has travelled outward for millions of years. Yet — now that it has been trapped in my eye — it has gone forever. Moments do *not* last."

Peter had meanwhile returned to his place by the lancet window. While his father was speaking, he noticed someone on the lawn below, a man, standing at one edge of the trapezium of light. The fellow had his back toward the house but when he turned sideways, toward Bea's bedroom, Peter realized it was none other than Henry Trewithen, the footman. Henry Peeping-Tom Trewithen!

An astonishing wave of anger swept over him — astonishing, because his first thought was not for Bea's honour but for Gemma's. He was outraged that Trewithen should be staring up at the lighted window — obviously in hope of catching a glimpse of her!

"I'll soon stop that!" he murmured, making for the door.

"Stop what?" his father called after him.

"Something I forgot to tell Bea earlier," he replied.

All the way downstairs his spirit raged at the thought that Trewithen might be a contender for Gemma's affections. Even if a marriage with her master was out of the question, she deserved someone far above the likes of Trewithen.

He was so shaken by what he had seen that he forgot to knock on Bea's door. He went bursting in, almost bowled Gemma off her stool, apologized extravagantly, and ran the remaining distance to the window, which was raised a mere four inches. At the last moment a sense of caution held him back and he slipped behind one of the wide-open curtains and moved his head slowly out so as to take Trewithen by surprise.

He was just about to shout a rebuke when he saw that the valet had been joined by someone else, a young man, who emerged from the shrubbery between the house and the stables. A moment later, Peter saw it was the stable lad himself, young Dixie Dixon. He stood just beyond the pool of light from the window and beckoned the valet toward him. Trewithen closed the distance in three strides and then passed something to the lad; it could have been an envelope, or just something wrapped in paper. Dixie took it without a word and went back toward the stables. Trewithen turned on his heel and returned directly to the house without so much as an upward glance.

What an extraordinary little scene! Peter thought. What could be in that envelope, or twist of paper, that it had to be transferred after dark? A love letter? Such things were on his mind. Perhaps Trewithen was soft on some female relation of Dixie's, and the stable lad was their go-between? Or perhaps she was a servant in some nearby house, to which Dixie had access while poor Trewithen did not? It was a rum do, anyway.

Peter became aware that both his sister and Gemma were protesting at his sudden bursting-in among them.

"Sorry," he murmured, turning from the window.

"What's the panic, anyway?" Beatrice asked.

"Oh ... nothing." Trewithen's business was his own affair.

"You're making a lot of fuss about *nothing!*" Bea chided.

"I thought I saw, er, foxes — a vixen and her cubs — playing in the moonlight. That's all."

He wanted Gemma to look up at him but she kept her head bent and her needle flying.

"That's *all*, is it?" Bea pointedly echoed his words and turned her eyes toward the door.

"D'you fancy a few hands of bezique?" he asked.

"I rather fancied the conversation Penhallow and I were enjoying a moment ago."

"Oh — don't let me stop you."

"Peter!" she said in an exasperated tone.

"What were you talking about?"

She and Gemma exchanged wearied glances. "What's the Roanokes' place like?" Bea asked. Her tone suggested that if he was insisting on staying in the room, he might as well tell them something interesting.

"A bit old-fashioned," he replied. "It's bound to happen if you don't rent your furniture, I suppose. You live among heirlooms. I imagine it's more to his taste than to hers."

"Oh?" Bea looked up with interest. "Do they not see eye-to-eye, then?"

"Not on most things, I imagine."

"Was her own boudoir decorated in an entirely different taste, then?" She nudged Gemma with the toe of her slipper. The two girls grinned at each other and Gemma glanced at him for the first time. "He's blushing!" Bea said.

"He is not blushing," he replied.

"Why won't you answer, then?"

"I have a reason. But does Miss Penhallow really wish to hear it?" he asked.

They both stared at him, slightly shocked.

"You're not to say that!" Bea chided. "You mustn't call her 'Miss' until it's been made official."

"Until what's been made ..."

"That Penhallow is to be my lady's maid. You may call her 'Miss' then."

He bridled at this gracious permission. "I'll jolly well call her 'Miss' now, if I feel like it. Unless *she* has any objection?"

"Which she has," Gemma said, again glancing at him briefly. He heard the beating of her heart upon her breath.

"But why?" he asked, glad to have *any* reason for talking with her. "Tell me."

"Because I do not have ideas above my station — that's why." After a pause she added, "Sir!"

"Stop embarrassing her!" his sister put in. "I should have thought you'd done enough in that line for one day. For one *year,* come to that."

"Ah, but what *is* your station, Gemma Penhallow?" he asked, ignoring Bea.

Gemma stared at him; she was either surprised that he knew her name or shocked that he should use it like that.

He went on: "Had it not been for a quirk in the law — or so I understand — you would be the daughter of a yeoman farmer. And woe betide the young gentleman who did not call you *Miss* Penhallow then!"

Gemma shot Beatrice an accusing glance.

"I didn't breathe a word to him," she assured the maid.

They both turned to him and Gemma said crossly, "That Mrs Roanoke!"

He nodded. "She told me, yes."

"Did she also tell you ... I mean, was that all?"

He restrained an impulse to tell her what he knew; instead, he replied: "It was a lively dinner table. Sustained conversation on any single topic was impossible."

"Why?" Bea's curiosity was piqued by his obvious evasion. "Was there more to tell?"

"No!" Peter and Gemma spoke simultaneously, then stared at each other in confusion.

Once again the astonishing colour and intensity of her eyes made his heart falter, stop, and then race. He could have gazed at her for ever — and she, for her part, did not seem eager to turn away — until Bea spoiled it by drawling, "I see-ee!" in a particularly irritating manner.

9 Gemma washed herself from head to toe every night and she changed her underwear daily. The other servants considered her rather too fastidious. If their mistresses made do with two baths and changes a week and their masters with one, then these daily ablutions carried the business a bit too far. Gemma's only response was to ask when any of them had last seen a master or a mistress sweating with exertion of any kind. The one thing she never said was that she did it because she enjoyed it and because she felt good afterwards. And clean and pure. To feel clean and pure was the basis of untroubled sleep.

Martha Unwin, with whom she shared the garret room, would wash her hands and face scrupulously enough, and see to her fingernails and things like that, but then she'd flop exhausted into her bed and give out huge sighs of creature comfort just to let Gemma, standing there all damp and naked, know what luxuries she was missing. Tonight, however, was different. Tonight they had to discuss and minutely dissect the de Vivians, the new enemies, and pool their observations of the family's individual strengths and weaknesses. So, while Gemma carefully flannelled, soaped, rinsed, wiped, and dried herself, portion by portion, Martha began.

"They aren't too bad, seemingly," she said. "I put the dust in the hearth and she seen I but she never said nothing. Mrs Walker, she seen it, too, but she never said a word."

" 'Twill be funny," Gemma replied, "having the master in the house all day. I'm not too sure about that."

"He do leave it all to she," Martha said confidently. "And she isn't that fussed. What do you think to the maid — Miss Beatrice, then? She do seem con-fortable, like."

"She's easygoing enough from *our* point of view, but *they'll* have trouble with her before too long, I daresay."

"How?"

"Well, she didn't open up much, not on the first night. She might have done if that great galumph hadn't come bursting in upon us with his tales of foxes and I don't know what, down in the garden."

"How are they going to have trouble with she?" Martha insisted. She wanted to get round to Master Peter, too, of course, but all in good time.

"Well, you know she's got two older sisters, both married? Florence and Charlotte."

" 'Es." Martha sat up, pulled a shawl around her shoulders, and hugged her knees to her. She envied Gemma's sturdy, athletic body; if she herself weren't so gawky and misshapen (in her own estimation), maybe she'd go in for more of this washing lark, herself.

"Well, you should hear her talk about *them!*" Gemma put a foot on the chair and sawed the flannel vigorously between her toes; she never felt really clean until the skin down there tingled. "She's just turned nineteen, Beatrice has, and she's still a spinster. She got a man last season. You heard about that, I suppose, did you?"

" 'Es. He fell off of his horse and died, poor feller. Mrs Walker told I."

Gemma set about making her other toes tingle. "Listen, Martha. I think they're going to make me her lady's maid — Miss Beatrice's. You don't mind, I hope?"

"Mind, my lover!" the other replied scornfully. "How should I mind?"

"Because you've got the seniority, that's how — by age, anyway. I'll say no if it would upset you. Truly."

"You go on, cooze. I shan't be niffed. I'd be frighted for my life to do lady's maid work. I'd only make a caunch of it. Honest I would."

"You wouldn't, you know. You'd manage very well. You only think you wouldn't."

"Never you mind all that. I do know what I do know. The cobbler should stick to his last and let who will go first. How are they going to have trouble with she?"

"Well, both her sisters were married and mothers by twenty, so the master and mistress think there might be something wrong with little Miss B."

"Something amiss with a miss!" Martha laughed too loudly at her own joke and then clapped her hand over her mouth and held her breath.

Both girls waited for Mrs Walker to bang on the ceiling below with a broom handle but this time they were lucky.

Gemma, dry at last, slipped into her nightgown and carried the candle to the rickety whatnot between their beds. It was the new smokeless kind, so things were looking up at Number One. She slipped beneath the blankets and pumped her legs in a running-on-the-spot motion to warm up the sheets. From then on they spoke in near-whispers, which was easier now, with the whole world silent and their heads only feet apart.

"She says that the things she hears from her sisters about the blessed state of matrimony make her want to stay single for ever and ever."

"Stay *single?*" The vehemence of Martha's whisper showed she was having difficulty with the very idea. "A spinster, you do mean? All a-purpose? An old maid for ever?"

"Something along those lines."

"Is that what she said — just in so many words?"

"Not in so many words, no. She went on about one of her friends, back up Plymouth way, who ran off with her father's chauffeur and they started a taxi business in Bristol and they're now as prosperous as she would have been if she'd married the man her parents chose for her. And then she told me of another friend — or friend of a friend — who did something terrible two seasons backalong ..."

"Like what?"

"I never asked. Went out for a stroll in the park without her maid or something, I daresay. Or wore coloured gloves instead of white? I don't know. Some really terrible crime, anyway."

"So they can't put she back in the ring? And she done that all a-purpose?"

"Exactly. That's what Miss B says it is, too — an auction ring. But what's that wicked young lady in question doing now? Living in her own apartment, free as a bird, and binding books for her living in the British Museum, that's what. Making her own way in the world and mingling with people who know about books and art and music and who never mention foxes nor hounds nor grouse nor guns."

"Hark at you!" Martha raised her head, grinned slyly at Gemma, and then blew out the light.

"What?" Gemma asked.

"Was that Miss B talking then — or Gemma Penhallow?"

Gemma chuckled. "Bit of both, I daresay. I should admire a man who can play the piano well and talk about music and painting and books and things."

"*You* can play the piano," Martha pointed out.

"I can tinkle the keys, Martha. I mean a man who can really play. And a man who can look at a picture and, even though it's not as good as a photo, he can tell you why it's even better than one. D'you follow? Or who can read a story ..."

"No spinsterhood for you, then!" Martha interrupted.

Gemma sighed. "Nor no chance of finding such a man, neither. Though ..." She hesitated.

"What?"

"Sometimes people can surprise you. I was talking with Trewithen this morning while we were at the silver. What he doesn't know about heraldry and family crests and that isn't worth knowing. Did you know he was like that?"

Martha laughed grimly. "I know what Trewithen's like, all right," she said.

"How?" Gemma was puzzled.

"He's out for Number One, is our Henry Trewithen."

"Oh? I find him quite chummy."

"'Es! Like a cat when you've got your hand to the pantry door. He's all purring and no heart — and talk about tight with his pursestrings!" Martha was far more interested in the de Vivians. "So you don't reckon much to the young master, then?" she asked.

"No!" Now it was Gemma's turn to be brusque.

"Nothing good to say for'n at all?"

"Rich young idlers with nothing to do and nothing to fill the space between their ears!" Gemma said. "I'd stand them all against a wall and shoot them."

"Oh my gidge!" Martha did not know whether to be impressed or to giggle.

Gemma, realizing where her passion had inadvertently led her, lightened the mood with a laugh. "But that's me all over — a hopeless idealist!"

Martha's laugh brought the long-expected bangs on the ceiling below at last.

"Us'll catch it in the morning," Martha said. "G'night, my lover. I'm gwin say me prayers now — 'tween the sheets. I aren't gettin out in the cold."

"Nor yet me, neither. G'night, Martha."

Gemma included the usual prayers for her masters and mistresses, all by name. She hesitated over adding Peter's but then, realizing that her antipathy for the young man had nothing to do with God, prayed for him, too, at last.

She felt better then; her soul was now as clean as her body. She even felt able to think about the young master without annoyance — and, she realized, she really ought to think as calmly as possible about the embarrassing scene on the front drive that afternoon, just so as to be ready in case he sprang anything like that on her again.

So, although it made her cringe with embarrassment, she forced herself to relive the whole ghastly business. It played in her mind like those pictures printed in sequences in little books, so that when you riffled the pages, the pictures appeared to move. You could stop at any page and make it happen again from the beginning. She did the same trick mentally with Peter as he worked his way down the line toward her. She couldn't yet face that moment when his eyes first met hers, but she took several runs toward it, just to work up the courage.

It surprised her to feel how swiftly her heart began to race in anticipation of that moment. At length the discomfort of it made her go on, to meet his eyes as they turned toward her. It was one of those rare moments in life when everything that happens is indelibly printed on the memory. She had once seen a child fall into the harbour and drown off Custom House Quay — before she herself had learned to swim. She'd swear she could remember every ghastly moment of that event even now, ten years on. And the time Ruby told her she was looking for Roger Deveril's babby ... she could see the clock hands now, and each individual flower in the vase, and the badly ironed corner of the table runner. Every little detail was locked away forever in her mind's eye. And it was so now with that afternoon's encounter with Peter.

She could see his eyes, the bored eyes of a bored young man, making commendable efforts to be nice as he followed his parents down the line of welcome. She could see them settle on her. And how would one describe the change that came over them then? How can you say that the boredom fled, when boredom itself has neither size nor shape? No flicker-book could have captured it and yet, from one brief instant to the next, he changed utterly. And so, to be honest, had she; that was how she knew what had happened to him, too.

A sharp-eyed outsider might have dismissed it as something much more commonplace, a simple encounter in which a normal, healthy young man spotted a good-looking girl and got that sudden sparkle in his eye. It happened every day, scores of times. Gemma herself had been quite ready for that — ready, that is, to freeze him out with an icy stare and a cold formality of speech. Perhaps he had been expecting something shallow like that, too, having caught the merest glimpse of her as the family descended from the cab? At all events he was utterly unprepared for whatever it was that *had* happened between them when at last he set eyes upon her.

'Whatever it was'?

No, she would not name it. It had no name. It was like nothing she had ever met before. Something more than sudden. Something beyond deep. Something absolutely ... absolute. It could not be love, of course. She would not be at all reluctant to name love when it finally came to her. Love made you want to hold him and never let him go; but she didn't really want to even touch Peter de Vivian. Love made you say, 'Whithersoever thou goest, there also will I go'; but if she heard his voice in the next room, she would start thinking of reasons to avoid going there, herself.

And yet *something* had flashed between them — quite literally in the twinkling of an eye. *Something* had compelled him to reach out a hand toward her, not necessarily to shake hers, just to reach toward her. That had been no mere prank. She knew it because that same something had made her respond just as unthinkingly. It was good to know these things, good to admit them, because then she could get her thinking straight. It was good to know it wasn't love, either. Love was unstoppable, but this ... well, one could take precautions to make sure it did not develop into anything like that.

10 Peter woke briefly several times during the night, which was unusual for him. Each time, he felt a moment's confusion. *Something is new,* he thought. *There's a big, new ... something in the air.* Then the memory would come to him: Gemma Penhallow! As soon as he remembered her he felt comforted and reassured and fell back to sleep — until that sense of a vast and unknown novelty prompted him to awaken once more.

Her name was on his lips again when he woke up in earnest, the following dawn. He intended rising at once and going down to the beach for an invigorating swim, but the sweetness of her name held him there. Gemma! She was no longer a shadowy memory in the night but a real person, somewhere in the house, also waking to the day, perhaps. He remembered unashamedly her hand in his; how warm it had been, how soft, how real ... and her eyes — her amazing eyes! Oh, Gemma! He folded a spare pillow to the shape of a head and hugged it close to his.

An hour or so later he awoke again, still head-to-head with 'her.' There were stirrings outside on the landing. Trewithen, no doubt, bringing round the shaving water and first post. Peter closed his eyes and pretended to be asleep, nine-tenths hidden in the bedclothes. The man opened the door without knocking, crossed the room, and began setting out the shaving things. Peter pretended to stir himself awake. Then he remembered the mysterious little scene outside, last night, and a new explanation suddenly popped into his head.

"Are you a betting man, Trewithen?" he mumbled from beneath the blankets.

"Pardon, sir?"

It was Gemma's voice! He peeped out over the edge of his sheets and saw that it was, indeed, the maid who had brought his hot water and was laying out his things.

She saw his two startled eyes peering at her between the counterpane and his unruly shock of hair. It was so comical she only just managed to keep a straight face. *Fancy waking up beside something like that!* she thought — and then pushed the notion angrily aside. Such sentiments, even when contemptuous, were full of danger.

"I thought you were Trewithen." His voice was muffled from under the bedclothes.

"Will that be all, sir?"

"*Is* he a betting man?" Peter, recovering from his surprise, wanted her to stay and talk.

"I wouldn't know anything about that." She took a step toward the door.

"I say!" He sat up, eager to stop her from leaving.

She paused and stared at the floor.

Look at me! he tried to will her but she would not. "Hand me my dressing gown, if you please," he said. "*Are* you going to be a lady's maid?"

He meant, of course, that a lady's maid did not simply stand about, waiting for orders. She had to think ahead and anticipate all the things her mistress might need — and have them ready, without being prompted, when the time came. The fact that he was quite right only made his remark the more annoying to her.

"I'm sorry, sir," she said as she peeled the garment off its hook and brought it to him.

She was much too too dignified to offer him any sort of excuse for her lack of thought; he gave her full marks for that. But now he had run out of easy ways to keep her there, so, taking his courage in both hands, he blurted out, "I must also apologize to you, Miss Penhallow, for the stupid way I behaved on the front drive yesterday afternoon."

There was just a hint of panic in her eyes. He thought of her sister and young Deveril. Was she thinking of them, too?

"Let's say no more about it." She spoke calmly as she turned to go.

"That's not going to be easy," he said before he could think better of it. He saw ... not panic but a kind of pleading in her gaze. God, but she was lovely! He relented. "But I'll do my best," he added, forcing a smile.

Gemma closed the door behind her and, after glancing up and down the passage to make sure she was alone for the moment, leaned back against it. She had actually wanted to stay and talk to him, she realized. And her only reason for leaving so swiftly had nothing to do with ... past events; it was that, if she had lingered, Mrs Walker would have disapproved and would have arranged for Martha or even little Bridget to take his shaving water to him in future.

Still, it showed she could control herself — and self-control was the most important virtue of all in a maid.

Shaved and dressed, Peter went down to a hearty breakfast of porridge, kippers, and kedgeree. His father was less than a minute behind him.

"I've been thinking, m'boy," he said as he ladled out his own porridge and sprinkled the salt.

They ate the dish in Scottish fashion — standing with their backs to the fire.

"And what I've been thinking is this," he went on. "I've been thinking that if you dined with *Mrs* Roanoke and company last night, but without your host, you are more-or-less obliged to call on the house this morning, to leave your card and inquire after him."

"Oh?" Peter's heart leaped up at this officially approved chance to meet Guinevere again so soon, but his manner was dismissive. "She said they weren't too fussy about such things here in Falmouth."

"Just as I said — NQOC," he responded. "But that doesn't mean *we* have to behave like yahoos. You cut along there this morning and do your social duty properly."

Peter, fearing his eagerness to see Guinevere again would show, continued to raise objections. "Suppose she doesn't *want* to be interrupted? Is it 'social duty' to force unwanted attentions upon people?"

"Oh, dear boy!" His father was exasperated. "I'm not suggesting you *see* her. Or him. Or anyone — other than the maid who answers single knocks."

"But you said to inquire ..."

"Give me strength! You simply write the words, 'To inquire after Mister Roanoke' on the back of your card and hand it in to the maid. D'you want me to come and hold your hand?"

"No, sir." Peter lowered his eyes, duly chastened. At least no one could now say he seemed eager to get back to that house.

He spent the first part of the morning in a workman's boiler suit, starting the long job of clearing out the cellar he intended to turn into his workshop. He chose the one at the end because it ran the full front-to-back width of the house *and* had a window large enough to pass the completed hull of his dinghy out onto the back lawn.

The job was not actually a long one but he made it so, for he wanted to be sure Guinevere would be up and about by the time he called. Also, the more he delayed, the less they would suspect him of actually *wanting* to see either of the Roanokes. His father dispatched Trewithen twice to remind him of his social duty. At eleven o'clock Miss Eddy, the cook, sent Martha down to him with a cup of tea and a slice of the fuggan she had just baked.

"Oh, Unwin, you were never more welcome," he said when she set them down on an old upturned tea chest. As he spoke, he reached out and squeezed her arm, briefly and casually — as if it meant little or nothing. He had decided to diminish the shock of yesterday's behaviour by showing he was that sort of person — given to impetuous little intimacies toward one and all, acts of no particular significance.

The maid was surprised but, because he made so little of it, hardly embarrassed. "It do break up the day, sir," she said. "Oh, and your father says ..."

"I know, I know. I really will break off now — don't worry." As
he spoke he pulled the fruity slice of fuggan in two and passed
her the larger half, adding, "Tell me something of yourself,
then. Were you born and reared in Falmouth?"

"Oh, sir!" She looked hungrily at the slice, not daring to
accept it.

He glanced down and appeared to see for the first time what
his hands had done. "Oh, go on! It's too much for me."

She ate with relish, her mouth open. In anyone else it would
have disgusted him but she did it so artlessly, with such joy, he
was not even offended. He felt like a missionary tolerating
strange, savage customs. Her open mouth, pink and wet and
warm, was sensuously touching.

She also spoke while she ate: "Not 'zackly Falmouth, sir. We
do live in Falmouth now but I was borned and reared in Flushing,
'cross the river from Greenbank, where the yacht club is. My
father, he had the rowboat ferry to Greenbank afore he moved
us over this side."

"And what does he do now?"

"Please sir, he's got a ship's chandler's down Fish Strand
Quay, by the gasworks."

"Ah! I daresay I'll be seeing quite a lot of him, then. I suppose
you know I'm going to build a racing dinghy down here. I've
planned it for some time. That's why I'm working so hard now.
Will you have a word with him?" He winked. "Make sure I get
his keenest price, eh?"

Somehow his manner and gestures persuaded Martha there
was 'no harm in him' — as maids judge these things. Her
wariness vanished and, though she did not flee to the other
extreme and become overfamiliar, her manner was perfectly
natural and easy from then on. They spoke a while longer about
his dinghy, and the sea, and the things he might soon be buying
down on Fish Strand Quay ... until his father's voice came
booming down the cellar steps and rolled like thunder along the
passageway: "Pe-ter!"

Twenty minutes later, washed and spruce again, he retraced
his steps to Wodehouse Terrace. He tipped his bowler back on
his head and swung his malacca cane with panache as he strode
out. There were so many things he wanted to talk about with
Guinevere now.

He could not have arrived at a better time for his ostensible purpose — to inquire etc. — nor a worse one for his real purpose. A dogcart was waiting at the kerb and, as he drew near, a tall, well-built gentleman in a morning coat and topper emerged from the house and started to descend the brief flight of steps toward it. He walked with an athletic swagger, swinging a silver-knobbed cane as if he meant to do damage with it. He could only be Mr Roanoke.

Peter decided to pass on by, as if he did not know the house, but the man raised an eyebrow and then broke out in a smile. "Young Mister de Vivian?" he asked. "Come to do your duty? My, my! You are commendably punctilious, sir!" He held forth his hand. "Henry Roanoke."

His grip was strong, his features were salt-browned and weatherbeaten — as was to be expected, of course. Peter could easily imagine him standing at the tiller in a full gale, roaring out commands. He said, "Peter de Vivian, your servant." He contrived a smile to suggest that nothing could have made him happier than this meeting.

"My new *crew,* I hope," the man said. "It's a step lower than a servant, actually — pretty close to a slave!" He laughed. "Care to come down and look at her? I'm on my way to the club now, in fact." He opened the dogcart door and held it for Peter. "Not for a sail, I'm afraid. I'm auditing the bar stocks."

"If you're quite sure, sir?" Peter glanced up at the house. Guinevere was standing at one of the upper windows, gazing down at them. When she saw he had spotted her, she smiled and raised both hands in a gesture that plainly said, 'Hard luck, but there's nothing we can do about it!'

"I saw her becalmed off Trefusis Point yesterday evening," he said as he climbed into the vehicle.

"The *Guinevere?*"

"No!" Peter, not realizing that Roanoke had named his yawl rather than his wife, almost yelped his denial.

"My tub, you know," Roanoke said. The young man's discomfiture amused him. "Did you think I meant ..." He nodded vaguely backward as he took up the reins and shook the pony to a trot.

"Of course not, sir," Peter assured him. "Well, I mean ... I knew you couldn't be referring to Mrs Roanoke."

"You mean *she wasn't* becalmed!"

Peter decided to ignore the jibe. "But then I wondered. So — she's called the *Guinevere,* eh?"

"*She* chose the name — and launched her," he replied, keeping an eye as much on Peter as on the road ahead.

"You had a fair number of oars out," Peter remarked.

"Five pairs before we finished," Roanoke confirmed. "The breeze just died, completely."

"She looked pretty standard from a distance. Have you modified her, sir?"

"Not a bit. She's built to G. L. Watson's design of eighteen ninety-four, you know."

"Yes, I've seen it in Dixon Kemp — the latest edition. Very nifty off the wind, he says, but not weatherly."

From that point onward their conversation left most of the English language behind as the air thickened with talk of fore burtons, storm foresails, reefed mizens, clinker planking, and the run of the hull. Peter gathered that, if he joined the crew, he would start at the bottom — quite literally, for it would be his task to shift anything up to a ton of iron pigs and wet sandbag ballast from side to side, as wind and weather dictated.

"It'll give you the big, brawny shoulders you'll need when you move up to the oars," Roanoke said. "We usually keep one or two galley slaves pulling away on the lee bow when we're running on the wind."

They were approaching the end of the road and, although the harbour was to their right, Roanoke was positioning the dogcart so as to turn left, away from it. Peter sat up and craned his neck to see if he was correct about the direction of the water. Roanoke followed his gaze and misunderstood. "Vernon Place," he said, drawing the pony to a halt. He inclined his head toward a terrace of houses on the very crest of the hill, all with their shutters still closed. "You've no doubt heard its reputation?"

From his tone Peter knew they were talking about *that* — which would also explain the shuttered noonday windows. "No, sir." He eyed them with new interest.

"Well, it's the sailors' first port of call in *this* port of call." He clucked the pony to walk on and completed the left turn into Wellington Terrace. "Ah yes, indeed! 'Nuff said, eh? Women — God bless 'em! We need 'em, but not for very long."

"So, is this the only way down into the town?" Peter asked.

"The only way for vehicles. You can thank Falmouth's hills for that. We've got more hills than Rome, you know. But if you were on foot, you could go through Vernon Place. Or you could also have gone straight ahead, in fact. Did you see the little passage where we turned? That's the top of the famous Jacob's Ladder — you've surely heard of that? A hundred and fourteen granite steps from the Moor up to the top there — the scene of many a tipsy challenge. And almost as many heart attacks among the contestants, too. I used to run the full rise of it when I was your age, two steps at a time. Mind you, it'd kill me now." He laughed to show he didn't really mean it.

Peter's disbelief must have shown in his face.

"I assure you it would," Roanoke promised him. "How old d'you take me for?"

Peter thought swiftly. Guinevere was thirtyish — thirty-one or -two at the most. Roanoke looked fortyish, which was probably his actual age, too. However, his manner of asking the question suggested he was under the impression he looked quite a bit younger. So Peter guessed thirty-eight or -nine.

Roanoke gave him a withering look.

Surely he did not imagine he seemed even younger?

"*Over* forty?" Peter asked incredulously.

"Over fifty!" came the stout rejoinder.

"No!" Peter laughed to show he was not quite as credulous as all that.

"Fifty-three," Roanoke insisted.

Peter stopped laughing. "Really?"

If it were true, then it was, indeed, remarkable. "Fifty-four come September," the man insisted. He was having to haul quite hard on the brake now for, although this meander avoided the steepest hills, the gradient was still severe.

Peter remembered what Guinevere had said about her husband last night — how he needed to prove his manliness and virility all the time. And why. But for that reminder, the man would have impressed him greatly.

"I'm looking forward greatly to meeting your father," Roanoke went on.

"Ah, I'm afraid he shows only a passing interest in yachting, sir. That is — he's interested as long as it's passing him by."

"I thought your manservant, Trewithen, had looked out the *Roseland Belle* for him?"

"Oh dear!" Peter pulled a face. "She's not what one would call a *yachtsman's* yacht, I hope?"

"No, but she's a good, solid tub."

"Ah, that's better. If she floats and has a poop where he may sit under an awning and read his astronomy journals, he'll be happy enough with her."

"You get on well with your father, do you?" Roanoke asked. They had reached a gentler slope and he could relax his grip on the brake.

The question took Peter aback. "Better than most chaps, I imagine, sir," he replied.

"And why d'you suppose that is?"

Peter said the first thing that came into his head. "Most chaps' fathers *do* something. Even if they don't need a salary. They volunteer for this and that ..."

"Your father's on the board of the de Vivian Bank, isn't he? Isn't that *doing* something?"

Peter just grinned at him by way of reply.

Roanoke laughed. "You are commendably frank, young fellow. But I don't see the connection between fathers working and ..."

"Oh, well, when men have positions of trust and responsibility, it seeps into their bones, I think. They become grave and remote and aloof *all* the time. Some chaps don't even know they *have* a father until they leave the nursery and go away to school — when this whiskered foreigner in a stovepipe hat presses a fiver into their hands and tells them not to blub when they get swished. But I've often thought my pater wishes I was just a couple of years his junior."

"So you can talk to him freely, eh?"

They had reached the Moor, which, despite its name, was a low, triangular area between two hills; it served as the town's only attempt at a market square. Peter stared up at the crowded ranks of houses on either side, and their long, steeply sloping gardens. He was amazed that their dogcart had descended so far in so short a time.

"Your father?" Roanoke prompted his memory. "You can talk to him freely?"

"Pretty much so, yes, sir. About anything except messing about in boats, of course. Actually, I'm thinking of building my own boat — a singlehanded racer. Shell hull, varnished. Fourteen foot. A dinghy, really."

"How will she be rigged? Fore-and-aft?"

"I was going to try Bermudan — plus a spinnaker, if it could be managed."

Roanoke was silent awhile. Then, as they started up the High Street — the final hill before the yacht club — he said, "Single-handed sailing!" and shook his head. "Somehow it seems to go against the whole spirit of the thing. To me, sailing is a fine crew of fit, strong chaps, young and old, all pulling together ... singing shanties ... working with a will. All earthly and domestic cares forgotten. And not a wife in sight — that's what it's all about!"

11 Gemma's initiation as a lady's maid was to wash, bleach, blue, and lightly starch the lace collar and cuffs of Mrs de Vivian's morning dress. While she unpicked them, the lady herself looked on and outlined some of her other duties. "I subscribe," she said, "to *The Lady's Companion, A la Mode,* and *Fur and Fashion.* You will read them, too, and keep a little commonplace book in which you will note any new trends in styles, colours, materials, and so forth. You'll make at least one trip a week through the town, visiting the leading milliners, haberdashers, and the like, picking up little tips from them and discovering how well *they* are keeping abreast of the times. We don't rely on them, of course. That's why it's important for you, yourself, to know what's going on in London and Paris. I have known milliners with a glut of grey serge on their hands to swear it was all the rage in London when the magazines were full of pink organdy or mauve chiffon or something."

Gemma told her that Mrs Deveril had taken *The Lady's Companion* and had sometimes let her read it, too.

"The worst part of your job," Mrs de Vivian went on, "is that you will know your fashions inside-out — at least, you will if you do your homework properly. You will be able to date this or that trend to the very hour and minute of its birth. It is very hard for a woman to *know* what is the latest fashion and yet to deny herself the joy of wearing it. But that is precisely what you will have to do, Penhallow. I hope that is understood? You must *never* seek to apply this rich fund of knowledge to your own person — except in very minor, unostentatious ways. Nothing is more ridiculous than a lady's maid who apes her betters. The French lady's maids are dreadful in that respect. One sees them in London during the Season, out walking with their young mistresses, and one cannot tell them apart. They look like cousins. Apart from anything else it's most embarrassing. One sees a young lady to whom one has been introduced at some ball or other, apparently out for a stroll with her cousin, and one stops for a brief conversation, and one smiles at the 'cousin' — as would be only polite to do — and waits awkwardly for an introduction ... which never comes. Because, as it turns out, the 'cousin,' though dressed in the very height of fashion, is no more than a French lady's maid! I have been caught more than once by such intolerable behaviour. Impertinence is what I call it. So don't you ever be tempted."

She spoke with such passion that Gemma could understand how humiliated she must have felt. "I'm surprised the ladies who employ them tolerate it, ma'am," she remarked.

"They have to," the other said crossly.

Gemma waited for more and then said, "Oh?"

"Yes." Mrs de Vivian explained reluctantly. "A good French maid *knows* so much. She can turn any woman's goose into a swan. Oh, Miss Penhallow! You have no idea what competition there is for suitable husbands during the Season. And to think we have to endure it all over again this year — having been quite sure we had put it all behind us last time! We shall hire a French maid, again, of course — no matter what it costs. But we'll take you, too, as her assistant — *if* you prove suitable over the coming weeks, of course. I don't suppose you speak French?"

"Hardly, ma'am," Gemma replied — meaning, in the Cornish usage, that she had a smattering of the language. It was not uncommon for Falmouth people to have a smattering of several languages, for it was a slack day in the port on which you did not hear French, German, Dutch, or Greek spoken *somewhere* about the town. And, of course, she was taking lessons with Miss Isco-Visco of the WEA. So her 'hardly' was more modest than truthful.

But her mistress understood her to mean, in the more general English usage, that she could hardly be expected to speak *any* foreign tongue. "Never mind," she said consolingly. "They speak English quite well enough when they know they have to. I shall expect you to stick by her side and learn all you can. It'll do you no harm, either. Really skilled lady's maids are becoming as rare as hens' teeth — though I suppose I oughtn't to be telling you that."

Gemma, realizing that the woman had misunderstood her reply, was about to correct herself when it struck her that it might be to her advantage if the misunderstanding remained; her mistress might say things in French that she did not wish her maid to know. And knowledge was power. And no one yielded power for free.

Then, reverting to the earlier part of their conversation, Mrs de Vivian said, "It's even worse when people don't simply *dress* out of their class but marry out of it, too. It upsets the whole apple-cart. Don't misunderstand me, Penhallow. I'm no snob, I hope. Merchants' daughters have married into the aristocracy. Go-ahead butchers' sons have married squires' daughters. And that's fine. There has always been a little judicious mingling at the edges — unlike Europe, which is why they have revolutions every twenty years and we don't. But when the younger sons of dukes and earls marry actresses and shop assistants ... well, that's altogether different. Especially the actresses. They pick up our superior manners and more refined language in no time. It's so deceptive."

She paused and then, as if changing the subject, said, "I've been wondering about Mrs Roanoke — the lady who called to welcome us yesterday. What do we know about her? Was she ever an actress? *Is* she a lady?"

"Her father was a tooth-puller," Gemma said. "From Helford up to Truro he pulled teeth by appointment. He had a regular day in certain towns and villages ..."

The other woman pounced on this tidbit with delight. "What — 'teeth pulled every Thursday at two pee-em at the White Hart, Penryn' — that sort of thing?"

"Well, ma'am, it was the King's Arms, Penryn, but, yes — that sort of thing."

Mrs de Vivian clapped her hands and said, "How delightful!"

Gemma repeated certain parts of this conversation to Beatrice that same afternoon. She gave out some of Mrs de Vivian's thoughts as if they were her own, just to see how the younger mistress responded.

Beatrice said that some of her mother's opinions — though utterly, utterly worthy, of course, which went without saying — were very much of her generation; girls of her period had been the last to grow up in the shadow of the old queen. "I have no time for all that old Victorian fustian," Beatrice said. "If this were my household, I should not dream of calling you Miss Penhallow, which sounds terribly cold to me. I should call you … Gemma, isn't it? And you should call me … well, you'd continue to call me Miss Beatrice, of course. But in all sorts of *other* ways we should be less formal and reserved, I think. After all, what is the fascination of tales like Cinderella, if it isn't the thought of a scullery maid sweeping out ashes one minute and dancing with the prince himself the next?"

The huge mental leap between this last question and what had gone before startled Gemma. Mrs de Vivian claimed she was shocked when actresses married into the aristocracy; but Miss Beatrice was merely 'fascinated' at the thought that a scullery maid might marry a prince. Was this the new way of thinking among the younger members of Society? If so, then the world was no longer the rigid, unchanging place she had always thought it to be.

"In fact," Beatrice went on, "I think — when we are alone together — I *shall* call you Gemma. Unless you object?"

"Well, miss …"

"And you needn't keep saying Miss Beatrice or even just 'miss' all the time — just once or twice — when we're alone. After all, I don't keep saying 'Peter' or 'brother' when I'm talking with him, do I! I just talk to him. So … yes, I think that will be very satisfactory. Don't you?"

"If you say so …" She had to force herself not to add the 'miss.' Then, when she realized that Beatrice was waiting for it, despite all her fine words, she laughed. They both laughed.

"Also …" Beatrice went on "… I mean, how much land did your family have over there at Penhale Jakes?"

"A hundred and twenty acres — which is a big farm for Cornwall. Lots of farms aren't even twenty."

"It's a substantial farm in any county, Gemma. Many squires wouldn't own that much land — which just shows how silly the whole business is. If your great-grandfather had died a year later — even if he *had* killed himself — your family would still own that land. And all sorts of young men would now be competing for your hand."

Gemma remained silent.

"What d'you think about that?" Beatrice pressed her.

"Could-have-beens in the head is not could-have-beans on your plate, miss. It does no good to rake up the past like that."

"I agree — except for this: You *know* your ancestry. You know what stock you descend from. It must allow you to hold your head higher than Biddy-from-nowhere."

Gemma shrugged awkwardly. "That could be."

"And the higher your head, the farther you can see. And the farther you can see, the wider grows your choice!"

Later, when Gemma mentioned these interesting conversations to Trewithen, he soon put them in a different light. "The only *fairy* story in Cinderella," he said, "is where the prince goes looking for her *after* he's had his fun. If you gave me the choice between two masters, one all stiff and aloof, who doesn't care if you're feeling on top of the world or dying of toothache, and the other all matey and concerned for my welfare, I'd pick the first one every time. These 'democratic' masters will always be masters. They'll call you Gemma and smile at you, fit to cut their heads in half, but you'll still lick their boots. They'll always let you down in the end. Don't never be deceived, maid. They'll be friendly enough until you do something as threatens them … threatens their position. Then you'll hear the shutters and gates clang loud enough to deafen you."

Gemma turned pale at this, for Trewithen was describing precisely the way the Deverils had treated Ruby when she asked them to give their grandson an honest name. Had someone given away her secret shame?

The Deverils had been masters of the 'kindly, democratic' kind. "Our servants are like members of the family," they had said more than once; but when Ruby told them their son had put her in the *family way,* the poor maid had discovered that the word was most elastic in meaning. It did not include girls who were 'no better than they ought to be' — whatever that meant.

Nor girls who set out to dazzle and seduce their naive and susceptible young masters — which Ruby most assuredly had not done. And anyway, to call Roger Deveril 'naive and susceptible' was like calling a wild boar 'dainty and unassuming.' Yes, she reflected, in Ruby's case the shutters and gates had certainly come clanging down loud enough to deafen them all — including her own father and mother, who had turned her out to fend for herself without a second thought.

Poor Ruby! Where was she now? And did she have that baby? If only she'd write and let her know she wasn't dead. Just that. She needn't write directly if she were afraid of compromising her sister; there were plenty of third parties known to them both. Or if she sent poste restante to Falmouth, someone down there would let her know, especially after she'd gone in to inquire every week in the first months after Ruby had vanished — and still did so from time to time. Miss Harvey, behind the counter, or Billy Carney, who did the window flower boxes and telegrams — either of them would surely get notice of it to her. But never a word had she written.

Gemma's response wavered between anger and anguish. There were times when she thought that, no matter how bad things were with Ruby, the girl could at least put pen to paper and let her sister know she wasn't actually dead. Even from prison she'd be allowed to write. It made Ruby's silence seem merely perverse, which fired up Gemma's rage. But then at other times she'd get to thinking that things must be parlous indeed if Ruby could not even write. Or would not. She'd spy some wretched young girl lying drunk in a gutter down Smithick Hill or behind Vernon Place — or one of those slums of Falmouth through which even the most respectable people could not help passing from time to time — and she'd think at once of Ruby, knowing very well that, if their paths in life had been exchanged, so that she, Gemma, were now reduced to that pitiable state, the last person to whom she would write would be her twin sister, no matter how much love might remain in her heart. Pride alone would prevent it.

And these latter thoughts would, in the oddest way, comfort her. If Ruby were in those wretched circumstances and yet still had enough pride *not* to write, then all was not lost. She, Gemma, always inspected them closely, those pathetic bundles of lost humanity, just in case one of them was Ruby. She would not put it past her sister to return to Falmouth, not to batten on her own family, nor to rely on former friendships, but to multiply her own punishment — to live so near and yet so far, to tantalize herself with memories of all that she had made forfeit in that one scarlet moment with the Devil Deveril. In that respect, Gemma knew Ruby as well as she knew herself, for the two sisters were alike in their inclination to condemn themselves and pile on the punishment.

So Trewithen's words reinforced her own notions about how to behave toward her new employers — it must be coolly and with dignity. She already had the most powerful reasons for avoiding even the most minor intimacy with the young son of the household, despite — or perhaps because of — his pleasant manner and his devastatingly good looks; now she had equal reason to remain cool with the mistress and the daughter, too. 'They'll always let you down in the end' — she should imagine those words hanging like an embroidered text above her bed, reminding her of the basic fact of her life both on dreaming and on waking up afterwards.

Trewithen said one more thing that turned itself over and over in her mind during the following weeks: "You'll notice," he said, "that the mistress told you it was all right to get pally with this temporary French maid up Lunnon — but she never suggested hobnobbing with other lady's maids here in Falmouth, did she! You'd learn just as much for your own good from them — but that's the last thing they want — all us local servants getting together for a bit chat. If you don't believe me, just try asking leave for one of the upper servants in some house in Wood Lane to come calling on you, and you'll see what a dusty answer you'll get. But then ask for the same privilege for some clerk down the town hall or in one of the shipping offices — someone of the same social standing, see — and it'll be all smiles and blessings on you. Domestic servants and office clerks can't get talking together, can't go making comparisons, can't combine on wages and hours, see!"

Gemma thought it marvellous that a simple remark like that, intended half humorously, could stir such profound thoughts within her. Until then she had assumed, without giving it a second thought, that the social order was in some way ordained and unchangeable. Whether it was by God's will or the Devil's or the government's or simply by near-universal agreement, it didn't really matter. You either accepted it and got on with your life as best you might or you struggled to change things and led a pretty miserable existence in the meanwhile. But Trewithen's observations opened her eyes to the possibility of something in between. Deep inside herself she *could* refuse to accept the social order even though she made no bones about accepting it from day to day; she could still get on with her life as best she might, while all the time preparing for something better. It was all a matter of attitude.

In a way, that was what Miss B had said, too. What was it — the higher you hold your head, the greater your choice of the good things in life? Something like that.

12 The London Season was one of those typically British institutions that start out as one thing and evolve into something completely different — into its exact opposite, in fact. Back in early Georgian days the great aristocratic and landed families had all congregated in London for the parliamentary session that began after Easter and ended in August. Dinners and other entertainments accommodated themselves to parliamentary time, so that a member could go straight from the tabled amendment to the tabled pheasant. In those days the king held afternoon levées at which the aristocracy and gentry presented members of their family who had undergone some rite of passage — coming of age, marriage, the birth of an heir, and so on. It was a private ritual, enabling the king to keep in touch with his larger 'family,' the five hundred or so people who ran the country in his name.

The first breach in the ramparts of this intimate custom came in Regency times, when the court reporter of the official *London Gazette* was graciously permitted to hide behind a curtain and copy down the names off the cards that were left by those being presented to the king. From the moment when 'presentation at court' stopped being a private, family matter and became a public affair, those who stood just outside the charmed circle clamoured for it to be widened enough to let them in. *Just* enough, of course. And the loudest noise of all came from the clink of gold on its passage from pocket to pocket — or, rather, from dowry to marriage settlement.

Wider and wider the circle grew. Throughout the following century old money snubbed and humiliated new money with gusto but could not drive it away. The interlopers kept coming back for more. More parties. More balls. More operas. More seeing and being seen — at the Eton—Harrow match, at the Royal Academy's private view, at the Epsom Derby, at Henley regatta, at Cowes, at Glorious Goodwood — the occasions of extravagance multiplied year by year. And the court reporter no longer skulked behind his curtain; indeed, the palace itself now issued Certificates of Presentation at Court, which were carried triumphantly back to the provinces and shires, to hang, no doubt, among the achievements of earlier years — the gymkhana rosettes, the pigeon-shooting cups, the sawn-off oar blades, and all the other trophies of a richly fulfilling and socially useful life.

By the time the old queen died and her son Edward ascended the throne there was no longer the slightest pretence that the Season was anything other than a three-month extravaganza for the rich — and anything up to three months of purgatory for each of their unmarried daughters, whose torment could not be ended until an acceptable gentleman asked her parents' permission to slip a ring on her finger and murmur the magic words in her grateful ear.

The de Vivians, having only one spinster-daughter left — and she going up for her second time — decided not to take in the full Season. There was a general agreement that a girl going up for her second time ought not to present herself in the early weeks, for that was when the fledgling swans took their first well-chaperoned flights upon untried wings. So Ada de Vivian decided to depart for London during the first week in May. They would not rent a house; the price of a good address was quite outrageous. Instead, they would stay in St James's Square at the house of a distant cousin who fled the metropolis annually at that time, saying he preferred the society of salmon and trout in Ireland to Society in London. "And," de Vivian commented, "since he does nothing but slaughter those Hibernian species, Society in London has much to be thankful for!"

When Peter told Guinevere Roanoke of this arrangement, adding that he would be going up, too, she stamped her foot and said it wasn't fair. Being able to talk to him so freely had altered her life out of all recognition. She no longer felt herself at boiling point and ready to explode all the time. She even came down to the yacht club, singing to herself all the way, and she could happily wave at the yawl, her namesake, knowing she had at least one friend aboard her. But now Peter was going away for God knows how long ... it could be months ... it simply wasn't fair.

What would she do without him?

What would *he* do up there? Nothing! Live in idleness and acquire evil habits. Falmouth was bad enough, being a seaport, but at least it was all kept behind closed doors and shutters; the streets were as pure as any Methodist watch committee could desire. But London's streets were awash with enticements of every low kind ...

At which point she stopped and a thoughtful look crept into her eyes. Peter thought her tantrum was just becoming interesting; in fact, he was on the point of challenging her to justify her denunciation of London with a bit of chapter and verse when she said, "Conrad Wilkes!"

"I beg your pardon?"

"Conrad Wilkes — of course! My cousin's husband. He's taking Devoran House in July, but ... oh, and there's Graham Melchett, too — another cousin!"

"I'm afraid I lost the fox some while ago, Guinevere," Peter said. "Who are all these cousins?"

She explained then that Conrad Wilkes was married to her cousin Teresa, by whom he had three daughters. They lived in Bayswater, overlooking Hyde Park, and they had a country cottage near Maidenhead. Teresa was 'not with us very often' — Guinevere did not elaborate on that cryptic dismissal. Conrad was a hatter in quite a big way. The daughters were twenty, eighteen, and sixteen; the two elder ones would probably be taking part in the Season and, what with Teresa's 'problem,' Conrad would be delighted if she, Guinevere, came up to chaperon them.

Graham Melchett was a second cousin to the three girls; therefore a cousin to Guinevere, too. He was highly spoken of in the colonial service, and he'd be staying with the Wilkeses in Bayswater for much of the summer. He'd also probably come down to Cornwall with them in July, unless he'd found a wife by then — which was his principal reason for taking home leave this summer.

People said he was destined for the highest ranks of the service. He would certainly 'pull' a knighthood one day and very probably a baronetcy.

"Anyway," Guinevere concluded happily, "I have excellent reasons for joining in the London Season — so, contrary to what I may have hinted at earlier, I find I heartily approve of your mother's intentions to take you along, too!"

"And what of the enticements that abound in London's streets?" Peter asked.

"Oh!" she said dismissively. "London isn't half as bad as people like to paint it, you know. Besides, I'll be there to look after you!"

'To look after you'! He had noticed lately that Guinevere enjoyed using ambiguous phrases like that, especially in ambiguous circumstances; it was as if, by toying with ideas, or mere suggestions of ideas, she could keep the reality behind them at bay.

Or alive?

Ada de Vivian was not in the least bit pleased at this development — especially at the news that Guinevere Roanoke, the tooth-puller's daughter, had a cousin who was such an eligible bachelor and who would, moreover, be coming to London this Season for the express purpose of finding a wife. One day, he'd be Sir Graham Melchett, Bt! And his wife *Lady* Melchett! That would be enough of a feather in any daughter's cap. But, to gild the lily, he also had an income of twenty thou' a year and never drew his salary. Bachelors hardly came in more eligible form than that.

How dare Guinevere Roanoke be the daughter of a mere provincial tooth-puller! It was so vexing. Now she, Ada, would have to be as friendly as possible with the woman, tolerate her disgraceful habit of dropping in at any hour of the day with never a by-your-leave, and try to overlook her humble origins — to say nothing of those arch and frivolous conversations she indulged in with Peter.

Beatrice took against Graham Melchett from the very moment she heard of these machinations, in the same way as she took against books that people recommended in over-enthusiastic gushes of praise. To put her off any particular course of action, all one needed to say was, 'Simply *everyone* is doing it. You *must* try it for yourself, my dear!' It worked better than the strictest outright prohibition.

"He will be short, fat, and prematurely bald," she sneered — until Guinevere produced a photograph that revealed him to be tall, handsome, and curly headed. Then she said she was sure his breath would be offensive — which, of course, a whole album of photographs could not gainsay.

"They go on about his wretched private income, as if they think it's exciting," she complained to Gemma when they were sure of not being overheard. "It would be more convincing if we were poor. But we are not."

The maid delicately cleared her throat.

Beatrice, knowing what question was implied by her reticence, responded as if Gemma had asked it frankly. "I don't know. They never discuss such things — certainly not in front of us. But you can't sell thirty-five flourishing banks for mere pocket money! I know *I* have a private income, too, but they won't tell me how much it is — which they would if it were something tiny, like a thousand a year."

Tiny! Gemma thought. A thousand a year would pay all the servants at Number One several times over.

"My sisters were settled with sixty thou' each on their marriages — I know that much, though I'm not supposed to. It's all in trust, of course. They can't actually touch it. Women could not possibly be allowed to manage such dizzy-making sums all by their little, muddle-headed selves! Their husbands can't touch the capital, either — fortunately — though they do enjoy the income." After a silence she added, "Don't feel you have to hold your tongue, Gemma. No one else is listening. The whole thing infuriates me. Why *should* a lady be shielded forever from such things? Why *should* I be passed from the care of my father — or of my *brother,* for heaven's sake, if my father should die — to the care of a husband and never pollute my mind with thoughts of filthy lucre? The whole thing is just so preposterous, don't you think?"

"This petticoat cost fifty pounds!" Gemma said. She wondered if she dared add that it was more than double what she was paid in a year.

Beatrice gave it the briefest glance. "Ha!" One after another she picked the 'evening confections' (no one wore gowns or robes any more) that had been bought, made, or altered for her London ordeal. She handled them with a curious mixture of awe and contempt. "Two *hundred* pounds, this one. A hundred and eighty for this. And, oh, here's a cheap one — this one was only a hundred and fifty. But this one now — this one is more like it: two hundred *guineas!* That's what? Ten times as much as we pay you in a year?"

"About that," Gemma said. Then, with another delicate ahem, she corrected her reply: "Eight times what I was *promised* on being promoted, anyway."

"I'll remind my mother about it," Beatrice assured her.

"No!" the maid put in hastily. "Best not."

"Oh, I shall do it most tactfully, fear not. And" — she spoke warily now — "there *is* something you could do for me, Gemma — equally tactfully, I hope?" Her tone turned the statement into a question.

"Yes?" Gemma's tone was equally guarded.

"I know servants have ways of finding out things their masters would rather they didn't. It's a well-known fact. So if, by some circuitous mode of inquiry, you could discover the true size of my income, I should be utterly beholden to you. D'you think you might?"

"I shan't go prying into drawers and things," Gemma warned.

"Fortunately, that's not what I mean."

Gemma just went on staring at her until the penny dropped.

"Oh!" Beatrice laughed at her own slowness. "You mean have *I* tried prying open drawers and locked cupboards? The answer is yes."

"And?"

She shook her head. "No luck. My father still has an office at the bank in Plymouth. It's probably there."

Gemma remembered that a second-cousin of her mother's worked in that same office, but a moment's further reflection convinced her he'd never risk his entire career on such a whim. "I'll put on my thinking cap," was all she'd promise.

That evening in the servants' hall, just before she left for her French classes, she broached the subject with Trewithen. She did not, of course, admit that she had been commissioned to discover the size of the settlement that produced her mistress's income; she merely mentioned the fact of it and wondered how anyone would go about finding out more.

"Was it bequeathed by way of a will?" the valet asked. "Or was the trust set up by someone in his lifetime?"

Gemma shrugged. "What would be the difference?"

"Wills are published on grant of probate," he replied. "Anyone can go to Somerset House in London and look them up. I'm not so sure about deeds of trust. They must be on the public record somewhere but maybe the details are not disclosed. Why? Did the young lady ask you how she might find out?"

"No!" Gemma knew her denial was too effusive. To recover herself she added, "She just mentioned the fact and said she had no idea what the size of it was. And I just thought it would be nice to surprise her if ever she says such a thing again. You know — just come straight out with it."

A couple of hours later, she returned from Miss Isco-Visco and the WEA with her head full of verbs that took *ne* plus the subjunctive. *"Il fait beau maintenant, mais je crains qu'il ne pleuve,"* was her favourite — and would come in very handy one day, considering the tendency of the Cornish weather to rain at the slightest excuse. She found Trewithen waiting for her with yet another suggestion. This time it was more direct.

"You know this Graham Melchett they're all talking about?" he began.

Her eyes raked the ceiling; no other reply was necessary. The entire house had rung with nothing but the name of La Roanoke's cousin for days.

"Well, if your mistress has an income of any great size, and if her mother is truly dedicated to ensnaring the said G Melchett, I imagine she'd find some way of making sure the man knows about the settlement, don't you? I never met a rich man who wasn't interested in being richer, did you?"

Gemma saw the point at once. What better way of letting the Melchett family know how well endowed Miss Beatrice de Vivian was than to pour news of it into the ear of the man's cousin — who happens to live just round the corner!

"Oh, Trewithen — you're a darling man!" she cried, impulsively flinging her arms around his neck and hugging him tight. She was even about to give him a chaste kiss, but she was mortified to feel his whole body stiffen, as if in distaste. It was his genuine, unpremeditated response.

A moment later, the civilized man took over and forced him to relax again as, unpeeling her arms, he said, "And you're some darling maid, Miss Penhallow."

"I'm sorry ..." she stammered as the blood rushed to her face. She felt sure her cheeks were quite scarlet. "I didn't mean to ..."

"Don't *you* be sorry," he said vehemently. He still held her by the wrists, which he now shook to emphasize his words. "Not *you.* 'Tis *I* must apologize — for being ... the way I am. Not outgoing, you know. Not ... I mean, it's not *you*. My old mum used to try and hug me and I'd go like this." He did a perfect comic imitation of the way in which a young boy might wince on being ordered to kiss an aunt with a heavy moustache. Gemma laughed but the mood remained awkward.

He continued talking, to cover it up. "You do know that Sally Kelynack, don't you?" he went on. "Mrs Roanoke's maid."

"By sight," Gemma replied. "She dropped a glove in church once and I gave it back to her. But those are the only words we ever exchanged."

"She'd help, I'm sure." He paused before adding, "Or ..." He hesitated again.

"Or what?"

"No." He shook his head firmly.

"Go on," she urged. "Say it, anyway."

"Well, I was thinking. Master Peter sees quite a bit of the Roanokes ..."

"You mean I should ask him to ..." Gemma bit her lip and shook her head.

Trewithen's main purpose in raising this possibility had been to gauge her response to Peter's name and to the possibility of using her hold over the young master to get the information out of the Roanoke woman.

That Peter was obsessed with Gemma he did not doubt. How much Gemma realized it, and what she, in turn, felt for the young master, was much less certain. But there was always electricity in the air whenever those two were in the same room.

She never lost a chance to sneer about him and she would always leave his company on the smallest pretext if her duties did not require her to stay. But she would not let anyone else take him his morning shaving water and she often lingered there to enjoy some petty argument with him. It was never an ordinary, pleasant conversation — always something aggressive and insubordinate. If the young master wasn't so taken with her, he'd have had her dismissed weeks ago. And she would come out of that room with her breast heaving and her eyes shining. Even on her day off, once a fortnight, she wouldn't leave the house until she'd performed at least that one chore. If the Walkers weren't so busy bickering with each other at that same hour, they'd have spotted it at the start.

"He'd do it for you, if you asked," the valet risked saying.

"What do you mean?" she said pugnaciously.

"No more than I say: Master P would do it for the asking."

Her eyes flashed angrily. "I'm not interested in him," she said in her haughtiest manner.

He raised both hands in a small gesture of submission. "Did I say you were? Did I even hint it? I just stated a fact about Master Peter."

"I know my station," she went on. "As for all that foolery about family crests and my yeomen ancestors, that's just kitey nonsense. I'd be daft as a wagon hoss to think anything else, Mister Trewithen."

She usually scorned her native dialect except when, as now, she could use it to make a point.

"Miss Penhallow — on my word — I never thought of you as anything other than ..."

Gemma interrupted him. Taking her heart in her hands she said, "The sort of man who interests me is a man of my own station in life — a modest man with one eye to better himself and the other firmly fixed on the limits beyond which he may not aspire." And she kept her own eyes firmly fixed on him as she added, "An upper servant like yourself, for instance."

He closed his eyes and turned his head away. "*Not* like myself," he said.

"Why?" she asked.

His immediate rejection of the very idea was a shock, not least to her self-esteem.

He stood awhile in silence, not looking at her. Then he crossed the room to the door, closed it firmly, and, facing her at last, said, "What I'm about to tell you must never go beyond these four walls — all right?"

She swallowed heavily and nodded.

"You spoke out plain to me, Miss Penhallow — words that cannot have come easy. So I owe it to you to say you do *not* want an upper servant like me ..."

"Oh but ..." Gemma tried to object.

"You want one who *isn't* already married!"

She stared open-mouthed until the meaning of his words sank in. "You?" she whispered.

He nodded. "Me."

"But ... how? I mean ..."

"I was eighteen, she was sixteen — that's how. You don't get a second chance to make such a mistake."

"Is she ..."

He shrugged. "Who knows? She ran off with ... someone, four years ago. That's the last I saw of her. I am not an uxorious man, Miss Penhallow. You are a nubile young woman. Take my word for it — you do *not* want someone like me. Nor" — he cleared his throat diffidently — "do I think you want any kind of upper servant, neither."

"Who then?" she asked.

But he shook his head. "Another time, maybe. Now, I'm going out to smoke a bit baccy. I'll lock up when I come back."

He squeezed her arm as they passed, she making for the servants' stair, he for the rack where his hat and inverness cape were hung to dry.

Her eyes were full of tears as she mounted the stairs. She tried to sob quietly but Peter heard her.

She was not to know that he waited near his door every night for the sound of her retiring footsteps; somehow he could not settle to sleep if he knew she was still up and about the house. He realized how stupid it was and he mocked his nightly dependence on this pointless little ritual, in which he pressed his ear to his door and listened to the whisper of her passing. But he could not give it up.

She had barely started on the final flight of stairs, the steep one that led from the third floor up (where the Walkers and

Trewithen slept) to the female quarters in the attics above, when he caught up with her.

"Gemma!" he whispered hoarsely.

She stopped and turned round in a panic.

"Go 'way!" she urged in the most vehement whisper she dared. She hiccupped once or twice in the aftermath of weeping.

"What's the matter?"

"Go away!" Now she spoke the words, softly but deliberately. "Nothing's the matter."

"You were crying."

"I wasn't."

"You were."

"I ... I twisted my ankle."

"That's a lie!"

Without thinking, she hit him. It was a mild enough slap on the cheeks but something unforgivable between servant and master. His involuntary cry was loud enough to stir Mrs Walker from her sleep.

Gemma pulled the offending hand tight against her and held her breath, waiting to see what Peter would do next.

All he did was repeat her name — "Gemma!" — in something of a pleading tone.

"What now?" she asked. She had meant to use a weary tone but it did not come out like that; indeed, it made her sound quite tender. Her guilty conscience, of course.

"This is no good," he said, trying to take her hand.

She would have let him, too, if she had not spied Mrs Walker's shadow emerging from her room ahead of her. "You're right," she said. "It will not do." She winked and darted her eyes meaningfully over his shoulder.

He heard the soft tread of carpet slippers behind him and caught on at once. "So!" he said, all brisk again. "You're sure you're all right? I'll gladly bring you a bowl of cold water to bathe it."

"What's all this, then?" Mrs Walker asked suspiciously.

"I think she turned her ankle, Mrs W," he said. "Didn't you hear the clatter?"

"I never *clattered,*" Gemma said at once.

As Peter turned to go he looked at the housekeeper for sympathy. "Whatever I say, *she* has to contradict it!"

"Is that a fact?" the woman asked in a thoughtful tone. "Is it hurt? Let me see?" She waited for Peter to avert his eyes before she lifted the hem of Gemma's dress. "No swelling," she said.

Their eyes met and Gemma knew there were other kinds of 'swelling' on the woman's mind. "Nor there won't be, neither," she replied.

"Betterfit you go to bed, then." Mrs Walker turned about and waited until Peter had gone back downstairs before she, too, returned to her bed.

The following morning he was up and respectably clad in his dressing gown by the time Gemma appeared with his hot water. "That was a rum do last night, Gemma," he said.

"Who?" she asked in a challenging tone, without even looking at him.

"Very well, then," he replied wearily. *"Miss* Penhallow. Why were you crying?"

"I wasn't." She stood at his washstand, three-quarters turned away from him, staring out of the window. *If I was rich,* she thought, *I'm sure I'd spend a lot of time standing at windows, wondering what to do next.*

"Don't start all that business again. Something made you cry — or some*one.*"

"That's none of your business. Can I go?"

"I'm not stopping you." He took an elaborate step to one side though he had not been blocking her way before. *If I were poor,* he thought, *none of these barriers between us would exist.* He moved closer to her, not with any particular purpose in mind — just to be nearer.

She continued to stare out of the window, trying to ignore the little thrill she felt at his closeness. A movement in the garden below caught her eye. An azalea shivered and a moment later Trewithen stepped gingerly out upon the lawn. He turned and glanced back over his shoulder. Gemma followed his gaze and saw young Dixon, the stable lad, standing at one of the loose-box doors. He gave the valet a cheeky thumbs-up and tugged his forelock in a distinctly ironic manner, as if he were mocking Trewithen's superior station in the hierarchy of servants.

"Well, well!" Peter murmured at her elbow.

She turned in some alarm to face him. "What d'you want?" she asked brusquely.

"Did you see that?" He nodded at the now deserted garden.

"Mmh." She turned to look that way, too.

Dixon flung wide the stable door and started to fill the gardener's barrow with the overnight dung. He glanced up at the house but the reflected brightness of the sky must have obscured them from him; at all events he gave no sign of noticing his two puzzled spectators.

"Is Trewithen a betting man?" Peter asked.

That must be the most likely explanation, she thought. To keep it secret from the Walkers he'd get the lad to place the bets for him. "I never heard him talk of it, nor yet saw him place a bet," she replied.

"And now we know why — perhaps," he said. "D'you know what I'd like to do, Gemma?"

Alarm renewed itself as she turned to him again.

"I'd like to compile the true diary of a house like this. Just covering one day, minute by minute. And record all the comings and goings of *everybody* — masters, mistresses, housekeeper, butler, upper servants, lower servants, outside servants — the lot! All the little secret criss-crossings. The jokes and tricks, the little acts of kindness and spite, the likes and dislikes ... everything! Wouldn't that be jolly?"

The suggestion intrigued her, much against her will, but she wasn't going to let him know it. "So nobody among us could look another in the face, ever again!" she sneered.

"My goodness!" He laughed. "Are things as explosive as *that* beneath our calm, unruffled exteriors!" Then, more seriously, he added, "On the other hand, we might all understand one another so much better, don't you think? We're all so dishonest with one another."

Gemma said nothing to that.

"Children are dishonest with parents. Parents never tell the full truth about anything to their children. We gang up to conceal things from you servants — and you never let us know half of what's going on among you. Don't you see? We're all living in a fog of half-truths and misunderstandings."

"I've got to go," she said suddenly, and this time she suited action to her words.

"Someone's got to break the pattern," he called after her departing back.

13 Early one morning in the week before they all set off for London, Gemma brought Peter his hot water, as usual, but was surprised to find him dressed and ready-waiting. He must have shaved in cold.

"What now?" she asked suspiciously.

He put a finger to his lips and beckoned her to follow him outside — which she did, rather hesitantly. Her reluctance increased when she saw he intended to lead her up to the forbidden territory of the observatory.

"Just a couple of minutes," he whispered when he saw her hold back. "It's a very nice surprise, I promise."

"No funny business?" she asked.

"Oh, suit yourself," he said crossly as he turned from her and raced to the top, three steps at a bound and as silently as a cat.

Curiosity overcame her caution and she followed him up, one careful step at a time. He already had the telescope adjusted by the time she arrived. But, although she saw the direction in which it was trained, she did not make the connection until she put her eye to the lens — and then the sight that greeted her took her breath away.

"Oh, my gidge!" she murmured. "Is that …?"

"Penhale Jakes," he said.

"They're bringing in the cows." Her breathing shivered. "Well, I never!" She gave a little giggle. "It's a much bigger place than I thought."

The bend of her cheek, the slight flicker of her one closed eye, the delicate curve of her lips as they broke into a smile — all made him quiver with longing to touch her face and caress her hair, just with his fingertips, so gently that only he would know it.

He said nothing to break the spell while she watched, enraptured. It was so sweet to give her pleasure.

"Twenty milkers!" she said at last. "And followers. They're not short of a shilling."

"And it *should* all be yours," he said.

She rose from her half-crouched position and rubbed her eye. "That's silly talk," she said crossly — though he sensed she was not actually cross.

"Did you see a dairymaid there, bringing in the cows. A girl about your own age?"

"I might have."

"She was there yesterday, too. I thought she looked rather like you."

He knew exactly what thoughts this innocent-sounding remark prompted: Ruby! Had she gone and found work as a dairymaid at the old family home? He could almost see the brain-cogs whirring behind Gemma's eyes.

She came straight to the point. *"She* told you, didn't she! That Mrs Roanoke."

He nodded. He wanted to say about three things at once and ended up saying none of them.

She drew a deep breath and, avoiding his eyes, asked, "What d'you want of me?"

He had to fight a desperate urge to tell her everything, all at once; only the thought of her taking fright, giving in her notice, moving to another place prevented him. "Not to be so ... I mean, sometimes all I need do is look at you and ... whizz! You're like a hedgehog with all your prickles up. Keep off! I understand your fear of me, of course — knowing what I do. But ... I just wish ..." He shrugged.

"Don't stop there!" she exclaimed. "You wish ... what? Let's have this out, once and for all. Just what is it exactly that you wish for ... with all this sighing and stuff? You know that anything of a serious nature is impossible. And as for anything of a *not*-serious nature ..."

"Listen — don't you go putting words into my mouth, Gemma! Impossible? That's not what *I* say."

She hesitated!

He saw a flicker of wild hope in her eyes, just for an instant. Some part of her wanted to believe that an honourable love between them was, indeed, possible; but the rest of her, which had its feet on the ground and its head well out of the clouds, soon came to the rescue.

"Well, I *do* say it," she countered. "So there! And that's the first and last of it. I'll thank you for showing me that." She tilted her head toward the telescope. "And now *some* of us have work to do."

"Wait!" he called after her.

But she went without another word — and he had to stay and readjust the telescope to the bearing and elevation at which his father had left it last night.

There was so much to do in getting the two ladies of the household and their six trunks of gowns ready for the London Season that, once the de Vivians were stirring, Gemma hardly had a moment to herself. It was quite amazing, therefore, the number of times she found herself down in the kitchen around eleven o'clock each morning, at precisely the time Miss Eddy prepared a tray of tea and biscuits for Master Peter, working away down in the cellar.

Because of the 'interruption' of the Season, as he saw it, he was toiling day and evening to finish as much of his solo racing dinghy as possible before they left for London. If he could at least stretch her shell and varnish it, he could finish the rest when they returned and still get in a decent bit of sailing before the autumn; indeed, in the sheltered waters of the Fal estuary, he did not see why he shouldn't sail through the winter, too, on all but the roughest days.

His 'lady,' as he called his creation, now had all her ribs, braced between her risings by two of the four intended thwarts; and he was halfway through bending her strakes to the diagonal; as a result, the floor was always knee-deep in shavings by the end of each day.

He was, without doubt, a natural craftsman in wood. It was the only school subject at which he had excelled, which distressed his parents far more than it pleased them. Even though the school had called it 'sloyd' to distinguish it from common, working man's 'woodwork' or 'joinery,' it was still too manual for comfort. In any case, a gentleman should try not to do anything *too* well; it smacked of professionalism. His skill surprised the servants, too. Those who sneaked down to the cellar on this or that pretext, but really to watch him at his work, expected to see him fiddle-fiddle-fiddle like any dedicated amateur before he got the parts of his boat to fit and look right; and for there to be five times the wastage that a professional would create. Instead they were amazed to see that he got almost everything right first time. 'Measure twice, cut once,' was his motto. So that, shavings apart, the wastage of solid timber would not have kindled many fires.

"He's after shaving one of they ribs by eye," Bridget Condron said after taking him his afternoon tea one day. "Never tried 'n. Just used his eye. But when he tapped 'n home, I couldn't pull 'n out. Not for my life, so I couldn't."

So the remarkable speed with which he shaped the basic frame of his dinghy soon ceased to be a subject for comment. Peter himself thought little of his skill. It was something he had held, not in his mind but in his hands and fingers, for as long as he could remember — ever since their old gardener had taught him to whittle dolly pegs, spinning tops, and fishing floats in their former home in Plymouth. As he toiled and perspired in the dusty gloom of that cellar his imagination carried him down the hill to the wide waters of the Fal estuary. There he pictured himself, alone at the helm, tacking upwind or racing before it with a taut sail swelling and groaning above him and the waves slap-slapping beneath him as her sharp bow cut them in two and shouldered them effortlessly aside.

Later in that same morning of their clandestine visit to the telescope, Gemma brought him his usual mid-morning cup of tea and a slice of Miss Eddy's heavicake. He was shaving out the next diagonal strake, so he did not hear her approaching. She paused in the door a moment and watched him at his work. His movements were firm and graceful, and the play of light and shade upon the rippling muscles of his bare forearms was ... *un plaisir*. The word just popped into her head.

Then, as one word conjures another, she recalled the song Miss Isco-Visco had taught them the previous week: *'Plaisirs d'amour'* by Martini. Its sweet, haunting melody began at once to echo in her mind: 'Pleasures of love abide a mere moment. The pain of love endures your whole life long ...'

Was it true? Or was it just the sort of thing people say so as not to tempt fate — the way they say 'We'll pay for this later!' on glorious summer days, or the way parents say 'This will end in tears!' when children are enjoying themselves hugely? Even if it were true — a truth universally acknowledged — it didn't seem to stop people falling in love.

Had she fallen in love with Peter? She certainly thought about him a lot — and would do so a great deal more if she didn't control herself. It would be so different if he pursued her — the way Roger Deveril had pursued poor Ruby, making her feel like the most important, most attractive, most lovable girl in the world. She, Gemma, would be triple-proof against such blandishments. But Peter was quite the opposite — being either shy and hesitantly respectful or jokingly argumentative. The incident with the telescope that morning had marked something new — a way out of the rut into which their behaviour had fallen.

It was as if he had wished to give her a present, knowing that anything material, such as a handkerchief or a pretty comb, would be inappropriate. It made her want to penetrate his reserve, to strip away all those conventions of class and gender that held them apart, and have a *real* conversation with him. But, remembering Ruby, it also made her doubly wary of doing any such thing.

Day by day, as she watched his boat taking shape, she indulged in daydreams of climbing aboard with him, down on Custom House Quay, and sailing out into Carrick Roads, watching Falmouth dwindle away behind them, and, with it, her place in Society, his place, her history, and his — in short, everything that now kept them apart. Then, shyly at first, they would each discover what the other was really like and … who knows? It was only a daydream; there was no need to pursue it to socially acceptable conclusions.

Standing there, watching him at work, wanting to touch his arm and feel the muscles ripple, and knowing what a mountain lay between that wish and its *safe* fulfillment, she felt not actual tears but that pressure at the top of her nose which always warned of their imminence. She sniffed and held her body rigid, getting a grip on herself.

"Oh, you gave me a start!" he exclaimed, noticing her at last. "Have you been there long?"

"Oh yes, very likely!" Brusquely she set the tray down on his workbench, slopping the tea a little. That annoyed her even more, of course.

"You ran off pretty smartly this morning," he went on.

"And you never followed me."

"I had to put the telescope back, pointing the way my father left it." He nodded at the nearly completed hull. "What d'you think of her? I'm going to call her *Gem* — the first of the *Gem* class of racing dinghies. Nifty name, eh?"

The idea thrilled her, though she was careful not to show it. "How do you bend the planks?" she asked. When she stood near him, all that side of her body seemed to tingle faintly, wanting to draw nearer still.

"It's not all that difficult once you know the trick. I steam the planks in a length of old cast-iron drainpipe. The really tricky part will be tomorrow, when I have to stretch a skin of wood over those planks — a thin, unbroken shell of veneers and marine glue. I've never done it myself, only seen it done." He cleared his throat and added, not looking at her, "It's going to take two people, I think."

"Fancy that!" she said, forcing herself to move a little away from him. "You know what you talked about the other morning — about all the secrets and cross-currents in this house?"

"Yes?" He grinned and broke the heavicake in two, passing the larger half to her.

She hesitated before taking it. "Well ... I was thinking ... something your sister said ..." She bit off a corner of the 'cake' — which is actually more of a biscuit — and watched him warily.

"Yes?" he said again.

"About her own income — from her trust."

He was taken aback. "But ... I mean, she shouldn't discuss such things with you."

"Well, *sir,* she's not the only de Vivian who discusses things with me that they shouldn't."

"Touché!" He hung his head and pretended to suck a finger.

"You'd best not try walking through Constantine," she warned him, naming a village between Falmouth and Helston. " 'Cos I've heard they're short of a village idiot and they might just decide to keep you. Anyway, the thing I was thinking was ... do you know the size of your sister's income?" She held her breath for his reply.

A slow grin spread across his face. "Has she asked you to find out for her?"

"Never you mind. Yes or no?"

"No — as it happens. Next question: Do you want me to find out for *you?"*

She nodded. Her pale eyes seemed to burn with a lambent fire in the dim light of the cellar. He had never wanted so much to take her in his arms and hold her to him, to look into those magical eyes from inches away, to see nothing but himself reflected there, to put his lips to hers ... to tell her she had someone in this world who loved her to distraction and always, always, always would.

Voices inside him were urging him to it, saying the moment was perfect and assuring him she would not resist ...

Whether or not he would have heeded them he was not to know for, at the very moment when urge might have yielded to impulse, they both heard Guinevere Roanoke call his name at the head of the cellar steps.

"Oh, God!" Peter grumbled, pulling a face. Then, raising his voice and forcing himself to sound cheerful, he called out, "Come on down!"

"What's up?" Gemma stared at him in bewilderment. " 'Tis only Mrs Roanoke."

"*Only* Mrs Roanoke! She'll want to *talk*. And when I say 'talk' ... well, you've no idea. Listen! Stay here — please, *please* don't leave me! Stay through thick and thin — no matter what. I'll give you a quid if you stay."

Gemma did not know whether to laugh or to pat his arm in reassurance; she had never seen him like this. "You may keep your money," she replied scornfully. "But if she says I'm to go, I can't rightly stay."

That was true, of course.

In any case, the woman herself was fast approaching — or as fast as her hobble skirt would allow. He stood like a trapped animal and counted down her mincing paces to the door — five, four, three, two ... "Why, Peter! What on earth are you ... oh! And Miss Penhallow here, too, I see!" Her tone switched from teasing pleasantness to frosty observation. "What's that you're doing, girl?"

Peter turned to find that Gemma had picked up his measuring tape and was standing there with it, and a pencil, at the ready. Quick thinking! With equal speed he added some likely explanation. "We had a disagreement ..." he began.

"What a novelty!" she interrupted coldly. "I understand you have little else."

The comment surprised Gemma. Had Peter been telling her about the petty squabbles with which they seemed to start most mornings? And if so, was that a good thing?

Meanwhile, he was explaining: "Miss Penhallow suspects the hull will be too large to go out via that window when I've finished her."

Guinevere's eyes switched back and forth between the incomplete hull and the window. The ostrich feathers in her hat skipped the opposite way each time she moved, like demented children playing tag with her coiffure. She was wearing a blouse of perfectly translucent pink gauze; a tight bodice outside it prevented the display from being *totally* indelicate.

She's only a tooth-puller's daughter! Gemma could not help thinking. She remembered Mrs de Vivian's delight at discovering the fact — and the woman's later chagrin at having to overlook it, all because of that eligible cousin who was going to be a baronet one day. Then came the depressing thought that she, Gemma, had no such redeeming cousin, and that people would never accept her in Society if she were ever to marry above her station. Her sneers about Mrs Roanoke, all in the secrecy of her own mind, would be turned upon her, too; and they would ring all over Cornwall.

"Well, I think the girl's right," Mrs Roanoke said. "But I'd prefer her to prove it some other time — if you don't mind, Miss Penhallow? There are things I wish to say to your master. Go on now, girl!"

"Oh, let her finish, do," Peter said jovially. "I just want to see her face when she realizes she's wrong and I'm right."

Guinevere hesitated. She had no desire to humiliate Peter, which she would do if she insisted on having her way. "Very well," she said, suddenly pleasant again. "What shall we talk about instead? What have we all in common?"

"Humanity?" Peter suggested.

She ignored him. "I know — the Season! Are you looking forward to your first Season, Miss Penhallow?"

"Very much, ma'am. And if I may say so, I do admire your costume. I'd welcome your advice on adapting a dress for ..."

"You surprise me when you say you're looking forward to London." Guinevere interrupted her. She was determined not to get shunted into a conversation about fashion, especially after that word 'adapting.' The sharp-eyed creature had spotted at once that her hobble skirt was, in fact, last year's model, hastily adapted with a couple of pinned tucks. "But then," she went on, "perhaps you have not heard the latest news — that the Deverils have returned to England? You never had much liking for them, did you!"

Gemma stood stock still, staring into the bottom of the boat. She no longer pretended to be measuring anything.

"Your employers are almost bound to run into them — present and previous owners of this house, you know. They are almost bound to run into ... all sorts of people."

Gemma flung the tape down upon the workbench. If the look she shot their visitor was anything to go by, she would gladly have flung it at her, instead. She stumped out of the cellar without a word.

Peter ran after her. He was so angry with Guinevere that he might well have said something highly ungentlemanly if he had stayed. "It doesn't *matter!*" he cried as he caught up with Gemma. He grabbed her arm and repeated the words: "Ruby and Roger Deveril ... it doesn't matter."

"It does to me," she replied.

"Then it shouldn't. Listen! Suppose Ruby is still with young Deveril. And suppose they are in London for the Season. If I find them first ... if I warn him off ... if I bring Ruby to you ..."

She glanced over his shoulder and he heard Guinevere's mincing steps on the flagstones behind him. She jerked her arm free and ran up the cellar steps, leaving him to stare after her. For an instant he had seen the hope in her eyes, and a sort of provisional gratitude for the promise he had been about to make. Unable to stop himself he reached out a hand and caressed the precious space that had so recently held the rare magic of her presence.

"Oh, Peter!" Guinevere said softly, standing some way down the passage behind him. "Why do you persist? No good can ever come of it, you know."

"That's a matter of opinion," he said disconsolately as he returned to the workshop.

"You never spoke a truer word," she told him. "Opinion with a capital O — society's opinion. And take it from one who knows: You ignore it at your peril."

He picked up his by now tepid cup of tea and sipped. "And what d'you think society's opinion will be of that pneumonia blouse of yours?"

"D'you like it?" She smiled down at herself and ignored his question. "The sales ticket called it 'seductive' — honestly! Some milliners have no shame these days."

He picked up the tape and pretended to measure the hull, though he could have recited every dimension in his sleep.

She watched him awhile, thinking how odd it was that, when they were apart, she had daydreams of seducing him (or, rather, of permitting him to seduce her, for she could not, even in fantasy, take the lead in such an immoral enterprise); but when they were together, all those exciting impulses gave way to fear and uncertainty. She shied away from taking the initiative; and he, for his part, was too diffident to act.

It was because of the Penhallow girl, of course. She jerked her head contemptuously — having no idea what a mocking dance the feathers made behind her. In the beginning she had tolerated his infatuation with some amusement. She thought it would all blow over soon enough and, meanwhile, it gave Peter an incentive to seek her out and tell her all about it — for whom else could he tell? But now, when it showed no sign of blowing over, she was less and less tolerant. She could not, however, decide whether contempt or laughter offered the best means to bring him to his senses. Or shock?

"I wonder if your obsession with this servant girl will outlast the London Season?" she mused.

"She's coming, too," he replied — an answer that clearly surprised her. But surely she had known it?

"I know *that,*" she said angrily. "But what I mean is that, er, this relative's house you're staying in, in St James's Square — it's a big sort of establishment, I imagine. Lots of servants. *And* all the demands of the Season. You won't enjoy the free-and-easy ways available to you here." She smiled, warming to her theme. "To say nothing of all the pretty young débutantes you'll be meeting!"

"Well — it's obviously going to be a testing time," he said vaguely. "For all of us."

"And don't imagine you'll have too many chances to sneak away for clandestine meetings. People fondly believe that London is this great big ...".

"Honestly, Guinevere, it's not really uppermost in my mind just at the moment. If I don't manage to ..."

"People fondly believe," she insisted, "that London's a big, anonymous place where they can get away with anything. Well, just be warned — it isn't. Not for people of *our* class. The West End is one vast drawing-room for the Upper Ten Thousand. It might as well be roofed over and carpeted. Whatever you think of getting up to — someone will see you."

Tired of this conversation, he patted the hull. "I want to get her varnished before we go. Have you and the mater decided on an actual date?"

"Next week — Friday, the sixth of May."

He smiled and relaxed. Barring unforeseen accidents he could easily manage the varnishing inside that time. "That's the day I'm down to crew on the *Guinevere* — quarter-finals of the Harbourmaster's Trophy."

She turned on her heel and accidentally clouted him with the dancing end of one of those long feathers. He snapped at it jokingly, the way dogs snap at flies, not meaning to catch it, though that is what happened. He spat it out again but now it hung soggy and low.

"I couldn't help it," he said. "I ran into your husband at the club last night. I could hardly ..."

"My husband?" She frowned and pressed her gloved knuckles to her brow. "Oh yes! Tall fellow. Dashing chap. *Looks* extremely virile — is that the bloke?"

"Guinevere!" He stretched out a hand and gave her a sympathetic smile. "You know whose side I'm on. I think he treats you abominably. But what can I do? I can't strike him down in public. The days of duelling are over. I can't even cut him. I just wish there was something I *could* do. Just talking about it doesn't seem to help much, does it?"

She couldn't believe he was working up to suggesting they should no longer meet and talk from time to time, yet his question implied that possibility. It frightened her into saying, "Oh, but talking with you is an enormous help to me — you've no idea. Every time I'm sure I'll burst with anger and loathing, I only need to think of you — that you're there — that you'll listen — and it calms me down again."

He took off his bib and braces, to assure her he was stopping work for the present. "I'm listening," he said as he took her arm and started walking her toward the door.

But she resisted and held her ground. "This morning ..." she began hesitantly.

"Yes?" He still wanted to get her out into the garden somewhere, to be in public.

"Before we rose this morning, he ... he *embraced* me ..." She hesitated again.

"'Embraced'," he said. "Does that mean ..."

"No, it does *not!*" she replied angrily. "Not all the way. I thought he was going to break the habit of ... well, of more months than I want to count. But he wasn't fully awake. The moment he realized what he was doing, he sprang from the bed and fled to his dressing room. Why I didn't follow him and cut his heart out, I do not know. Well, of course, he hasn't got a heart, so that's why."

"Oh, Guinevere! I just wish ... you know, that there was ..." He did not complete the thought because he had been going to say that he wished there were something he could *do* — which, of course, there was.

But she replied as if he'd made the offer, anyway. "Just hold me, will you?" she said, close to tears. "I promise it won't mean anything and it won't lead to anything — promise, promise, promise. But I just want someone — a man, a *real* man — to put his arms round me and tell me I'm not" — her final words were muffled against his chest — "something men just want to *shun*. I'm not, am I?"

He kissed the stiffened silk of her hat, to reassure her.

She felt it and, quick as a flash, whipped out her pins and shook the ridiculous creation to the ground — a gesture that brought her lips within inches of his.

Still he hesitated.

"Please?" she begged. "Just once. It won't be the start of anything. I'm so alone, Peter. You've no idea."

He kissed her. At first he tried to salve his conscience by closing his eyes and pretending she was Gemma; but then, realizing that was a kind of sacrilege, he opened his eyes again and kissed for kissing's sake.

There was not only the thrill of kissing a rather beautiful woman, there was the added piquancy of knowing she was another man's wife — that he was stirring her in ways her husband could no longer manage. But it — the piquancy — did not last long, unlike the kiss itself, which seemed to go on for ever. Very soon she ceased to be Guinevere, just as he ceased to be Peter, and they melted, instead, into nameless, elemental woman and man.

Guinevere must have felt it for she stiffened suddenly and pulled herself away. "I ... I ..." she stammered. "I didn't mean that to ..."

He shivered and leaned against his workbench for support. "Nor did I."

Each was thinking, *But it has happened — and neither of us is going to be able forget it very easily.*

"Pee-terr!" It was his mother's voice from the head of the stair. "Is Mrs Roanoke with you down there?"

Guinevere stepped away from from him, grabbed up her hat, and, in her haste to pin it back, stumbled, because of the hobble. He was unable to prevent her from falling but he caught her in time to soften her landing. The pins that had turned last year's straight-sided dress into this year's hobble tore out of the cloth with a sickening rip.

"Yes!" he called out to his mother. "Stay there! We're just about to come up."

But she had come downstairs and was already approaching along the passage. By the time she appeared he had his carpenter's brush in his hand and was dusting the sawdust and shavings off Guinevere's dress — a sight that robbed her of speech for a moment.

"Why, Peter!" she exclaimed, aghast. "What on earth d'you think you're doing?"

"It's my fault entirely, Mrs de Vivian," Guinevere replied. "I tripped on this." She kicked petulantly at a bit of four-by-two.

Ada suddenly noticed that the skirt was last year's, and that it had simply been pinned in. "I see," she said after inspecting it closely. "That *is* clever."

Guinevere said, "There's no point in having a lady's maid if she can't make last year's fifty-pound creation look like this year's two-*hundred*-and-fifty-pound model."

"Peter!" Ada had just noticed that her son was actually *holding* one of Mrs Roanoke's nether limbs while he brushed the sawdust away. "That is not seemly. I'm astonished at you. Go and call Miss Penhallow down here."

"No — please do not trouble!" Guinevere protested. "You are kindness itself, Mrs de Vivian, but the maid may brush it off in the garden. Isn't your son clever! Just look at the way his little yacht is taking shape!"

Ada surveyed her son's handiwork and was reluctantly forced to agree that it was turning into something pretty remarkable. "His father built a model of Lincoln cathedral out of fifteen thousand matchsticks, once," she said. "That's where he gets it from, I daresay."

"Mater!" Peter said decisively, as if he were taking command of the situation. He linked arms with her and started guiding her back toward the door. Then, as a humorous afterthought, he offered his other arm to Guinevere, who accepted it warily. "I've been thinking a lot lately and what I've been thinking is this. I've been thinking that people who might be interested in seeking my sister's hand ought to know the size of her income. Don't you agree?"

"That's between your father and me," his mother replied frostily. She tried to extricate her arm but he held tight.

"Ah," he drawled. "So when eligible young chaps take me aside and ask me, in the strictest confidence, what she's worth, I'll just refer ..."

"Peter!" She could not have cried out more sharply if she had trodden on a nail. And this time she managed to shake her arm free of his.

"Well, they do, you know," he went on, calmly letting go of Guinevere's arm on his other side. "It has already happened down at the yacht club a couple of times."

He turned toward Guinevere as if for confirmation. She made sure that Ada was not looking before she gave him a wink and a barely perceptible nod of reassurance. "How disgraceful!" she said. "People seem to think of nothing but money these days — money, money, money! By the way, Mrs de Vivian, did you hear that the Deverils will be in London for part of the Season? Their son Roger will be rowing in the sculls at Henley. A *solitary* sport! He is so versatile."

"How nice." Ada's tone was lacklustre enough to let all the world know how little she had taken to the Deverils — although she had liked their taste in wallpaper enough not to have changed a single one of the hangings at Alma Terrace.

Moments later Guinevere was standing on the lawn, with Gemma squatting beside her, brushing and hand-picking the sawdust out of the velvet pile of her dress. Peter was indoors, taking a lecture from his mother on topics one did and did not discuss in front of outsiders.

"Young Master de Vivian is an extraordinary man," Guinevere remarked. "Don't you think?"

"That boat, you mean?" Gemma said.

"Yes, that too."

Gemma paused — long enough for the woman to say, "Well? Have you done?"

"I don't believe you about the Deverils," she declared. "You just said that to test if …"

"How dare you! You forget yourself entirely, girl!"

Gemma rose and slipped the brush into her apron pocket. "You're clean enough on the *outside,* anyway," she observed. "So I suppose that'll have to do."

"Besides, Roger Deveril *is* rowing at Henley — or didn't you hear me say that?"

"Yes, well, Henley isn't London and the regatta isn't the Season. Why did you tell Peter about Ruby?"

The woman gasped at this fresh impudence. "I … I …" She blustered. "I really must ask you to adopt a more respectful tone, Miss Penhallow."

"Why did you?" Gemma persisted.

"I shall have to speak to your employer, if you do not."

Gemma stared unflinchingly. "What did you hope to gain by it?" she asked.

"Did you hear me?" Guinevere countered. "I shall have to speak to Mrs de Vivian."

Gemma smiled pleasantly and said, "We both know that's the very *last* thing you'll do, Mrs Roanoke. Either you had a good reason for telling him or you just enjoy stirring up trouble for people. The only thing I know at this moment is that you don't seem to care which I believe."

Guinevere turned a shade or two paler still; the girl's confidence had shaken her. Why should she, Guinevere, care which explanation the maid believed? The implication was that she ought to care. But why? Because the girl would discuss it with Peter? And he *would* pay attention to Gemma's beliefs? That was also implied. In short — if she, Guinevere, wished to stay on good terms with Peter, she had better keep Gemma Penhallow on her side, too, because he would never stay friends with anyone who upset his darling!

Gemma must be very certain of her man to offer such a challenge. Did Guinevere feel confident enough of her own claims on Peter to meet it with a challenge of her own? She decided she did not.

Or not *yet.*

"We'll talk about this another time, Miss Penhallow," she said. "Soon, I promise. Meanwhile, I ask you to accept it was not simply to stir up trouble."

She waited for Gemma to signify that she accepted the assurance, but the maid merely replied with another veiled threat: "I'd rather stay on good terms with you than bad, Mrs Roanoke."

Part Two

Rotten Row

14 The following week — on the first Friday in May — at a quarter past seven in the morning, the four de Vivians and Mrs Roanoke took the train from Falmouth to Truro, where they changed to the mainline express for London. It was a day that few who lived in Britain, or her Empire, were ever likely to forget.

They had reserved an entire first-class compartment for themselves, which left one seat free for a luxurious pile of newspapers, magazines, books, and chocolates. The servants — Gemma, Trewithen, and Sally Kelynack, Guinevere's maid — travelled second, two coaches away. Six large trunks of clothing had gone ahead of them 'per luggage-in-advance' and had been collected by the servants at St James's Square, which Ada's cousin had already vacated in favour of the Irish mayfly.

The party left Cornwall on a bright, sunny morning, which perfectly matched their mood of excited optimism.

Ada knew that nothing had been spared which might bring to the third finger of Beatrice's left hand the adornment she, Ada, so ardently desired to see sparkling upon it.

Beatrice, for her part, still had no ambitions in that direction, and thus was free to be quite cheerful about the coming Season, win or lose.

Her father daydreamed contentedly of trips to Greenwich, visits to the Science Museum, and long, happy hours among the library shelves of the Royal Astronomical Society.

Peter had so many happy thoughts to chase that his mind flitted from one to another like butterflies in buddleia. First, there were the balls where no one would be expecting him to propose, not for some years yet, and where he would thus be free to flirt with whomsoever he pleased — all without fear of misunderstanding. Then there were old schoolfriends to look up, seniors he had hero-worshiped from the lower depths of the fourth and remove. These were men who had swished him for burning their toast or whistling to their annoyance; but now they would treat him as an equal — knowing that he, in his turn, had become a senior and had swished other juniors for burning *his* toast, wearing their waistcoats with the bottom button done up ... and all the other heinous crimes of their schooldays. Then, too, while his father saw nothing but stars and his mother thought of nothing but galas, fêtes, balls, and presentations, there would be chances for unobserved conversations with Gemma — even if their words turned swiftly into arguments, at least it made their hearts race and set their eyes aglow. The only fly in the ointment was Guinevere.

He had not forgotten that passionate kiss — nor the panic in her eyes when she realized how much it had carried her away. He dreaded the thought that she would want to repeat the experience the moment they were alone together (and there would surely be such moments in the weeks ahead). Or, to be utterly honest, all his better instincts dreaded the thought; but his baser self — the Peter his old Plymouth cronies would recognize — was much more sanguine at the prospect. In unguarded moments it confronted him with all sorts of expedient arguments in favour of a repetition ... and more. After all, he and Guinevere *liked* each other quite a lot ... enjoyed each other's company ... and there was no possibility that *love* or anything so profound might develop between them ... so why not? Every man had to acquire a bit of experience in that line, if he wasn't to make a complete fool of himself and mortify his bride on their wedding night. And the usual way of acquiring it was, frankly, rather sordid. He knew that already because he'd tried it a couple of times and could not recall either occasion without a sense of shame. So there were *those* ghosts to lay, as well. And it wasn't as if he'd be cheating old Roanoke of something he actually valued — quite the reverse. Indeed, you could say that any husband who so cruelly ignored his wife's needs deserved cuckolding.

His baser self would have made a fortune in any barrister's chambers — among its equals, one might say.

Guinevere was equally torn between her nobler impulses and the needs Peter had awakened, or revealed, within her during that same kiss. What an act of folly it had been! And yet how sweet! And wasn't Roanoke just asking to be deceived? And wouldn't it be a capital revenge to present him with a child he could not disown without making himself a laughing stock! She sat in the compartment, reading a magazine, staring at the passing landscape, and stealing an occasional happy glance in Peter's direction.

Two coaches behind them, Trewithen had lost himself in the new edition of *Debrett*, while Gemma sought advice from the more experienced Sally about how best to deal with the French maid the de Vivians had engaged — 'at ruinous expense,' as Ada complained to any who would listen — for the Season. But she listened with only half her mind, since nothing could really be decided until they had met and Gemma had discovered what sort of woman she was 'underneath all that French polish.' The remainder of her thoughts dwelled on the frightening prospect of meeting Roger Deveril again — for, despite her brave words to La Roanoke, she had to admit such a meeting was not impossible. One of the reasons she had taken so strongly against Peter de Vivian was that he had, at first, reminded her of Roger. Not that they resembled each other in looks. Where Peter was dark, lithe, and wiry, Roger was curly-fair, broad-chested, and muscular — 'no more than a fit young yard bull,' was how Mrs Walker had dismissed him.

On the morning when Ruby had announced she was looking for his babby, she, Gemma, had seen him standing on the terrace, staring out to sea and thinking God knows what dark thoughts. It was a frosty day and the steam was coming out of his nostrils. That was when Mrs Walker had joined her at the upstairs window and come out with her description. Gemma had never heard anything more apt; suddenly she knew what that look in his eye had been every time they met — it was the hopeful-cum-arrogant look a yard bull gives every cow and heifer they drive toward his pen. And it was the look she had seen — or imagined she had seen — in Peter de Vivian's eyes in that first moment of their meeting.

Now, of course, she knew different, though it had not been a direct change of mind. Indeed, when she realized — quite early on — that Peter was not simply another Roger Deveril, she had feared he was worse, not better — a *more* cunning kind of seducer. On his very first evening in Falmouth, Guinevere Roanoke had told him about Ruby; so he must have realized from the start that she was triple-proof against the charms of all the Roger Deverils in the world. Therefore, she believed, he had tried a slightly subtler approach — pretending he was really interested in *her,* as a person, and not at all looking for a bit of you-know-what.

That belief was only just beginning to yield to the thought that he might be quite genuinely in love with her — which she wanted to believe with all her heart. In some way, she told herself, his behaviour in London would reveal the sort of person he truly was. *Then* she'd know what to believe about him. Then, too, she'd know what to do about it. Meanwhile, she decided, she would neither encourage nor discourage him; it was going to be a difficult line to tread.

After a while Sally became aware that Gemma was listening to her with only half an ear. It was a pity, she thought, that the noise of the train made a more intimate, and interesting, conversation impossible. She glanced toward Trewithen but did not trust his apparent absorption in his book; any servant who'd been at the game as long as he had would be able to listen to every nuance of another's conversation while seeming to be deaf or miles away.

"Care to stretch a little?" she asked Gemma, inclining her head toward the corridor outside — a suggestion to which Gemma readily agreed. As soon as the door slid to behind them, she added, "There are things a lady's maid can't discuss in front of a valet."

There was a welcome movement of air in the corridor; Gemma realized how warm it had been in the compartment and she flapped her shawl to ventilate all around her neck and shoulders.

"Like what does your Miss Beatrice really think of the Season?" Sally went on.

"Why?" Gemma was guarded. "Has your Mrs R said anything about it?"

"There's all this talk of an alliance between Miss B and her cousin, this Graham Melchett."

"Yes, what's he like? Have you ever met him?"

"He stayed a week last year," Sally replied. "He's got no time for sailing, I know that much. He quite disgusted Mister R."

"That'll make him popular with my lady. She can't abide either of them — sailing nor your master."

"Well, I'd say if she wants to be popular with Mister Graham, she should learn up all she can on Nyasaland and the Cape and that part of the world."

"I'll tell her. I can't see her doing it, though. She's not too fussed if she doesn't get a stone on her finger — nor this year nor next nor ever."

"Yes, I heard about that tragedy last year. Fell off his horse and died. Is she still grieving on that?"

Gemma shook her head. "I don't think she loved him. Not ..." For want of a word she rapped her breastbone with her knuckles. "Not in here. She'd more or less resigned herself to marrying him because her mother said he was the most suitable one to ask for her hand. I think she can't abide the idea of going through it all again. So if she doesn't get knocked silly by some dashing young suitor — head over heels, you follow? — she'll just as soon come home and ..."

"And what?"

"I don't know. No more does she, yet. She wants to *do* things, she says. Not just *be* someone's wife. She doesn't say it too often, though, because it drives her mother to distraction."

Sally stared out of the window for a moment or two and then prefaced her next words with a chuckle. "It seems to me that mothers and fathers haven't cottoned on to how things are changing, don't you think?"

"How?"

"Well, when *they* hitched up, it was for advantage. I don't know about your master and mistress, but mine would *never* have spliced the knot for *love*. It was advantage all the way — especially for *him*, by God! She was only a tooth-puller's daughter but hers is a big family and she came into some great legacy, I can tell you. He had all that blue blood in his veins but he was drowning in red ink, and that's a fact. He only gets the income. He can't lay a finger to the capital. That's all what's keeping them together."

Gemma was distracted a moment by the passing scene. They were traversing the wooded hills near the romantic ruins of Restormel Castle, where, at one moment, you stare down into bosky little dells, and, at the next, you are face-to-face with an almost vertical plantation of oak and rhododendron; the purple flowers seemed luminous in the gloom beneath the canopy. "I wonder if that isn't best?" she mused. "To marry for advantage."

"Instead of love?"

Gemma nodded. "Like your master and mistress."

"Ha!" Sally's laugh could hardly have been more scornful. "You never saw them together, did you! If they get closer than three feet, you can almost *feel* their flesh begin to crawl."

"But they must ..." Gemma halted in confusion.

Sally, knowing very well what she had been going to say, smiled. "Just because they're man and wife, you mean?"

Gemma blushed. "I didn't mean anything."

"You'd rather not discuss that topic?"

"That's right."

An awkward silence followed; then Gemma said, "You mean they don't? Not ever?" She did not look at Sally.

Sally did not look at her, either, but she could see her reflection sidelong in the window, every time the train plunged into the woodland dark. "Do Mister and Mrs de Vivian?"

"Oh, my gidge!" Gemma exclaimed. "How would I know a thing like that?"

"Yet you think *I* would!" Sally laughed. "You're right, though. A contented woman has no need to open her mouth about it. But one who's not fulfilled can talk of little else."

"And Mrs Roanoke?"

"Talks of little else." Sally chuckled drily. "Not dirty, mark you. I never heard an indelicate word pass her lips, but she'd leave you in no doubt all the same."

After a while Gemma said, "But she must also have married to have children — not just for social position. Surely every woman wants children?"

"Do you?"

Gemma blushed. "In due course. I want a stone there first." She displayed her ring finger. An image came into her mind of Peter putting it there; she shook it away angrily.

"Still, you're right about her," Sally went on. "She did want babbies. So did he. But the way she tells it, his family is ... you know ... unfruitful."

"It could be her that's barren."

"That's what he'd like to believe. She says that's why he's so vain about staying young and athletic and doing all those manly things. But he's got half a dozen aunts and uncles — on both sides — and all of them childless."

"Sans progeny ... no issue ..." Gemma recalled snippets of genealogy from conversations with Trewithen.

"If you say so! But on *her* side it's like a rabbit warren. So there's no doubt in her mind which of them is the unfruitful one!" Sally glanced up and down the corridor and then put her mouth close to Gemma's ear. "She said they practically broke the bedsprings, trying for it, when they first got married. But now he won't go near her. Says she's barren." Another careful glance all round preceded her conclusion: "In my humble opinion, he's just asking for trouble. There's that light in her eye! You just take a good look at her next time. She's coming up to London to find someone who'll help her prove him wrong."

"Never!" Gemma was appalled that a lady could break her most solemn vows, not in the heat of the moment but by deliberate calculation.

"Serve him right, too!" In Sally's pugnacious tone and the determined lift of her chin Gemma could see echoes of La Roanoke — an authentic touch that convinced her the maid was speaking the truth.

Then she was struck by a horrifying possibility. "Did she say who?" she asked casually.

Sally chuckled. "Not a word to me, but I suspect she's got her eye on the young man in *your* house — Master Peter!"

"Oh?" Gemma forced herself to smile — as any maid would who had no reason not to. "Have they ... er ...?"

The other maid shook her head. "And he won't, either."

Gemma clutched at this straw. "Has he said so? Has she already tried?"

Sally shook her head again.

Gemma pressed her: "How d'you know, then?"

Sally shrugged. "It's a feeling I get — watching them together. You just study them if you get the chance. She talks to him like she talks to no one else on earth. And he doesn't look at his watch or his fingernails or ..."

"What do they talk about? Does he talk to her the same way?" She meant, of course, 'Does Peter unburden his heart to her when they are together?'

"My-oh-my!" Sally looked her up and down. "You're some interested!"

Gemma, realizing she was in danger of revealing herself, said the first thing that occurred to her. "What *I'm* interested in is finding out the size of Miss Beatrice's endowment and income.

She's made it a sort of test of my value to her, see? And I'm sure your lady has been told it. So I asked Master Peter to ... I mean, because ..."

"Yes, all right!" If it wasn't romantic, or scurrilous, Sally wasn't particularly interested. Gemma breathed a sigh of relief as her friend continued. "The point I was making was that your Master Peter ..."

"Not *my* Master Peter, thanks very much!"

"Are you going to listen?"

"Sorry. I just wanted to make that clear."

"Very well. *Her* Master Peter is a bit of a rarity among men. I mean — when a woman talks to him, he actually *listens!* As I said — he doesn't inspect his fingernails or look at his watch — he listens. Isn't he like that at home?"

Gemma, who was not at all pleased to have 'her Master Peter' substituted for 'your Master Peter,' admitted that he was the same at home. "I still don't see how that means he'll disappoint Mrs R when she flutters her eyelashes at him."

Sally shrugged again. "I may be wrong, of course," she admitted. "Like I say — there aren't too many men like him about, but the ones I've come across aren't too interested in ... you know." She looked all about them yet again and added, "It's not easy to express it delicately. I mean they don't go in for the sixpenny stuff ... the fumbler's feast. That's more the sort of thing that ..." She hesitated. The tips of her ears turned red and she looked about her, this time as if seeking escape.

Gemma knew what she was thinking, so she said it for her. "The sort of thing that Roger Deveril went in for!"

Sally expelled her breath in a rush of gratitude and put the flat of her hand to her chest. "My dear soul!" she exclaimed. "Miss Penhallow! What must you think?"

"It's all right, Miss Kelynack. Truly. I take no offence. I know what you mean — though I never saw it so clearly as now. But you've put your finger on it for me — the difference between Master Deveril and Master Peter."

"Talking of whom ...!" Sally murmured, giving a slight tilt of her head toward the corridor behind Gemma.

She turned to see Peter himself approaching them; she had learned so much about him during this conversation — or had come to understand so much that she had learned without actually digesting — that he seemed a new person. She actually managed to smile at him without being prompted.

Then she chided herself for it, remembering her resolve to neither encourage nor discourage him.

"Hallo, Miss Kelynack," he called out as he approached. "Don't let me break up a happy party. I just wanted to point out our old house to Miss Penhallow. It'll be in view soon."

Since Plymouth was still ten miles or more away, Gemma thought this was rather barefaced. "Why should I be interested in that?" she asked.

Sally stared at her in shocked surprise. She had never seen these two in each other's company before, so Miss Penhallow's rudeness took her aback. A scullerymaid might repel a young master's overtures so brusquely but a lady's maid should have a more refined manner. She did not doubt that Miss Penhallow was capable of being as refined as anyone could wish; therefore her rudeness was deliberate.

Why?

It was an interesting speculation, especially when coupled with the maid's protestations that he was not *her* Master Peter.

The young man laughed, more out of embarrassment than with humour.

Gemma was implacable. "Did you find out that other thing?" she asked, equally bluntly.

"That was also what I came to tell you."

This brief exchange — or, rather, the fire that flashed between their eyes during it — was enough to convince Sally that she was onto something. She would dearly have loved to stay and listen to them; but that, she realized, would afford no more than an instant satisfaction; in the long term, more was to be gained by withdrawing and watching them. They would speak much more freely if they were sure they were not overheard — a freedom that would extend to their looks and gestures, too.

"I think I'll go and take the weight off my feet," she said, and returned to the compartment. Trewithen's response was interesting, too. He glanced at the pair out in the corridor, raised his eyebrows meaningfully in Sally's direction, and returned to his book.

Peter and Gemma leaned against the handrail, side by side, a careful twelve inches apart. "Gemma?" he said softly.

"Miss Penhallow, please," she responded. "I don't mean to be unfriendly, sir, but it's not fitting we should be on such terms, you and I."

"Not fitting!" he echoed morosely. "If everything we did had to be *fitting,* we'd end up paralyzed."

"That thing I asked you to find out?" she prompted him.

"Oh, yes. You could actually have found it all out at Somerset House so, I'm sorry to say, I'm not doing you the great service I had hoped to perform. Our grandfather left me and each of my sisters a hundred and twenty-five thousand in trust. Invested in gilts it brings in five-thousand-odd a year for each of us. Mine and Bea's just gets added to the capital. I can't touch any of it until I'm twenty-eight. Granddad obviously thought I might be sensible by then — ha ha!"

She was listening with open mouth to all this; the sums themselves were unimaginable but the things that might be done with them were not.

To tease her he went on: "However — to get back to what interests *you* — my parents will also add a dowry of another hundred thou' — which will bring Bea's income up to almost ten thou' per annum. Actually, that bit you couldn't have got from the published wills. So I have done something to help. And now you know! And so, by this evening, will Beatrice, I suppose?"

Gemma just stared out of the window; her face, in profile, was unreadable. He wanted to stretch out and run his finger down the line of her nose and lips. He wanted to stroke her like a cat and feel her purr and lean into him. Would it ever, ever happen? "Well?" he asked.

"I shouldn't ought to have asked you," she murmured, more to herself than to him.

"Should I be sorry I heeded you, then?"

She closed her eyes and spoke more softly still. "We keep coming back to it — the question *you* can't answer ... and no more can I: What d'you *want* of me? I don't know what to do or say ..."

"I don't know, either," he told her. "I mean I do know what I *want,* but I don't see how it's possible. I don't know what it's *possible* for me to want — what I'd dare to want. All I do know is that ..." He hesitated. He seemed to be fighting to breathe.

"Yes?" she asked, still not looking at him.

"All I know is that you are *real.*"

"I should hope I am!" She laughed in puzzlement.

"No — I mean real. Really real. Don't you ever look at other people and wonder if they're really there at all?"

"No!" She looked at him for the first time — and became aware, out of the corner of her eye, that Miss Kelynack was watching them like a cat by a mousehole.

"Well, I do. Most people are like the chorus in an opera to me. Or bits of scenery that happen to move. They are *there* all right, but hardly real. D'you see what I mean?"

"A bit," she conceded reluctantly. "Pretend you're talking about the landscape, or the weather. We are being watched very closely. *Don't look!*"

"Sorry." He pointed meaninglessly toward a couple of circling pigeons. "I was saying — few people are entirely real to me, Gemma, but you are among them."

This time she did not correct him. But she did not wish him to pursue this line any further, either. That is, her wiser self did not wish it. Of course the eternal girl in her longed to hear she was the star of his show, always at the centre of his stage, always in the limelight for him. But, the wiser woman she aspired to become asked, what then? Where would such an outpouring take them? And did she really want to be there? Wasn't life already complicated enough? Didn't she need to digest the things she'd learned in the past half hour?

He waited for her to ask the obvious question and, when she failed to do so, said, "All right, Miss Penhallow. I shan't press this further. The only thing I'll say is that I'm glad you *are* real. I'm glad you're there. I'd love to ..." he swallowed with difficulty "... to talk with you. To know you better as a *person.*" His voice cracked. "Oh ... hell to it!" he exclaimed and, turning on his heel, walked away.

"Peter!" she called after him.

"What?" He halted and looked back at her, smiling that absurd, endearing, lopsided smile of his. Just because she'd spoken his name!

"Weren't you going to show me where you used to live?"

The smile did not falter as he waved a dismissive hand at her. "Why should you want to know that? I'm not a *person* to you — and probably never will be." He strode back to his own class.

15 THE KING: GRAVE NEWS said the newsboys' billboards at Paddington. But Mr Wilkes, Guinevere's cousin's husband, who had come to the station to meet her, said it couldn't be all that grave because, when it was *really* grave, they always came straight out with it — HOPES FADING FOR KING or even KING DIES. In his opinion, the king just had a touch of bronchitis. It had prevented him from meeting Queen Alexandra at Victoria yesterday and that was what had started this whole 'grave-news' scare.

Neither Ada nor Guinevere was cheered very much by these bluff reassurances.

"What was the queen doing at Victoria yesterday?" Ada asked. "She is supposed to be on holiday in Corfu."

"If they brought her back all that way," Guinevere added, "it must be serious, indeed. I think you should all wait here while I make one quick telephone call." She smiled wanly. "What is the point of having a friend at court if one cannot use her at a time like this?"

She went to the public telephone room, took a private booth, and put through a call to St James's Palace.

Friend at court! Ada thought. *She's probably no more than a chambermaid.* If Wilkes hadn't been there, she would have voiced the opinion aloud.

And as for Wilkes himself, he was sticking to his line. The palace, he said, was letting Witch of the Air, one of his majesty's two-year-olds, run in the 4:15 Spring Plate at Kempton Park with R. Marsh in the saddle. He, Mr Wilkes, had a fiver on it and could strongly recommend the nag if any of them wanted to put a call through to his turf accountant. They still had half an hour before the off.

Gemma and Sally exchanged weary glances. A royal death would mean that every lady's maid in the country would be working frantically with her needle long into the night — and black thread in black material is not the easiest combination to manage by lamplight.

Guinevere returned with a face as long as could be. "The gravest news of all," she said, "will never be reported in the newspapers." She took Wilkes and the two older de Vivians aside and added, "The queen has allowed Mrs Keppel to take her leave of his majesty."

To Gemma, who just managed to overhear Mrs R, the news meant nothing; but when she repeated it to Miss Kelynack the maid explained. Alice Keppel had been Edward's fancy woman for as long as anyone could remember. The queen would never have broken protocol to that extent unless she was convinced that her husband was soon destined for a place where such considerations were of no account whatever.

Then came the words they had both been dreading ever since they had seen those headlines:

"We must go at once to Shoolbred's or Maple's," Guinevere said. She had had several minutes to recover from the shock and was already thinking ahead, almost as fast as her lady's maids. "We must buy enough black silk to make dresses for Beatrice and my two — there will be a most fearful run once the news gets out."

"And" — Ada was thinking as quickly as Guinevere now — "we must send a telegram to Falmouth for them to put our mourning outfits on the night mail up to town. When does that arrive here? Six o'clock, isn't it? Trewithen?" She turned to him. "You can find that out now and then follow on to St James's Square with Miss Penhallow. And be sure to return here tomorrow morning early to meet that train!"

The valet bowed and left on his errand.

Wilkes's eye met de Vivian's and they smiled indulgently at this typical example of women fussing over nothing. But they humoured them and, after a small detour to drop Sally Kelynack off in Bayswater, went directly to Shoolbred's. There they were astonished to find that all the women in London were 'fussing,' too. The store had already sold out of black silk. They went at once to Maple's, where they were served from the very last bale in its capacious stockroom.

While these boring transactions were in progress, Wilkes leaned confidentially toward Peter and murmured he could do worse than back Lemberg to win and Greenback for a place in the Derby, which would be in three weeks' time, on the first of June. He had seen the young man's interest in his earlier tip for the Spring Plate.

Ada, overhearing the word 'Derby' but not what had gone before, said that if the king died — which God forbid, of course — the court would probably cancel the whole of Royal Ascot.

Wilkes just laughed and said, "Not if the royalties want to avoid a revolution they won't."

Then they parted company — Guinevere and Wilkes back to Bayswater, the de Vivians to St James's Square.

"What an exceedingly vulgar man," Ada said when they were at last alone. "Just what one would expect of *her* family, I fear. He makes hats, she says, and I can well believe it." She heaved an angry sigh. "It's a great pity we have to be on terms with him. I suppose we *do* have to?"

"We can hardly do otherwise, my dear," her husband agreed.

"Quite," Peter murmured. "The fellow probably has friends at court, too."

"Ha!" Ada then delivered herself of the opinion she had been forced to stifle earlier. "God knows I'm no snob," she went on, "and never have been. But we must try to avoid him, now that the damage is done."

Peter sighed wearily. "And we haven't even been in London an hour as yet!"

"I don't know what you mean by taking that tone," his mother snapped. "People up here have nothing to go on except the company we keep."

"'We must try to avoid him'!" he echoed sarcastically. "Why not just hire a couple of sandwich-board men to walk about the West End proclaiming the message that the de Vivians came over with the Conqueror and please don't judge us by 'the company we keep'!"

"Peter!" his father shouted angrily.

"What's got into the boy?"

"I'm just trying to add a touch of subtlety to what the mater was proposing, that's all."

She glared at him. Bea, at his side, was trying her hardest not to laugh.

"Any more of this and you'll be rusticated straight back to Falmouth," his father threatened.

"It's what he wants, unfortunately," his mother pointed out. "Just ignore him." She immediately ignored her own command by leaning across the growler and gripping his arm. "Listen!"

she hissed. "This news about the king has thrown all our careful plans into complete disarray. We have only a few short weeks in London — three months at the very most. And what's left of the Season may now be drastically cut back. Oh, it's *too* bad! We have less chance than ever to make our mark — to leave a favourable impression."

"But surely ..." Peter began.

"No!" she thundered. "You just sit quiet and listen. We've had quite enough of your smartness for one day. Whatever I have said of importance to you in your entire life ... *nothing* will prove more important than this. From now on, *everything* we do in public will count toward that impression. Every little social blunder we make will be noted by someone or other and may be set down against us."

"In a book?" Peter asked scornfully. Then, with pretend horror. "Or in the public prints?"

"Be quiet, sir!" Terence de Vivian barked. "Hold your tongue and listen!"

"In something much worse than a book," his mother replied dramatically. "It will be carried on the wings of whispers — from ballroom to *thé dansant* to At Home to ... yes, perhaps even to the court itself!" She glowered at her son and told him not to pull such faces. Every word she said was true. They were walking on eggshells from now until August.

"Wilkes makes hats *by the thousand,*" Peter said.

She looked at him as if he had spoken Chinese. "What are you talking about?" she asked.

"Wilkes. He manufactures hats. On quite a vast scale, if you want to know. You asked what he does and I'm telling you. It's not some workshop three flights up in Saint Giles's. He has whole factories down in the East End, where his workers all die of mercury poisoning, and ..."

"Peter!" his father thundered. "That will do."

The following morning the papers were all edged in black and the headlines announced that the king had breathed his last as Big Ben struck a quarter to midnight. His final words had been spoken several hours earlier: "That's good," he had said on being told that Witch of the Air had beaten the favourite in the Spring Plate. When Mrs Joseph, the housekeeper at St James's Square, brought *The Times* and the *Telegraph* to the de Vivians' bed, Ada roused herself and Terence at once and gave orders for Peter and Beatrice to be wakened, too — and all were to dress in full mourning, which Trewithen should have collected from Paddington by now or God help him!

Half an hour later, with nothing but tea and a few marie biscuits to fortify them against the morning chill, they went abroad for a constitutional, as far as St James's Palace, to read for themselves the death notice on the railings there. Gemma accompanied them, for she, wise maid, had actually brought a mourning dress with her. Ada was delighted to see that they were among the very few who were already in mourning; she felt sure that *someone* would take note of their patriotic devotion and make discreet inquiries as to their identity. At all events it would do their reputations no *harm,* she insisted in the face of her husband's head-in-the-clouds indifference and her son's patronizing smile.

They nodded and bowed gravely to all they passed, even to crossing sweepers and policemen. Normally, of course, it would have been a solecism to acknowledge anybody to whom one had not been introduced, but ... at a time like this ... the nation closed ranks and rank itself was abridged.

Beatrice was wearing her everyday mourning, of course, not the magnificent dress that was to be made up from the silk they had bought at Maple's yesterday. As they made their dignified promenade down St James's, mother, daughter, and maid discussed the finer points of that new gown.

Should it be in the new hobble fashion? Was the hobble going to 'catch on' — it was, after all, a Parisian rather than a London innovation and London did not always follow where Paris tried to lead, especially in the more *outré* styles. Whatever became of 'hareem' trousers, for instance! Those *jupes culottes* were still spoken of in breathless tones in all the ladies' magazines but had anybody ever seen an actual lady wearing them?

Besides, how could anyone be expected to curtsey in a hobble? And if you couldn't curtsey in a dress, you couldn't possibly wear it to court, and if you couldn't wear it to court, then it wasn't a feasible fashion.

Perhaps Beatrice's new mourning dress had better be made in the plain, straight-sided style, which was also *quite* a new fashion, being only two years' old.

Peter, remembering Guinevere's way of turning a straight-sider into a hobble, suggested doing the same with Beatrice's new costume. "Then she can be a slave to either fashion at the poke of a pin," he said.

An awkward silence followed before Ada told him not to remind everyone of that indelicate moment. Beatrice grinned and winked at him, but Gemma, for some odd reason, just stared at him, stony-faced.

It happened, he now realized, every time he mentioned Guinevere Roanoke. And it was especially marked since their arrival in London last evening. Or, to be precise, since the train journey — during which she and that Sally Kelynack must have enjoyed a good long chinwag, if not several. What had the maid told her?

Come to that, what had Guinevere told her maid?

He began to worry. He turned to Gemma and said, "What d'you think, Miss Penhallow? Could it be managed?"

Trapped, Gemma looked to Mrs de Vivian for support.

"That's enough out of you, Peter," she said. "Go and walk a little way away from us."

He halted and let them draw ahead of him as they went down into the Mall, to look at Buckingham Palace and see the flags at half-mast.

He had often heard his mother complain that one couldn't tell lady's maids from their mistresses these days. Now, with the whole town in mourning, he exulted in the thought that she was going to have an even harder time of it. Bea and Gemma were two silhouettes in Bible black, almost indistinguishable from each other; you'd almost have to get close enough to feel the quality of the material to be sure who was which.

Then, enjoying the grace of their walk, he became distracted by the beauty of Gemma's silhouette. The social question was kicked into oblivion. What *was* he to do about her? He could not endure this degree of longing for the next seven years, until he came into his inheritance and could kiss the family goodbye. Seven *months* would be hard enough. Seven weeks would be just about bearable. How did people survive those five-year engagements — assuming they truly loved each other, of course? No one could endure five years of this frustration.

He could borrow against his expectations!

The small spark of hope that was kindled by this fancy soon died. The banking world was a tiny clique; no one with the name de Vivian could borrow so much as a fiver without a flurry of jungle drums that would be heard equally well in St James's Square as in Falmouth.

They stared at the palace awhile, wondering which curtained window filtered its light onto the coffin. Then they turned about once more.

And now, to hide his face, Peter walked ahead of them, back to Pall Mall.

A moneylender, then?

At thirty percent a month? A de Vivian would sooner die.

Besides, Gemma hadn't seemed too overjoyed yesterday, when he'd artfully (as he supposed) let slip how rich he'd be one day. For reasons he could not have explained, he did not feel that gold was ever going to win her heart — which was admirable, of course, and only made him admire her the more; all the same, it was a bit of a nuisance in present circumstances.

He remembered Wilkes's tips for the Derby — Lemberg to win and Greenback for a place. He had about seventy quid saved up in the Post Office Savings — mostly winnings from card games in Plymouth; there was a lucky streak in him somewhere. It would be nice to have a good little pile tucked safely away, all unknown to the jungle drums. Cash, to be sure. But off-course betting for cash was illegal, and anyway, he wouldn't want to trust so large a sum to a bookie's runner. Could he start a line with a turf accountant — pretending he was already twenty-one?

He'd have a word with Wilkes — if he could just be sure Guinevere wasn't in the house; he wanted nothing to do with her if it was going to upset Gemma.

"Wait there!" Ada called out when he reached Pall Mall.

As they drew level he said he'd die if he didn't get some breakfast inside him soon.

Beatrice, who had not worn this particular mourning dress since Frederick Conyers's tragic death last year, was only too aware that it had not been let out to keep pace with her growth. She agreed heartily.

So their mother's suggestion that they should return the long way round, by way of Pall Mall and the Haymarket, allowing even more people to admire their patriotism, was voted down in favour of the beeline path. As they strolled back along the northern side of St James's Square, Terence de Vivian waved a hand across the heavenly panorama above them. In an azure sky, the waning moon was a narrow crescent just a few degrees ahead of the sun, which was just about to rise above the roofline of the buildings on the opposite side. It rays spread out in a golden fan, at the centre of which sat the dwindling moon, a diva in her limelight.

"Soon," he said, "Englishmen will be standing up there, planting the Union Jack and telling the moon creatures all about us down here. How little our lives matter in the face of such vastness, eh!"

"When is 'soon'?" Peter asked.

"Quite soon," he replied confidently. "It will be the first of many new conquests of space."

"Yes, well," his wife put in impatiently. "Before that happens we have a conquest of a more personal nature to make down here among us earth-creatures – and it is far from being a trivial matter, let me assure you!"

"I know just what you mean, Mama, dear," Peter said – as if offering an apology. He did not look at Gemma but he felt her gaze on his cheek like rays from a burning glass.

16 There were no dinner parties, no balls, no presentations, no soirées; the Season was in complete abeyance until after the funeral of the late king, which was set for Friday, the twentieth of May, two weeks after his death to the day. The lord chamberlain instructed the ladies of the court to wear nothing visible that was not black; not even purple gemstones were allowed. Naturally the rest of society followed suit. The daily parades of the rich and fashionable continued in Hyde Park, of course, for where else could one demonstrate one's patriotism if all other gatherings were cancelled? Even the carriage parade of the demimonde, around four in the afternoon, continued as usual; and the usual crowd turned out to stare in fascination as the pretty young mistresses of the old aristocracy and the new plutocracy paraded in black silks and satins and taffetas – a

colour which, all agreed, showed off their milky complexions, their pearly teeth, their rosebud lips to perfection.

The word was going about that society would remain in black until after Royal Ascot — specifically, until after Derby Day on the first of June. And even then, people would continue to sport some token of mourning, added to the gaily coloured gowns they had all brought up for the Season. Needles flew in St James's Square as Gemma and Mam'selle, the ruinously expensive French maid, made new buttonholes in sleeves and across bodices — not for buttons but for the black ribbons that were to be threaded there. Gemma was pleased to see that Mam'selle's needlework was no finer than her own, though she joined in the general conspiracy that held the French maid's to be superior; the poor creatures were so touchy and were apt to give notice on the spot, especially at a time like this, when replacements were not to be had for love or money.

From the moment of their meeting Gemma did not take to Mam'selle Antoinette Dupuy, to give her her full name. She had been fully prepared to be friendly and to go out of her way to help a young woman away from her home and native land; but all that goodwill evaporated the moment Mam'selle was introduced to Miss Beatrice. "We will speak French, mademoiselle, yes?" Mam'selle had said — in French. "When we wish this peasant maid of yours not to understand." And poor Beatrice had perforce to agree for fear of losing this precious adjunct to the Season.

Later Beatrice had sought out Gemma alone and assured her that she would tell her if Mam'selle said anything that she, Gemma, ought also to know. Gemma was on the point of telling her not to bother and that she had already understood everything Mam'selle had tried to keep from her; but then she held her tongue. It astonished her that Beatrice knew nothing of her attendances at Miss Isco-Visco's classes at the WEA. She was so used to living most of her life under the watchful eye of an employer that it never occurred to her that such an important feature of it would have escaped notice entirely. Who did they imagine read all those French newspapers she brought into the house — which her father begged from the newspaper shop when they were no longer saleable? Had they even noticed them? she wondered.

It struck her then that the de Vivians' watchfulness was a most selective faculty. What touched their pocket, their honour, their reputation, or their person — these commanded their utmost vigilance. What touched a servant's moods, feelings, or ambitions — these passed them by. What an education it was, this London Season, to be sure!

However, though she and Mam'selle did not exactly 'cop on' to each other like long-lost friends, Gemma was not so blind that she could not see the woman's skill in all things that related to her employment. And there, indeed, she was happy to place the laurels on the other's brow, and sit at her feet, and learn. Mam'selle took this deference as no less than her due, but, while it lasted, she was pleasant enough in her patronizing way with her young admirer, as she now thought Gemma to be. And so a cordiality somewhat short of actual warmth, an amity that was slightly less than true friendship, prevailed between them. And Gemma learned much that would make it hard for the de Vivians to refuse her a substantial rise in pay when they returned to Falmouth.

To give just one example. Beatrice had a 'pneumonia' blouse of pale pink gauze, which was all the rage that year. It was finished at the neck with silk bias, also in pale pink. Gemma's task seemed simple enough — to fashion a small bow of black velvet and sew it at the throat of this garment. But when she had finished, the knot of the bow pulled the bias away from the neck in an ugly curve and the wings of it drooped unevenly, with one side round while the other hung limp or twisted; and whichever she tugged into the desired shape, the other immediately sagged out of it. But the remedy seemed easy, too — a little piece of ribbon behind the bias, to strengthen it, and a discreet stitch or three to keep the loops of the bow stretched out evenly, like a pair of wings, on either side. Gemma was surveying the result with pride when Mam'selle pointed out that the loops now looked as if they were glued tight to the bias of the neckline. "They are not alive," she said with an expansive gesture of her hands. And she unpicked them and restitched them with a short stem in between — as there is between a button and its anchorage. Gemma saw at once that the bow now had a little independent liveliness, which made all the difference. She also began to understand how fine a line separates the excellent from the merely good — and what a long way she had yet to go. There were half a dozen such lessons every day.

One, in particular, amused Gemma; she made a note of it for use if she ever took a place away from Cornwall. Mam'selle showed her a letter, written by her sister but not dated, telling her that their mother was gravely ill and not expected to live. "Eef you need to leave your employeur in an 'urry," she said, "all you do ees write in ze date ... *et voilà!*"

In these circumstances she had no time for Peter — and told him so. Besides, his repeated attempts to find himself 'by chance' in the same room as her and to engage her in meaningless, if pleasant, conversation were dangerous. Mam'selle would soon twig that something was going on and, even if she said nothing at the time, she was the kind who'd store it up and use it to her advantage later.

For a while after that he mooched about the house, unwilling to go abroad and face the crowds, all with long faces and crêpe armbands. Worse, his mother's insistence that the de Vivians should go into full mourning, as if they were members of the court, would mark him out wherever he went. If he tried to have fun of any kind, people would look at him askance, for, if he were in mourning for a close relative, it would be unfeeling, and if he were merely parading his patriotism, the world would see how shallow it was.

And so, toward the end of the afternoon, he drifted once again 'by chance' into the maids' workroom and asked if he could do anything to help.

On an inspiration, Gemma told him they'd made a surprise discovery in the attic that afternoon — which was true. They had discovered about ten yards more of the black velvet ribbon than they were ever likely to need. So, she asked Peter, why didn't he go downstairs and telephone Mrs Roanoke and offer some of it to her?

"Don't let on we've got ten yards, mind," she warned him. "Say three. Ask should you bring it round."

Mrs Roanoke! Even from the way Gemma said the name he could tell how she felt. So he said nothing. He just went on staring at her. At that moment Mam'selle was with the laundry-maid in the basement, so this was a good time to have it out, once and for all.

"Go on!" she urged, not looking up from her work though she could feel his eyes as sharp as the needle in her hand.

"If you say the word, Gemma," he murmured, "I'll never see Mrs Roanoke again."

She stopped breathing momentarily and then said, as casually as she could, "What word is that, Master Peter?"

"You know very well."

"Do I now?"

"You know how things are."

"I've told you, Master Peter. Some people have work to do around here. Please don't make life more difficult for me than it already is. Please?"

"All right, all right! I understand how busy you are. I accept it. I accept that you're not just making some excuse to get rid of me. I promise I'll keep out of your way as long as you wish it. But you cannot be as busy as this for ever. They day will come when you have a little time on your hands ..."

"And then?"

"We're in London, Gemma. The possibilities are endless. I'd like to meet you ... somewhere out there. In the park, in Kew Gardens, at the v&a, in some cosy tearooms ... or a pleasure boat on the Thames. I'd like to meet you as an equal and talk with you. Just talk."

"And *then?*" she asked, more insistently.

"D'you want me to say it? D'you need to hear the actual words from me?"

She closed her eyes and shook her head. "Go and ring that Mrs Roanoke."

"Don't you understand?" he asked.

Her eyes remained closed and her lips were pursed so tight that she barely managed to squeeze the words out between them: "It's because I *do* understand. Now go! Go and make that telephone call."

"If I do, it will be because of you. *You* are now deciding that I shall go."

"Yes." Gemma swallowed hard. "I am now deciding that you shall go — Master Peter."

"Go to Mrs Roanoke," he insisted.

"Yes — go to Mrs Roanoke."

17 Despite Gemma's cold-shouldering, Peter did not at once telephone the Wilkeses at home — not on that day nor for many that followed it; nor did he cross the park to Bayswater merely on the off-chance. Instead, for some days, he took to roaming at large throughout the West End, looking ... for what? For *life,* he told himself grandly — and vaguely. Also for some honourable way of paying court to Gemma. At least more people were in full mourning now, so he did not feel quite so conspicuous.

He was not turning into a complete monomaniac, however. He also wanted to finish his dinghy — to sail her, to master the wind and the wave, to know that everything which lay between him and drowning had been fashioned by him. The palms of his hands itched for the feel of mallet and chisel, of plane and spokeshave once again. And yet, even as he yearned for that achievement, he knew it would not be enough. He would return after his first outing, make fast, and think, *What now?*

He began to suspect there was a void in his life that even Gemma could not entirely fill. Suppose the impossible were to happen and that she somehow became his wife — what then?

It was the same question. First the achievement, then the void that still cried out to be filled. The ambition to win her love had so mesmerized him that he had fallen into the trap of seeing it as an end in itself. But it wasn't, of course. Marriage was *for* something else. For children, naturally, and for ... something *other.* Even married to Gemma he would still face that question: 'What are you *for,* Peter de Vivian?'

The children would surely ask it. 'Mama, what does Papa *do?*'

'Hush, darling boy — your father does nothing, just like his papa before him. And if you're a good boy and eat up all your spinach, why then, one day *you'll* grow up and live in perfectly useless idleness, too!'

He stopped and stared at himself in a bookshop window. He flinched at the sight; would any girl on earth want to face such a vision over the breakfast table? A change of focus blurred his reflection and brought a title into focus: *The Descent of Man,* by Charles Darwin.

Had humans *descended* from apes — not ascended? In his present mood the word began to seem appropriate. At least apes knew what they were *for*.

Things had seemed so easy before they left Plymouth. Life in those days was shaped not by any impulse within himself but by the expectations of all around him. Even to call them 'expectations' was stretching things a bit, for most people expected him to do precisely what so many thousands of young men with rich parents and an income did, year after year: nothing! He would hunt when the fox ran, shoot when the pheasant took wing, fish when the trout and salmon rose, dance when the band played, sail when the wind stood fair; and in between he would display good manners, hit little white balls over the hills and fields, devise practical jokes with his cronies, and be extremely modest about any accidental achievement along the way.

Unable to face himself in the glass, he drifted into the bookshop and browsed among its shelves at random.

"Ah!" cried the bookseller, closing in. "Byron!" He glanced at the spine. *"The Corsair* — a happy choice, young sir!"

"Is it?" Peter asked.

"Indeed, it is." He wafted a hand at the front window. "There is Albermarle Street! You have just trodden very pavement where Byron once paced up and down in torment while Murray, his publisher" — he pointed vaguely away to his left — "read the final draft of that very book. There's glory for you!"

And, Peter had to admit, the hair was prickling a bit at the back of his neck.

"Did you actually see him, sir?" he asked.

"Do I look to be a hundred and ten to you?" The man laughed. "Never mind — it's glorious poetry. Read on!" He patted the book and wandered off again.

Peter opened the pages at random and read:

> *The spirit, burning but unbent,*
> *May writhe, rebel — the weak alone repent!*

"Bloody good stuff, this!" he murmured to himself and hunted eagerly through the pages for more, not just in *The Corsair* but in others of Byron's works. "She walks in beauty, like the night ..." he read aloud, thinking of Gemma, all in black, walking to

St James's Palace and back on that first morning. This poet surely knew a thing or two!

But when he opened *Don Juan* and read that 'man's love is of man's life a thing apart, 'Tis woman's whole existence,' he realized that Byron, too, had feet of clay. Any man who could say that women have but one fate — 'To love again and be undone' had obviously never met a determined, self-reliant woman like Gemma!

A couple of feet upstream on the shelves he discovered Robert Burns.

> *But to see her was to love her,*
> *Love but her, and love for ever.*

Wasn't that Gemma, caught to perfection?

> *What is life when wanting love?*

His feelings exactly. And how about this for a description of the idyllic life:

> *A youthful, loving, modest pair,*
> *In other's arms breathe out the tender tale,*
> *Beneath the milk-white thorn that scents the evening gale.*

'In *each* other's arms' he meant, obviously, but poets could break the rules like that. Duller minds just had to catch on. Poetic licence, it was called. Poets could break the normal rules because they had something too big, too important to say to be bothered by such petty restrictions. So why couldn't there be some kind of *social* licence — to allow someone like him to express a love so big, so important that it could not be held back by the usual petty restraints?

They were, indeed, heady days for Peter, those early days of the nation's mourning, when he wandered aimlessly through the streets and alleys of London, his soul on fire and his heart bursting with a love he could not declare, much less indulge. He hardly ate. He had visions of himself pining away to nothing. He imagined his family gathered around his bier, weeping bitterly and saying to each other, 'If only we had known! If only he had spoken out! Of *course* we would have let them marry if we had known it meant so much to him.' Oh, *then* they would be sorry!

People who saw him smiling at these bittersweet fantasies looked quickly away and hastened to get past him.

He accompanied his father on a visit to the Science Museum one day, hoping for an opportunity to broach the subject with him. But the man's head was so full of galaxies and orders of magnitude and something called 'relativity' that the occasion never arose. Peter wandered off into the natural history section, where he marvelled at the dinosaurs and decided that the dodo was more useful as a metaphor than it had ever been as a living bird. And then to the V&A, where he enjoyed many pleasant fantasies. He imagined himself and Gemma wandering hand in hand through all the historic rooms as if they were in their own house. Here they were a medieval lord and lady; there a renaissance baron and his ... châtelaine (or were châtelaines also medieval?); there a Tudor duke and his duchess. All that joyous afternoon Gemma wore the finest dresses, the richest silks, and the costliest jewels to be found in all Europe. Or in Kensington, anyway.

But, inevitably, a mood of depression settled on him as he walked homeward for tea. A nagging thought that had lain at the back of his mind now surfaced. The house in St James's Square was full of imperial bric-a-brac and sporting trophies — not unlike the Natural History Museum and the V&A. And the brass and ebony instruments so lovingly displayed at the Science Museum were very like the telescopes, microscopes, and sextants that had hung about his father's rooms for as long as he could remember. And once that thought was let free, there was no stopping it. Never mind the house in St James's Square and the museums in South Kensington, the whole of London's West End now seemed to him like one vast country house occupying several thousand acres yet still somehow enclosed.

In fact, hadn't Guinevere Roanoke said something along those lines to him back in Falmouth?

Suddenly, the people around him were no longer people. They, too, were stuffed animals, animated by some clockwork trick. The fact that so many were in mourning, and moved about with grave faces and solemn demeanour, made the notion seem even more reasonable. In other words, his idea —

that by leaving the house and roaming the streets he was somehow liberating himself from the constraints of home — was a delusion. Home, the values of home, the *clutch* of home, was always there. 'Yea, though I flee to the uttermost depths of ocean, there shalt Thou find me still!' There was poetry for you, too — though of a starker and more ancient order.

Was there *no* escape?

He had to ask someone, anyone. He had to *talk*. His brain had rung with these thoughts for long enough; it now heard nothing but echoes and re-echoes of itself and, as with any single word repeated often enough, the thoughts had lost all meaning.

But who?

He knew the answer, of course — Guinevere — but he would not admit it; he would not say her name and turn his feet toward Bayswater. He suspected she would be quite a different person up here in London, free of her husband and away from the prying eyes of her Cornish neighbours. That kiss, he told himself, had been no spur-of-the-moment affair. She had timed it deliberately so that mere kissing would seem old hat by now. He racked his brains to think of some way in which he might discover if she were out — without her discovering that he had inquired, of course.

So, unwilling to cross Hyde Park and risk a meeting with her, he had no choice but to wander on up Piccadilly. Slower and slower his feet dragged as he neared Devonshire House, by which time he realized he had no choice in the matter. There was no one else in London — indeed, in the world — to whom he could unburden himself. He just had to talk, and it would have to be with Guinevere.

He turned in at one of the alleys by the Army and Navy Club, intending to cut across Mayfair and come out a little way up Park Lane. And thus he discovered Shepherd's Market and the trade that has gone on there since brick replaced green field.

He looked for a way around and saw none. As he turned back toward Piccadilly a young girl stepped out of a doorway and, laughing at the fright in his eyes, said, "We don't bite, you know. Not unless you ask us to."

Her accent was straight out of some posh finishing school; otherwise he would have smiled and walked straight past her, back to the unchallenging freedom of the main road. Instead he hesitated. Perhaps it would be possible to speak his mind with a total stranger? Would she take money just to listen? He wasn't really seeking advice. He just wanted to know what his thoughts sounded like when spoken out loud; he needed to look into someone else's eyes while his words sunk in. She wouldn't be jealous, either — which Guinevere very well might be.

"Is that the way you usually speak?" he asked.

"I beg your pardon?"

"You're not just mocking *my* accent, are you? It is the way you normally speak?"

Her gaze hardened. He was trespassing upon ground where no amount of money could buy him admission.

"I'm sorry," he said, making to walk past her.

"What do you want?" She stood tall and threw out her chest. She had a fine figure and a pretty face — and she knew it.

"To talk," he replied awkwardly.

"Dirty?"

"No!"

Their eyes dwelled in each other's and for a moment, he thought, anything could happen.

What actually did happen was that Mr Wilkes, manufacturer of hats, stepped out of the door behind her, saw Peter, and came to an abrupt halt.

"I know you," he said. "Wait a mo' ..."

Peter opened his mouth to speak but Wilkes grinned and pointed the knob of his cane in warning. "No names, no pack drill," he said. "I've got you now. Remember me, too?"

"Yes, sir," Peter said.

"Care to quaff a pint of the foaming?"

"Just a moment, *sir,*" the girl said sharply. "There's unfinished business here."

"I don't think so," Wilkes said pleasantly as he took Peter's arm and started walking him toward a nearby alehouse. He swung his cane with an I-own-the-world sort of swagger.

Peter looked back over his shoulder and shrugged an apology. She just smiled back, an oddly knowing smile, he thought.

"Were you really thinking of going with her?" Wilkes asked.

"I don't know, sir ..."

"No need for the 'sir' — we're about to become drinking companions. Go on."

"Not to *do* anything. I just felt like talking to someone."

"Oh dear! Bad as that, eh? Lucky I came along!"

Peter laughed. "Why?"

"Well, old chap, for one thing, I'm cheaper. *Jenny* back there wouldn't stand you a pint, believe me! Have you eaten? Well, you'd better have some pie first."

Peter glanced back again just as they entered the alehouse door. Jenny had just linked arms with a fat, elderly man and was leading him indoors — through the same door from which Wilkes had just emerged. The smile on her face was precisely the smile she had flashed at him, not two minutes earlier. The sheer *indifference* of it shocked him — that it mattered not the slightest to her whether she went up to her room with a fat, doddery old toad or (not to be immodest) a slim, good-looking young man. It *was* lucky Wilkes had happened along.

"Just in case you're wondering," his new drinking companion said as Peter tucked into a large Melton Mowbray pie and a side plate of scotch egg, "I didn't. Not that I wouldn't. Not that I don't. But not today. It so happens that my turf accountant has his office on the ground floor of that house — and that was my business there — on my Bible, yer 'onour." He winked so that Peter no longer knew whether he was being offered the truth or a fiction to maintain at home.

"Take my tip," Wilkes went on. "If you haven't started sniffing around these mercenary skirts yet, don't! If, like me at your age, you're still pressing your nose to the shop window, keep your dreams intact. Nothing within half a mile of here could even measure up to the most commonplace of your dreams."

"D'you know that girl?" Peter asked. "You called her Jenny?" He cringed from the thought that at that very moment she was probably gasping under the weight of that old toad.

"I know Jenny," Wilkes assured him. "D'you imagine *you* want to know her, too? I advise against it."

"I don't mean 'know' in the biblical sense."

"I mean it in *any* sense. You don't want to know her. At all. Full stop."

"She speaks ... so ..."

"Like one of our class? Well, so she is. In fact" — he glanced right and left and an amused smile stretched his lips as he leaned toward Peter — "she's a bishop's daughter." Seeing the disbelief in Peter's eyes, he added, "I'd name the man, too — if I wasn't keeping him for myself. To blackmail, you know, if ever I fall on hard times." He chuckled. "What d'you think it would do to the dear old c of e if ever it got about!"

"But ... why?" Peter, believing the tale now, was intrigued.

"The said bishop has numerous sons and daughters so the fact that the name of one of them is no longer spoken probably doesn't get noticed too much. I say! How long is it since you last ate anything?"

"Too long." Peter pulled a face.

"I can believe you. Love, is it? Unrequited love? Is that what you were hoping to talk to her about?" He sucked a tooth. "You chose well. She could have told you all about *that!*"

"Cheer-ho!" Peter relished the first nectarlike draught of ale.

"A toast to both ends of the busk!" Wilkes drank deeply, too. "She fell in love with the coachman. Or footman. Some kind of manservant, anyway. They eloped. And then he tired of her. A neat reversal of the usual story, don't you think? The servants' hall takes its revenge."

"Good God! When did this happen?"

"Last Christmas."

"No! So she's only been ... Why didn't she just go home?"

"She took one look at this way of life and decided it was preferable to what she'd had to endure in the bishop's palace — so she says."

Peter had the impression that Wilkes was trying to think of something witty to say but that the seriousness of the matter kept getting in the way. In the end he gave up the struggle and added, "Can't say I blame her — can you? Upper-class women have a pretty shitty time of it, wouldn't you say?" Annoyed with himself he turned side-on to Peter and took another deep draught of ale — which allowed him to gasp with satisfaction and say, "That's better!"

"I understand you have two daughters, Mister Wilkes?" Peter dared to say.

"Wilkes, laddy, just Wilkes will do. I have three, as a matter of fact. Drink up and we'll go. You'll come back with me? Have a word with La Roanoke? She speaks very highly of you." He tapped the flagstone floor with his cane to emphasize his impatience to be going.

"Oh?" Peter ran a nervous finger round his collar.

"Says you're building a racing yacht all by yourself? The talk of Falmouth?"

"Hardly!" He laughed. "It's no more than a dinghy with the lines of a yacht. You didn't say whether you had other daughters — or shouldn't I ask? Can I stand a round, by the way?"

"D'you want more?"

Peter pressed his full belly and said no.

"You can be in the chair next time," Wilkes said as they left the bar and started to run the gauntlet of available flesh that stretched from there through Shepherd's Market and all the way up Curzon Street, almost to the gates of the park. "Talking of turf accountants, did you place a bet yet on those horses I tipped you?"

"Lemberg and Greenback?"

"You did! Good man! You won't regret it. The odds are shortening daily."

"Actually," Peter said. "I'm not yet twenty-one."

Wilkes looked at him askance, as if he thought the youth must be pulling his leg. "Well, well!" was all he said. "You do surprise me. No account, eh? Well, we can soon take care of that. How much d'you want to splash?"

Peter thought it over and suggested a tenner. He had two fivers hidden under the insoles of his shoes, in case the man asked for cash. They returned to the turf accountant's office. Beside its door a dark, narrow, uncarpeted stairway led to the floor above; a small red lamp glowed dimly at the half-landing. Wilkes pointed to it and said, "When it burns bright, she's free. Well, not *free* but you know what I mean."

A brass plaque on the door beside them said, *Gabriel & Co., Turf Accountants.* The office was dark and spartan — three bentwood chairs, one occupied by a crumpled edition of *The Pink 'Un;* a small strip of carpet; a partners' desk that had seen better days, tenanted by a cheerful-looking elderly clerk, whom Wilkes addressed as Jenkins; and a huge safe that must have been assembled in the room for it would never have been got in by the door; dusty hand-coloured photographs of classic winners graced the walls. Overhead the ceiling creaked with the unmistakable rhythm of humans climaxing in rut on squeaky bedsprings. Peter's heart began to beat wildly.

"We'll put a fiver on each," Wilkes said. "Lemberg to win and two-pound-ten each way on Greenback for a place. You won't be disappointed."

Jenkins recorded the bet in Wilkes's name and put Peter's in brackets after it; Wilkes said the young fellow could collect any winnings on those bets himself — and, if he came across any other loose change and wanted to get it on before the race, he could use the same subterfuge.

"The Falmouth yacht club is at a place called *Greenbank,*" Peter said. "So that's probably a good omen."

Wilkes shot him a withering look but said nothing. Jenkins smiled without looking up.

The clerk had a laborious hand so that the rutting upstairs was over before the each-way bet was recorded. Wilkes gave Peter the slips and he stuffed them in his pocket, being eager to get away. But the fat old toad made it to the foot of the stairs just as the two men were leaving the office. Peter almost vomited at the sight of him close-to; every inch of the man was an essay in foulness. The ogre paused to check his dress; his pudgy little hands barely reached his flies around his paunch. Peter heard the door open and close above, meaning that Jenny was about to reappear. Roughly he shouldered the creature aside and escaped into the alley. "I'll see you round the corner," he called out to Wilkes.

"Didn't want to meet his grace's daughter, eh?" the man commented when he caught up. "Can't say I blame you." He took Peter's arm, as if to steer him safely through the shoals of the flesh market ahead. Now he handled his cane less jauntily. "About my daughters. They are sixteen, eighteen, and twenty, by the way — and each and every one a paid-up member of the non-militant suffragists."

"With your encouragement?"

He shrugged. "What's a man to do? I've given them a good education in something more useful than water-colours, embroidery, and Chopin. Come the revolution, they won't have to do the same as poor Jenny back there."

"And if the revolution doesn't come?"

"Ah, well, that's the whole point, isn't it! They either face unhappiness as wives or equal unhappiness as rebels in society. Not much of a choice, is it!"

"Must it be unhappiness?"

"What d'you think? Talk to them about it."

Peter, having spent the past weeks depressing himself with the prospect that *all* roads in life lead to unhappiness, did not want to hear it confirmed by anyone else. "There must *be* happiness," he said. "Otherwise why have a word for it?"

"Careful!" Wilkes gripped his arm in apparent alarm. "We may bump into a Jabberwocky round this next corner," he added laconically. "If we do, try not to show your disbelief. It hates that."

Peter saw his point and chuckled. He was amazed that the girls were taking so little interest in them. Maybe there was a secret sign language — the way Wilkes wore his hat or something. "By the way," he said, "I've never gambled before — not seriously, like that. Just card games."

"No more have I," Wilkes replied calmly. "That wasn't gambling, laddy. Listen — I'll tell you a thing or two about betting. Betting on cards is folly — unless you're the sort of genius who can learn the odds against every single hand by heart. Then there's a good living in it. Betting on raindrops running down the window, flies landing on sugar lumps, the Boat Race ... that sort of thing, is for pennies. But betting on horses is in a class of its own. Why? Because the punters set the odds. If they all go mad and bet on a blind cart horse with three legs for the Grand National, it'll be an odds-on favourite. You may laugh, but that's only an exaggeration of what's really happening. The world is full of lunatics, men and women, who think they can pick winners with pins or because its name begins with the same initial as them or the jockey's wearing their favourite colour."

"Or because Greenback is like Greenbank!" Peter grinned.

"Just so — though I was too polite to say it. In other words, that office we were in just now is simply full of idiot-money — money that's there for the taking by people like me who *know* why geegees win races." He guffawed and slapped Peter on the back. "Here endeth the first lesson."

They had reached Park Lane and were waiting for a lull in the traffic before they crossed into the park.

"*There's* a symbol of our times," Wilkes said, pointing his cane at an enclosed garden inside the park.

"Nannies and babies?" Peter was puzzled.

"No — Hamilton Gardens itself — all enclosed behind iron railings. You can't get in unless you live in Mayfair and have a key. A little upper-class enclave among the commoners of Hyde Park. The privileged little mites clutch at their iron bars and stare out at *hoi-polloi* running free all about! D'you read H.G. Wells? He predicts we'll keep the upper classes for *meat,* one day! Yum-yum!" He smacked his lips ghoulishly and laughed. "Come on! You were going to tell me all the things you thought of telling the bishop's daughter."

And so, as they strolled across the park toward the Bayswater Gate, Peter told him all about Gemma — from that still-astonishing moment of their meeting right up to her most recent admonition to leave her alone. "You see, it's not the usual thing," he concluded. "It's not that I want a bit of slap and tickle in the spare room on the housekeeper's day off. I want to wake up beside her fifty *years* from now — and to feel this same … this same …" His voice faltered. "Damn!" he said.

They had sauntered to a halt during this last speech. Wilkes placed the tip of his cane against a daisy and murdered it. "What's stopping you?" he asked quietly.

"My youth. Her certainty that we could never find happiness — that people would never *let* us be happy."

"What people?"

"The people one knows."

"Why couldn't you get to know some other people? The world is full of diversity, after all."

"What would we live on? My parents would stop my income at once, I'm sure. Even if they didn't want to, they'd have to protect my sisters' reputations. They'd have to show the world that the de Vivians aren't *like that.*"

"You could build boats, couldn't you?" Wilkes laughed. "You could even sell hats. I'd give you a trial."

"In a shop?" Peter tried to keep the distaste out of his voice — just in case the offer became a reality some day.

"Wholesale. On the road. I make over a hundred thousand hats a year, you know. A salesman with a good accent is worth ten who speak like oiks. It's a very snobbish business." He punched Peter lightly on the arm and set off again. "Listen, Peter," he said. "May I call you that? Listen! All this is up in the air. What I'm really trying to say is that *if* this young maid truly is the be-all and end-all of your life, then you don't honestly have any choice. You *must* do something along these lines ..."

"But she would never agree."

"I suspect she would, you know. I suspect her resistance may be due to something you haven't even thought of yet."

"What?" Peter stopped and stared at him.

Wilkes took the young man by the elbow and pulled him onward. "Class," he said.

"Class?" Peter was puzzled. "But if she married me, she'd be moving *up!* Not that *I* think that way, mind, but if ..."

"Would she?" the other rupted. "You know my wife's cousin quite well, I think — Guinevere Roanoke?"

"Yes."

Wilkes grinned. "The tooth-puller's daughter who married above her station? Have you never heard anyone speak of her like that?" Peter's blush answered for him. "And," Wilkes continued, "is it possible that your darling Gemma may also have overheard such remarks from time to time?"

"My God!" Peter closed his eyes and shook his head.

"Put yourself in her position, once such remarks have sunk home. What thoughts would run through her mind if some upper-class young man came along and offered to marry her?" When Peter made no reply he said, "Eh?"

"Yes, yes — you're absolutely right. Actually, there's something else I haven't told you. Oh, dear! It's a dreadful thing to give away about the woman one loves, but ..."

"Don't, then. I'll accept that she has other reasons, too." He cleared his throat delicately. "To do with you, eh? Something you've done?"

"No." He beat his fist dramatically against his brow. "Not to do with me. Nor with her, in fact. But with another member of her family. She — this other girl — got into trouble with ... with a young man, just about my age. A young man from a very good Falmouth family."

"And?"

"I don't know. We've never talked about it, but I'm sure that's why Gemma's so scared of ... well, of even talking to me. She doesn't want history to repeat itself."

"How did you find out, then?"

Peter was in a quandary. He didn't want to say that Guinevere had told him because he was sure Wilkes would get all the details out of her in no time. He probably would, anyway, but there was no sense in handing it to him on a plate. "Servants talk," he said. "Other servants talk."

"D'you know the names of these runaways? Maybe they're blissfully happy! They could be your most powerful argument. Why d'you laugh?"

"I'm laughing at my own stupidity. I never thought of that."

"It's all sex, you know," Wilkes said suddenly. "Just you wait another thirty years and you'll wonder what all this fuss was about." He watched Peter's face and then said, "Yes, I know, old fellow. It's that 'thirty years' bit, isn't it! Well, here's the other answer." And he swung his cane toward a number of open carriages — magnificent landaus and phaetons — sweeping out of the park toward the Bayswater Gate. *"Voilà!* The demimonde on its way home to their love nests in Maida Vale. 'Love nest'! Isn't that an exciting brace of words? Wait just a few months, until you come of age, and then you'll surely have income enough to keep one of these deliciously scented creatures in a *love nest* somewhere. Falmouth must have its miniature equivalent of Maida Vale."

Peter stood entranced, hardly listening, as the carriages swept by. Was it rude to stare so? Surely, these perfumed butterflies were used to it — else why parade themselves down in Rotten Row at all? And distance no doubt combined with wishful fantasy to lend a certain enchantment, but they were quite exquisite in their black and purple mourning, with their milk-white skin, their bright bee-stung lips, and those eyes that could kill at a hundred paces.

"And the last is the prettiest of all," Wilkes said as he set out briskly to cross the final half-mile of grass.

Peter had been so entranced with the next-to-last girl that he barely had time to notice the final carriage and its fair occupant. Or auburn-haired occupant, rather. But when he saw her he just stood there with his jaw agape.

"Something the matter?" Wilkes asked.

"She looked rather like Gemma." He stared after the departing beauty, who was now just a pair of dainty shoulders beneath a frilly black parasol.

18   When it looked as if Guinevere was going to offer him her cheek to kiss, Peter hastily took up her hand instead, and kissed the air a fraction of an inch above it. "My, my!" she exclaimed frostily. "What refined ways we have learned in a few short days."

"It's second nature to me now," he replied smoothly. Behind her he could see three young ladies who were obviously dressed for amateur theatricals — the Misses Wilkes, presumably. They were taking their father's hat, gloves, and cane with an attentiveness that immediately suggested they were hoping for some privilege or permission. "I see we are interrupting something," Peter added.

"Not at all." Guinevere smiled broadly but he knew she was conserving her irritation until a more suitable occasion. "Let me present you to these three charming young ladies."

Sophie, at twenty, was the girl Guinevere was chiefly helping to bring out that Season. She was blonde, with a tall, slender figure and pretty, somewhat doll-like features, except for her eyes, which were cool and intelligent.

Felicity, the eighteen year old, could not have presented a greater contrast, with her jet-black hair and deep-blue eyes; she had the figure of a field girl — short, stocky, and powerful.

Tabitha, sixteen and still in the schoolroom, had long, dark-brown hair with a ginger tinge framing a narrow, freckled face; the effect of her thin, rather severe lips was contradicted by her hazel eyes, which sparkled with merriment.

Peter wondered what Guinevere had told them about him to make the two older sisters pretend to be so cool with him. He had met enough girls since leaving school to know that most of them were simply bored by men of his unmarriageable age; but this pretence at superiority was something new.

"What did you think you were interrupting, Mister de Vivian?" Sophie asked.

He waved a hand vaguely at them and said, "Charades?"

Wilkes burst into laughter. "Didn't I warn you!" he chuckled as, picking up the evening paper, he went into the drawing room. "Whisky-soda? Gin and It? Name your poison, laddy," he called out over his shoulder.

Each daughter looked down at herself and then at her sisters in a bewildered search for anything that might remotely suggest to anyone that they were playing at charades. But their surprise was feigned; they knew the cause of his confusion very well. They were all — even young schoolgirl Tabitha — wearing 'hareem trousers,' the notorious *jupes culottes* that Paris had been trying to impose on an unwilling British matriarchy for the past two seasons. And very fetching they looked in them, too — as Peter would have been the first to admit, if he had not already made it clear he thought they were mere dressing-ups from some attic lumber-room.

"I've poured you a whisky-soda, de Vivian," Wilkes called out from the drawing room. "Girls — do your duty."

Guinevere, all smiles again now, slipped her arm gently inside Peter's and led him through the tiger country of the three affronted girls.

"You could have warned me," he muttered when they were past the gauntlet.

"Why d'you think I tried to offer you my cheek?" she replied in a murmur.

He sighed. *"Touché!"*

"Yes." She even managed to murmur severely. "In future, where I lead, you follow — *laddy.*" Then, raising her voice, she spoke to Wilkes. "Conrad! What a fortuitous meeting this was! Did you bump into him on the pavement outside?" She smiled at Peter. "Were you *lurking* there?"

"We met near St James's," Wilkes told her. "We had a most amiable walk back across the park."

"So!" She now fixed her eyes on Peter. "We shall never know if you intended coming here of your own volition or not. Were you *ever* going to call?"

Sophie put Peter's glass in his hand, bending his fingers round it as if he were a mannikin in a draper's window. Her amusement was mocking rather than an apology for her earlier coolness. "Do sit down, Mister de Vivian," she said.

He raised a hand in mock alarm, to fend her off. "I am quite capable of bending my *own* back and knees, Miss Wilkes, I do assure you."

She tried not to smile but he saw he had struck home. Her head went back and her eyes sized him up, as if to say he might make quite a worthwhile sparring partner.

"I thought I might not be welcome here," he said as he proved himself capable of sitting down.

"How so?" She bridled.

"Not *just* here. I mean in any house in London where they are putting a daughter through the Season."

"I still don't understand."

"The king's death, the hugga-mugga, the brou-ha-ha, the fuffle." He described the feverish activity at St James's Square. "Didn't they send over some yards of the stuff?"

"Oh!" Guinevere wafted her hand. "We managed all that within the first day." She smiled at the girls. "All one needs is a certain dexterity ..."

"Please, Guinevere!" Sophie interrupted. "Do not so much as mention our facility with the needle. It is not an accomplishment to boast of — no more than a gentleman who has a certain facility for ... say ... *carpentry"* — she shuddered — "would dream of bragging about it in mixed company. Don't you agree, Mister de Vivian?"

Wilkes winked at him and gave a silent toast with his glass.

Peter decided that if these brittle young ladies were going to use the social rigidities as a bouncing board for their little barbs, the only thing to do was to ignore the rigidity. "I am intrigued by these theatrical costumes, Miss Wilkes," he replied. "I use the word in the sense of 'dramatic' or 'striking,' of course. And on you and your sisters they are also most fetching, if I may say so."

The two elder girls maintained their composure but Tabitha could not help nodding with approval. Her eyes gleamed when they met his and he guessed she had too often been the target of Sophie's darts when there was no suitable male around.

"May I ask what it is, in particular, that intrigues you about them?" Sophie asked. "Each outfit comprises, as you see, a pair of floral silk *trousers* ..." She paused to see if her use of that indelicate word shocked him. Disappointed, she went on, "... covered by a tubular silk skirt of the same pattern to just below the knee."

"*Trews,* Sophie, dear," Guinevere remonstrated. "Don't use that unbecoming word."

"Trousers!?" Sophie asked with belligerent but entirely fake surprise, making her voice rise, fall, and rise again, all on the one word.

"Trews *and* a skirt," Peter put in. "It is a judicious mixture — the best of *both* worlds."

While Sophie looked from Guinevere to Peter, wondering which to tackle first, Felicity jumped in. "You believe there *are* two worlds, then, Mister de Vivian? You think men and women are worlds apart?"

He was beginning to get the gauge of them. Sophie liked to bowl googlies and spinners; Felicity hurled them straight and solid, right down the centre of the pitch. Tabitha sat in the pavilion still, enjoying her elder sisters' discomfiture, no matter who or what caused it.

"I think you *must* meet my sister Beatrice," he replied. "Don't you agree, Mrs Roanoke? She would give her eye-teeth to have such jolly pals here in London."

She dipped her head gravely. "Indeed, that may be arranged sooner than you think. Your sudden irruption upon this household — however it came about" — and here a glance at Wilkes made it clear she did not believe his account of the matter — "is, indeed, fortuitous, for, had you not come, it had been my intention to ... oh dear! I've lost the thread of ..."

"You are all invited to Westbrook — my country cottage — for *next* Thursday-to-Monday. A week from today." Wilkes rose and picked an envelope off the mantelpiece. "Here's the actual invitation. Slip it in your pocket now so you won't forget. Graham Melchett will be there, too."

Peter started to say that, while he could not formally accept on behalf of his family, he did not doubt ...

But Guinevere cut him short. "Westbrook is just south of Maidenhead," she explained. "Catch the three-fifteen local train from Paddington and you will be met. I've scribbled all the details on the back. It's not many miles from Windsor, so we'll make up a party to attend the king's funeral, you see?"

"Naturally, it will not be a country-house party in the usual sense of the word," Wilkes warned. "There'll be no formal dances, no professional recitals, but we may still make our own modest entertainment."

"Yes!" Peter beamed all round. "Charades, for instance!"

19 During the following week the late King Edward lay in state in Westminster Hall while more than a quarter-million of his subjects filed through to pay their last respects. The de Vivians were among them, of course, as were all their servants at St James's Square. The grief of the people was quite genuine. It was only to be expected that all public buildings would be draped in black or purple, as is laid down for such occasions. But no protocol compelled a cabby to tie a black ribbon round his whip, or a shopkeeper to keep his shutters closed, even though the shop itself was open for business — or a private householder to keep the blinds drawn all day. These were the spontaneous tokens of a widespread and heartfelt sorrow that gripped the whole nation. Newspapers that had once railed against Edward as a gambler, a womanizer, a rake (all of which was true), now mourned the passing of England's greatest ambassador, the statesman who had always been able to bring his mad nephew, the German emperor, to heel (which was also true). And even now, the Kaiser still held his old tormentor in such awe that he ordered the Royal Navy's red ensign to be flown at half mast from the yards of every vessel in the Imperial German Navy. The kings and generals and ministers of every great European state were already eyeing one another uneasily, now that the Uncle of Europe was no longer there to bang their heads together. Indeed, though the skies were blue that long, sad week in London, the storm clouds were already gathering for those who had eyes to see them.

For Peter the lying-in-state brought a more immediate disappointment. He had not been able to forget the young demimondaine he had seen driving toward the Bayswater Gate on the day he ran into Wilkes in Mayfair. In that tantalizingly brief glimpse she had looked so shockingly like Gemma that he could only wonder if he had not, in fact, seen the 'disgraced' sister Ruby. It was an almost impossible long-shot, of course, and yet the resemblance had been so startling he could not rule it out. He simply had to go back and see her again, just to set his mind at rest.

And just suppose it was Ruby — what a feather in his cap it would be with Gemma, to be able to tell her he had found her lost sister! And if he could arrange an actual meeting between them ... well!

But when he arrived at the park he learned that all the carriage rides had been cancelled for the week — the respectable rides at two as well as the demimondaines' at four. So he turned his face north, thinking he might as well call on Guinevere — if only to escape yet more accusations, next time they met, that he was deliberately avoiding her. But, as he approached the Bayswater Gate, who should he see approaching him but the three Misses Wilkes! They were obviously entering the park for an afternoon constitutional. He stood and waited for them, hat in hand.

They saw him, too, and stopped. After a brief discussion they resumed their walk but, when they drew near, he saw that they intended to pass him by, pretending they had not seen him at all. He should have guessed they'd try to tease him in some way; he should have placed himself directly beside the gravel path instead of some twenty paces short of it. He put on his hat and stood there with his arms folded; he fixed his eye on Tabitha, the youngest, knowing that she would be the least dedicated to such a prank. And, sure enough, when they were almost level, she shot a glance his way, found his gaze already fixed in hers, and burst into laughter.

Felicity angrily released her young sister's arm but still did not look toward Peter. She and Sophie swept on, maintaining their silly pretence, while Tabitha stood uncertainly where they had dumped her.

Peter beckoned to her and she, with a daring glance toward her sisters, obeyed the summons. "Shall we share an ice cream?" he suggested.

She glanced again at her sisters and then said a defiant, "Yes!" as, without hesitation, she accepted his arm.

They set off across the grass, walking parallel with the two older girls.

"It will be perfectly acceptable to flirt with me," he told Tabitha. "Neither of us is in the marriage market yet."

"I'm not at all sure how one goes about flirting," she replied with a giggle.

He told her she was doing well enough so far.

At about that time her sisters turned around to tell her to catch up — and, at last, noticed what had happened. Sophie even stamped a foot in annoyance.

"She's magnificent when she's angry," Peter said, quoting a catch phrase from a popular song.

Sophie and her sister went into conference. The rules of mutual chaperonage gave them no choice but to stay with or near their sister; the only question was, how near? They obviously decided that twenty paces was near enough for, when Peter beckoned them to catch up and join the party, they both waved at him to go on.

"They think to snub me," Tabitha said.

"How would this be a snub?"

"They think you'd really prefer their company to mine, so they're punishing you by forcing you to make do with me. Don't you call that a snub?"

"No. I call it jolly decent of them — not to inflict themselves upon us and to let me enjoy your company unalloyed. I had not even dared dream of it, Tabitha."

She giggled again and said, "Sophie will be *mad!*"

"Only Sophie?"

"She rather likes you — though she'd scratch my eyes out for telling you. If you ever tell her I told you, I shall deny it. And I'll challenge you to pistols at dawn."

"Why *are* you telling me, then?"

After a pause she said, "Well, to tell you the truth, *I* rather like you, too."

He laughed. "That's good! You don't need any lessons, little face." When she did not respond he added, "Oh! Is it my turn to amuse us now?"

"I'm serious," she said quietly.

"Oh, dear," he responded. "Listen! I don't think that's at all wise, do you?."

She walked in silence at his side, staring dead ahead, for a long, awkward while before she reacted. Then she threw up her chin, shook her curls, flashed him a smile that would one day be devastating — and one day quite soon, too, he thought — and said, "You're right, Peter. I may call you Peter, mayn't I? So let's pretend then, shall we?"

"That's what flirting is, Tabitha."

"Let's pretend we are sort of unofficially promised to each other. Agreed?"

He shrugged. "I don't see why we should, but, just as long as that word 'pretend' is in there, I have no strong objection to playing the game. What then?"

"Well, I can write love letters to you — just for practice. And I promise not to copy them out of a book. And you can read them as a man and tell me how I might improve them — make them more effective."

"Effective for what?"

"For captivating a man's heart. For binding him to me for ever and ever."

"I see. And what would your darling suffragist sisters think of this scheme?"

She looked up in alarm. "But they are to know nothing of it. We shall also practise all the clandestine arts in maintaining our secret love" — she grinned as she added — "my dearest."

"Our secret *pretend* love, my most precious."

"Yes, yes!"

Peter began to feel twinges of discomfort at the unexpected turn their game had suddenly taken. If she was serious about sending him secret letters and if one of them were to be intercepted, her parents might not take so sanguine a view of his 'cradle-snatching,' as they would certainly see it. "What's in it for me?" he asked.

"You may write quite freely to me and I'll perform the same service for you," she replied. "Or we could meet somewhere and you could rehearse some flowery speech you propose making to your inamorata and I could point out ways to make it even more telling to a woman's heart."

He thought he saw a way then to scotch the whole idea, to kill it before it was fully born. It would also warn Sophie off, if she was developing any dangerously romantic feelings about him. He had nothing to lose, anyway. The Wilkeses were pleasant but temporary companions along life's way; nothing they did or said could have any permanent effect on him.

"I'm afraid my 'inamorata' doesn't exactly go in for flowery speeches, my dearest," he said mournfully. "In fact, we have the devil's own job to snatch even a few words together."

Tabitha was thoughtful but said nothing.

"Well?" he prompted.

"Well what? What can I say if I don't know the first thing about her?"

"She's poor," he offered.

"And?"

"She's Cornish. Her family is from old yeoman stock — small landowners, you know."

"Yes, yes! I know perfectly well what yeoman means. Do they still have the land?"

"No. That's the point."

"Is it? It seems point*less* to me. The *fact* that they once owned land is just so much wearisome historical baggage. Are you saying she's too proud to marry a rich man like you — just because her family's no longer rich?"

"Not in the least!" He thought it interesting that she should at once make the same point as her father had made — that Gemma might want to avoid marrying above herself.

She lost patience with him, for being so reticent. "You're making a very bad job of telling me about this woman, Peter. Either you're ashamed of her or you love her so much you don't know where to begin — which is it?"

"The second," he replied, chastened. "I love her to distraction. Her name is Gemma Penhallow. She is my sister's lady's maid. So now you know."

"That's better," Tabitha said quietly. "Go on."

"What more is there to say?"

"How d'you know you love her?"

"How d'you know you like ice cream? Where is the stall, by the way? I'm sure I saw it here before."

"Just beyond those trees. How did it all begin?"

"Oh God!" he murmured.

"Go on."

"It sounds so hackneyed but it was love at first sight — literally. The moment we arrived at our new house, with the servants all lined up to meet us. We traipsed down the line, shaking hands, blah-blah ... and then *bang!* My eyes meet Gemma's and her eyes meet mine and we're in love!"

"We? Has she confessed it?"

"No. But I know she loves me, too."

"Will she be at Westwood next weekend? I presume she will. I'll tell you then if you're right."

"You're not to speak to her about it!" he said in alarm.

She just smiled. "It won't be necessary but I will know."

"And you're not to mention a word of this to either of your sisters — please?"

"Oh." She was not quick enough to hide her disappointment. "Promise?"

She moved her hand out of his sight, crossed her fingers, and said, "Of course I promise it — *if* that's what you really want."

"Are you really only sixteen?" he asked.

She preened herself. "What makes you doubt it?"

He just shook his head. "If your sisters are anything like you, I think your father has raised three extraordinary young women, that's all."

He could see she wanted to deny that her sisters were remotely like her, but his tale of secret romance was too fascinating to drop for a second. "D'you suppose you'll ever be happy with your Gemma Penhallow?" she asked.

"I have no idea. But I'm absolutely certain I'll never be happy without her."

"Oh, Peter, I think that's simply beautiful!"

He glanced sidelong at her and was surprised to see a tear in her eye.

She grinned at him, a saucy, gamine sort of grin, and said, "And if it comes to nothing, my darling, do not despair. Remember — *I'll* still be waiting, ever-faithful in the wings!" And before he could stop her she reached up and gave him a quick peck on his cheek.

Behind them, Sophie and Felicity, who had been champing at the bit for some excuse to intervene without losing face, both cried out and ran forward to remonstrate. But when they saw the single tear coursing down Tabitha's cheek, they hesitated.

And Tabitha leaped into the breach. "Oh, Sophie!" she said breathlessly. "Oh, Felicity! Mister de Vivian has just told me the most moving story — the poor, poor man! It would break your heart to hear it."

"What? What?" Her sisters crowded her eagerly.

"Alas, he has made me promise on my absolute honour never to breathe a word of it!"

20 The de Vivians had imagined they might be among two or three other families invited down to Westwood to witness Halley's Comet and the royal funeral. But, as they discovered when everyone came to assemble on the platform at Maidenhead, the London party alone consisted of about thirty people and an almost equal number of maids and valets. They were met by two motorized charabancs, with a large horsedrawn dray to follow on with their luggage.

"It must be quite a large 'country cottage'," Beatrice remarked as the size of the party began to dawn on them.

"Not necessarily," her mother replied, looking about her with distaste. Their fellow guests had a distressingly commercial air about them; she couldn't be sure, of course — not without talking to them — but she prided herself on having a certain nose for such things. "I expect he'll put most of these ghastly people up in local hostelries. Mister Wilkes did not strike me as the sort of man who'd own a *large* country house. He himself called it a 'cottage,' didn't he, Peter?"

"Eh?" He had not actually been listening; instead he had been searching among the throng of lady's maids and valets for a glimpse of Gemma.

Beatrice stepped in to save him. "Mister Wilkes called Westwood a country cottage, didn't he?"

"Oh ... yes."

"Well, then!" their mother felt vindicated. "Their place in Bayswater is about his limit, I should think. Twenty rooms and a pocket-handkerchief garden." Her sharp eyes darted hither and thither, seeking out any mid-twentyish unattached gentleman who might possibly be Graham Melchett; the trawl left her hoping he was none of them.

Even then she had no high hopes of the man, no matter how many people tipped him for greatness. Anyway, they only had La Roanoke's word for that. She had no great hopes of this coming Thur-to-Mon, either. The things Peter had told her about Wilkes's ghastly daughters made her flesh creep. Wearing *trousers!* And actually calling them by that unmentionable name, too!

Her discomfort increased in the confined space of the charabanc. It was so embarrassing to be travelling among people to whom one would soon be introduced and to whom one could then talk but who, meanwhile, must simply be acknowledged with an awkward nod and no more than a hint of a smile. Unfortunately, most of their fellow passengers already knew one another; and to make things worse, they did not seem to understand the accepted conventions. They acknowledged the de Vivians' obvious superiority by allowing them first into the vehicle, but then they filed past with cheery greetings of a most familiar kind, which, though clearly intended to put the newcomers at their ease, had precisely the opposite effect — on the parents, at least.

The coach had hardly started on its two-mile journey when a man positioned himself in front of them, anchoring himself against an iron stanchion by the door. "Higgs is the name," he said cheerily, passing over a card that identified him as an importer of fine silks and damasks. "Can't say I remember seeing you before. What line are you in, old chap?"

"Ah ... er ..." Terence de Vivian floundered before deciding on, "Astronomy!"

Higgs's eyes narrowed. "That's a new one," he said. "Much in it, is there?"

Ada intervened. "Astronomy is Mister de Vivian's *pursuit*, Mister Higgs. His profession is banking."

"Crikey!" Higgs laughed. "I shall have to watch my PS and QS, eh! I'm glad the funeral's tomorrow, aren't you? It sort of gets the whole sad business out of the way and gives us the weekend to pick our spirits up again. Though, mind you, I could name several spirits I'd sooner *lower*, what? Eh?"

The conversation continued in this distasteful manner until they were well out of the town and into the new-leafy lanes of Berkshire. There Peter decided to rescue his parents. "This looks like good hunting country, Mister Higgs," he said.

"It used to be," the man agreed. "But it's too built-about now. The North Berks is gone, and the Old Berkeley's going the same way. People round here put their mounts on the train and go down to Salisbury Plain to hunt with the Craven. Unrivaled country, of course. Mind you — a young, fit fellow like you can always get a run on foot with the Eton and Windsor Beagles."

"Oh! What a jewel of a house!" Ada, grateful for her liberation, was trying to steer the conversation toward impersonal, exterior topics — such as the passing scene. The object of her delight was a stately home of some grandeur, a Victorian pastiche of a French château whose plans had become slightly mixed with an Italian renaissance palazzo — a blend, in short, of classical fenestration and gothic turretry. If her aesthetic eye had been as keen to spot a sham as her social nose was to sniff out a faker, she would have disdained this 'jewel' as cordially as she detested Higgs and his like.

"Ah, Mrs de Vivian," he said, "now I *know* you've never visited the Wilkeses in their little country cottage."

Ada looked at him in amazement, then back at the imposing pile on the slopes below them. "You mean ...?" she murmured in a daze. *"That* is Westwood?"

Higgs tapped the side of his nose. "Between you and me, dear lady, our host is a bit cagey as to whose name is on the title deeds. His father and mother *live* there — though they're away in Italy at the moment. They *claim* they own the place. They certainly behave like as if they do! But I'm not the only one as thinks it's hats as pays all the bills."

"I gather that he makes a hundred thousand hats a year," Peter threw in casually.

"Is that what he told you?" Higgs laughed. "A million is more like it. A hundred thousand in England alone — yes, I could accept that."

Ada stared again at the house, which was now becoming difficult to see, for the charabanc was entering a stately, leaf-green tunnel of beeches and elms. A profound, if hasty, re-evaluation of their host was in progress behind her probing eyes. What else had Peter said about those three daughters? They must have *some* redeeming features, surely? They had no brothers — there was one! But, alas, the eldest of them was coming out this Season. She'd be snapped up, of course. Well, she'd be too old for Peter, anyway. One that got away.

Unless, mind you, there was a good *strategic* reason (she avoided the word 'commercial,' even in her own silent thoughts) for an alliance. Did this vast hatmaking industry need more capital? She knew few industries of any kind that didn't. How swiftly had he grown? Rapid success had overstretched many a company. Was his credit dangerously extended? It would be worth the de Vivians' while to move anything up to a couple of hundred thou' out of gilts and into a profitable *family* business, especially if it cemented an alliance with a family that could still afford to own and run a house and estate of *this* size. And even more especially if that family had no sons to carry it on!

She had entirely forgotten Higgs's existence by the time they reached the magnificent entrance to the estate.

The gatelodge was another romantic fantasy — a turreted portcullis that resembled nothing so much as a model artisan's dwelling perched atop a Tudor castle wall. As the charabanc swung in beneath the menacing spikes of the portcullis itself, Ada took the opportunity to look around at her fellow passengers. She had surveyed them earlier, it is true, but this time she had a purpose. Social training from the nursery upward had taught her to take a mental snapshot in less time than a Kodak needs for the real thing. As the tyres scrunched down the long and immaculately raked gravel drive, she pored over the image now etched in her mind. To her dismay she discovered no fewer than five young or youngish men who could be put in the eligible-bachelor class. At first sight, anyway.

How infuriating that Peter and Paul had waited until *after* two of their sisters were born. Perfect gentlemen, she had always joked, but it wasn't so funny now. The youngest girl — what was her name? Sophie, Felicity, and ... Thomasina? Tallulah? Tabitha! Tabby the cat — she should have remembered. Peter said she was just a playful little kitten. She'd have to do if the worst came to the worst, but you couldn't beat an alliance of capital on one side and the *eldest* daughter on the other — as most of the families in *Debrett* could tell you!

"Good heavens!" she exclaimed aloud.

"What, my dear?" Her husband had been trying to explain the vastness of the light year to Higgs, who kept trying to transpose the figures into pounds, shillings, and pence because, he claimed, that was the only way he could grasp numbers of any kind.

The whole of the Wilkes family — except for the enigmatic Mrs Wilkes, of course — was waiting beneath the arcaded portico to greet them, Guinevere among them. Ada shivered with distaste. Such a welcome should only be put on for royalties.

And, to compound the crime, the Wilkes girls were flapping their arms about as if they were gathered on the arrivals pier at Southampton — where such behaviour was just about tolerable. Had they never heard of the word 'decorum'? At least they were wearing modest, straight-sided dresses today, not the unmentionables Peter had described.

As the charabanc drew to a halt beside the vast portico, the *valet-du-jour* stepped briskly forward and opened its door. The de Vivians were first out, of course, but even in that brief sweep of her eyes, as the vehicle pulled up, Ada had already summarized the three daughters in her mind.

Sophie, the Miss Wilkes, was the pale, neurasthenic type who had painful menstruations and a succession of other internal complaints by the bucketful. A possible nagger. But well worth a Westwood and a million hats.

Miss Felicity was a stocky little heifer who looked as if she could breed until she dropped — not that young couples did such a thing, these days. People had criticized de Vivian and her, Ada, for stopping at five; few couples even reached such a figure today. Felicity would probably litter a high proportion of males, though; she had that lantern-jaw look.

And as for the little tabby kitten — heavens above, what *did* she think she was doing, bouncing up and down like that, waving her arms and knocking her hat awry! She was getting much too big in the chest to bounce at all — and someone ought to tell her so.

"Mrs de Vivian! Mister de Vivian!" Wilkes did not simply shake them by the hand, he clasped his own around theirs, in turn, and pressed them warmly to emphasize his words. "I cannot begin to tell you how welcome you are!"

Perhaps he wasn't such a bad fellow after all, Ada mused. His heart was in the right place.

"You haven't met my daughters, Mrs de Vivian. Allow me to present them to you."

At least he knew which way round to present people. She positively beamed at the three girls. "I've been *so* looking forward to meeting you, Sophie ... Felicity ... Tabitha. Peter has said such complimentary things about you, I quite expected to find you flying above us on your wings!" She was careful not to single any one of them out for particular praise — not yet.

The girls laughed prettily, thanked her, and then hurled themselves at other arrivals — with whom they were clearly *very* familiar. The kitten-girl included Peter in her effusiveness and then lingered at his side. Ada did not hear her murmur, as she planted a kiss on his cheek: "Which one is Gemma?"

The servants' charabanc was just disgorging its passengers, a respectful hundred paces away. The maids were descending first and Gemma was among the leading half dozen.

"There!" Peter said proudly. "The tall, beautiful one with pale auburn hair."

"Not the sour, dark creature she's talking to?"

"No, that's Mam'selle."

Tabitha surveyed Gemma critically for a moment and then said, "I hate her already."

"Call them over," Peter said to his sister. "They should accompany us indoors and learn who's in what room."

Tabitha chuckled. "Don't worry about that in your sister's case. Hallo, Beatrice — I'm so delighted to meet you at last. What a gorgeous mantilla! I feel we are already friends — Peter has told me so much about you."

"You must give me every opportunity to disprove it all!" Beatrice laughed. "Why should I not worry about the maids not knowing my room?"

"Oh, they'll know! There's no mistaking the vestals' rooms. They're at the top of a locked staircase which you reach by creeping past six maids' rooms and the housekeeper's."

"Creeping?" Beatrice asked as she beckoned to the two maids. "Must we creep?"

"Not you," the girl replied. "The bachelors. You'd never believe the obstacle course our grandparents erected between their quarters and the vestals."

Ada, who had listened to this exchange with increasing distaste, placed herself pointedly between her daughter and this hoyden — not that Tabitha noticed: she had eyes only for Gemma, who was now drawing near. During most of that brief walk, she noticed, the maid stared at Peter; but as she and Mam'selle drew close, she switched her attention to Beatrice and avoided Peter's eye entirely.

"Well, Kitten?" he murmured when his mother was safely engaged in giving out instructions to the two maids.

"It looks hopeful — I have to admit it."

"Miss Tabitha," Ada said. "Fascinating though my children may be to you, you must not let them monopolize your time."

"Ah, Mrs de Vivian!" There was a slight catch in Tabitha's voice. "You are so right to chide me." She curtseyed and wandered off, saying, "I have forgotten what it is like to have a loving mother to put me right from time to time."

Ada stared defensively at her two youngsters. "Chide her?" she echoed angrily. "I simply reminded her."

Trewithen joined them at that moment and Guinevere, noticing it, returned to them with Felicity in tow. She said, "Let me show you to your various rooms. Felicity, dear — you take Beatrice and Mam'selle. Trewithen and Miss Penhallow should know where Mister and Mrs de Vivian are. Then I'll show Master Peter to his quarters."

She beamed all round as she swept them up the grand flight of steps to the imposing portico. Ada kept up an automatic conversation while her mind whirred with quite different notions. She was thinking that Graham Melchett was only a second-cousin to Sophie; so a union between them was quite acceptable — not least to her and her plans, which now included finding a suitable match for Peter. A match with a million hats and a fine estate like Westwood was decidedly suitable for her son. It would be worth sacrificing Beatrice's chances with Melchett if the fellow showed the slightest interest in his second-cousin; that would neutralize Sophie quite effectively; a colonial administrator tipped for high office wasn't going to chuck up his career, title and all, not even for the sake of a million hats.

Which would leave Felicity, the jolly, buxom, rosy little heifer; she looked a distinctly possible bet for Peter.

And then again, one mustn't deny the kitten an outside chance; she had a poise and a presence of mind beyond her years. Ada had already forgiven her that elegant rebuff, and was ready to overlook a great deal more — as long as the outcome was satisfactory.

While her mind thus seethed, her eyes took in the splendour of the interior. The hall was, in fact, a vast picture gallery that ran the full three-storey height of the house and most of its length. It was illuminated by three glazed lanterns among the turrets on the roof above. A cast-iron footbridge, supported by decorative chains from the side walls, spanned the full length of the gallery at the level of the first floor up — presumably to allow one to see the higher paintings from a better vantage. At the farther end a grand marble staircase doubled as another gallery, this time for suits of armour, swords, claymores, shields, arquebuses, crossbows, and blunderbusses ... they had never seen so many instruments of sudden death all at once.

The armorial shields especially fascinated Trewithen. He had already promised himself he would discover which of the Westwood servants was responsible for polishing them — and that he would offer the fellow his help.

"It's no place for a family given to quarrels!" Gemma murmured to him.

Peter, who had hung back as close to her as he dared, overheard and turned to smile at her remark. But the glance she gave him in response put a damper on his spirit. 'Please!' her eyes mutely begged. 'Don't do anything silly while we're here!'

"You're in the *chambre d'honneur,* of course," Guinevere said as she halted before a huge walnut door.

It grated on Ada's nerves that this woman of no particular breeding was, effectively, the châtelaine of this grand house and could open its doors with a flourish that said, 'Yours for four days, mine whenever I like!'

But it was a room to take one's breath away — spacious, richly marbled, deeply carpeted, and — its ultimate glory — endowed with a balcony that opened, not onto the damp English countryside, but into a huge palm-house that was built right against the main pile. It filled the room with the exotic perfumes of half a dozen tropical plants then in bloom.

"Oh!" Ada could not help clapping her hands in delight. "If I owned this house, I should never leave this room!"

"Mama!" Peter cleared his throat awkwardly. He took her aside and explained that, rather like the mad Mrs Rochester in *Jane Eyre,* Mrs Wilkes was permanently in that unhappy situation.

Meanwhile Guinevere was tactfully showing Mr de Vivian various arrangements to do with the electrical gadgets, the mechanical skylights, and the house's own interior telephone system. Then she took Peter and the two servants back to the head of the marble staircase, where Trewithen left them to go and assist with the luggage.

"You walk straight on down this corridor," Guinevere told Gemma, "through two doors, and you'll arrive at the rooms for the lady's maids. You and Mam'selle are in number three, which you will find immediately beside the stair leading up to the young ladies' rooms."

"The vestal chambers," Peter murmured as she led him off at last to his quarters.

She told him that only fluffy-headed sixteen year olds said things like that.

They crossed the landing at the head of the staircase and started along a minstrel gallery that led the full length of the farther wall, running parallel to that long, cast-iron footbridge. Halfway down this gallery was a wide gothic arch, which opened upon a winding wooden staircase, broad enough for four people abreast. They paused in the archway a moment. The echoes that bounced between the cliff-like walls were disheartening.

"The governess's room," she said, pointing to a heavy oak door just inside the arch. "Or so it was in the days when there was a nursery and children here. The bachelors' rooms are up those stairs."

Peter turned and gazed back into the vast space of the gallery. If his sense of direction were right, the lady's maids' rooms were diagonally opposite, beyond the far corner of the gallery-cum-hall — where, he now noticed, there was a door. Tracing a path with his eye, he saw that the minstrel's gallery did not traverse the hall at that end. So that door could not be reached from here ... unless ...

He looked back to the landing at the top of the marble staircase and saw that from there one could walk the full length of the cast-iron footbridge, from whose farther end a small gallery gave access to the door in question. He wondered if it really did lead to the lady's maids' rooms.

Guinevere, following his eyes, had little difficulty divining his thoughts. "It almost outdoes the ordeals those fairy-tale princes had to undergo to win the hands of their princesses, eh?" she mused. "An amorous bachelor had to creep down these winding stairs, past the governess's door — and I'll bet she was a light-sleeping old battleaxe, too — and out into this vast hall. And remember, the house was patrolled by two night-watchmen in those days. Then he had to walk the full length of that iron bridge and pick the lock at that far end. And even then he still had to get past the housekeeper and a dozen lady's maids."

"How long has Wilkes owned the place?" Peter asked — to give her the impression he was not interested in all these architectural details.

"About eight years. He bought it from Lord Datchett. It was the Datchetts who guarded their spinsters' virginities so assiduously." She laughed. "Maybe too assiduously — the line died out with him last autumn."

"Tabitha said it was an obstacle course," Peter remarked.

"Yes. Between ardent bachelor and shy maid ..." She paused in mid-sentence as the door at the farther end of the gallery opened. A woman peered out. It was Gemma. "... a huge gulf stretches," she concluded.

Peter grinned at her. "But it can obviously be bridged, Guinevere." He waved a salute at Gemma.

The maid withdrew her head and closed the door. She leaned against it a moment and stared blankly into space. The image of Peter and La Roanoke was still vivid in her mind's eye. She realized she was foolish to entertain the slightest hope of an honourable association between herself and Peter. As a pleasing fantasy it could just about be sustained in a small, domestic setting like Alma Terrace. But here, where sixty regular servants, augmented by thirty lady's maids and valets, managed a household scaled like a large, international hôtel, the social gulf between her and Peter could be seen in its true proportion. Even if she were that yeoman farmer's daughter Peter kept telling her she was 'really,' she would still have to call at the tradesman's entrance of Westwood — whereas Peter and his family were shown in first as the guests of honour.

Sad as it was to face these truths, she was glad she had accompanied the family for the Season, otherwise she might never have realized her folly.

"Vous avez perdu quel'q'chose, Mam'selle Penhallow? Hein?" Mam'selle's question roused her from her reverie.

She almost forgot herself and replied. Just in time she remembered to look blank.

"You 'ave lost someseeng?" the woman repeated.

"Oh, nothing of importance," Gemma assured her. "It was only of *sentimental* value — as we say."

21   The Bard never has been, and probably never will be, quoted so widely as he was throughout the land that night: 'When beggars die there are no comets seen,' people told each other in the tones of an Irving or a Tree. 'The heavens themselves blaze forth the death of princes.' And, indeed, it was remarkable that Halley's Comet should have made its once-every-seventy-five-years' visit in the very month of King Edward's funeral — also that it should come close enough for the Earth to actually pass through its bright tail. It was surely the most spectacular visit of that or any other comet in recorded history — a second Milky Way, spanning most of the sky. The waxing moon was four-fifths full yet still the comet outshone it. Truly, the firmament did blaze forth the death of a mighty prince that night, and, in passing, it also marked the importance of Britain and her monarchy for all the world to see. Those who stood on the balconies and terraces of Westwood to witness it were stirred by twin emotions — awe at the celestial display and patriotic pride at its especial significance for them.

"Old Kaiser Bill must be tearing his hair out in rage tonight," Higgs said happily. "Down there in Windsor Castle."

"Uncle Bertie gets the heavenly fireworks," said another. "But old Fritz will be lucky to get a single shooting star when he kicks the bucket."

"Fair's fair," put in a third, who had a large import-export business with Germany. "He did order the entire German fleet to fly the Royal Navy ensign at half-mast."

"Guilty conscience," said the implacable Higgs, "for all the grief he caused our king."

"Old Higgs ain't exactly keen on the Germans, is he!" Peter murmured to Beatrice.

Wilkes, overhearing him, chuckled. "The Turks are his biggest suppliers," he explained, also in a murmur. "But they play him off against the Germans. He'd be happy to see Germany rocqueted off into the shrubbery, leaving the field to him."

What vulgar, squalid people, Ada thought, with a shiver that had nothing to do with the night's chill. She did not dare so much as whisper the words to her husband at her side, though.

There would be no point, anyway; a sentence that was not sprinkled with the odd 'elliptical orbit' or 'space-time' stood no chance of penetrating her husband's euphoria tonight. For at last something was actually *happening* up there; the dotty panoply of heaven's fixed vault was changing day by day.

It was doubly annoying to Ada because she so desperately wished to discuss with him the thoughts inspired by Higgs's revelations on the charabanc ride that afternoon. Should she sound out La Roanoke on the idea of encouraging a union between young Melchett and the eldest Wilkes girl — steering Peter toward Felicity, instead? And then find someone else for Beatrice — preferably not from among these wretched commercial people?

It distressed her that the tooth-puller's daughter should play such a pivotal part in these intimate family decisions, but fate had placed her there, so it was pointless to complain. Where romance and dynasties mixed, it always took an age to get from the germ of an idea to the actual moment of decision. And if La Roanoke looked with favour on her plans, it would certainly shorten that time.

On the other hand, if the woman opposed her, she would have exposed her hand — and then an uphill task would become an upmountain one, instead.

Decisions, decisions! They were surely the most vexing things of all. Any decision to do X automatically prevented you from doing Y or Z; whereas, if you put it off, you kept all those possibilities open. So, even making the correct decision did not help, you also had to know precisely *when* to effect it. She gazed at the comet, wondering if Paul were up there, too, riding its tail and looking down on her, trying to project the light of his cosmic wisdom into her dull, dark, and weary brain.

The servants were allowed outdoors, ten at a time, to marvel at this astronomical phenomenon of the century. Ten menservants were followed by ten females, then ten more men, and so on; but, inevitably, there was a little overlap and a lot of giggling. One of the Westwood footmen, a fellow named Horace Wall, had taken a shine to Gemma and was trying to impress her with facts gleaned from the newspapers he had ironed that same morning. He ironed the papers every morning and so had an encyclopedic knowledge of current affairs, though it was all in headlines. The moment he came out he spotted her among the maids who were about to go back inside.

"Ah, Miss Penhallow!" he exclaimed, stepping in her path. "What a grandiloquent sight, to be sure!" He waved at the sky as if he had personally taken a hand in the production.

"To be sure, Mister Wall," she replied. She was thinking that she wouldn't mind if he kissed her because, for one thing, they would part company after next Monday and she'd never see him again and, for another, he was very good-looking.

"Forty years ago," he said, "that comet was three thousand million miles away from the sun!"

She did a rapid calculation. "That's about ten light-days," she replied. She had been taking astronomy lessons by proxy from Trewithen, who had been dipping into their master's library.

"Eh?" He was nonplussed. It was a man's job to impress a woman and a woman's job to be impressed, not to cap him.

Gemma laughed and then, with a boldness born of limited time and opportunity, murmured, "Come on — give us a kiss!"

On the other side of the hedge Peter heard her laugh and was powerless to stop himself from drifting in its direction.

The box hedge had three little alcoves cut into its otherwise sheer face; if Gemma and her temporary swain had skipped to either of the others, Peter would never have seen them.

She did not see him, though — standing there, staring at the scene in shock.

Trewithen did, however. Until that moment he had merely had his suspicions about Gemma and Master Peter; one glance at Peter's face was enough to confirm them — on the young man's side, at least.

"Hellew, hellew, hellew!" he exclaimed, clapping and rubbing his hands as he approached the kissing couple. "All the jolly jollies, eh!"

Gemma pushed her partner away and looked guiltily about her, but by then Peter had gone. "Just a harmless bit of fun, Mister Trewithen," she said, trying to pass it off with a laugh.

The footman advanced on Trewithen and, not realizing that Gemma was following right behind him, muttered in his ear, "Piss off, you! I'm on to a right cleaver here."

Trewithen laughed and turned again to his fellow valets, who were enjoying their brief permission to view the comet. "All is for the best in the best of all possible worlds," he intoned cheerfully as he went.

"Miss Penhallow!" the footman called after her. "Where are you going?"

"To wash my mouth out," she snapped. "Yours could do with some neat carbolic."

He stared after her in bewilderment as he cupped a hand before his mouth and sniffed his own breath. "What's bleedin' wrong with that?" he asked himself as he swaggered back to join his fellows. "Bleedin' women, eh! Always pickin' on somefink. Well, bollocks to the lot of 'em!"

On the other side of the hedge, people were beginning to drift indoors, for the skies were clear and the night was turning cold. Besides, someone had started a gramophone and one or two enthusiastic couples were already to be seen twirling past the ballroom windows. Somewhere out in the stables the generators were having trouble in coping with the demand for electricity. The roar of the motor hunted up and down and the lights were following the same curve.

A new thought occurred to Ada. Perhaps she could use Peter as a sort of stalking horse; he seemed to get on pretty well with the Roanoke woman. *He* could sound her out without tipping anybody's hand — not by asking her directly about these specific proposals, of course, but just ascertaining her views in general. He could, for instance, ask her if she considered Beatrice and Graham to be perfectly suited — or where she thought friction between them was most likely to arise. Concerned brother looking after sister's interests ... that sort of thing.

She drew her son aside just as he was about to re-enter the house. "I want to show you something," she said, leading him up the terrace toward the end of the building.

His silence surprised her but she passed no remark on it.

"There!" she exclaimed when they arrived. She pointed to the enormous palm house for tropical plants, built like a giant conservatory directly against the end of the house.

"But I saw it this morning," he said.

"Oh, of course! Sorry, I forgot." Now she had the whole walk back in which to talk to him.

"It must cost a small fortune to heat a great glasshouse like that," he observed morosely.

"Is that the *first* thought to cross your mind?" she asked irritably. "These mercantile people are having a most distressing effect on you."

He gave an apologetic shrug. "So ... er ... is that all you wanted to show me?"

"Yes, I suppose so." She sighed. "The scents in our *chambre d'honneur* are quite heavenly. Frangipani and bougainvillaea and jacarandas and I don't know what else."

"It sounds like *Against Nature.*" he commented.

"How can you say such a thing?" she protested. "It's *using* nature, surely?"

Peter had meant the decadent novel by Huysmans and the obsession of its aristocratic hero, des Essentes, with exotic perfumes. He did not bother to correct her, though. What would be the point? What was the point of anything, now — with his entire world just blown to smithereens?

Ada, annoyed at his lacklustre behaviour, swallowed her feelings and took his arm, to slow his progress back toward the house; she hadn't even started on what she really wished to discuss as yet. "You're shivering," she said, suddenly concerned. "I hope you're not sickening for something."

He responded with a single dry chuckle. "Maybe I'm just getting over something."

"Good!" She was brisk again, for time was short. "Would you say you're pretty intimate with Mrs Roanoke?" she asked.

She felt him stiffen at once. "God, no!" he exclaimed fervently.

Ada stopped dead and gripped his arm tight to make sure he did not escape. "What did you think I meant?" she asked in a voice loaded with suspicion.

"Well ..." He cleared his throat and looked awkwardly all about them; no one else was near so he had no reason to stay silent. "It's a pretty ambiguous word, isn't it."

"*That* particular meaning had not even entered my mind, Peter, and yet it is the one which *immediately* occurred to you. I am bound to ask why."

"You're not bound to ask anything at all, Mater. Look — just tell me what you want to know about her and I'll answer to the best of my knowledge."

But she was implacable now. "It is the *degree* of that knowledge which I am obliged to question, Peter. You may come of age in a

few months' time but until then you are still in our charge —
which, in practice, boils down to *my* charge. So let me ask you
bluntly — is there any kind of romantic intimacy between you
and Mrs Roanoke?"

"A true gentleman would never submit to answering such ..."

"You may turn *that* tap off!" she exclaimed. "Tell me plain —
is there?"

He detected a curious edge to her voice, almost as if she'd
approve of it. "Well," he replied cautiously, sticking a toe in the
water, "I *have* thought of it."

"Has she encouraged you in that direction? And don't tell me
that a true gentleman ..."

"Her marriage is not at all happy," he pointed out, sticking
two toes in.

"That's hardly a secret."

He swallowed hard and immersed the entire foot. "I have
occasionally gained the impression that she would not be averse
to a little ... er, comforting."

"Good!" Brisk again, she relaxed her grip and resumed their
walk. "You're obviously not going to tell me the full story, but
that's good enough for the favour I'm going to ask you."

"Ah?"

"Yes. The fact is, we're going to have to rely on that woman
quite heavily during this Season. And I'm not *entirely* sure she's
utterly on our side."

"So, assuming there *is* a certain sympathy between her and
me, you'd like me to cool it down just a little?"

"*No,* darling! Quite the opposite. Cultivate that sympathy.
Extend it."

"Really? But why?"

"So that you can play your part as a good brother and dutiful
son! I want you to stay close to her whenever possible. And be
nice to her, darling. Nice as pie. You can do it if you put your
mind to it, I know. If she wants someone to run little errands,
you run them. Any little favour she wants, *you* do it — and do it
without complaint. Get her to *need* you for those little things ...
to rely on the fact that you are always *there.* Now I don't know
what sort of programme *you* had mapped out for yourself this
Season, but I'm telling you now — this cancels it. This takes its
place. And you must note any little thought she lets drop —

about her cousin, about Wilkes, about his daughters, about Beatrice. Note them all, however trivial, and pass them on to me. D'you understand?"

"Mmh-hm."

"You don't sound too certain."

"I was just thinking. Not that I wish to be a cad about it, but ... since we are being terribly blunt ... just suppose she desires a greater degree of intimacy than I ... you know?"

She gave his arm a confidential squeeze. "You must make up your own mind about that, my darling. You'll very soon be twenty-one, after all. I know it's not an easy thing to talk about. Shall I ask your father to ..." She hesitated, afraid he might say yes. "On the other hand, we're almost there already, aren't we. So, at the risk of embarrassing you, I'll just say this. Every man has to gain experience somehow, so as not to hurt or embarrass his bride on their wedding night. We all know that, though we never say it in so many words. So you have two choices. You can either employ the services of an Unfortunate or you can find a complaisant married woman. A young widow with a bit of life left in her would be best of all but we don't happen to know any just at the moment. Both choices have their good and bad points. I'll get your father to talk to you about the first. As to the second choice — the married lady — let me just say this: Be very careful! Do nothing that, in our grandfather's day, would have led to pistols at dawn. Infidelities went on then, of course, just as they do now, but as long as it was done in secret, nobody felt obliged to duel over it. Just don't imagine that the days of duelling are over. Nowadays it's careers and reputations they kill — and it's far more effective, believe me."

She released him, for they had reached the terrace door. "Now go in and do your duty. I don't suppose there's any actual *programme* for these dances — beyond a casual stack of gramophone records. These ghastly people have no social graces whatsoever. So just go inside and pick the first wallflower you set eyes on and ask her for a dance, be she never so plain."

He gave a baffled laugh. "Mater!"

"What now?"

"You're not such a bad old stick, are you!"

Pleased and embarrassed, she gave him a token push. "And walk properly," she added.

22 The first 'wallflower' his eyes lighted upon was Tabitha Wilkes. "Care for a trot?" he asked.

She almost fell into his arms in gratitude. "This is the first ball I've ever been allowed to attend," she said. "I was so afraid no one would ask me."

He was about to tell her it was hardly a ball but then he realized how important this petty rite of passage was to her. Instead he said, "I like the way you've piled up your hair."

She dug him sharply in the ribs and laughed. "It's not 'piled up.' It's coiffed. It took ages to do."

"Well, it was worth it. I like it very much. Hang on — is this a two-step?"

"No, it's a foxtrot — forward-side-together-side, back-side-together-side — see?"

"Got it!"

They set off again. The lights were still hunting up and down.

"Isn't modern engineering just wonderful!" she sneered. "That great motor roaring away out there, just guzzling petrol, but if you switch on more than half a dozen lights — pfft! Daddy says we could get ten times the value if we used the same amount of petrol in lamps instead."

"I see the servants are setting out a few strategically placed candles," he said.

"Spoilsports!" she exclaimed. "And talking of sport, how are you getting on with you-know-who? Perhaps one shouldn't say this for fear of making you all swollen-headed, but you dance very well, you know."

"I was going to say the same to you. We both dance well."

"We are obviously meant for each other." She gave him an odd look, half coy, half supercilious, wholly ready to jump either way, depending on his response. She added in a mock dramatic whisper, "Do give up this mad dream of yours, my dear! You cannot honourably court a servant girl."

He was determined not to think about it — to push it from his mind entirely. He forced himself to smile at her and say, "Isn't it a wonderful discovery?"

"What?" she asked, a bright-eyed child again.

"That a pretty girl can say the most outrageous things and no one — no man, anyway — will take her to task for it."

"Am I pretty?" She preened herself.

"Devastatingly," he assured her. "Especially with your hair all piled up like that."

"Beast!" She pinched the lobe of his ear quite sharply.

But his cry of pain was masked in a general hubbub of minor shrieks and shouts as the generator finally gave up the ghost and all the lights failed at once. The clockwork gramophone played on, mocking their paralysis.

"Sorry-sorry-sorry!" he heard her say above the tumult all around. "Let me kiss it better."

A moment later he felt her lips settle not on his earlobe but on his mouth; they were soft, warm, and fragrant with some pastille she must have been sucking earlier. She devoured him with a passion that left him astonished.

Someone nearby struck a match. It failed to light but the spark and the noise of it alerted them. Their faces were inches apart when, on the second attempt, the match flared into life. Its momentary brilliance, reflected in her eyes, gave them a predatory gleam. And it froze her smile in his vision, too, which was an unequivocal smile of triumph.

Candles began to cast their flattering light on the entire company but the gramophone was now broadcasting the even crackle of the playout groove.

"Little face," he said while someone changed the record. "I think we must have a chat, you and I. Quite a serious chat, in fact. Would you be allowed a walk in the shrubbery?" He inclined his head toward the palm house.

"I don't see why not," she replied as she took a step in that direction. "Let's get a cordial on the way, shall we?"

They danced a half-circuit by candlelight, which brought them to the buffet. There he helped her to a raspberry cordial and soda.

"*You* can have wine, of course," she said.

He took a raspberry and soda, too, telling her he rather thought he needed to keep his wits about him.

The lights came back on and held steady; she commented that someone must have gone around all the bedrooms, switching

off unwanted lights up there. "But at least no one could object
to our taking a stroll among the palms now," she added.

He saw that there was, indeed, a dim form of lighting dotted
around among the specimens. Arm in arm they drifted through
the door, carrying their cordials with them.

His mother had been right about the tropical scents; the air
was suddenly cloying, humid, overripe.

"Every time I stroll in here," she said, closing her eyes and
inhaling deeply through her nose, "I think of the young Baron
des Essentes and his obsession with recherché perfumes — in
Huysmans's *A Rebours*. You know it?"

Of course, she *would* have read it in the original French! It
was amazing what a ballgown and a bit of piled-up hair could
do. She was actually quite beautiful, despite her immature
years. So beautiful, in fact, that the dim lighting, which would
have flattered many an older woman, did her a disservice.

From the way she opened her eyes he realized that she knew
he had been looking at her. He was probably the first man who
ever told her how pretty she was. She must still have been
thinking about it, for her first question was: "Am I really?"

He knew he ought to say yes — no quibbling; but there was
something in him that suddenly wanted to punish her, or not
simply her but *all* women, just for being women, for exercising
the irresistible power of their beauty over him. So he said, "No,
you're not *really* beautiful. You're just ordinary-beautiful. D'you
know what marks out the *really* beautiful woman?"

"What?"

"She never needs to ask. Why not? Because the answer is
already there in men's eyes. It's there in the licence they give her
to behave outrageously. It's there in the way they accept her
unfeeling cruelties. It's there in every act of arrogance and
selfishness she perpetrates as she sweeps uncaring through the
world ..."

He choked on his own words and apologized. "I didn't mean
to say any of that."

"I shouldn't have kissed you," she said. "It has spoiled ...
absolutely everything."

"It was very pleasant," he offered.

"Yes, I agree. But it has still spoiled everything. You're the
only man I know who I can talk with. *Whom* I can talk with?

With whom I can talk? You know what I mean. All the other young men develop that ghastly glacial smile and try to talk about the weather and the Eton—Harrow match and *stuff* like that." She gave him a sidelong smile. "D'you want to hear something nice?"

"Why ask? You're going to tell me anyway."

She pouted. "There's a definite curmudgeonly streak in you tonight, Peter."

"Sorry! Yes, I'd love you to tell me something nice."

Her eyes gleamed with promise. "You know my maid, Gwynneth? Well, I've put her on the sleuthing trail!"

He was suddenly alarmed. "You didn't tell her ...?"

"Calme-toi, chéri! I said nothing. I simply asked her to get chummy with you-know-who and to chat about romantic things and see what she says. That's all."

"Even so!" He was only half relieved. "She must wonder *why* you're interested."

"She'll assume Cousin Guinevere wants to know. Don't worry. I did the right thing, didn't I? You *are* still interested in discovering her true feelings?"

"Yes." He sighed. "God help me, but I am still interested."

23 He could not sleep, of course. His emotions blew alternately hot and cold. In the heat of anger he cursed the day his life and Gemma's had crossed, and the light that burned in her eyes, and the sweetness of her face, and the willowy grace of her body ... and the treachery of that kiss with some oik in livery; in cooler, more reasonable moments, he remembered the beauty of her eyes and the sweetness of her face and the willowy grace of her body ... and told himself that Tabitha had kissed him with just as much apparent passion and yet, it seemed, had meant nothing very serious by it. So if Tabitha could do experimental things, why couldn't Gemma?

But when was love's pain ever soothed by mere logic?

If all Gemma wanted was to experiment with someone, she knew where she would find the most willing collaborator in all the world. Why choose a person she'd never see again after this visit to Westwood?

At last, when he had twisted and turned so much that his sheets were bunched into a hopeless knot, he rose, put on his dressing gown and slippers, and crept down the stairs. He had no very clear purpose in mind, apart from a vague memory of crossing a bridge somewhere on their way up the long drive; if that were a river, and a deep enough one, he supposed he might still his feverish thoughts with a chilly swim.

He paused at the foot of the first flight, where the gothic arch opened out on to the long gallery, and glanced across at the door — *the* door — in the far corner. *Gemma!* He tried to project his thoughts in that direction. *If you're there ... if you can hear this plea ... if you're sorry ... if you've got some explanation ... unlock that door and show yourself ... now!*

He stared at the door until his fatigued vision dissolved in clouds of flying black needles.

Now! he shouted again in his mind.

And again, *Now!*

Nothing happened.

He became aware of two bats flying around in the moonlit hall; they flew stolidly back and forth, not with the erratic darting so typical of their kind. Perhaps they were juniors, just learning to fly?

Learning to do what adults do — there it was again!

Somewhere in the house a door clicked softly, surreptitiously. To his right? To his left? He could not tell.

A floorboard creaked. That was behind him, quite definitely. He spun about but could make out nothing. Already the pale, silvery light in the hall had night-blinded him to the dark of his own stairwell. He listened hard but heard nothing, either.

The very air was alive with secrets tonight; the house had taken on a secret life of its own ... secret movements, secret assignations, secret *tendresses* in the whispering dark. This was the wild, orgiastic counterpart to that rigid daytime life in which women, crippled by their corsets, changed dresses four times a day and moved through public rooms with never a word or a hair out of place. And gentlemen were gentle men to the tips of their white kid gloves.

He heard a sharp click, and again it came from somewhere behind him. In a moment of irrational panic he imagined some cuckolded husband was cocking the hammer of a pistol! That was his mother's talk of duelling, of course. He froze in the act of flinching and forced himself to turn round.

"Getting cold feet, are we?" asked a voice — Guinevere's voice, he realized with some shock. She was speaking from the door of the governess's old room. Even in the dark he could hear the smile on her voice, which was as soft as the purr of a contented cat.

"Good heavens!" he exclaimed. "You!"

"Shush!" She put a finger to her lips and took a couple of steps forward, into the light. "D'you want to wake the whole house, my darling?"

"I had no idea you were sleeping there."

Or was she sleeping there, he wondered? Perhaps she was leaving the scene of an earlier rendezvous ... putting a brave face on it?

"There's an excellent reason for your ignorance," she said.

"What?"

"You never asked me! I declare, I felt quite slighted by your disgraceful neglect." She came all the way to him. Then, running a teasing fingernail up and down the back of his upper arm, she added in a pouting, provocative tone, "Are you going to slight me once again, my darling man? Or are you going to make it up plus interest? *Are* you interested, mmm?"

He swallowed heavily. His heart began to pound — which was just as well, because the increase in blood pressure was needed to sustain certain other physiological changes about his person. From that moment on, events acquired an undeniable air of inevitability.

"No," he whispered.

She slipped her arm through his. "Why, my dear boy — I do declare you're shivering!"

He seemed to be gliding across the space toward her door. "Fever," he said. "I'm on fire."

"Me, too! Oh, Peter! I thought this would never happen. I've longed for it ... from the beginning. I can't tell you how much. But I thought it would never ..."

Standing in her doorway he smothered her words with a kiss, the most passionate kiss he had ever given any woman in his life.

When they broke off to breathe, she laid her head beside his and rubbed cheek-to-cheek — again it was very like a cat.

Over his shoulder she saw the door at the farther end of the hall open, to frame a female in a white nightdress. In that dim light she could not be certain, yet something told her it could only be Gemma Penhallow.

Sly old Peter!

Had they arranged a tryst? Had affairs progressed that far between them? And had he given up waiting?

He became aware that she had stopped her cheek-massage and was gazing at something over his shoulder. He straightened up, intending to turn around, but she, in a sudden panic, fell backwards into the room.

Whether she actually intended it or not, her action had the effect of pulling him down on top of her.

"Impetuous boy!" she laughed as she stretched out a foot and pushed the door shut. "Can't you even wait until we're decently in bed?"

Part Three

Black Ascot

24 Washed and shaved, Peter felt on top of the world, physically, at least. His emotions, by contrast, were in shreds. He had betrayed Gemma, and none of the arguments he could advance in expiation was worth a bean. She had betrayed him, too, with that kiss; but, as Tabitha had demonstrated not half an hour later, it might not have meant all that much, anyway. Certainly it could have been nothing so stirring, so fulfilling, so unique, as the night he and Guinevere had just passed together. Nothing he had ever read on the wonders of carnal union, nothing his Plymouth cronies had ever told him about it, had come anywhere near to preparing him for the glory of the act itself.

The awe that now dwelt within him was almost religious — but so, too, was the guilt. Yes, it was miraculous, but no, it should not have happened with Guinevere; it should have been with Gemma, and they should have been lawful man and wife. Well, it was never going to happen again, unless ...

No! He was not even going to think of her parting words to him at dawn. They had nothing to do with love, or tenderness, or even good old rabelaisian enjoyment of the flesh; they were spoken in pure hatred of her husband — and he wasn't going to have any part of that.

Four men were at the breakfast buffet helping themselves. The large dining table was supplemented by smaller ones around the edges of the room. Peter joined the line and considered the selection: porridge, bacon, scrambled eggs, fried eggs, poached eggs, coddled eggs, devilled kidneys, kedgeree, kippers ... and there was more in silver tureens that no one had even opened yet.

The man ahead of him politely inquired if he had *slept* well. His emphasis on the word made Peter aware he was not referring to the unconscious kind of sleep. He wanted to boast about his graduation in the university of life but all he said was, "Like a log. How about you, sir?"

"Me — I find it very difficult to sleep well in a strange house," the fellow replied — and winked at him.

Peter wished he'd thought of some such reply.

Melchett joined the line and said, "Sit with me, young de Vivian? If you wouldn't mind. I want to take you up on a couple of points from last night."

"Delighted," Peter said with sinking spirit. What the hell had they talked about last night? Melchett had the room next to his in the bachelors' tower and they had had some slightly tipsy conversation on the landing. Something about feudalism. The word made him think of servants. Then of Gemma — which led to more self-accusation and renewed vows of fidelity.

"Sleep well, old chap?" Melchett cut across his reverie as he set down a huge plate of victuals.

"I find it difficult to sleep in a strange house," Peter replied with a wink.

"Ah! Quite! Good, good! At least I didn't keep you awake with my snoring. I dropped off the moment my head touched the pillow."

It was such an insistent statement that Peter wondered if the man hadn't done a little night-crawling himself.

Guinevere, in black from head to foot, entered the breakfast room at that moment, took a few uncertain steps, saw them, and veered toward their table. Both men rose at her approach.

"Just a little toast and some lime marmalade, please, Graham," she said. "There's a dear."

"Allow me." Peter, nearer the buffet, sprang to the commission.

"Did you sleep well, cuz?" Melchett was asking when he returned to the table.

"Like a log," she answered.

The room was filling fast now, with everyone in black, of course. Sophie was the latest to enter. She saw Guinevere and started toward her table; then she recognized the two men and hesitated — until Guinevere beckoned her. Peter, who had seen her falter, wondered why. "What may I get you, Miss Sophie?" he asked.

"No, no, old fellow!" Melchett beat him to it this time. "People will begin to think you're a footman."

Footman ... valet ... Peter did not welcome the reminder.

Sophie saw what Guinevere was having and asked for the same. "People seem quite cheerful," she said, looking around the room after Melchett had gone.

"It's mourning without actual grief," Peter said. "We regret the passing of the king but it doesn't touch us personally."

They were still debating whether this was true when Melchett returned. He, of course, had quite a different point of view. The late king had been the uncle or great-uncle, either by blood or by marriage, of no fewer than eleven reigning monarchs, including the Russian emperor, the German Kaiser, and the kings of Greece, Spain, Rumania, Yugoslavia, and all the Nordic countries. At least eight of them would be attending his funeral in person at Windsor that day. All had admitted that *he* had been the only one who could bang their heads together and bring about agreements when all other resources had failed.

In his, Melchett's, view today's funeral would mark the onset of Europe's disintegration. The cat was away and the mice would play — and the play would get ever-more boisterous until, before long, it would descend into open war. Within five years the new king and the old Kaiser, who would walk side-by-side in Windsor today, would be at each other's throats — metaphorically speaking, of course.

He smiled at them, lingering especially, Peter observed, on Sophie. The modest jollity she had noted at other tables was nowhere in evidence at theirs. Peter drew breath to join in but Melchett's upraised finger silenced him.

"Moreover," the man continued, "because the great European powers have redrawn the map of the world in their own favourite colours, this coming war will involve the rest of the world, too. It will be the first-ever *world* war."

He was speaking to impress Sophie, of course. Peter was fascinated at her response. The surprising thing was that Melchett himself, though he must have known the Wilkes girls, on and off, all their lives, was still somewhat taken aback when Sophie turned the tables and started lecturing him back. That had not been Melchett's intention at all. He had set out to parade his knowledge before an admiring and impressionable young female.

Instead he found himself having to sit there and smile his way through a lecture on the history of the Balkans that would have left most people in the Foreign Office looking rather thoughtful. And at breakfast, too!

Melchett could just imagine poor old Buffy Campbell, Governor-General of Nyasaland, wilting under the fire of such a brilliant impromptu lecture at some formal dinner party in Government House, Blantyre. No, no — Sophie would not do, second cousin or no, fortune or no.

"I see you are something of a specialist on Central Europe, cousin," he said in the first available conversational niche.

"Oh, not really," she assured him earnestly. "I'm actually more familiar with Greek and Turkish history — where, of course, the problems are analogous ..." And she was off again, proving it.

Peter and Guinevere exchanged surreptitious glances of delight but said nothing that might spoil their enjoyment of Melchett's comeuppance.

After a while, however, Melchett's interest began to rekindle. He realized that, if the dear girl's distressing propensity to fire off a polished and lucid position paper at the drop of a hat could be tamed — so that she merely uttered the usual feminine platitudes to all and sundry, and reserved her needle-sharp observations and encyclopedic knowledge *for his benefit alone,* then no post in the Colonial or Foreign offices would lie beyond his grasp, not even Viceroy of India ...

Lord Melchett, Marquis of Westbrook ...

He gazed around the huge, stately breakfast room with new eyes. A magnificent place like this was *not* beyond his grasp, after all!

25   Even in Windsor such pomp and pageantry were rare. And for such a sombre occasion there were astonishing splashes of colour, too — beginning with the coffin itself, which was draped in both the royal standard and the Union Jack and mounted with sceptre, crown, and orb. Then there were the heralds. Bluemantle and Norroy were there, and Portcullis, too ... Richmond and Rouge Dragon, Somerset and Ulster — all in their sumptuously embroidered tabards, evoking the splendours of medieval England beneath the massive, sunstruck walls of England's finest medieval castle. The Guards were there, of course — every regiment in the brigade. Their black bearskins, together with the grey astrakhan caps of the Russian Cossacks,

were the perfect foil for the silver helmets and red plumes of the German officer corps.

The contrast between this rich panoply and the simplicity of the party that drew the gun carriage could not have been greater, for they were simple blue jackets, ordinary seamen in striped canvas trews and straw boaters — straight out of Nelson's navy. Half of them hauled the gun carriage from in front while the rest steadied it from behind. As Ada said in a whisper to Guinevere, they provided that simple touch which was lacking in so many *foreign* ceremonials — which was, of course, why *they* often appeared so overblown and *vulgar.*

The Westwood party had taken a position by the forecourt of the Great Western station, where the procession formed up. From there, accompanied by the massed bands of the Guards playing the Dead March from *Saul,* it wound slowly uphill by way of Barry Street, River Thames Street, the High Street, and Castle Hill to St George's Chapel, inside the castle walls. In that same chapel the late king had been both christened and married, so it was in every sense a homecoming for him to be interred there, too, in a vault within its walls.

Immediately behind the last of the blue jackets came the new king, with the Kaiser at his right, followed by a lavish selection of equerries and aides. And behind them, as Melchett had said, marched no fewer than seven other sovereigns, all related to King Edward by birth or marriage — right down to young Manoel, the boy-King of Portugal. Also the Archduke Franz Ferdinand of Austria and the Hereditary Prince of the Ottoman Empire. And that wasn't the half of them, for, as these nabobs among nabobs moved off in slow time, a grand rally of Imperial Highnesses, Royal Highnesses, Grand-Ducal Highnesses, and Serene Highnesses formed up behind them, eventually stretching to no fewer than fifteen files. From Hesse they came, from Teck and Saxe-Coburg, from Prussia and Saxony ...

The parade took an age to move off, so Peter had plenty of time to work his way surreptitiously through the crowd until he was, at last, standing beside Gemma, who was, naturally, at Beatrice's side.

"What *do* they think they look like!" he murmured to her.

"Shush!" said a shocked Beatrice.

Gemma stared stonily ahead.

Look! he thought. *Who betrayed whom here?*

True, he had betrayed her last night — or *also* betrayed her — but she wasn't to know that. So how dare she get on her high horse with him now?

"We can't ever *talk* together properly," he whispered to Gemma. "You and I?"

"There's nothing to talk about," she replied.

"But there is!"

Beatrice shushed them again, even more vehemently.

Gemma still refused even to look at him.

"I miss you," he whispered.

"So I've noticed!"

A little squirt of fear curdled his half-digested breakfast. She was so positive. What had she seen? Or learned?

The dirge-music swelled as the cortège passed into Barry Street; he took advantage of it to ask, "What can I do, Gemma? Just tell me."

She put her lips close to his ear and whispered. "You can leave me be! That's what you can do."

The whole of that side of his body nearest her was suffused with a rich glow. It tingled just to be near her. He would do *anything* to have her say she loved him. Yes, anything! Give up his friends, his family ... everything. Perhaps that was the answer? If Wilkes and Tabitha were right about her, then it *was* the answer — no perhaps about it. She'd never marry above her class because she'd 'know' everyone was sneering, even if they weren't. But he'd happily marry beneath his class — for the very good reason that he'd never consider a marriage to Gemma to be *beneath* anything.

Now, when he looked back at the official funeral procession, the tail end of which was just vanishing into Barry Street, he no longer saw the pageantry, the dignity, the splendour of one man's funeral. Rather he saw the funeral of an entire civilization, old and decrepit, marching itself off the stage of history.

Get rid of class itself — that was the answer!

Who were they, anyway — these Serene thisses and Arch thats and Grand the-others?

They were nothing but an hereditary clique of inbred boobies whose mere existence helped to perpetuate the status quo — including the stifling conventions that kept people like him and

Gemma apart. How he would love to make this, their meta-phorical funeral, real!

Think of it! One rogue machine-gunner up there on the castle walls could do more during the next minute for the sum total of human happiness in Europe than all the so-called diplomacy of all its so-called statesmen! A single howitzer in Windsor Great Park could free the world! Such chances do not come every day. If Melchett was right about Europe's immediate future, such a chance would *never* come again.

As the ordinary citizens shuffled onto the forecourt to form the unofficial tail of the parade, Peter took advantage of the crush to press against Gemma. She must have known it was him and yet, to his surprise, she did not push him away. Instead, her fingers found the fleshy part of his palm and, for one delirious moment, he fancied she was going to take his hand. But all she did was pinch him there, as hard as she could. He darted a look of wounded surprise at her — at her tight-clenched jaw and the grim line of her mouth, in profile. Then, without returning his gaze, she mouthed the words, 'Go away!' clearly enough for him — for anyone — to lip-read.

"I love *you!*" he whispered desperately.

Exasperated, she drew out one of the three long pins that held her hat. Then he moved away. Immediately she placed herself on the far side of Beatrice and repinned her hat.

Melchett stepped at once into the space she vacated; now he was at Beatrice's side he turned to her and asked if she were warm enough.

What he would have done about it if she had said no was anybody's guess; taken off his coat? But, since she was at that same moment wishing she had brought a fan along, the implied offer was never tested.

Melchett nudged him and pointedly gazed at the upper storeys of several nearby houses. "Scotland Yard," he said.

The windows were crowded with mourners, most of whom had paid handsomely for their places and who therefore divided their attention between the procession and the 'sweaty multitude' below — to see if their privileged elevation was being accorded its due measure of envious glances. But among them stood a number of men in black. Stood *out*, one could say, for they clearly did not belong in the ranks of the pampered rich. They were big, bearded, burly men in tight suits. They stood with folded arms and gazed incessantly about them, now at the fringes of the crowd, now at the windows and rooftops of neighbouring houses. There were others of a similar stamp among the castle battlements, Peter saw. And every now and then they would exchange cabbalistic gestures and signs.

He had not noticed that the slow reshuffling which occurs in any crowd had brought Wilkes to his other side, until the man himself leaned close and murmured, "I'm not the only one to have worked it out, then — that a single competent bombardier, strategically placed, could do the world more good today than the entire Salvation Army."

"I was thinking of a howitzer in Windsor Great Park," Peter told him.

Wilkes grinned and punched him on the arm. "Man after my own heart," he said.

Melchett stared at them, aghast.

Peter realized that Wilkes was, quite unwittingly, spoiling Sophie's prospects of a match with the future star of the Colonial Office — prospects that had taken a decided turn for the better at breakfast that morning.

But, then again, perhaps it wasn't as unwitting as all that. Would any loving father wish a husband like Melchett on his beloved daughter?

Come to that, what about any loving brother whose sister faced such a possibility?

26 The afternoon of the funeral was goffering time for most of the lady's maids — ironing the frills that would trim the gowns for all those splendid balls, which would recommence now that the old king was decently laid to rest

Tabitha's maid, Gwynneth, found Gemma down in the laundry, looking somewhat lost, for she had never been in such a big establishment before.

"The housekeeper said I'd find a spare set of goffering irons down here in a drawer somewhere — but just look!" Gemma pointed to an array of drawers that would not have disgraced a safe-deposit vault.

Gwynneth laughed and opened the one Gemma was seeking. "I remember the first time I came down by here," she said. "I couldn't believe it. Did you see the drying racks?"

Without waiting for a reply she crossed the flagstones to what looked like an array of polished vertical planks, four inches wide, ten feet tall, and hanging an inch or two clear of the ground; each had a polished brass handle at around waist height. She grabbed one at random and gave it a tug. It moved outward, being hung on trolley wheels from overhead iron rails, and Gemma saw that it was, in fact, a rectangular frame with horizontal washing lines stretched across it, front to back, at roughly eighteen-inch intervals. Three gent's shirts hung from the line that was at head height. Gwynneth tugged at the next one, which contained a single linen sheet, hung from near the top. Gemma herself pulled out the next one, which held a few items of lady's underwear.

"See?" Gwynneth pointed to a woven bronze grille, which formed the floor beneath these sliding racks. "There's hot water pipes running under there. Gets everything dry in no time. And the heat and the moisture goes on up through the floor of the palm house." She giggled. "Nothing wasted here, lovely!" She looked Gemma up and down. "You're Cornish, aren't you?"

Gemma nodded. "And I'd never guess you're Welsh!"

"D'you speak Cornish?" When Gemma shook her head, she added, "And I can't speak Welsh, neither — so we're both a fine credit to our nations! Did you bring the frills down here? It's a bit steamy and sticky, don't you think? Would you like to come up and do it in my workroom? Don't tell any of the others but we've got one of these new 'Rapido' goffering sets up there. It's a marvel — you can do a foot at a time!" She held her hands vertically, eighteen inches apart. "We'll be finished before we start, practically, so we can put our feet up and have a good long chat, eh? And another thing — from up there we can see all the quality people having fun — *their* idea of fun, anyway, though, speaking for myself, I'd prefer a wet afternoon on the sands at Port Eynon anyday ..."

She maintained a steady stream of chatter all the way up the female servants' stair to her needlework room. On the way past the housekeeper's parlour an imperious voice called from beyond its closed and forbiddingly solid door, "Jones! Don't you ever stop talking?"

"Yes, Mrs Gostelow," Gwynneth said mechanically, barely interrupting her own flow. "I'll help you if you like. We got two irons so we can go at it, hammer and tongs. I always say any work goes easier with two. I know it looks lazy not to press each frill individually, but honestly, with the 'Rapido' the result is much better and it's results that count in the end, isn't it?"

Gemma said she'd welcome any sort of help because she hadn't done much in the goffering line, even with the old-fashioned tongs. She'd only started her new life as a lady's maid a few weeks ago.

"Is it a big place like Westwood?" Gwynneth asked, throwing open the door to the needlework room at last.

Gemma saw that it 'overlooked' the croquet lawns and the badminton court only in the sense that if you sat like a tailor on the workbenches and didn't slouch, you could just about see them. But then Gwynneth raised a full-length swing mirror in a gallows, which had formerly been used for raising fully dressed crinoline hoops and lowering them onto a body; then, with a little adjustment, the two of them could stand at the ironing table and, by glancing overhead from time to time, still watch the world at play.

"Nothing's impossible, see?" Gwynneth commented. "All it needs is that you go about it the right way. It makes everyone look left-handed, but that's the only drawback. Look — there's our Cousin Guinevere and Miss Tabitha playing croquet with your Master Peter and Miss Beatrice."

"Not *my* Master Peter," Gemma said mechanically as she took the pieces to be frilled from her bag and assembled them in what she thought was the order of difficulty — linen first, then cotton, then silk.

"Is that a fact?" Gwynneth asked as she kindled a spirit burner and then was careful to carry the matches and fuel well out of harm's way.

Because of the maid's singsong accent, Gemma could not tell if this was a question or a comment. "I think this will be easiest," she said, holding up the linen.

"It's all easy if there's two of us, lovely. Start with the linen and let it cool down. That's right. I think you *have* done this before! Anyway, it's hard to go wrong." She adjusted the air inlet until the flame settled and she wiped the initial film of black off the iron.

Gemma was about to remark that it looked like any old ordinary iron when she saw that its underneath was rippled like a washboard.

Gwynneth, meanwhile, brought out what looked like a foot-long toast-rack. Gemma now saw why she had held her hands wider apart, because it had flat platforms at either side. "See?" Gwynneth said as she set it down on the ironing table. "This is why it's easier with two. You stretch it between these two platforms and hold it firm while I press the iron into these slots. If you're single-handed, you have to use these clamps and it all takes time. Besides, it's boring if there's no one to talk to, don't you find?" She held the iron near her cheek and said, "Let's try it." She held it near Gemma's cheek, too. "No, no, silly! I'm not going to burn you! Just feel the heat — that's right for linen, see? Stretch the cloth, now."

"Do I need to damp it?"

"Sometimes. Let's see. It's quicker dry — if it'll hold." She pressed the iron to the cloth, fitting its washboard ripples to the slots in the 'toast-rack' part." She lowered her voice. "So — what d'you think of my three ladies? I say 'my three' but really only Miss Tabitha's mine, but we share and share about when nobody's looking."

"Is that done?" Gemma asked nervously.

"Probably." She plucked up the iron and said, "Yes — almost scorched it." She giggled. "Move it on, lovely!" She pressed the iron down again. "They're a hoot, don't you think, the three Misses Wilkes? What does your Miss B think? You don't object to me calling *her* 'your' Miss, I hope?"

"No," Gemma agreed. "Just ... no, I don't object to that."

"Just *him,* you were going to say! Trouble, is he? Your ... I mean that Master Peter?" Her eyes raked the ceiling as she lifted the iron again. "I've known some like that in my time, I can tell you! Got more linen, have you? I think I'll heat it up again. Yes — terrible they are. Pushing you into doorways. Shoving their knees where they think it'll excite you ..."

"Oh no!" Gemma cried out, anxious to stop her before it all got too graphic. "Nothing like that."

Gwynneth stared at her in amazement. "Nothing?" She stretched the word over almost two octaves. "You mean nothing at all?"

"Oh dear!" Gemma adjusted her lace cap and then readjusted it back to where it had been.

"Sorry, lovely!" Gwynneth cackled and held the iron near her cheek again. "Ready! I know I talk too much. Pay no attention. My father says I'd talk the hind leg off a donkey. Still, I think it sometimes helps. People ask me what I think about this or that and I tell them I don't know, not until I hear myself saying it. Can you think in silence inside your head?"

"Usually," Gemma managed to slip the word in — for Gwynneth did not stop, not even when she lifted the iron for the cloth to be moved along.

"I find that almost impossible, look you. I just go round in circles, agreeing with myself. But if there's someone else there, listening like, then I can watch their eyes and tell when they don't agree, and then we can have it out together. Like getting off one set of rails and onto another, don't you think? I do."

Gemma laughed. Clearly the only way to stop Gwynneth's monologue was to contribute something of her own. And, since they'd probably never meet again after this Season, where was the harm in talking over her problem?

It amazed her to see how the loquacious Welsh girl turned into a Carmelite nun once she, Gemma, started her tale. Only when she had brought it right up to date, with the events in Windsor that morning, did Gwynneth say anything more than 'Mm-hmm' ... 'Uh-huh' ... and 'Go on!' By then they were goffering the cottons.

"Is that all?" she asked.

"Isn't it enough?" Gemma asked in surprise.

"No, I mean have you told me all?"

Gemma stared at the overhead mirror. Mrs Roanoke and Peter were now playing Beatrice and Tabitha at badminton. What a dull, futile existence! she thought.

"Only there was talk going on in the servants' hall last night," Gwynneth added.

"Talk?"

The maid shrugged. "I suppose you've more right to know than anyone. That Horace Wall was calling you ..."

"Dirty, filthy man!" she snapped.

"Yes, we all know that! Anyway, he was calling you a stuck-up young prig. Well, there's two other young maids here know what he means when he says a thing like that!"

"Oh, very well!" Gemma sighed. "I suppose I'd better tell you absolutely everything."

And she did — including Peter's nocturnal visit to La Roanoke's room.

"And Trewithen told you — definitely — that Peter saw you spooning with ..."

"I wasn't spooning," Gemma objected. "Well ... yes ... I suppose I was ... in a way. But I didn't mean anything serious by it. I was just ... I mean, I knew I'd never see him again after next Monday, so why not?"

"Your Mister Peter doesn't know that, though, does he!" Gwynneth was interested to note that this time there was no objection to the 'your' nor any comment on the change from master to mister.

"I suppose not," Gemma admitted.

"And if he really and truly loves you — tne way a man ought to love — the way he says he *does* love you — I mean, put yourself in his shoes. What's he going to think, seeing you and Harold Wall like that?"

"I know." Gemma sniffed and swallowed heavily.

"I think a woman — a good-hearted woman, which I'm sure you are — would forgive a man anything he might do in the twenty-four hours after such a shock, don't you?"

Gemma laughed drily, mainly to prevent any further slide toward tears, for she was determined not to make a spectacle of herself by weeping and wailing all over the place. "Only the first twenty-four hours?"

"Oh, yes!" Gwynneth was suddenly pugnacious — as if an errant suitor stood before her at that very moment. "I'd tell him!" She wagged a finger at the empty space where her imagination had placed him. "I'd say, 'You pay one more nocturnal visit to Mrs Roanoke — or any other female, my boyo — and that's you and me washed up for *ever!*' See?"

Gemma laughed, mainly at the comical contrast between the savagery of her imaginary warning and the delight with which she uttered that final, 'See?'

She held up the first of the silk frills but Gwynneth said they'd let the iron cool a bit.

"I could never tell him *that,*" Gemma said.

"Why not?"

"Well, it'd be the same as saying that if he behaved himself, it *wouldn't* be all washed up between us."

"And what's wrong with that, lovely?"

"What's wrong with it is that there is *nothing* between us — nothing to be washed up or *not* washed up."

Gwynneth sniffed. "That's not how it sounded to me. Maybe I should get my ears tested."

"You think there is? But how can there be? How can a servant girl like me and a man like him — I mean, there are de Vivian banks in every town in Cornwall. I'd be a laughing stock. He goes on about my yeoman ancestry as if it's the answer to all those sneers but it'd only make things worse. There's a lady in Falmouth everyone laughs at behind her back because she never stops talking about 'the duke' — the duke does this and the duke says that and the duke thinks the other. And all she is is she's something like third cousin twice removed from a duke's maternal uncle. They'd only laugh at me — at *me,* not him — every time he spoke of my yeoman stock. And I just won't have it."

Gwynneth was uncharacteristically silent awhile, busying herself with blowing on the iron to cool it faster. "That's the only objection to him then, is it, lovely?" she asked at last. "The opinions of others?"

"It's big enough, don't you think — as objections go? I mean, I don't see a way round it. Do you?" There was a plaintive note of hope in the question.

"If he was someone else — I mean, if he was the same *man* but closer to our class. Say he was … I don't know … chief engineer on a ship. No! Not at his age, of course. But let's say he was the sort of young man who could one day rise to chief engineer — see what I mean?"

Gemma nodded. She could barely glimpse the shape of the argument but Gwynneth's confidence suggested to her that it really was going to answer her problem.

"But in every other way he's the same Peter — the man you know and like. You *do* like him, don't you?"

Gemma nodded miserably. Once again the pressure of incipient tears was in her eyes and this time she did not know how to roll them back.

"So, he pops the question, as they say. And what do you reply — after the traditional 'let-me-think-it-over' and all that rubbish? Will you have him?"

Gemma nodded and swallowed heavily.

"There's your answer, then! Simple as one-two-three. Now we can polish off those silks."

"But how is it my answer?" a bewildered Gemma asked.

"If he wants you — *really* wants you — he's got to sacrifice his present position and inheritance."

"Oh, my gidge! I could never ask that of him!"

"Oh?" Gwynneth appeared to be losing interest in the whole question. "Then it isn't your answer, after all. I don't know what is, I'm sure."

Later, when she was 'piling up' Tabitha's hair for dinner that evening, her young mistress said, "Well, and did you have a fruitful afternoon, Gwynneth?"

"More fruitful than you, I should think," was the reply. "Don't you ever get tired of nothing but games and walks and chatter and ..."

"... and minding my PS and QS? You know I do. But it's only for the weekend. So tell me what you discovered. Has Peter got a hope with her?"

Gwynneth did not at once reply. Instead she asked, "Why are you helping *her* — that Gemma Penhallow? He's a good man. He'd do very nicely for you one day. And you're more than fond of him, I can tell."

"Oh, don't be so sentimental! There's plenty of time for me — and lots and lots of good men for me to ..."

"Don't you believe it! Men like him are snowdrops in June."

"Maybe. But he's not unique. And I'm not going to tie myself down with any sort of engagement at my age — it's absurd. Why should I? I'm going to have fun before I settle down. So you can just stop all this and ..."

"I had to be sure, that's all."

"Very well. I do appreciate your concern, really I do. But now you *are* sure, you can forget all that and tell me the truth. What does she feel about Peter?"

"She loves him. I don't believe in this love-at-first-sight myself but it seems to have worked in their case."

"That and all the obstacles placed in their way!"

"That, too — yes."

"But? I could hear a great big 'but' on the way."

"Not really. She'd marry him tomorrow if he gave up his rank and inheritance and prospects. Not sink to the lower depths of domestic service like me and her, mind!"

"Oh, yes — ho-ho-ho! Very amusing. But? This is where you say 'but,' am I right?"

"But I think if he had enough patience and stuck it out and gritted his teeth against all the times she's going to turn him down …well, I think, in the end, she'll give in and marry him on any terms."

Tabitha sighed ecstatically. "It's as bad a case of love as that, is it?"

Gwynneth shook her head sadly and admitted that she'd never seen worse.

27 The weekend passed in the usual empty pursuits of the leisured class — promenading up and down the terrace; taking tea; playing at tennis, croquet, and badminton; changing their outer clothing four or five times a day if they were women but a mere twice or thrice if they were men; sipping sherbet; going walks in the garden (well chaperoned where appropriate); admiring the tropical profusion in the palm house; and dancing to gramophone records, playing billiards or pingpong, or doing party pieces round the piano in the evenings. And, of course, when interest flagged, one could always look forward to the next meal.

For those who could not hold out for the five long hours between breakfast and luncheon a selection of cold meats, pies, and pickles was served at eleven, when the more abstemious or figure-conserving members of the party made do with sherry and biscuits. Luncheon was a frugal five courses and only three wines were served. But even those who privately criticized Wilkes for his parsimony had to admit that the buffet he laid on at four, for those who could not be satisfied with a simple tea of hothouse strawberries and cream, scones, bath buns, crumpets, and six kinds of cake, was a compensation not to be sneezed at.

And even the world's most dedicated guzzler and swiller could lay no complaints against the magnificent eight-course dinners that were served every night from seven until ten o'clock. Wilkes was reputed to have the finest cellars in the county so there was no surprise at the seven fine wines that accompanied the repast; they entirely soothed away any lingering resentment people might still be feeling at the niggardly scale of their luncheon.

Notwithstanding all this, members of the Westwood party would have been enraged if some envious, rabble-rousing scribbler had noted that their time was passed entirely in playing games badly, gossiping cruelly, and gorging unhealthily — while putting their maids and valets to the considerable labour of preparing and after-caring whole trunkfuls of clothing each day. For the truth was that these seeming diversions were the mere accompaniment to the really serious business of the day, which, though nothing like so glamorous, was essential to the running of the country and to the prosperity of all — including, they would point out, rabble-rousing scribblers. In short, the true purpose of these seemingly mindless frivolities was to assist in the promotion of commerce and the formation and cementing of alliances.

True, nobody brought an actual order book to a weekend party; the commerce being promoted was not at that mundane level. But when men whose whole lives are wrapped up in business affairs meet, they are bound to discuss recent movements on the exchange, the political outlook in Argentina, a new tariff in America, an assassination in the Balkans. And when they tire of such lofty discourse, it is inevitable that two or three should put their heads together to discuss a fourth:

"What's your opinion of young Smith? I heard he got his fingers burned badly in the Gold Coast bubble last year."

"He's recovered pretty smartly — was careful not to have too many irons in that particular fire. And his speculation at Kalgoorlie has just soared."

"Bit of a speculator, what?"

"No speculation, no accumulation, old chap."

"Wants to borrow a couple of thou', unsecured."

"Well, if I had a couple of thou' I could kiss goodbye to without too much pain, I'd lend it to him. He could turn it into ten within a year."

"And bring it back to nothing a year later!"

" 'Twas ever thus, old bean."

After finding himself on the periphery of many such discussions all that Saturday, Terence de Vivian said to Ada as they were dressing for dinner that night, "D'you know, my dear, I'm beginning to regret that I ever got out of banking."

"But you are not out of banking," she replied in alarm. The last thing she wanted was any upheaval in the settled portion of her life. "You are the chairman of …"

"Yes, but we all know I am only a figurehead there. The farmers find the de Vivian name comforting. That's the only reason I'm there. What I mean is I'm sorry to have left the day-to-day business of banking without ever really trying it."

"Oh, dear!" Ada sat beside him and laid a hand on his brow. "What has brought this on?"

"Mixing with these chaps. Listening to them talk. I thought commerce was all sums and ledgers and logical decisions but it's not. It's people. It's judgements. It's more art than logic. I'm surprised more women don't get into it, despite the hostility of the men who are already there."

Ada bridled. "And do you imagine we are not?"

"Mind you, I suppose, if these wretched suffragists have their way, we shall have ladies in business and commerce before you can say Jack Robinson."

"What do you think Peter would do with the estate he will one day inherit — if it wasn't for what *I* shall do first to ensure he makes a good marriage? And d'you imagine *your* parents didn't select *me* with the greatest care as the one person who could keep your predilection for the stars and planets within reasonable bounds? It is absurd to say we women do not already play an absolutely central — though always ladylike — role in the affairs of the nation."

"Perhaps there would be some place for Peter in this fascinating world of commerce?" he mused. He was not exactly ignoring her but he had long been accustomed to letting all her opinions go out unchallenged, unless they touched upon the stars and planets, of course.

Ada's response to this inflammatory suggestion surprised him. Instead of telling him he was talking through his hat, which he was sure she'd have done at any other time, she asked him if he truly believed it — almost as if she actually wished to discuss the matter.

"The time and place could hardly be more propitious," he replied guardedly, for she occasionally pretended to be interested in his ideas merely to drag him in deeper before she pounced.

She held out her diamond necklace for him to manage the clip. "Did you see Mrs Huxtable was wearing diamond earrings at *luncheon!*" She shuddered. He made no comment. She addressed the point at last. "Peter's friendship with the Roanokes has been no disadvantage until now — and yet I wonder if he needs to pursue it quite so assiduously in future. There is something" — she shuddered again — *"decadent* about that woman. Don't you feel it?"

"Tie my tie?" he asked. "What's going through your pretty little head now, my dear?"

Her mouth was a thin, grim line as she replied, "I'm wondering what's going through *another* pretty little head not a light-year away from us at this moment. Do you suppose *la belle* Guinevere has much influence with Wilkes?"

"A bit looser, if you don't mind. This collar needs no assistance in strangling me. Influence in social matters, d'you mean?"

"In business, say."

"I would think not. Why?"

"Perhaps Peter should cultivate Wilkes a little more and La Roanoke a little less. I wonder if I did the right thing?"

He realized she was talking more to herself than him, so he did the usual thing — made vague noises of agreement: "You almost always do, my dear."

"Do try to contribute!" she snapped.

"I would if I had the faintest ..."

"Just think! Wilkes has this enormous business in hats. He has no son but he has three nubile daughters. We have an unmarried son who sorely needs an occupation — and who could certainly bring a great deal of capital to any enterprise. Can you not see a pattern in this constellation of circumstance — you, who can make bears and archers out of dots in the sky!" She gave his tie a final tug. "There!"

He crossed to the window and gazed at the comet for the umpteenth time. "What if he's grooming one of his daughters to assume control of the business?" he asked.

"Don't be absurd!" she said.

"He is not a conventional man. And nor are they conventional young ladies. Shall we go down and mix before dinner?"

"We'll wait for the ten-minute gong. Ten minutes of mixing with these ghastly people is quite enough torture, I believe. Also I've been thinking ..."

He chuckled. "I do not doubt *that!*"

"Poke fun if you like! We cannot leave these things to nature or chance."

"Nature has a way of winning in the end, my dear."

"Quite! That's why we invented civilization — to keep her firmly under our thumb. Talking of which, I wish you'd have a word with Peter about ... well, the things that only a father can tell a son — gaining experience — you know. Tell him where to go ... what precautions to take. Are you listening? Do come away from that wretched comet!"

"Consider it done, my dear," he said easily as he returned to the room.

"However, that's not what I started to say. We know that Wilkes and his daughters are leaving London at the end of June and — by happy chance — are taking Devoran House. And I suspect this Season is going to be a bit of a damp squib, anyway. So I think that we'll cut our own Season short, too, and return to Cornwall. I wonder if Melchett will be coming down with them? La Roanoke said he would but she may not be reliable — there as elsewhere."

"How fortunate that Devoran House is so close to Falmouth!" he mused.

"Four and a half miles by boat. The ideal sequence of events, from our point of view, would be for Melchett to become engaged to Sophie. She has a keen interest in political affairs. Peter says she wiped the floor with him — with Melchett, I mean — at breakfast the first morning. Some argument about the Balkans. She'd make him an ideal partner. I'm sure the idea has already occurred to him. I've seen his eye on her. And neither of them would be interested in hats. Which would get Sophie neatly out of the way and leave the field clear for Peter.

Felicity would make the more suitable wife but, ever perverse, he seems more friendly with young Tabitha."

"And what about our own little Beatrice?" Terence asked. "Have we overlooked her?"

"Oh, we'll have no difficulty with her. I shall tell Mam'selle and Penhallow that she comes with a dowry of two hundred and twenty-five thou'."

"You mean you haven't already done so?"

"Not while there was a tacit sort of understanding between La Roanoke and us, about an alliance with Melchett. One must behave honourably in these matters."

All Terence said was "Hmnh!"

She asked him if he had no more enlightening contribution than that to make.

"I just wonder if you're right about Sophie's suitability for Melchett? Isn't she a bit modern and free-thinking to play the hostess in a colonial governor's house? There'd be one scandal after another. Melchett needs someone like Lady Delamere's daughter, what's her name? Hermione! A Victorian termagant of the old school. Men have sought refuge in New South Wales after one withering glance from her. That's the sort of wife a colonial governor needs."

"Yes, dear," she said impatiently. He was right, of course, but she wanted her own view of things to prevail nonetheless. "D'you think you might have a word in Wilkes's ear? Sound him out about his daughter's wedding portions? The future of his million-hat empire? That sort of thing."

"A word with Wilkes ... a word in Peter's ear ... I have a talkative evening ahead of me!"

"For once!"

His chance with Wilkes came after dinner, when they faced each other over what seemed like half an acre of green baize and set about one red and two white balls with gusto. After a few well-chosen remarks about the recent limitations on the power of the House of Lords and the revolt in Albania, Terence remarked, apropos nothing in particular, that society and its ways had greatly changed since his young day. Wilkes laughed and said it certainly had. In his case, he was born and raised in a terrace of poky little brick houses in Gospel Oak.

"So you didn't inherit the hat business?"

"There was no hat business to inherit, man. I built it all up from one small shop in Kentish Town. I did inherit that, though."

Terence paused, though it was his turn with the cue, and gazed toward Peter, who was playing at another table at the farther end of the room. "I often wonder about that lad," he said. "Have we done right by him?" He went in off red and spotted his ball again.

"In what way?" Wilkes asked, peering at Peter as if the alleged neglect or ill-treatment might be visible in some way.

"I was brought up to go into the bank but I suppose I didn't start low enough down the ladder. I didn't meet the people that banking exists to serve. All I saw were the books and balance sheets." He cannoned off white on to red.

"Shot!" Wilkes said.

"So, of course, I got bored. Just fooled around."

"You played quite a lot of billiards, I should guess!"

Terence smiled. "Among other things. If I hadn't developed an interest in astronomy, God knows how far I should have gone off the rails."

"And now you're worried about your son?"

Terence expected Wilkes to add that he was lucky to have a son to worry about — which is what ninety-nine out of a hundred sonless fathers would have said. But he didn't. "I've a mind to put him in the bank," Terence said. "Down at the level where he'll be dealing with people. Perhaps he'll see how fascinating it can be." He potted the red again.

"As a matter of fact," Wilkes said casually, "*I* offered him a job the other day. On the road, selling my hats." He misinterpreted Terence's expression, which was one of amazement that the conversation should have leaped so swiftly to his desired point. He took it for one of horror, so he mischievously added, "Wholesale, of course!"

"And?"

Wilkes was amazed to see the other hanging on his answer as if the entire de Vivian fortune depended on it. "Well ..." He waved a hand. "I wasn't being entirely serious — though I must say I'd take him on like a shot if he really were interested."

"Oh." Terence was crestfallen at the first half of this statement and encouraged again to hear the second half. In his confusion he went for a cannon and missed.

"You mean you wouldn't object?" Wilkes lined up a cannon of his own and got it.

"My dear fellow! It would be the crowning of the boy — much better than banking, where he'd always be under my shadow." He saw a fleeting skepticism in Wilkes's eyes and pointed out that even figureheads cast shadows. "And you'd be as hard on him as needs be, I daresay? He'd take it better from you than from me."

Wilkes cannoned again and said, "I'm sure I would — otherwise there'd be no point. Life was never meant to be easy for any of us, was it, old chap! But see here, this is all passing clouds, is it not? The lad himself will have to agree, surely?" He was in danger of potting Terence and so walked around the table twice, looking for a way to avoid such a fate.

"Yes," Terence mused. "If he gets so much as a whiff of my approval …"

"What would Mrs de Vivian say — if I may interrupt?"

"I haven't discussed it with her — well, obviously not. But she was fairly keen for him to make something of himself before *anno domini* placed a substantial inheritance in his hands." He waited for Wilkes to take the bait; it would show how genuinely interested he was in alliances — or whether he was simply offering his wife's cousin's friend a bit of a helping hand in a scheme that would cost him nothing.

Wilkes managed a cannon off three cushions that ended by nudging Terence's white clear of the pocket. "And I *never* got bored with my business," he commented with a smile. "Inheritance, eh?" he echoed.

"Large enough to ruin a young man if it had nowhere useful to go — and even more so if that young man had no experience of the world outside football, cricket, and sailing."

"Terrible," Wilkes said complacently as he managed another cannon. "A terrible dilemma — I can quite see it."

"You must have *something* of the same problem?" Terence suggested. Would the fellow *never* bite?

"Me?" He cannoned again. The balls were now set up in such a way that he could cannon back and forth almost indefinitely. "No. I solved my problem long ago. My daughters will inherit nothing but a pension of a thousand pounds a year each on their sixtieth birthdays …"

"What?" Terence's scandalized cry brought a momentary hush to the entire room.

"That's right." Wilkes was calmly notching up cannon after cannon now. "Not one of them gets a penny before then — unless she's stricken down with some incapacitating illness. I've insured against that. Everything else goes to charity. They must find husbands who aren't looking for money from me, or they must fend for themselves. They've always known that." He smiled genially at his guest. "Keeps the bounty hunters at bay like nothing else! That's how I solved *my* problem, you see? If you don't give *them* any illusions, they can't shatter yours."

28 The news that Westwood was to become a public amenity, endowed out of Wilkes's hat business, and that his daughters were to inherit nothing of either asset brought Ada close to an apoplexy. The idea was so monstrous, so unthinkable, that Terence had to tell her about it in several different ways before it sank in.

She kept saying, "What ... *nothing?*"

To which he grew tired of replying, "That is what the man said, my dear."

"And what is to become of his girls?" she asked when at last she accepted this unthinkable thing.

"They must find their own husbands or make their own way in the world, just as he did."

"But he inherited a shop — didn't he say as much?"

"Yes, but he explains that a *true* inheritance is a parent's gift to a child. His gift to them has already been made — their education. They must make what they can of it. And that, he says, is a better inheritance than any that *he* enjoyed."

"Oh, those poor girls!" Ada paced the room, wringing her hands. "Those poor, *poor* girls! Who will have them now?" A new thought struck her. "Certainly not Peter! We must prevent all further intercourse between him and any of them. How could I ever have imagined they would make him a suitable partner? I should have trusted my first instinct. That gleam in their eyes ..."

She paused and ran her fingers over the handblocked silk of the wall hanging, a costly replica of a *toile de Jouy* from Versailles. "And to think of this magnificent property simply being *given away* to the public! The *public,* my God! Can't you just see them clodhopping through here on a Sunday afternoon, gawping at all this? Bert with the beer suds still clinging to his walrus moustache, and Elsie with her fairground false teeth and the chicken feathers in her hat, and a string of *kids* with running noses and impetigo, all bleating for a treat of ice-cream. Eurgh!" She shuddered. "It will simply stoke up their envy of their betters. The man is worse than a socialist. He's a ... he's a ..." But she could not actually think of anything in all the world worse than a socialist.

After that she found it almost impossible to remain civil to a man who proposed to do so much to destroy the very fabric of society and the nation. Indeed, without her innate good breeding and her years of practice at being courteous toward people who, to be quite honest, hardly deserved her civility, she would never have managed it.

She was also helped by the intrusion of a certain tactical problem, which left her little time to brood over fundamental things like the future good of society — namely, the refocusing of her efforts to secure a match between Melchett and Beatrice. Peter — who seemed to have achieved an excellent rapport with Guinevere Roanoke, bless him — would have to tread a painfully fine line between cultivating his friendship with her while shunning any advances from the three young ladies in her charge, all of whom she now saw as the worst kind of 'gold-diggers' (a vulgar Americanism yet somehow quite appropriate to these girls and their situation).

She decided that her best plan was to take her son entirely into her confidence and leave all details of action (and inaction) to his good sense. She did not entertain this plan with whole-hearted joy but the lad was past the age where simple parental commands were enough to secure his obedience, so what choice had she?

That Sunday morning, shortly after Peter had received his new 'standing orders,' he saw Beatrice out walking with Gemma and Mam'selle in the rose garden. There would be no opportunity of speaking with Gemma on her own, of course, but the chance

to be near her without arousing suspicion was too good to
forgo. As he went out to join them he decided to pick a rose for
each and say something gallant, in the hope that Gemma would
understand that it was a kind of apology or peace offering,
intended for her alone.

However, he caught his jacket on a thorn and it made a small,
triangular tear in his pocket. Gemma, who always carried a little
'housewife' with her, took out a needle and some black thread
and, seating herself on a nearby bench, told him to take his
jacket off.

Beatrice, believing he had contrived the accident, smiled
approvingly and winked as she took Mam'selle farther on down
the path.

Gemma, too, thought he had done it on purpose, but she was
not so sanguine. "You're like the fellow who burned down the
pigsty just to get roast pork," she said.

"Well ..." he sighed. "Nobody's going to believe me but it *was*
a pure accident, I swear it. However, it gives me the chance to
say I'm sorry."

"What for?"

He laughed awkwardly. "What d'you mean — 'what for?'
You know what for."

She looked up from her sewing and fixed him with her eye.
"For you and Mrs Roanoke?"

He felt the blood drain from his face. "What d'you mean ..."
he began.

She resumed her sewing. "I mean it was an understandable
thing to do — for you — in the circumstances."

"Ah!" He realized he'd stopped breathing a little while back;
he made up for it now with one huge draught of air.

"Trewithen told me you saw."

"I wasn't, you know, spying or anything."

"I didn't say you were. It doesn't matter, anyway. As I was
saying — the business with you and Mrs Roanoke was understandable *in the circumstances*. However, since those circumstances aren't going to be repeated ... well, need I go on?"

It took a while for him to absorb all the implications of this
warning. "You mean ..." he began, not daring to spell it out.
"You're saying ... I mean, the implication behind what you've
just said is ..." He still did not dare voice the thought.

"I mean things aren't entirely hopeless. But all I'm saying is I'd like to meet you somewhere. Away from all these eyes and tongues. I'd like to talk. I want to know you better. But that's all. I'm not making any promises beyond that."

"At least you believe I'm not ... well, just another Roger Deveril. Talking of which ..."

"Yes, I'll grant you that. I believe you're sincere ... Peter." She smiled at being able to speak his name, just like that. "Sorry. You were going to say?"

"Oh, yes. Talking of Deveril, I *think* — only think, mind you — I know how to get in touch with Ruby."

She froze. She was just finishing off the mend and her needle was poised in mid-stab.

"If I manage it ..." he went on.

"Yes?"

"Would you like to meet her?"

"Where?"

"How do I know? I'm not even sure I can trace her. I'm just saying if."

After a pause she said, "Maybe Ruby won't wish to see me. There!" She handed him back his jacket.

"I'll tell you one thing you won't die of, Gemma, and that's optimism." He inspected the mend. "Goodness! It's invisible! How d'you do that?"

"It's a hopsack weave," she told him. "One of the easier ones to mend."

"Can I ask you one thing?" He slipped the jacket on again. "It's a free country."

"How did you know about me and Mrs Roanoke?"

Gemma did not wish to lie, but nor did she wish to admit she'd been so foolish as to contemplate making the long, dangerous walk from her room to his in the small hours of the night. In any case, she doubted she'd have got farther than just beyond the first door; but even that was more than she cared to admit. "You may think me over-cautious," she replied, still thinking of Ruby and how her sister's fate had cramped her life. "And I'm sure you imagine you were not observed. So it's a warning to both of us."

By now, Beatrice and Mam'selle had completed a slow circuit of the garden and had picked up Tabitha on the way.

"Just look!" Peter cried as they approached. Proudly he showed them the invisible mend.

Mam'selle inspected it minutely and he could see she was trying to find fault somewhere. *"La weave est sac de houblon,"* he told her with great authority and no attempt whatever at a French accent. *"Très simple."*

She stared at him blankly and shrugged.

"What can you do for broken hearts, Miss Penhallow?" Tabitha asked, clutching at Peter's arm. "I think I've lost this man to another fair charmer. Ah me!"

Gemma smiled. "I'm told that broken hearts mend all by themselves, miss," she said. "And the younger the heart, the easier it mends, they say."

"That's enough!" Beatrice wagged a finger at Tabitha. Then, turning to her brother, she went on, "I say — guess what! Tabitha says I could lodge with them if I got a place at one of the London art schools. D'you think the mater and pater will agree to it?"

"No," he replied at once.

They all looked at him in astonishment.

"They have other plans — as well you know."

"But that's just it — I don't know. I am never consulted. Do *you* know what they are?" She turned to Mam'selle and Gemma. "Has either of you heard anything?"

"They won't have." Peter intervened. "Mater and Pater have changed their minds — yet again — and they've only just told me about it."

"And?" She stamped her foot. "Am I going to have to drag it out of you, syllable by syllable?"

"I think I should go," Tabitha said.

"No, stay," Peter cried, though she had not actually stirred at all. He turned back to Beatrice. "I'll tell you everything, I promise. It's just so ridiculous. I don't know what they're thinking of … I mean, how they think it can possibly work. We must just make sure it doesn't, that's all." He turned again to Tabitha. "And that's where you can help, too — it'll take your mind off your broken heart."

She pulled a face at him and laughed. Then she spied Gwynneth, hovering in the gateway. She beckoned to her, but the maid was approaching anyway. "If this is a council of war,"

Tabitha told the others, "there's no better head than Miss Jones's. Don't you agree, Miss Penhallow?"

"I'm sure you'd hear no argument from her on that point, miss," Gemma replied.

"I know exactly what our parents are thinking of," Beatrice said with some feeling. *"Their* parents arranged their lives for them — and they didn't make a very good job of it. So now they're trying to do the same for us — except that they want to do it better. But they don't realize that that is exactly what *their* parents thought they were doing. It's an endless vicious cycle."

"No, it's not," Peter said. "Because we can break it." He smiled at the new arrival. "Miss Jones — welcome to the coven! I'm only visiting. We are trying to prevent our parents from making too big a mess of our lives. *Our* parents — not Miss Tabitha's." He saw she wanted to say something but was holding back, rather nervously. "Go on," he said.

"Oh ... it's nothing really, sir." She looked around with embarrassment as she added, "I was just wondering if I'm worth a handshake, too?"

Peter darted a glance at Gemma, who stared uncomfortably at the ground. "I see!" he said slowly. "All sorts of things are becoming just a little clearer! Of course you're worth a handshake, Miss Jones. Forgive me for needing to be prompted." He shook her hand warmly and then turned to Tabitha. "And so to business. Wouldn't you agree that, of all the eligible spinsters we know, your sister Sophie is the one most suited to marry Graham Melchett?"

"Indubitably!" the girl replied.

"If she can just hold back from lecturing senior colonial administrators on world history," Beatrice put in.

"Quite. She could be the effective governor-general of Canada, or something like that — through him."

"He's a bit of a booby," Beatrice added. "But she'd soon give him some spine."

"She will," Tabitha assured them. "Once she understands which side her bread is buttered on."

"So!" Peter looked at each in turn. "We are all agreed, I hope, that we will do nothing to hinder and everything to further an eventual union between Graham Melchett and Miss Sophie Wilkes? Yes?"

"Agreed," they murmured in ragged unison.

"Why is it so important?" Beatrice asked.

"Because *our* parents want him to marry *you!* They've reverted to that old plan."

"Ha!" It was almost a scream — loud enough for her to clap a hand to her mouth and look fearfully all about.

"They're baiting you with ten thou' a year," he added.

Her lip curled in a sneer but she forbore to speak the words that occurred to her.

"Well?" He turned to Tabitha. "D'you think he'll be tempted by that?"

"What man wouldn't be?" she responded glumly.

"Especiallee when eet goes with a so-beautiful bride as Mam'selle Béatrice!" Mam'selle added.

"Yes," Tabitha agreed. "I was just about to say the same. But his advancement in the colonial service is important to him, too. It may even be more important. It's a more certain path to honours and titles and so forth. So he might still choose Sophie, after all."

"You don't think your father would change his mind and throw in a good marriage settlement — just to make the whole thing certain-sure?"

Tabitha shrugged. "He's a law unto himself. If he wants something badly enough, he'd never let previously declared principles stand in his way — I know that much. But I wouldn't dream of actually *predicting* any particular course of action from him."

Peter nodded. "That's something for *me* to work at, perhaps. Finding out, I mean. But the main thing is that we all know where we stand — right?"

"May I say something?" Gemma asked.

"Of course! Anybody may. You lady's maids are just as important in this."

"A diversion would help?" Gemma suggested. "A distraction? Something to interrupt and confuse them if your plan looked like failing." She stared directly at Peter. "We should keep something like that up our sleeves, don't you think?"

He smiled back at her. "Maybe you're right. We must put on our thinking caps, eh? I'm sure that — between us — we can come up with the very thing!"

29 Between the Windsor funeral and Ascot there was little social activity. There were none of the usual large subscription balls, for instance; and very few society people went to the theatre or opera. There was a general consensus that a period of withdrawal was called for and that a subdued Derby Day on June the first would restart the Season. Presentations to the new king continued, of course, but, as Beatrice had been presented the previous year — and had since then undergone no change in status that would call for a fresh audience at the palace — she was not involved with that. So the de Vivians, like hundreds of other families in London that summer, had no choice but to become ordinary tourists, filling in their days with visits to Kew, to Hampton Court, to the Tower, to Westminster Abbey and St Paul's.

The days were warm, and the sun, pouring down on the black of mourning, made everyone and everything feel hot. Tempers grew short in St James's Square and Peter did his best to stay out of people's way. Twice he went to the Naval Museum at Greenwich and, for the first time in his life, planted his foot in the Eastern Hemisphere. It looked no different from the good old familiar Western Hemisphere, actually, but at least he could say he'd done it. There, too, he daydreamed for himself a career in making model ships of incredible accuracy for discerning collectors ... perhaps even for Greenwich itself. The wonderful thing about not deciding on any particular career was that *all* possible careers — from building racing yachts to model shipmaking to selling hats — remained wide open.

Now that he and Gemma had reached a vague sort of understanding, the pressure to meet her 'accidentally' on every possible occasion became easier. That freed him to consider his plans for the longer term. All of them depended on having more money; but he would have to gain it, somehow, without his parents' knowledge. The only way he knew how to get it in so short a time — legally — was by increasing his stake on Lemberg, the horse Wilkes had tipped to win the Derby. He just hoped the man knew what he was talking about.

He dithered for a day or two and then bit the bullet. These were all-or-nothing times for him. The odds on Lemberg were steadily shortening. His fiver to win had gone on at eight to one, so he stood to gain forty quid if the horse won. Now, however, they had shortened to five to one; and they could shorten still further, even to odds-on, by the day itself. So, on the last Thursday in May, with just under a week to go, he decided to stake his all — seventy pounds on the nose at the best odds he could get.

He did not even hesitate as he turned into Whitehorse Street, despite his distaste at the thought of meeting Jenny, the bishop's daughter, again. He reached the door to Gabriel & Co, Turf Accountants, without incident. Jenkins, the clerk, remembered him, and even remembered to ask after Mr Wilkes.

"I'd like seventy pounds on Lemberg, to win," Peter said, pleased to hear he sounded much more nonchalant than he was feeling. "I have my Post Office Savings pass book with me if you wish to see it?"

Jenkins thanked him for the offer but said that his friendship with Mister Wilkes was guarantee enough. He added that Peter was doing a wise thing to get his bet in early; the odds were still five to one but they'd shorten to evens by the weekend, and if Lemberg beat Maid of Corinth and Rosedrop in the trials on Saturday, the odds would go 'on' by Monday, he was sure.

Peter kept an ear cocked for sounds of life in the rooms above — which was only prudent if he wished to avoid an uncomfortable encounter in the passageway outside.

"Don't it bother you?" he asked the clerk, jerking his thumb at the ceiling. "The noises-off, you know."

"Bless you, young sir!" the man laughed. "I should think her business up there doubles our business down here. Why, I couldn't begin to count the number of gentlemen who comes down them stairs and pops in here to lay a bet — just so's they can walk out, bold as brass, tucking our receipt in their waistcoat pocket for all the world to see." He chuckled.

It was not welcome news to Peter, who was just about to walk out of the door, doing that very thing.

"And," the clerk continued, "it cuts the other way, too. Many a punter turns right instead of left after collecting his winnings here. One kind of spending leads to another, as I always say!"

Peter laughed dutifully and made for the door. But, just as he reached it, he took a hasty step back and hid behind it instead. His sharp ears had picked up the gentle closing of a door above and the rustle of silk along the landing. Moments later the stair treads began to creak, one after another. Through the gap between door and jamb he saw her sail past, as proud and stately in her silks and satins as the huge model galleons in full sail he had seen in Greenwich the day before. Her tiny bustle was in the height of fashion — it could have been the very one Mam'selle had selected for Beatrice last week. So, too, could the dress, which tapered to a hobble that even Guinevere would have turned pale to see. But when a divine figure like Jenny's was poured into such an outfit — and given a little discreet assistance from a tiny bustle — the result was so heart-stoppingly, mouth-wateringly feminine that, for a while after she had gone, he could only stand there, struggling to calm his heart and breathe normally again.

Behind his back the clerk watched with great amusement — and jotted a reminder to himself to let the dear girl know what effect her mere passing-by had had on this shy young man. As he had just remarked — what boosted her business up there also boosted his down here.

When he was sure she had gone, Peter hastened into the street, pulled down his hat, and scurried back toward Piccadilly, even though it added at least a quarter-mile to the walk, compared with the shorter cut through Mayfair.

The parade of the demimondaines had meanwhile resumed its daily round, so he had timed today's walk across the park to Bayswater to coincide with that fifteen-minute period during which the girls, having shown themselves off to the fashionable world, left Rotten Row and scattered to their love nests in that hinterland between the Harrow Road and Maida Vale.

But, as open carriage after open carriage passed him by, his hope of seeing the young lady who had so vividly reminded him of Gemma — and who, naturally, he thought must be her sister Ruby — began to fade. Several phætons and landaus held young ladies who, at a distance, raised his spirit — only to dash it once more as they drew nearer. He was just about ready to abandon his vigil when, toward the tail of the procession, he saw her once again.

And now there could be no doubt about it. She did not simply remind him of Gemma, she was Gemma's *Doppelgänger* in every little detail. She paid him no heed, of course. Those haughty ladies looked neither right nor left. They were there not to see but to be seen. But who else could she be but his own darling's disgraced sister?

As her turn came to sweep past him without a glance, he could not prevent himself from crying out, "Gemma!"

She heard him. No doubt about it. Her whole body stiffened — or what was visible of her above the coachwork. For an agonizing moment her *hauteur* prevented her from turning her head but, eventually, curiosity got the better of her and she glanced back over her shoulder, scanning the rather sparse crowd of promenaders for any man who looked as if he might have shouted that name.

He repeated his cry. "Gemma!"

She saw him and tapped her driver's arm.

The carriage stopped and she turned again for a better look.

He started toward her, keeping to the grass beside the carriage drive, for other carriages were now pulling out to pass her.

The moment she saw him moving in her direction, something like panic showed in her eyes and she set off again toward the exit gate.

Disappointed, he slowed to a halt.

She thought better of it and stopped once more.

He stared at her; she stared at him; each in a separate quandary. Eventually, she broke the deadlock by hooking a finger at him. Slowly, warily, he approached her, picking his moment to cross the drive and draw near the carriage on the farther side, where it had halted beside the grass.

How much should he say? he wondered. Should he come straight out and tell her all he knew of her story? Or pretend he knew nothing — beyond the obvious fact that she was the living image of his sister's maid? There was no time to consider such questions now. He should have thought it out before uttering that impetuous cry.

He took off his hat as he came close and, frowning at her in amazement, said, "Gemma?" He wished his voice was not quite so shivery.

"No?" she responded, giving the word a questioning lilt.

"Oh, then I beg your pardon," he stammered. "But you do bear the most astonishing likeness to a ... a lady of my acquaintance." He put a question into his next words, too: "Miss Gemma Penhallow of Falmouth?"

She moved to the end of her seat, nearest him, so that she could peer over the side of the carriage and see the whole of him. He knew exactly what was going through her mind: This fellow was clearly a gentleman, not some jumped-up little clerk putting on airs. He dressed like a gentleman, spoke like a gentleman, carried himself with that indefinable — and inimitable — air, which any English man or woman can recognize at once as the genuine thing. And yet he called Gemma Penhallow a *lady!* What could it mean?

"A lady, you say?" She looked him up and down again.

He nodded. "She is to me."

"I see." Her tone was flat; her mind was obviously racing. "May I presume to ask *your* name, then, Miss ...?"

She weighed the request a moment or two before she replied, "I'm called Sapphire."

He decided it was time to make a clean breast of it. "Gemma," he said. "Sapphire. Precious stones all. Gemma is like a diamond, I would say. I wonder ... is there a *Ruby* somewhere?"

Her expression hardened and for a moment he feared she was about to order her coachman to drive on and leave him standing. But, if such had been her intention, she thought better of it and instead said, "Suppose you tell me who you are — and what this is all about?"

"May I climb in and ride a way with you?" he asked. "I'm getting a crick in the neck."

She laughed. Until then he had not thought her voice at all like Gemma's; it was much too posh. But their laughter betrayed their kinship to any who knew either one of them. *"Neck* is one thing you are not short of," she told him.

"May I?" he repeated.

"Not if you value your good looks. My protector takes his business seriously."

Did she mean the driver or the man who was keeping her in her gilded cage? Either way he did not want to risk it. "Then may I invite you to climb down and take a stroll with me? It really is giving me a crick in the neck."

"Not without a chaperon," she said firmly.

He looked about him despondently, for what hope had he of finding a familiar face among the London millions?

But wait! His heart leaped up to see ... a good way off, still under the trees, but coming toward him ... Tabitha Wilkes!

He waved at her. She picked up her skirts and ran excitedly toward him. She was Tabitha, all right.

"*Deus ex machina!*" he said to Sapphire-Ruby with an apologetic shrug.

"We had one of those once," she replied, "but the cat ate it."

Tabitha slowed to a saunter as she drew near. "I was expecting you. I saw you from the nursery window ..." she began; but then she spotted the carriage and its fair occupant. Her jaw dropped as she took in the woman's features. "Gemma?" she asked incredulously, coming at last to a halt.

Sapphire, as Peter had now decided to think of her, was beginning to suspect that the pair of them had staged this elaborate ambush. "Who is this young lady?" she asked Peter. "Come to that, you still haven't told me who you are."

Peter introduced himself and Tabitha; he did not, however, complete the introduction by giving Sapphire's name.

Tabitha noticed the omission, of course, and blurted out, "You *must* be Gemma's sister."

"Must I!" Sapphire said sharply.

"Oh, Peter — how exciting!" cried the irrepressible Tabitha.

"Wilkins, stay here, please," Sapphire commanded. Then, without waiting for or even noticing the driver's nod, she rose to make her descent from the carriage. It impressed Tabitha that she placed her feet in the air without looking to see whether or not Peter had yet unfolded the step on which she was about to tread. She simply assumed he would have done so. And even when she reached the ground she was still unaware that he had only just kept ahead of each of her descending paces.

Tabitha took her arm at once, trespassing on the freemasonry she assumed to exist among all young ladies of fashion. "But it *is* extraordinary," she prattled, "that Peter should find Gemma Penhallow's sister here in the heart of London." She turned to include him and asked, "Have you been looking for her or is it pure coincidence — though, of course, there's no such thing as *pure* coincidence."

Sapphire turned to Peter, too. "I should also like to hear the answer to that question, Mister de Vivian."

"Gemma would be delighted to see you ..." Peter began.

But Tabitha interrupted him once again. "In case you don't know," she said. "Gemma is ..."

"Kitten!" Peter interrupted, laying a firm hand on her arm. "Please allow me to deal with this."

"No, no, no!" she begged. "Let me. I can say it without embarrassment." She continued in a gabble: "Peter has a sister called Beatrice, and Gemma is her lady's maid, and Peter is in love with her. So there!"

"Oh, my God!" Peter took off his hat again and ran his fingers through his hair.

Sapphire received this news quite calmly. "Is it true?" she asked him.

"Of course it's true ..." Tabitha began.

"Let him say it." Sapphire gave her arm a gentle squeeze.

"It's true," Peter responded flatly.

"And how does Gemma feel about it?"

"Oh, yes, that's what I was going to say," Tabitha began, but, once again, Sapphire gripped her arm and she fell silent. "Can you think of any *reason* why Gemma would wish to avoid you?" she asked Peter.

"Yes, I can," he answered. "I'm sure it's the one you have in mind, too."

"What? Who?" Tabitha could keep silent no longer. "You never told me."

"No," Peter agreed. "I never told you."

"What? Tell me now!"

"It's not for me to speak," he replied.

"*I'll* tell you," Sapphire said. But she turned first to him. "It's all becoming clear now. When you called out Gemma's name a moment ago, you knew, didn't you! You knew I'm her sister, Ruby. You know all about that."

"So you *are* her sister!" An excited Tabitha poked her head forward for another good look at Sapphire. "I knew it at once. Didn't I say so?"

"Shush!" The woman smiled indulgently at her. "*I* am the reason that Gemma will have nothing to do with your friend here. May I ask what your ... association may be?"

"Oh," Tabitha replied airily, "I was going to marry him myself once upon a time. That was before I knew about him and Gemma, though. Now we just flirt with each other. Gemma doesn't mind."

Sapphire laughed.

"I'd know you were Gemma's sister, even in the dark, if you laughed like that," Tabitha told her. "But why are you the reason she won't ... you know?"

"She won't because I would! In fact, because I *did!* I fell for the young master ..." She broke off and asked Peter: "Are you the people who moved into Number One, Alma Terrace, when the Deverils moved out?"

"We bought it from them, yes."

"And it was love-at-first-sight, you know," Tabitha went on. "Normally, I wouldn't believe in such a ..."

Sapphire shushed her again and continued addressing Peter. "Then that's double the reason for her to have nothing to do with you. The same house! Good God — she'd see it like history repeating itself."

"I know. We are only just beginning to be able to talk without that ... what can I call it? — that ghost of Roger Deveril rising between us."

"Who's Roger Deveril?" Tabitha asked. "Have you told me about him?"

"We did just now," he replied. "If you'd only listen more and talk less!" He turned back to Sapphire. "Deveril is no longer your ...? I don't wish to pry but Gemma is bound to ..."

"He is no longer anything to do with me," Sapphire replied.

"She misses you very much, you know."

The words floored Sapphire for a moment; her step faltered and she didn't know where to look. "Has she actually told you that?" she asked.

"Yes. But I'd have known it anyway."

"How?"

"Because you're twins. I'm a twin, too — or was, once. My brother died when I was fourteen. So I know all about it. Of course she misses you." After a pause he added, "And I'll just bet you miss her."

The two females stopped and stared at him. Sapphire reached out and touched his arm — lightly, as if she were just making sure he was really there. "When did she actually tell you about me, then?" she asked.

"She didn't. I heard it first from Mrs Roanoke."

"Cousin Guinevere?" Tabitha asked, excited again. "Does she know all about this, too?"

They resumed their aimless stroll.

"Mrs Roanoke was very kind to me," Sapphire told them. "She's one of the few truly *good* people I know."

"Hear-hear!" Tabitha said.

There was a silence while Peter wondered how to suggest that she and Gemma might meet. He realized that he first had to know a little more about her present arrangements.

"If Deveril's out of the picture," he said, "then may I ask ..."

"D'you really need to?" Sapphire half turned and gestured toward her carriage.

"I should have looked more closely at the coat of arms," Peter said.

"John Thynne, sixth Baron Carteret," she told him. Her tone was so neutral he could guess nothing as to the warmth or otherwise of their liaison.

"Would he object to a meeting between you and Gemma?"

"I shouldn't think so."

"And you? I find it very hard to ..."

"Tell me one thing, Mister de Vivian. If I say I have no wish to meet my sister, will you tell her of this encounter?"

"No, of course not."

"Then will you tell her you *think* you've seen me ... perhaps bring her here to Hyde Park, where she can make the discovery for herself?"

"If you don't wish to see her, then I promise you I shall say nothing and do nothing to go against your wishes, Miss Penhallow. Why do you ask?"

"I begin to believe you actually do love her. Very well. I will now answer your question. Of *course* I long to see her. Perhaps, as you say, only another twin could understand how intense the longing is. My only doubt is whether she will be so eager to meet me again. What I did cannot have made life easy for *her.*"

"I say!" Tabitha suddenly asked Sapphire. "Are you going to the Derby next Wednesday?"

"I expect so," was the rather guarded reply.

"With Lord Carteret?"

She shrugged. "Either way, there will be times when he will be absent — which is really what you're asking, isn't it. He'll hardly take me into the royal enclosure!"

Tabitha turned to Peter. "And all your family is bound to be there, too. And Beatrice and your mother will certainly take both Mam'selle and Gemma with them. So ... if, between now and then, I can prevail upon cousin Guinevere to distract your mother on the day and you can meanwhile persuade Beatrice to cooperate ... well, Bob's your uncle!"

She smiled graciously at both of them, as if she had solved *all* their problems.

30 Black Ascot they called it that year. It was like walking through a photograph in which they had tinted the easy bits — the grass and the sky and the jockeys' colours — but had left in black-and-white the more difficult ones — the ladies and gentlemen in all their usual finery. The Derby had never before been run during the initial month of deep mourning in the royal court; or, if it had, no one now alive could remember it. The royal enclosure was open but the royal box itself was closed and no royal standard flew over the private stand.

The sombre and almost universal monochrome affected everything. The braying guffaws of the gentlemen and the adenoidal jollity of their ladies were muted to gruff chortlings and carefully pitched chuckles — when any laughter was called for at all, that is. Ladies who won on the early races that morning restrained their elation by tapping their black fans against their black-gloved palms and saying, 'Heow splendid!' Only the very youngest among them risked a little jiggle of excitement as well.

But the death, even of a much-loved king, had done nothing to dampen the spirits of the regular Derby Day crowd. Give or take a dozen changes in fashion since then, they could have modelled for the famous painting by Frith, fifty-two years earlier. Jugglers, acrobats, three-card-tricksters, seltzer sellers, tipsters, newsboys, vendors of lucky rabbits' feet and Cornish piskeys, piemen, pickpockets, end-of-the-worlders, Band of

Hopers, urchins, mind-your-horsers, drunks, swells, mashers, gypsy fortune tellers, Bankside tarts and *grandes horizontales* — all were there alongside the bookies and their tictac men, to share or spoil the fun as their calling or character required.

By coach and charabanc they came, on foot or by car or special train, all crowding in on Epsom Downs until you might wonder the earth itself did not wobble and tilt. Respectable folk who would not bet a farthing on any other day of the year brought their shillings and half-crowns to the bookies' stands on that special day, knowing that one flutter a year was closer to salvation than to sin.

And what a mighty hubbub they all created! The bookies had to shout at the tops of their voices to make their "Four to one bar one" and "Six to four the field" heard above the roar of the lighting-set dynamos, the calliopes, the cries of the hucksters, the wails of children in tantrums, the neighing of horses, the backfiring of motors, the shrill of police whistles, and, while any race was on, the frenzied shrieks and catcalls of the crowd, who had anything from a fleabite to a fortune riding on one or other of the runners.

While the great unwashed enjoyed their fun, society packed the royal enclosure, where they minded their PS and QS and walked on eggshells and eyed each other like predators at some watering hole. 'Do I know you?' — the unspoken question would start a silent mental terror at the sight of each vaguely familiar face. 'Did I see you at Tattersall's? Are you a member of my club? Were you at Lady So-and-so's dinner last month? Did we mop our brows side by side at the Academy private view? Or have I merely seen your picture in the *Illustrated London News?*'

Eyes frantically begged eyes as bodies drew closer: 'Please help me! Smile in recognition. Open your mouth to remind me of your name and where we met. Or look away and smile at someone else. I know you are undergoing the same torment as me. One of us has to end it!'

"Why do we make things so difficult for ourselves?" an exasperated Peter asked after a mere hour of such torment. "We should all wear our names on our hats and carry lists of all the occasions we've attended during the past two years. We could pin them between our shoulderblades."

"Don't be tedious," his mother said. "You should be out there, mixing, talking to people, finding suitable men for your sister to meet."

"Mother!" Beatrice said wearily.

"I thought we were hunting with just one bullet up the spout," Peter said.

Ada gave a weary glance heavenward. "Only you could speak quite so frivolously."

"Can I put a bet on for anyone?" he offered brightly.

No one took him up — but it was not part of the plan that they should, either. Not yet.

When the morning's racing was done the meeting broke for luncheon. Half the people in the royal enclosure gravitated toward the refreshment tents; the rest left and went in search of their carriages and the hampers they had brought.

The de Vivians had purchased a ready-packed hamper from Messrs Fortnum & Mason — an extravagance that, at two whole guineas, mopped up more than one hundredth part of their daily income. Still, it was only once a year, and Ada did so enjoy the envious glances and suppressed murmurs of astonishment from less fortunate onlookers as Trewithen and Penhallow unpacked the quails' eggs, the larks' tongues in aspic, the steak tartare, the asparagus in olive oil, the Roman pies, the cheddar, the stilton, the fruit trifles and ice creams and sorbets, and, of course, the chilled Sillery and Montrachet, the Châteauneuf-du-Pape, the Bollinger and Veuve-Clicquot without which no Derby Day could be called complete.

Normally Peter would have eaten his way through each course with some relish but today he picked at his food and brooded until Beatrice, as arranged, said she might like to put a shilling on one of the nags in the big race.

Her mother, as expected, told her she could not possibly be allowed to do such a thing. The very idea! Peter must go and place the bet for her.

Peter asked why Penhallow couldn't be sent to do it.

Ada told him to keep quiet if he really had nothing sensible to contribute.

Beatrice said it wasn't just the *fact* of betting on the horse that was exciting to her. She wanted to see how it was done. Couldn't she go with Peter and stand back and watch?

No.

Why not? That was heartless.

Because she couldn't stand back *alone* and she couldn't go forward and stand by her brother when he placed the bet, among all those rough, vulgar people, so there was an end to it.

Well then, at least Mam'selle could come with her and be with her while she stood back and watched. No?

Fortunately, one look at Mam'selle's disgusted face put paid to that suggestion.

Penhallow then?

Eventually they wore their mother down to a state of grudging agreement, but only after she had stipulated in absurd detail how many paces around each bookie's stand was forbidden territory. And, she added, Beatrice was not to engage in conversation with *anybody,* no matter how friendly they seemed nor what tales of distress they spun to engage her sympathy.

And what if they happened to meet Graham Melchett?

Then, of *course,* Beatrice had leave to stay in his company! Really! Did she have to tell them every little obvious thing?

As they left, when it was too late for his mother to retract the permission, Peter added casually that he wasn't just going to plonk the money down with the first bookie they ran across. He was no fool! He was going to shop around for the best odds he could get. That was to explain why they did not simply go straight to the nearest bookie and back, which would have occupied no more than ten minutes.

Guinevere had been watching them all this time from the Wilkes's carriage, which was several rows away and, fortunately, nearer the bookies' ranks. The moment she saw them leave she told her cousin Graham she had a mind to put a guinea on this horse that Wilkes was so absolutely sure was going to run away with the rosette, and would he kindly escort her?

He offered to do the whole thing. She needn't discommode herself at all.

She gave much the same reasons as Beatrice had given for wanting to witness the transaction herself.

And so, with a precision that surprised them all, they converged in a meeting that surprised only Melchett and Gemma.

There was, of course, no point in shopping around for good odds. The frantic signalling among the tictac men ensured that no single bookie was left more exposed than any other. Melchett stayed to squire the ladies while Peter put Beatrice's half-crown and Guinevere's guinea on Lemberg to win. The odds were now down to seven-to-four — not quite 'on' but that was because of a late rush of bets on Lord Roseberry's Neil Gow, who had beaten Lemberg in the Two Thousand Guineas. With Neil Gow's odds at eleven-to-four, they were the only two horses in the real betting; the remaining eleven runners were all longer than ten-to-one.

"Don't you think we should be wiser to hedge our bets with a little flutter on Neil Gow, too?" Guinevere asked when Peter rejoined them.

"I wouldn't," Melchett replied confidently, like a man with inside information. "Neil Gow is trained at Percy Peck's stables at Exning — Lord Durham's place, which was overwhelmed by a colony of rooks this spring. And Durham gave orders to shoot the lot — which they did. The rooks, I mean, of course."

He clearly considered that to be the end of the story, until he met the blank stares of the others. "Well," he went on, surprised at having to state anything so obvious, "very bad luck, that — shooting a colony of rooks. Lord Roseberry is absolutely furious — and who can blame him?"

Peter recalled what Wilkes had said about the idiot money that goes into racing and just lies there waiting for clever people to come along and scoop it up.

"Miss de Vivian," Melchett said, "may I escort you back to our carriage? I'm sure my cousins would enjoy meeting you again — every bit as much as I."

He offered Beatrice one arm and Guinevere the other.

As Beatrice left with them, she told Gemma she could return to the de Vivians' carriage with Peter.

"Something's going on," Gemma said as soon as they were alone. "I never saw anything so contrived in all my life."

"Can't you guess?" Peter asked.

"Only too well!" She laughed and waved at the vast multitude on every side. "You've got me all alone at last!"

"Not that," he said.

"I'll tell you one thing you *can* do for me." She produced a sovereign from the palm of her glove. "Put that on Neil Gow for me — please."

He shook his head. "It's not worth it, love. Even if it wins — which it won't — you'll only get fifty-five bob at these odds. Is it worth the risk of a pound?"

"What *is* going to win, then?"

"My horse — Lemberg. It's a cert. I've got seventy-five quid riding on it."

She pursed her lips in a silent whistle. But she told him even more firmly to put it on Neil Gow. *"One* of us has got to have something to take home," she said.

"You're sure?"

"I wouldn't ask you if I wasn't. Go on, or the odds'll shorten even more."

Tempted though he was to switch her bet at the last minute, he did as she asked and then returned to her. The delay had only added to his excitement.

"You've got a strong heart, I hope?" he asked. "You don't swoon away at the slightest surprise?"

"You mean, like neither horse winning?"

He shook his head. "And what about a big, big surprise? What is the biggest surprise you could have at the moment? It's something we've talked about quite recently. Something you want — probably more than anything else in the world?"

Her eyes narrowed with suspicion. "To do with you?"

Again he shook his head. "Nothing to do with me."

He saw a sudden excitement in her; she had guessed, but she did not dare say it aloud in case it was not so.

"Yes," he said. "Ruby. I've found her and she's here."

She half reached her arms toward him and for a moment he thought she actually was going to swoon; then he realized that what she really wanted was to throw her arms about him and give him a hug.

But her courage failed her at the last. "And she wants to see me?" she asked, putting her hand to her chest to quell the beating of her heart.

"Every bit as much as you want to see her again. Are you ready? D'you want a bit longer to gather your wits?"

Tears were now welling in her eyes and she shook her head as people do at receiving news too vast to assimilate. "Oh, Peter! Peter!" she murmured.

"What?"

"I've been so meany to you."

"You haven't!" Embarrassment made him brusque. "Come on!" He offered his arm but was surprised when she took it. He hugged her hand tight against him and said, "Isn't this nice?"

His awkwardness helped her recover from her emotion, enough, anyway, to giggle. "Did you think I ever would — take your arm like this?"

"I never for one moment doubted it," he joked, pretending to an arrogant sort of clairvoyance.

She punched him playfully and said, "You!"

"That's better," he said, serious again. "Save the emotions for Ruby — though I should tell you that she calls herself Sapphire nowadays and that she is — well, to put it delicately — a very close friend of Lord Carteret."

She stopped dead, pulling him to a halt. "You mean ...? What does that mean — 'a very close friend'?"

He nodded. "Exactly what you're thinking, Gemma. Does it make a difference? She's still your sister — your twin."

"Can she see us now?"

"Why? Are you thinking of turning back?"

"Just answer. How close is she?"

"About a furlong," he replied, without taking his eyes off her. "Shall I tell you the strangest thing? She is so like you that it's uncanny. But when I look at her — even though I marvel at the resemblance — I feel *nothing!* None of those feelings that even the haziest sight of you can stir within me."

She did not smile. "I can't think about all that now, Peter. I've got to ..." She closed her eyes and shook her head. "Has she got the baby with her? What about the baby?"

"I'm afraid it was stillborn. She had a very hard time after Deveril deserted her. Carteret's been marvellous to her — or so she says. I've not met him yet."

A new thought struck Gemma. "You didn't just run into her by chance and immediately arrange this, all in haste, did you!"

"Of course not. I've met her two or three times — riding in Hyde Park. She told me from the start that she longed to meet you, but I wanted to make sure no harm would come to you if I agreed. No, not harm — but unpleasantness. If you think it will be unpleasant, we can turn about now. I've made no promises to her. D'you want to go back?"

Gemma slumped, so much so that her hand almost fell from his grasp. "No," she intoned. "I suppose not. Not having come this far."

They resumed their stroll.

"What she's doing ..." Gemma said, "I mean — it *is* immoral. You can't say it isn't."

"Ha!" was his only reply to that.

"But it is!" she insisted. "She accepts money from this Lord Carteret and in return she ... you know."

"Makes herself available to him."

"Yes."

"And putting ten thou' a year on Beatrice's head and touting her around the balls and concerts and theatres of the Season — that's not immoral? Or contracting an arranged marriage — accepting security and pin money in exchange for unlimited availability in the bedroom ..."

"Peter!" She looked all about them in alarm.

"What d'you call that?" he insisted. "I'll tell you what I call it."

"Only if it's repeatable," she warned.

"I call it a thoroughly *dis*honest version of what your sister is *honestly* doing. Anyway, Carteret's only waiting for his wife to die before he marries Ruby. Or Sapphire. Remember to call her Sapphire."

He had no idea whether this last statement was true. It probably wasn't. It was something Sapphire had merely hinted at. But he felt he had to overcome Gemma's prudish scruples somehow. Once she was reunited with her sister, they wouldn't matter, anyway.

They continued to thread their way among the crowd to the small knoll where carriages for the more raffish elements of society were laagered. And now Gemma stepped out so eagerly that conversation became too difficult. Not that Peter minded. The willing grip of her hand in the crook of his arm and the occasional crushing together of their bodies, sometimes accidental on her part, sometimes not, he thought, was all his heart could desire at that moment.

As for Gemma, her mind was in such a whirl of competing kinds of happiness that she hardly felt her feet touch the ground. But she certainly felt it when her hip brushed against Peter's, which seemed to happen whether she were in step with him or out of it. A magical sort of glow had descended on the day for her, bringing with it a feeling of recklessness — or what, in a cautious young maid like Gemma, would pass for such. Every now and then she contrived it so that her body deliberately brushed against his, which was something she would not even have contemplated before today — to do such a thing deliberately. But oh, what a sweetness it was! What powerful, electrifying feelings surged all through her every time it happened! God forgive her for thinking it, but she could wish that Ruby — or Sapphire — were a *hundred* furlongs distant; she would gladly walk every yard of them like this!

It was curious how things sometimes came together at just the right moment. When Sapphire had first fallen under Roger Deveril's spell, she had tried to describe her feelings to Gemma. But she had merely stopped her ears and dismissed her sister's talk as filth — an attitude she had maintained, though with dwindling conviction, until today. But now, in these brief moments of contact between herself and Peter, she felt, for the first time in her life, the majesty, the power, and above all the *goodness* of what her sister had tried to describe.

And then Gemma knew she could meet her without the smallest lingering trace of reproach in her heart.

"There she is," Peter said suddenly.

And suddenly Gemma was afraid to look. "Peter?" she said, turning to him.

"See? Waving to us."

"Peter?"

"What now?"

"I think ... I mean, I *thank* ... you. I'll never be able to say how grateful I am for this."

He choked on words he longed to utter. Looking down at her, gazing into the mysterious green fire of her eyes, he thought she was surely the most precious person on earth. It required a superhuman effort of will not to take her in his arms, there and then. As a token of things to come, he leaned forward and kissed her lightly on the brow — and even that was an intoxication almost beyond bearing.

31 At last Gemma felt able to turn and seek out her sister. She found her at once, which was no great feat, even in that milling throng, for Sapphire could have stepped straight out of the pages of any haute-monde fashion magazine — a skin-tight tube of black silk frills and furbelows from neck to ankle, topped by a black hat that could have sheltered an elephant howdah, trimmed with black ostrich feathers that could have reached down and tickled the same elephant's belly. Funereal though the colours were, anything less mournful than their excited, rosy-cheeked wearer would be hard to imagine; she was standing in her carriage, waving like a field telegraph and blowing kisses like a diva.

"Oh, my gidge!" Gemma exclaimed.

"I'll wait here," Peter said, giving her a gentle push.

"You will not!" Gemma replied firmly. "Not with *him* there."

Peter had not noticed the man before but it could only be Lord Carteret — five centuries of inbreeding lying to attention in the carriage and watching his mistress with a supercilious smile. As they approached, his lordship reached up with his cane and prodded the coachman in the back; it was Wilkins, the same coachman who drove Sapphire to Rotten Row and back each day. The man leaped down, squatted behind the carriage, and rose again with a bottle of champagne and a salver bearing four glass flutes.

"Gem! Gem!" Sapphire, unable to restrain herself any longer, leaped from the carriage and, snatching her veil up to her forehead, flew into her sister's embrace.

"Lipstick!" she warned when Gemma tried to kiss her on the mouth; instead, she kissed the air on each side of Gemma's head and then set about hugging her to death. There were simple tears on Gemma's part and tears and running eye-black and ruined powder on Sapphire's.

Peter, feeling *de trop,* moved beyond them, nearer the carriage.

"So!" Carteret called out to him. "That's what she looked like before she was ruined, eh? I've often wondered. Not bad. You must be Peter de Vivian." He stretched out a languid paw. "John Thynne."

"Lord Carteret." Peter gave a minimal bow as he shook the fellow's hand. He expected something limp and was surprised at the firmness of his grip. "I'm very pleased to make your acquaintance, sir."

"My bulldog here" — he nodded in Wilkins's direction — "thought you were making a bid to replace me, young fellow. However, I'm happy to see I needn't have worried."

Peter realized the man intended this as a slight on him, but he saw a way to turn it into a compliment.

"No, you're right there," he replied genially as he leaned against the door, tipped back his hat with the knob of his cane, and crossed one boot nonchalantly over the other. "I'm not the sort of fellow who likes to brag, old chap, but I do believe *I* have the pick of the litter."

He did not look at Carteret's face but the smirk on the lips of a nearby lounger told him he'd struck the mark.

His lordship turned away in annoyance, seeking out the Penhallow twins. "Champagne, girls!" he snapped.

"Thank you, thank you!" Sapphire said as she passed Peter on her way back into the carriage; as an afterthought she pecked him quickly on the cheek.

Gemma, grinning fit to split her face, raised her hand to Peter's and wiped off the smear of damp powder her sister had left behind — not realizing that her own face needed much more attention.

"Here!" Sapphire opened her parasol and vanished beneath it. " 'old this, my lover."

The perfect upper-class English of her 'heah!' followed by the pure Cornish of the remainder, symbolically spanned her present and former lives.

Carteret, recovering from his annoyance, smiled tenuously at Peter, sizing him up after having been worsted.

"Fancy anything for the big one?" Peter asked.

"Do I?" the fellow asked his coachman.

"You have a hundred guineas on Neil Gow, my lord," he replied stolidly.

"Only a hundred?" Carteret shrugged and turned back to Peter. "Obviously I don't feel too strongly either way. How about you?"

"I've put my shirt on Lemberg."

"Me, too!" Sapphire cried from beneath her parasol. "You know your trouble, don't you, Carteret — you're much too kind to all those lame, blind, spavined, broken-winded geegees." She emerged, a porcelain doll once more, into the light of day, which no longer held terrors for her. "Honestly!" she said to Peter. "He lavishes a fortune on them." She grinned at her protector. "Mind you — I don't think he knows their condition when he parts with his money."

Carteret joined their laughter, not altogether wholeheartedly, and said, "Climb aboard, young man. I think I'm going to be in need of some masculine support here. Let's drink to the winner, whatever colours he's running under."

He kept up this sort of edgy but entirely inconsequential badinage for the next fifteen minutes or so. Peter tried to distract him by drawing his fire but he kept including the two women, who thus found it impossible to hold any serious conversation between themselves.

An exasperated Sapphire was just about to propose a future meeting at which she and Gemma could talk at leisure when Beatrice and Melchett turned up. "Peter!" she called out from a little way off. "Curfew time, my dearest brother! You can't stay away any longer!"

Her voice trailed off toward the end of what was obviously intended as a firm command. Peter followed her eyes and saw they were fixed on Lord Carteret — who seemed equally fascinated by her; it was the first sign of animation the man had shown since Peter's arrival.

Beatrice, who had originally stood outside that invisible circle within which an introduction might be sought, now stepped firmly inside it and said to Peter, "New friends? What fun!"

Melchett looked most unhappy at this.

"Allow me to present Lord Carteret," Peter said reluctantly. "My sister, Miss Beatrice de Vivian."

"John Thynne," he murmured as he shook her hand. Then, glancing over her shoulder, "Melchett, isn't it? Come and join us in a festive bumper. Allow me to present a good friend of mine ..."

But Beatrice was already reaching her hand toward Sapphire. "I feel I already know you," she said, glancing rapidly from one twin to the other. "The resemblance is quite astonishing."

"Actually" — Peter held out a hand to help Gemma down — "we were just about to leave, anyway. Have you two arranged another meeting?"

Gemma nodded.

Beatrice was about to insist that her maid should stay, to chaperon her, when she caught sight of Peter's anxious expression and changed her mind. Instead she turned to Sapphire and, nodding toward Gemma, said, "Don't you wish to walk with her a little?"

But Sapphire declined the bait, for she, too, had seen the glance that passed between this very pretty young lady and her protector. "Thank you, Miss de Vivian, but we'll be able to enjoy a good long chat tomorrow," she replied, blowing a kiss at the departing Gemma.

Peter offered her his arm but she did not take it until they were well swallowed up by the crowd. Then she risked hugging him tight and even laying her head briefly upon his shoulder. "This is the happiest day of my life!" she sighed. "And I owe it all to you."

"The happiest *so far,* " he said. "Listen, Gemma! At the risk of pushing my luck a little too far for one day — do you actually want to go back to our carriage at once?"

"Do I *want* to?" She laughed grimly. "What I want doesn't ever come into it much!"

"Well, that's what I'm asking you now — I'm giving you the chance. Do you want to?"

"Or what?"

"Or let's go across the course to the Hill and watch the start of the big one. They say you haven't really seen the Derby unless you've watched it from among the crowd on the Hill."

"How long before it starts?" she asked.

At least she wasn't saying an outright no.

"In fifteen minutes, if they stick to the programme. Also, we can get a better view of the finishing post over there."

"*You* could get a good view from the stand."

"I'd rather be beside you — just to rub your nose in it when Lemberg kicks dust all over Neil Gow!"

She dug him sharply with her elbow but she was clearly still tempted. "There'll surely be trouble," she objected, but not very strenuously.

"Perhaps," he said as he deviated their path toward the point where they could most easily cross the course. "Does it really worry you?"

"Of course it does." When he stayed silent she added, "Why? D'you think it oughtn't to?"

He shrugged. "Perhaps we should no longer be *quite* so secretive? Don't you think?"

He felt her stiffen. "It depends what you mean. I think we should be *more* secretive, if anything. I mean, there has been precious little between us to hide so far, hasn't there! Apart from bringing you cups of tea, I've been slamming the door in your face every chance I got — and making no secret about it!"

"Well ... people may have noticed that, too. After all, there's such a thing as protesting too much — as well as too little — don't you know."

"No young maidservant ever got dismissed for resisting a young master — and that's a fact."

He tried another tack. "So what is it you think we should be *more* secretive about, then?"

"About the fact that I *do* now want to meet you." She moved her hand down his arm and linked fingers with his. "I *want* us to go on walks together."

"And talk."

"Yes. Find out what you really want out of life ... find out what *I* really want, too, because that's another thing I don't know. But that's why I think we've got to keep it all secret, still. In case it should all come to nothing — which it might."

He made no reply to that.

"It might." She pressed him on the point. "You've got to admit that, Peter. We're not starting some secret engagement here and now. Just a little exploration, that's all."

He noded glumly.

"Say it," she insisted.

He sighed. "We're not starting an engagement — just a friendship that may lead to one. And, yes, we ought to keep it secret still. But hardly from Bea — I mean, she knows already. Most of it. Also we're going to need her help, I'm sure — like today, for instance."

"Yes, all right. But no one else. None of the other servants — especially none of them. Promise me, Peter? Promise you won't do anything 'brave' in front of your parents — because it wouldn't be brave at all. It'd be very foolish."

"In that case, we're taking a risk now."

"Why? Who'll spot us in this crowd! If I thought there was a risk, I shouldn't be with you at all. The only risk is if we go back together. If we go back separately, I can tell the truth — I can say I met my sister who I hadn't seen for more than a year. Your mother may be annoyed but she'll hardly punish me for it."

"True," he admitted. All the same, he wished she wasn't insisting on being quite so damned sensible. Where was her sense of romance?

"You didn't promise yet," she reminded him.

"Promise what?"

"That you intend to be sensible?"

He heaved another sigh. "I promise!" He leaned forward to glance up and down the course. "Safe to cross now, I think," he added. Then he laughed. "Crossing the Rubicon, eh!"

32 They interlaced their fingers again as they threaded their way among the crowds on the Hill; most people were drifting in the same direction — toward the starting line on the farther slope. He lifted her hand in his and shook it gently. "What is so utterly special about *this* hand?" he asked. "It's flesh and blood and bone like any other and yet it is so ... unique, so *precious.*"

She raked the heavens with her eyes.

"Am I being silly?" he asked.

"Yes!"

"Can I ask a serious question, then?"

"No. It's too near the off. Anyway, I'm too happy to be serious. Next time it rains you can ask."

In fact, she wanted to avoid any serious question because she considered they had already progressed quite far enough for one day — if progress it was. "I almost backed Malpas at a hundred to one," she said. "You know there's a village called Malpas up the Fal, near Truro?"

"Why didn't you?" he asked, amused.

"Because I saw another one called Greenback, which is almost like Greenbank, and then I thought two coincidences was too much."

"So why did you choose Neil Gow?"

"Because Lord Roseberry's already won the Derby three times — eighteen ninety-four, ninety-five, and nineteen-oh-five — so he knows what he's doing. But mainly because that Mister Melchett said it couldn't possibly win."

Peter laughed. "That's the best reason of all — though I still don't think it'll beat Lemberg." He looked her up and down, as if seeing her in a new light. "So Trewithen *is* a betting man, after all!" he said. "Remember I asked you that once and you said you didn't know?"

She realized that by showing off her improbable knowledge of Lord Roseberry's previous wins, she had given the game away. Still, he had been remarkably nimble to make the leap from that to Trewithen as her likely source. Peter obviously had the sort of mind one needed for success in business — the mind that can somehow tap into what the other fellow was thinking.

"Servants never give away unnecessary information about each other ... sir," she said.

They reached the top of the Hill at precisely the moment the race should have started, but, from the melee on the course below it was quite clear there had been a delay.

"Shall we go down nearer?" he asked. "Though if we stay here, we'll be better placed to dash for the finish once they're off. Here — have my glasses."

They were so powerful she could not resist the urge to reach out, as if to touch the horses. "What are Lemberg's colours?" she asked.

"White tunic, red sleeves," he replied. "Red and white segments on his cap."

"Got him! Oh my!"

"What? Let me look."

"Nothing." She leaned away to stop him from taking the glasses. "It's just that he looks every inch a winner."

"Neil Gow's jockey is wearing ..."

"I know his colours. I've seen him already. He looks pretty good, too."

She started jiggling on the spot with excitement.

Looking at her he wondered yet again why the overpowering tenderness of his love for her never seemed to exhaust itself; every time he saw her — every *single* time — his heart seemed to overflow once again with a feeling no less powerful than that very first time. "They don't look like settling to starter's orders," he remarked. "I need no glasses to see that."

"They seem to be rewinding a knee bandage on one of the horses. Look." She handed him back the glasses at last.

While he peered through them he said, quite casually, "I'm going to ask you that serious question, anyway. Here it comes. You must have known, long before today, that I had no ulterior motive toward you — that I was not another Roger Deveril. Why did you wait until today?"

She made no reply. Indeed, she continued staring down at the starting line as if he had not spoken a word. The reason she had said nothing before now was, of course, the one Gwynneth Jones had teased out of her — that the only way she would ever marry Peter was if he were willing to live at a level where she would not be ridiculed. But if she gave him that answer now, he would agree to do it at once, without a second thought. And that was no use to her. He had to realize it for himself. It had to be his decision, completely unprompted by her — else there might be bitterness between them in years to come, and he would say she had forced him to give up his rank and inheritance.

"Well?" he prompted her.

She shook her head. "I'm not going to answer that, Peter, so it's no use your asking."

"What — never?"

She shrugged. "Maybe one fine day — if you haven't worked it out for yourself by then."

He let the glasses hang by the neckstrap again and turned to her with a grin. "A guessing game!" he said. "Good — I love guessing games."

She did not smile back, though. "It's more than a game, my love. And it shouldn't require any guesswork, either."

"What, then?"

"Simple understanding. Just put yourself in my position and ask what would make me hold back — even after I knew you weren't another Roger Deveril — which I calculate I knew by the second or third day!"

"What?"

His astonished cry drew the attention of several groups nearby. Embarrassed, they moved away to a similar vantage farther along the ridge.

"What?" he repeated less vociferously.

"You just work it out," she said.

"Hmpff!" Mildly annoyed, but also intrigued by her challenge, he raised the glasses to his eyes again and fretted aloud for them to be off. He tried not to think what it would mean to his life if neither Lemberg nor Greenback were placed.

He had beautifully curved lips, she thought, being now free to look at him without his knowing it. She wanted to reach up and run the tip of one finger over them. She wanted more than anything to feel them on her lips, pressed in a kiss, caressing each other lightly there. Suddenly there was a great hollow feeling inside her, accompanied by a slight difficulty in breathing. She uttered no sound, she was sure of that, and yet he somehow became aware of the change in her.

He lowered the glasses again and said, "All right?"

"Just excitement," she replied, jiggling up and down again to prove it. "Aren't you excited, too?"

"I was just thinking about that," he said.

"You don't *think* about excitement. You feel it."

"I was thinking that I don't really mind if Lemback wins or loses now. I've already won − if that's the right word − the most wonderful thing in the world. I want this day to last for ever, don't you? I can't imagine it coming to an end."

She smiled at this but there was a sadness in her voice as she said, "It will end, though, my darling one − in just about half an hour. And then we have to go back to being Miss Penhallow and Master Peter. And you" − she raised her fingers and touched his lips at last − "must stop grinning like the cat that got locked in the creamery!"

A great roar set in down near the starting line and swiftly spread up the Hill − and then, at the speed of sound, to the stands on the far side of the course.

"Only fifteen minutes late!" Peter struggled to sound calm. "In less than three minutes we'll know our fate."

The track formed a long horseshoe shape, running away to their left, then curving round at the infamously tight Tattenham

Corner to return to the finishing line between the Hill and the grandstands.

"What's happening? Tell me!" Gemma cried.

"Nothing much yet. Lemberg and Neil Gow are both off to a good start but it's Greenback out in front. Then three colts — Admiral Hawke, Charles O'Malley, and Wildflower the Second — I think."

"How close?"

"Hard on his heels. It's not looking good for either of us. With four ahead of him and Tattenham Corner yet to come, I doubt if even a brilliant jockey like Bernard Dillon can bring Lemberg to the front."

"What about Maher on Neil Gow? Where's he?"

"Just behind Lemberg. If Lemberg has a chance, so does he."

He lowered his glasses. "I can't see them any more. Let's go nearer the finishing post."

There was no need to ask the way, for the whole Hill seemed to be seething in that same direction. They went as far as they could, until the movement of the crowd set in a sort of human traffic jam.

There was no resisting the pressure now. She let herself be pushed against him, body to body at last. It thrilled him, too, she could tell — though he pretended not to notice. So, too, did she, come to that.

"Can I use these, if you aren't going to?" she asked, plucking at the straps of his glasses.

He passed them over, but she was not tall enough to see over the hats of the people in front.

"Shall I lift you up?" he asked, slipping behind her and putting his arms round her.

She just grinned at him and shook her head. "Sufficient unto the day ..." she told him. He shouldn't have asked. She passed the glasses back saying, "They must have come into view again by now."

He put the glasses to his eyes and, after a moment's hasty scan, cried out "Oh, no!" in a tone that suggested disaster.

If the Fates were guiding his destiny that day, they were preparing to twist the knife in the cruellest possible way, for, although Greenback was still slightly out in front, Lemberg was now the challenger.

"What?" Gemma gripped his arm fiercely. "What's happening? Tell me."

"I can't believe it. Two furlongs to go and Lemberg is challenging. God, what a jockey! What a man!"

"Yes? Go on! Don't stop!"

"Well ... Lemberg's gaining on Greenback. There's only a length — no, *half* a length — in it. No, now it's down to a *neck!* And now they're level. It's Greenback and Lemberg, neck-and-neck, with only Neil Gow to challenge them. But he's tiring and Charles O'Malley is moving up. He hasn't a hope, though. Not of winning. It's Lemberg out in front now. Lord, what a sprint! There's grass between him and Greenback. He's *got* to win! He's got to win!"

"Lemberg!" Gemma shrieked, almost splitting his left ear drum. "Come on Lemberg. Good old Bernie Dillon!"

He moved the glasses away from his face and stared at her in amazement. "You're on Neil Gow," he said. "Remember?"

"*We* are on Lemberg. Go on!"

The moment he focused on the field again he let out that same cry: "Oh, no!"

"What now? Don't say he's ..."

"He's tiring. Oh, come on, Bernie! You can get more out of him, surely?"

"Where's Greenback now?"

"Yes," cried a short fellow to Peter's right. "Keep up the commentary, young fellow. You were doing fine, so you were."

Peter resumed: "Greenback's swallowed all the grass between them. There's a furlong to go and Lemberg is still tiring. But Greenback hasn't all that much steam left in him either. Lord, this must be the fastest Derby ever! It's going to be which of them tires first. That'll decide it. Neil Gow has fallen right back to fourth. O'Malley's third but he's two lengths behind Greenback who's only half a length behind Lemberg. Neil Gow is still fourth. Oh, God, I can't *bear* this!"

He held the glasses with one hand and felt for his handkerchief. Gemma pulled hers from her sleeve and wiped his brow.

"Thanks," he gasped. "Half a furlong to go and Lemberg is still falling back. Still leading but falling back. Bernie Dillon's doing all he can but both horses are tiring. Either of them could drop back now. Fifty yards to go and there's half a length in it.

Come on, Lemberg! Just hold it there! And for God's sake, Gemma, stop jerking my arm!"

She was gripping him tight and jumping up and down, trying to see the finish with her own eyes. She was so far beside herself with excitement now that Peter, unable to resist the temptation, let the glasses fall on their sling, and, gripping her around the midriff, lifted her above the throng.

"Here!" cried an angry man behind them, who had enjoyed a perfect view until then.

But they were both too exhilarated to pay him any heed.

Gemma went on shouting, "Go on, Lemberg! Go on, Bernie! Yes! Yes! You'll do it! He's doing it!" while Peter closed his eyes and luxuriated in the unbelievable preciousness of her body, there in his embrace at last.

A moment later he received a violent thump in the back and he had to let her drop.

"Sorry, matey," said the man behind, defensively. "But it's not as if I didn't warn you."

"And so say all of us," cried the man behind him.

Peter suppressed an impulse to knee the man in the groin and asked Gemma, urgently, who had won.

She was still trying to get her breath back after all the excitement and shouting — and being dumped back on her feet like that. "Dead heat, I think," she said. "It looked as if it was going to end that way."

"No, it was Lemberg by a neck," the man in front of her said.

"Well, *I* thought it was a dead heat," said *his* companion

"And I thought Greenback was ahead by a nostril," said the man to his left. He was holding a stopwatch up to the daylight and squinting at the fine divisions. "Two minutes thirty-six!" he exclaimed. "If that's right, it's a record."

"It was still the longest two-and-a-half minutes of *my* life," Peter said.

There was another agonizing wait, which seemed even longer, before the numbers went up.

Five!

"Lemback!" A great roar went up all over the Hill — and from the stands, too, no doubt, but the Hill drowned it out.

Peter and Gemma were like a pair of children, jumping up and down and shrieking, "We did it! We did it!"

Gemma threw her arms around Peter's neck and, caring nothing for the crowds all about them — and nothing, too, for all her earlier words of caution — pressed her lips firmly to his.

How long their kiss lasted, neither of them knew or cared; it could well have been another course record. They did not stop until the crowd thinned to the point where they began to feel alone and exposed.

"I love you, Gemma Penhallow," he said as their lips parted for the final time.

"I love you, Peter de Vivian," she replied. "And I reckon I always will."

On the far side of the course, seated comfortably in the de Vivians' open carriage, Mam'selle lowered her glasses and tucked them away with a peculiarly self-satisfied smile. She had spotted young de Vivian and the Penhallow creature by sheer chance, while scanning the crowd on the Hill for anything that might be called fashionable. She had had her suspicions about those two for some time, and now they were suspicions no longer. The only remaining question was how and when to use this shameful secret to her best advantage?

Part Four

Twin Desires

33 Peter's winnings amounted to £125 on Greenback and £400 on Lemberg, or £525 in all — enough to buy a pretty decent house somewhere, if he so wished. Together with his original stakes he now had just over £600 of capital. He and Gemma could marry on that much and live modestly for several years in a rented house, or even longer if they stayed in rooms. There was, however, no possibility of stretching it out for the next seven years, after which they could kiss financial worries goodbye for ever. Therefore, he would have to eke it out by taking some sort of employment.

Employment! It was a novel thought. An exciting thought. And, he had to confess, a slightly frightening thought. It was hard to fail at idleness. A man with no talent for golf could make up for it on the ballroom floor; a poor cricketer could still keep his yachting trophies polished; even an amateur dinghy-builder could bask in the praise of others when no customer was hammering at the door asking why his boat was not yet delivered. To do the identical work knowing that your wife and children would go hungry if you made a mess of it or failed to win repeat orders, was quite another thing.

Still, there was no gainsaying those winnings — £605, presumably lying ready in that huge safe in the offices of Gabriel & Co., Whitehorse Street, Mayfair. It was earning him nothing there, which, to any de Vivian, was a scandal.

Jenkins, the clerk, stared at Peter's slips, turning them over and over as if he doubted his own handwriting. "And will you be returning to Cornwall after the Season, sir?" he asked sorrowfully.

"Before, actually." Peter, surprised at the question, was wary. "Why d'you ask?"

"Mister Wilkes, you see, sir, he doesn't so much bet to win as to show how much cleverer he is than what other punters are. Of course, winning's part of it, but he wagers small amounts, see? The winnings are just a barometer to him, if you like."

"And?" Peter thought the information interesting but not particularly relevant.

"Well, sir, a young man intent on *living* off of his winnings here in Lunnon, and with Mister Wilkes's tips to help him …

that would not be too pleasing to my masters." He unlocked the safe as he spoke, and took out an unsealed envelope containing the full amount. Wilkes's name was written on the front, with 'P. de Vivian, Esquire' in parentheses beneath it. "I'd be obliged if you'd count it at once, sir," he added. "To avoid any unpleasant misunderstanding later."

Peter laughed at the sight of so much money, and all of it his. As he counted it he told Jenkins his masters needn't worry about any further losses. "Seventy quid was my entire fortune. These last weeks have been a nightmare since I placed those bets. I'll never willingly do it again. I don't need to now, anyway." He lifted the envelope by way of proof and licked the gummed flap to seal it.

Jenkins slammed the safe door with excessive force. Peter thought he was annoyed; the man's true purpose did not become apparent until a short while later.

"I'd better get this into a bank pretty smartly," Peter said as he tucked the envelope into an inside pocket. "Where's the nearest office?"

"There's a branch of Barclay's in Berkeley Square," Jenkins suggested. Then, when he saw the face Peter made, he added, "Is something the matter, sir?"

"Barclay's own all the de Vivian banks in Cornwall. My parents would hear of it before sundown today."

"Ah! And that would put the proverbial fat in the proverbial fire, would it?"

"I'd be roasted — and it would be more literal than proverbial, too. De Vivian isn't a name like Smith or Brown exactly."

The man nodded sagely. "Mind you ..." He studied the ceiling as he spoke. "It's every Englishman's natural-born right to choose a different surname every day of the week if he likes. You could be Smith all day if you wished, and Brown tomorrow — *and* break no law by it."

Peter's eyes lit up. "Or Penhallow! That's it, of course. Thanks! You've given me the perfect idea." He shook the man vigorously by the hand, patted his bulging pocket again, to make sure he wasn't dreaming, and prepared to leave.

Jenkins sprang to open the door — and then his violent treatment of the safe door was explained, for there, pretty and clean and ready to please, stood Jenny, the bishop's daughter.

"Hallo, Charley," she said. "Flush with success, are we? Still want to *talk?*"

"Good morning, Miss Jenny!" Peter flattened himself to squeeze past without brushing against her.

At the street door he turned to bid her a cheery, no-hard-feelings farewell, but the look of desolation on her face was so touching that, instead, he took a step back toward her and said, "I'm sorry, honestly ... but ..." He shrugged.

"You don't *even* want to talk," she said bitterly.

He stepped into the street once again and tilted his head toward Shepherd's Market. "Over a cup of coffee?" he suggested. "If any of those places are open yet."

She cheered up at once and joined him, taking his arm and turning him toward Shepherd's Court. He tried not to think of the countless men that dainty little hand had touched since last December. "I want to bank some money first," he said. "I shan't be easy until I do. Which way is Berkeley Square? To the right, isn't it? By the way, my name is Peter."

"The National Provincial in Curzon Street is nearer," she told him. "That's where I'm going."

"You?" He did not know why he was so surprised.

"I have to do *something* with it," she replied sarcastically as she jingled a leather pouch, heavy with coins.

"Forgive me. Actually, the National Provincial would suit me even better than Barclay's. They have branches in Cornwall, too. I'm sure I saw one in Falmouth."

"Falmouth," she said, as if the name meant something to her.

"You know it?"

"No-o," she replied.

"You don't sound very certain."

"It just sounded a nice name."

She hardly exerted herself to make this explanation sound convincing, but he did not press her. Could her father be the Bishop of Truro? he wondered. They emerged into Curzon Street and she turned him left for the bank, which he now saw on the opposite side of the street.

"The friend I went off with the other day ..." he began.

"Conrad Wilkes."

"Yes. All right. He told me something of your story. I think I was supposed to feel pity for you, but I don't."

Her grip tightened to the point where it was almost painful.

"Sorry," she said when she realized it. "I don't know what to say to that. What d'you expect me to say?"

"Nothing, really. I just thought you ought to know. We can go back to talking about nothing in particular, if you prefer."

There was no traffic to speak of and they crossed the road without hurrying.

"So! You don't feel pity — and you obviously don't feel what most men feel when they ..."

"But I do! I'm just not going to give way to it, that's all. Don't get the wrong idea."

"It must be love," she said bitterly. "I only hope it lasts."

They entered the bank. "Ladies first," he said.

"A very good morning to you, Mister Watson!" She greeted the clerk by name.

"Good morning, madam," he responded gravely as he helped her into the seat — just as he would have treated a lady. When she tipped out the contents of her pouch, Peter understood why. It must have been the best part of fifteen pounds. A single night's earnings? He cringed inwardly to think of it.

Watson counted the money and entered the total in her pass book as well as in his daily ledger. She rose and beckoned Peter to take the seat.

He took the envelope from his pocket as he crossed the floor to the business table, opened it casually with his thumbnail, extracted the notes, and tossed the discard into the waste-paper basket. "I want to open an account in the name of a friend," he said. "And can it be held in your Falmouth branch rather than here in London?"

The clerk replied that the account had better be opened and established in London first; any request for a transfer to Falmouth would then be more easily handled from down there — if that were convenient?

Peter said it was. He gave his name as de Vere and opened the account in the name of Miss Gemma Penhallow, Number One, Alma Terrace, Falmouth. He signed an astonishing number of documents as her proxy and took away a sheet on which Gemma was to give specimens of her signature.

Before they left the bank, Jenny darted back to the business table and retrieved the envelope Peter had thrown away. "A keepsake," she explained to Watson. But the smile on the man's face told her she was already too late.

"What's this?" Peter asked when she handed him back the empty envelope.

By way of reply she pointed to his name, written on it in Jenkins's neat copperplate below that of Wilkes.

"Lord — thanks!" he said.

"It may already be too late," she added. "Watson's as quick as a travelling rat."

He stared morosely across the road, at the buildings which formed the outer edge of Shepherd's Market. He felt a sudden reluctance to return there, though he still wished to talk to Jenny herself, despite her profession — or, perhaps, because of the contrast between it and her upbringing.

"Spilt milk," she said when he hesitated at the kerb.

"There's a little café in Hyde Park," he said. "We could have a coffee there — and an ice cream, if you like?"

She, too, hesitated, running her eyes over the buildings opposite. "Yes, I know what you're feeling," she said.

"What?"

"There are at least three dozen girls plying the same trade as me, just in that small market. And there's a hundred more here in Curzon Street, between where we are now and Hyde Park. I still find it hard to believe sometimes. The *unendingness* of it. Did you ever stand on the Embankment, watching the Thames flow by, and wonder where all that water could possibly be coming from? It's like that."

He recalled the fat old toad who had so disgusted him. "And it's just as unpleasant as the Thames, I suppose."

She shrugged. "I'm sure the water police and lightermen don't even notice it any more, either."

"Hyde Park, then?" he asked.

"Why not!" she exclaimed brightly. "Today is a red-letter day for me, too."

"Should I ask why?" He offered her his arm as they set off.

"I'll tell you over coffee." She slipped her hand into the crook of his elbow. "Are you sure this is wise?" she asked. "Will Miss Gemma Penhallow mind?"

He stopped dead and stared at her. "How d'you know her name?" he asked, appalled. "Were you able to eavesdrop?"

She smiled and pulled him onward. "I didn't simply retrieve that envelope," she replied. "I can also read mirror-image writing on a piece of fresh blotting paper. Number One, Alma Terrace, Falmouth — is that her address or yours? Or both?" She smiled archly at the suggestion.

"My God!" he exclaimed bleakly. "Talk about being an innocent abroad!"

"Yes, Mister de Vivian, that does rather sum you up — quite well, I'm afraid."

"But surely there's such a thing as banking confidentiality? In *our* family it's a byword for absolute and unswerving loyalty among the bank's servants."

"I hope you're right," she replied airily. "But I doubt it, somehow. Put yourself in Watson's position. There he sits at the business table one bright Thursday morning in June and suddenly he realizes he's got the son of a prominent banker sitting opposite him. And he's opening an account in the name of a spinster in Falmouth. And he's paying into it some pretty large winnings on horses."

"How does he know that?"

"He knows Jenkins's writing as well as he knows his own."

"Heigh ho! Go on!"

"Well — you speak of loyalty, but what does it mean from Watson's point of view? Isn't it whatever earns him promotion? Tell me, which is more likely to further Mister Watson's career with the National Provincial? Keeping your little secret to himself or passing it on to his chief clerk so that he, in turn, can earn a little gold medal by passing it still further up the line?"

She broke off and frowned at him. "Is your father in town for the Season?"

Peter nodded, thoroughly miserable by now.

"And he'll be attending a City banquet or two, no doubt?"

"All right, all right!" he grumbled. "No need to rub it in."

"Not *now*, there isn't!"

She was pretty ruthless, he thought. His gaze was a curious mixture of annoyance and admiration as he asked, "When did all this occur to *you?* If you're so clever."

"No, Mister de Vivian, I'm not especially clever — not by the standards of the commercial world. I get by, of course, but I am pretty average, I'd say. Gamma-plus or beta-minus."

"And I don't even get an epsilon-minus, I suppose."

She offered no contradiction. "You were going to say earlier …?" she reminded him. "You don't pity me and you don't feel an overwhelming desire — so what do you feel? If anything."

"Admiration," he replied. "Many another young woman would have crawled home and put up with a lifetime of humiliation rather than do what you've done."

His praise embarrassed her. She had hardened her soul against abuse and slander, leaving it wide open to applause. She gazed all about her, as if seeking inspiration for a change of subject. Then she remembered what else she had been going to ask him: "Miss Gemma Penhallow," she mused. "Was she what you wanted to talk to me about?"

"When?"

"You know when. The first time you clapped eyes on me — when Conrad Wilkes took you off for a drink instead."

"Yes. All right — she was. But it's all resolved now."

"Then I guess she *would* object to my walking arm-in-arm with you like this?"

He thought of replying that she must be well used to the company of men, each of whom had another woman in his life — a woman who would not be too happy at a situation like this. But then he remembered what people who live in glass houses are supposed to avoid doing. "I don't think she'd be too glad," he agreed.

"Then why are you risking it? Not for the usual reason, quite obviously."

"May I ask — are you really a bishop's daughter?"

"I asked you a question first."

"Well, this is part of my answer, actually. Are you?"

"Is that what Conrad told you?"

"Yes. Do you and he … I mean, is he one of your …?"

She looked at him reproachfully. "You should know better than to ask such a thing."

"Yes. I'm sorry."

"I wouldn't give tuppence for honour among bankers, but there really is an honour among whores, you know."

"All right. I said I'm sorry."

She nudged him and said in a conspiratorial voice, "But how much will you give me if I answer your question?"

He glanced at her sharply.

She laughed. "I still wouldn't tell you. I just wanted to see you smile. As to my origins, I am the daughter of a rural dean — not a bishop. Or he's not a bishop yet, anyway. Conrad was just trying to protect me, bless him. *Now* can you answer me? Why is it important, anyway?"

"Because, as I said just now — you had a chance to go back home and you deliberately chose not to. That's right, eh?"

"I suppose so. It was a bit of a Hobson's choice — whoever Hobson was."

They had reached Park Lane. Peter pointed out Hamilton Gardens, the little upper-class enclave for Mayfair residents only (and only *some* of them, at that). "You know what struck me the moment I saw that?" he asked her.

She answered him at once: "That the Upper Ten Thousand are the *real* prisoners of the British class system!" She grinned and added, "Sorry, my dear! I, too, have walked this way with Conrad, more than once."

Peter smiled ruefully as he led the way across to the park. "But he's right," he said. "I've been thinking about it a lot lately — and about you and the choice you made. That's why I'm 'risking' this conversation, as you put it — because, in a way, I'm in the same boat."

"Heavens!" she exclaimed. "I hope not!"

"Well, similar. Gemma Penhallow, you see, is my sister's lady's maid ..."

"Oh, yes?" The question had an understandably sarcastic ring to it.

"Don't you start!" he warned. "It's taken me the best part of two months to convince *her* I'm sincere. I'm not going to go through all that again. You'll just have to take it on trust that I am. I've loved her from the very moment we met, and I'm absolutely determined to make her the next Mrs de Vivian — laugh if you will."

She sighed.

"Not even a chuckle?" he asked.

"You've convinced *me* in two minutes," she replied. "Miss Penhallow must be just a little slow in the uptake, eh? A bit simply furnished in the top floor?" She leaned forward and peered up into his face to see if she had managed to anger him.

"She's even brighter than you, I think," he replied with a smile. "If she had been with me this morning, she'd have prevented my stupid errors *before* they happened. However, there are certain complications."

"Complications? In a love affair between a young master and a lady's maid? You *do* surprise me!"

"Oh, *those* complications are a mere bagatelle, believe me. The real stumbling block is that she has absolutely no desire to live the life of an upper-middle-class lady."

"Well, that's one statement I *don't* have to take on trust. Good for her! I take back what I just said. But poor you! I suppose *you* have no skill or trade at which you could earn a living! Well, I know all about that, too!" She laughed. "I *knew* you and I would find something in common before too long, Mister de Vivian!"

He patted her hand to show he did not mean his words unkindly. "Sad to say, Miss Jenny, you are wrong there, too. I could make quite a good living building racing boats for the idle rich. I could do even better *designing* and building them."

She glanced at him quite sharply now and there was a new light in her eyes. "You've actually done such a thing?" she asked. "Built a boat and sailed it, I mean? It's not just talk?"

"I've finished the hull. She just needs the mast to be stepped and rigged. Believe me, I can do it — and in weeks, not months, if that was to be your next question."

A hoop came rolling toward them over the grass. Peter reached across her with his cane and deftly turned it in a U around them, sending it back with a flourish to its embarrassed owner, a little boy of about nine.

"You seem to have no difficulty, then," Jenny said. "Unless … have you come of age yet? And has she?"

"I will in October. She's only eighteen but I don't think her parents will object. My difficulty is that I think she is wrong. She is rejecting the only kind of middle-class life she knows — stuffy, petty, provincial, and boring. I agree with her there. I reject it, too. But I don't think the life of a lower-middle-class artisan is all that brilliant, either. Building boats is a wonderful hobby but would I still think it quite so marvellous if I had no escape from it? Especially when so many other possibilities beckon."

"Name one," she challenged him.

"Travel, for instance. Not in grand style but simply. Counting the pennies, even though we wouldn't need to. Making it a challenge to see how cheaply we could do it. Perhaps even taking casual work along the way. Harvest work ... waiting on tables ... buying things in one town, selling them in another — that sort of thing. See the world a bit before we settle down. The real world — not just one grand hotel after another."

"Have you suggested this to her?"

"Not yet. It's almost impossible to be alone with her. You know what a lady's maid's life must be like in the middle of the London Season. I'm really just thinking aloud. What d'you say? Is it just the sort of thing a man would love and a woman would hate? The roving life versus the domestic?"

She did not respond at once.

"Eh?" he prompted her. They were approaching the tea garden now.

"Let me put it this way, Mister de Vivian," she answered at last. "If she says no, and if you then find you still prefer the wandering life to a settled one as a married boatbuilder — and if you want an uncomplaining companion ..." She squeezed his arm and laughed rather than complete the sentence.

They chose an outdoor table under a spreading vine that was already furnished with luscious bunches of half-mature grapes.

"Shall we have coffee and some cream cakes?" he asked her as a waiter approached.

"Mmm!" she purred.

"I'm sorry," he said as he seated himself. "I seem to have monopolized our conversation. You said, some time ago, that this is a red-letter day for you?"

She stared at him in silence a moment, as if sizing him up. Arrived at a decision, she opened her pocket-book and took out the little red pass book from the bank and passed it to him, saying, "I must be mad. You're the only man I've ever shown this to — the almost daily record of my shame."

Miss Jennifer Diver was the name in the long oval window on its cover.

Being a de Vivian he riffled the pages at once until he came to the current total. The book was almost full. Today's entry, he was pleased to note, had been £15 4s 7¾d — bringing the grand total to £1,004 16s 9¼d. He whistled.

The waiter appeared with their order; Peter slipped the book onto his knees beneath the table.

"Thank you," she said when the man had gone. She lifted the coffee pot. "Shall I be mother?"

He raised a sardonic eyebrow at her choice of words. "I told you — no danger of that from *me!*"

She laughed, against her will, and poured out their coffee.

He, meanwhile flipped back through the pages and saw that she generally accumulated a sum between £10 and £20 — usually close to £15 — and then paid it in; it never took her more than four days; sometimes she managed it in two. She seemed to work without a break for three weeks and then take a whole week off; he was about to ask why when the reason occurred to him. He blushed at the crass *faux-pas* he had so nearly committed.

She set down the coffee pot and helped herself to cream before passing the jug to him. "It's a red-letter day," she said, "because I always vowed I'd stop when it reached a thousand."

"And you've done it in seven months!" he marvelled. "That's a better rate of pay than a high-court judge — or anyone but a field marshal in the army! And my mother calls you 'Unfortunates'!" A new thought struck him: "And how many did you say there are in Mayfair alone?"

Her lip curled in a sneer. "Not one who can work and save like me! They drink themselves into oblivion. They go to opium dens in Limehouse. They give each night's takings to worthless men — who beat them black and blue if they consider it too little ... so then they can ask the punters for even less ..." There was flint in her eye and steel in her voice.

He shivered to see her implacable spirit so nakedly displayed. "So ... what next?" he asked. "It'd give you an income of fifty a year, wisely invested. I suppose you could just about live on that — modestly, mind you."

"Modestly?" She laughed at his naivete. "I've almost forgotten what the word means." She lifted a dainty bite of viennese pastry on her fork. "Avert your gaze," she commanded. "I'm about to make a pig of myself!"

He took a bite of his own pastry, a cream horn. "Not modestly, then," he said.

"*Mode*-ishly — I'll accept. In short, I intend to open a little establishment devoted entirely to the very latest in fashion."

"In London?"

He was about to point out that the competition here was ferocious, and that she might easily be recognized and exposed — as if such thoughts had never crossed her mind!

Fortunately, she corrected him before he could make such a fool of himself. "I shall move to some provincial town," she said. "Somewhere that has never seen such an establishment. It will not be a shop — though, naturally, I shall sell the very latest in fashions. But it will be more as a doctor sells pills from his own dispensary — *after* the consultation. I want people to think of me for fashion ills and complaints as they think of their doctor for the bodily kind."

"And of the mental kind, too." Peter recalled his father's interest in psychology and that sort of stuff.

"Even better!" She looked at him admiringly. "You seem to understand exactly what I'm hoping to do, Mister de Vivian."

"You explain it so well, Miss Diver. Jenny Diver? I don't suppose that's your real name?"

She paused and then said, "It's Divett, actually. Now you'll be able to look in *Crockford's* and discover where my father is dean!" She laughed. "I was young and naive, too, once. I actually started to write my real name when I opened that account. I got as far as d-i-v-e before I realized my folly. So then I made it 'Diver' — like one of MacHeath's molls in *The Beggars' Opera!* I hope you will look up 'Divett' in *Crockford's.*"

"Why?"

"Because then you'll discover he's rural dean at Durham — and then you'll perhaps believe me when I promise you I had chosen to set up my little fashion establishment in Cornwall long before I knew you even existed! You can't get much farther away from Durham than that, can you!"

The announcement stunned Peter, of course, and yet he could not decide whether it was good or bad news. The romantic, adventurous side of his character welcomed the possibility of further meetings, and the chance to watch her blossom in this new business; the sensible, down-to-earth parts of him wanted no part of it.

"When you say Cornwall …?" he began.

"Yes," she replied. "I was actually thinking of Falmouth — which is why I gave a start when you mentioned the name."

34 The Wilkeses intended going down to Cornwall at the end of the first week in July. Graham Melchett was to go with them and so, since Ada had not changed her mind yet again about his eminent suitability for Beatrice, the de Vivians decided to return home as well. The Royal Academy, the Eton – Harrow match, Henley, and Goodwood would simply have to manage without them. To make sure the world knew of their departure they resolved to hold a grand ball at a venue yet to be decided.

They consulted Conrad Wilkes on the matter, hoping to learn of some magnificent location that would, nevertheless, prove quite inexpensive. He said that the Empire Rooms in Bayswater had an excellent reputation — and, curiously enough, he just happened to be a controlling shareholder. He could arrange for them to have it 'at cost.' In fact, they could have it at one-quarter cost if they combined with him in a joint ball for Beatrice, Sophie, and Felicity. Kill four birds with one stone, ha-ha.

Much as they detested the man and his notions about the proper provision for his daughters, this was the sort of offer the de Vivians always found it hard to turn down. Besides, Peter had proved remarkably obedient to their wishes that he consort with the Wilkes girls as little as possible, so their chief fear in agreeing to a joint occasion was allayed.

The grand ball was set for Monday, the fourth of July. Mam'selle and Gemma worked all the daylight hours on their ladies' gowns, petticoats, underwear, stockings, fans, handbags, dancing shoes, capes, hats, overcoats, mantillas, gloves, handker-chiefs, and jewelry — not forgetting their own costumes, simple though they were; for they would be there that night, too, waiting patiently behind the scenes to be sent on last-minute errands or to assist in any emergency, whether it might require a needle or a bottle of smelling salts.

Gemma at first refused to sign the papers Peter had brought from the bank. She felt it put her too much in his debt and encroached on her sense of independence. But he argued patiently with her, pointing out that if he put the money in the bank in his own name, his parents would surely hear of it; and they had legal power to do what they liked with it until he turned twenty-one. And the moment they learned he had acquired it by betting on horses, they'd send it to the African Missions or some such charity. Also, if he was run over by a bus, he wanted her to have it without any legal fuss. Also, she could, if she preferred, regard herself as merely looking after it safely for him until October. Also ...

Eventually she agreed and gave him specimens of her signature to return to the bank. By then, though, Mam'selle, who had been spying on them ever since Derby Day, had not only overheard enough of their conversations to know what was afoot but had also discovered the drawer behind which Gemma sought to hide the pass book and other papers.

When Mam'selle heard that Cornwall was very like Brittany (whose very name made her shudder) and that the two had once been part of the same Arthurian kingdom, she secretly vowed that not all the money in the de Vivian banks would drag her down there. So time was getting short if she wanted to put an end to La Penhallow's grandiose ideas. And yet she held back — not out of fear that she might be doing the creature an injustice but because she hoped that if she waited just a little longer, she would glean that extra nugget of intrigue which would prove beyond all doubt that Master Peter was behaving perfidiously and that La Penhallow was abetting him at every turn. The fact that he had not tried to flirt with her, Mam'selle, once in all these weeks rankled with her every time she saw him. It was a French maid's traditional right that the young master should lose his heart to her.

Her patience was rewarded on the Saturday before the grand ball. Beatrice had discovered from Peter that, on Saturdays, it was Lord Carteret's custom to go to Rotten Row during the hours reserved for the demimonde and return with Sapphire to Maida Vale. Beatrice, knowing that Carteret had taken more than a passing liking to her, had some primitive notion that she might be able to run across his path 'by accident' and invite him home to an impromptu dinner, instead, leaving Sapphire out in the cold — or out in Maida Vale, anyway, all on her own.

Mam'selle knew nothing of these machinations, nor even of Sapphire's existence; but she had endured her mistress's prattling of Lord Carteret's this and Lord Carteret's that until she was sick of it. So, when Beatrice summoned her that Saturday afternoon and said she'd like to walk in the park, Mam'selle — guessing at least something of what was afoot — agreed at once to chaperon her.

Beatrice was taken aback; Mam'selle had almost made it a condition of her employment that, while she was willing to accompany Beatrice into St James's Square gardens, which were just outside the front door, to chaperon her anywhere farther away would be Miss Penhallow's task.

"Oh!" Beatrice exclaimed. "Are you sure, Mam'selle? It is a very hot day, you know. I thought Miss Penhallow would ..."

"Mees Pen'allow, she ees buyeeng coloured tweests and reebons for ze gown."

"I'll wait," Beatrice said considerately.

"Eet's no trouble, Mam'selle. I come wees you ... *allons!*"

It was a miserable mistress and an intrigued maid who set off for Hyde Park under that pitiless July sun. If Mam'selle were to discover Sapphire's existence, Peter would never forgive her. As they approached Rotten Row, she saw them all — her brother, Melchett, Carteret, Sapphire in her carriage, and others — all in the same laughing, lounging gaggle. She dragged her feet as much as she dared, hoping that Peter would notice their approach; he was the only one who would see any significance in Mam'selle's presence.

He spotted them at last, just as she was about to abandon hope; and, God bless the man, he responded swiftly enough. He gripped Carteret by the shoulder and said, "No time to explain just now, old chap. I have to get Sapphire out of the way while Beatrice and Mam'selle are here." He then sprang into the carriage, and told Wilkins to break the record for getting to the farther end of the Row. The man probably did, too — but, unfortunately, not before Mam'selle got a distant glimpse of a young girl she was almost sure was Penhallow.

In fact, who else could it be — especially when Master Peter whisked her away in such guilty haste? Obviously the maid had deputed her marketing to some other servant — bribed her, probably, with money from her lover, Peter. Then she had changed into those fancy clothes and come to parade in the park with him, bold as a pageboy. It was all Mam'selle had been waiting for.

And when she heard of the arrangements for proceeding by carriage to the grand ball, she realized she had the perfect opportunity to end La Penhallow's delusions of grandeur once and for all. They were to travel in two carriages, one large, one small, and both were to arrive at a quarter to eight, fifteen minutes before the official start of the ball. Madame de Vivian, Miss Penhallow, and she, Mam'selle, were to travel ahead in the larger coach; Beatrice and her father were to follow in the smaller one, which could not accommodate a gentleman and *two* ladies in full ball gowns. So she could beguile the half-hour or so between St James's Square and the Empire Rooms by telling Madame — in French, of course — precisely what sort of peasant schemer was tearing her family apart behind their backs. And she would tell her tale with so many smiles and sympathetic looks at Penhallow that the ignorant little creature would never know! Was that not exquisite?

The wheels were barely turning before Mam'selle began.

First she produced her emergency letter — the one from her sister to say that their mother was gravely ill in Paris and was not expected to live beyond another week. She swallowed her tears bravely and said that of *course* she would never dream of letting her dear Madame down on this big night in Mam'selle Béatrice's life, but she would be eternally grateful if her dearest Madame would see fit to release her from the remainder of her contract — in these melancholy circumstances. If Madame agreed, she would leave by the boat train in the morning.

Of course Madame agreed. What terrible news! One must hope that her sister had misunderstood the doctors and that their mother was less gravely ill than she indicated.

Gemma suppressed a smile — not only at the elegant simplicity of the ruse and the fact that it had worked like a charm but also at the thought that, from tomorrow on, the household in general and she in particular would be free of this Mam'selle, this monster of selfishness, greed, and arrogance.

Her pleasure died abruptly at Mam'selle's next words.

Did Madame realize she had a serpent under the flowers? She, Mam'selle, could not, in all honour, depart without acquainting her with certain facts.

Serpent under the flowers? Gemma thought rapidly — something she was by now used to doing whenever Mam'selle broke into her native tongue. 'Snake in the grass'? She stared out of the window — making it plain she was not listening — and peeled her ears for more.

No, Madame did not realize that. Who did Mam'selle mean? She must feel perfectly free to speak. No word of it would get back to the person concerned. She had Madame's personal word on it.

If it did get back, Mam'selle told her, it would have *very little way* to travel. The female in question was not in a thousand other places than here.

Gemma fought to maintain her air of indifference.

Pray continue, Madame commanded. But Mam'selle should be very certain of her facts. She, Madame, had the highest opinion of the said person and was very satisfied with her.

Then Madame could not possibly be aware that the female had lately been given a substantial sum of money by Madame's own son?

Indeed? What might 'a substantial sum' to be?

Around five hundred pounds. Perhaps six?

Madame could not help laughing. Mam'selle must have misunderstood. Where would her son have acquired so much? He would have had to save his allowance for as long as …

From betting on the horse-race they had all attended recently — and perhaps others. Mam'selle did not know. But he certainly had accumulated over *four* hundred pounds. And he had certainly given it to the aforementioned female. If Madame did not believe her, she had only to look in the top drawer in the chest of drawers in that female's bedroom. She should pull the drawer right out because the papers were hidden in an envelope glued to the back of it. Perhaps Madame would modify her high opinion then!

Madame certainly would — *if* it were true. She would reserve judgement on that and meanwhile she'd be obliged if Mam'selle would remember that *nothing* — not even this news, true or otherwise — must be allowed to spoil this evening of all evenings.

"Gemma!" She turned to the maid with a radiant smile. "I'm so sorry. It's very rude to go prattling on over your head like this, but my chances to keep up with my French are so limited. You do understand, I hope? We're not talking about anything of importance, anyway."

Gemma replied that, of course, she understood.

Mam'selle, angry that Madame was being so even-handed in the matter, asserted that she could not possibly be mistaken.

Madame, reverting to French, replied that, while she may not be mistaken as to *fact,* she could not be so sure as to *motive.* For example, her son might very well have won this money by betting on horses. She had no difficulty in believing that much. And, being under twenty-one, he would know he had no legal right to it — if his parents decreed otherwise. He would also know that, in his particular case, any attempt to open an account in his own name would immediately be commented on throughout the banking profession and would reach his father's ears in no time. And so, knowing the young rascal as she did, she was sure *he'd* think it no end of a joke to persuade a servant girl to bank it for him in her name. In other words, the young female they were discussing might be his innocent dupe. She, Madame, would wait until she could have it out properly and calmly with the girl. And that — she must repeat — would not — *could* not — take place before tomorrow at the earliest.

Mam'selle then played her final card. Would an innocent dupe go carriage riding in the centre of London, dressed like a grand lady in the very height of fashion, when she had been sent on errands to buy ribbons and twists and things?

What on earth was Mam'selle talking about? When did this highly improbable event take place?

Last Saturday afternoon. And she saw it with her own eyes — when she chaperoned her young mistress to the park. Madame's son was sitting in a carriage with the young female in question — and she was dressed as Mam'selle had already described — and, the instant he saw her and his sister approaching, he drove off at high speed, leaving a cloud of dust behind.

Well, it all sounded very melodramatic and even more improbable, but Madame must now repeat for the third and final time that it must all wait until tomorrow. *Nothing* was to interfere with tonight's grand occasion.

A bitterly disappointed Mam'selle, who had hoped for some sort of cataclysm within the family, preferably on the very steps of the Empire Rooms, could not even bring herself to look at Gemma, much less soothe her with a synthetic smile, as they descended from the growler.

Peter had gone ahead to squire one of the Wilkes's two carriages. Having done his duty by them, he was waiting under the awning for his own family to arrive. It was a fine, warm evening and he was going to dance with a lot of splendid girls and the champagne would flow and he'd surely find some way to enjoy a brief stroll round the square with Gemma, once it got dark. And then it would be goodbye London! And they'd be back in Cornwall by Saturday and then ... and then a whole new life awaited him and Gemma.

This happy mood did not survive his first glance at her face as she descended from the growler, which drove onward at once to park in the square.

"Trouble?" he murmured as she passed him.

She, knowing Mrs de Vivian's eyes must be upon them, murmured, "The worst," and stood well away from him, waiting for Beatrice and her father to arrive.

Mam'selle joined her, managed a genial smile at last, and, waving a hand across the deep, cloudless blue of the evening sky, said, *"Ah, qu'il fait beau ce soir!"*

It was the phrase Gemma had waited months to hear — the one Miss Isco-Visco had used as an example when teaching them the very swanky use of *ne* and the subjunctive with verbs like *craindre* — to fear. Without pausing to consider whether or not it was wise, she smiled back and said, *"Ah, oui, Mam'selle. Il fait beau maintenant mais je crains qu'il ne pleuve!"*

Mam'selle stared at her aghast. *"Quoi?"* she said, as crudely as any of those Breton peasants she affected to despise.

Gemma obliged sweetly, enjoying herself even more this second time. *"J'ai dit qu'il fait beau maintenant mais je crains qu'il ne pleuve comme la vache qui pisse!"* Her deliberate addition of this gross crudity (which she had overheard when Miss Isco-Visco, thinking she was alone, had emerged from the TA drill hall one typically wet Cornish night) almost gave Mam'selle a fit of the vapours.

Peter, aware that something more than a minor contretemps was under way between the two maids, did his best to distract his mother's attention with questions and comments that would keep her eyes trained in any direction but theirs. It worked for a while but, eventually, her concern that they should be on hand and alert when Beatrice arrived caused her to look toward them. She, too, realized at once that something was wrong. Gemma had the look of an avenging Fury; Mam'selle looked like a woman on the threshold of the Last Judgment.

Had Miss Penhallow understood Mam'selle's revelations in the growler? Surely not. They had been so careful not to mention names.

Perhaps she had caught enough of the gist of it? No — she had given no sign of it during the entire journey. Nor, indeed, when they arrived.

So it must have happened since their arrival — in the last couple of minutes. Mam'selle must have told her! Oh, the spiteful little cat!

Without further thought Ada went to where they stood. "Mam'selle!" she snapped as she approached them. She was cautious enough to speak in French, just in case she were mistaken. "Have you taken leave of your senses?"

Mam'selle drew breath to protest as best she could but Gemma got in first: *"Ma chère soeur ... "* she began, and went on to quote the letter Mam'selle had shown her during those early days in St James's Square — not verbatim, of course, but close enough in spirit to leave Ada in no doubt.

Of the two surprises — namely, that Miss Penhallow did, after all, speak French (and pretty good French, too) and that she knew the contents of a letter that had only arrived that evening and which she had, presumably, not yet seen — Ada addressed the lesser one first. "Did Mam'selle tell you about that letter?" she asked.

"She showed it to me," Gemma agreed before adding the sting in the tail: "Sometime early in May."

Ada's nostrils flared. "Is this true, Mam'selle?" she asked.

"If you examine the date, I expect you'll see it's written in a different ink," Gemma added helpfully.

By now Peter realized that his mother was engaged in something more serious than resolving a little domestic tiff between two servants. He joined the group while she was demanding the letter from Mam'selle. Gemma took advantage of her distraction to put a finger to her lips, warning him to say nothing unless he absolutely had to.

"Voilà!" Mam'selle shrieked, pointing at them. "See! They make secret signs behind your back, Madame!"

Distracted — and not a little distraught by now — Ada turned to Gemma, then to Peter. Seeing nothing but innocent faces, she was reduced to saying, "Will someone please tell me what is going on?"

"I tell you already what ees going on!" Mam'selle cried.

"I'll tell you what's going on," Peter remarked, almost casually. "The carriage with Pater and Beatrice has just appeared at the end of the street."

It ended all discussion, of course. Peter and his mother returned to the edge of the pavement; the maids stood in readiness, a couple of paces behind them.

"Don't you think it might be for the best, Mam'selle," Gemma said, "if you were to catch tonight's boat-train instead of waiting until the morning?"

The woman hesitated.

Gemma continued: "Your salary *will* be paid — and a little *bonne bouche* on top of it, I'm sure."

"Oh, *you* are sure!" she sneered.

"Yes, of course. You are a professional lady's maid. You have your reputation for discretion to keep up. And our mistress will not wish to give you any reason for doing otherwise."

It was true, of course, and if Mam'selle had not been so upset, she would not have needed Gemma to point it out.

Seeing her hesitate, Gemma went on. "You could go back to St James's Square as soon as we're sure everything's going well here. The boat-train leaves at half-past ten. I'm sure Trewithen will help you to Victoria."

"*Tiens!* And you geeve me permeession now!"

"I give you advice, Mam'selle — good advice, I think. You'll regret it if you ignore it just because it comes from me."

Mam'selle tossed her curls angrily but both of them knew the woman had no choice.

Meanwhile, Beatrice and her father had arrived — to face a barrage of questions as to what had kept them. Ada was sure it had been some last-minute fussing by Beatrice and directed most of the fire at her; but it was her husband who answered. He levelled a finger at Peter and barked: "Don't you run away and hide, young man!"

Peter laughed and assured him he had not the slightest intention of doing so.

"You may — when you hear what I heard on the way here!"

Peter looked accusingly at Beatrice, who started to protest that it had nothing to do with her. "We were stuck in Mayfair," she said, "and a fellow in another carriage recognized the pater and ..."

"Enough!" cried her father, who had been retrieving his hat and gloves from the carriage. "*I* shall deal with the matter in my own way and my own time."

"Oh! Was there *ever* such an ill-starred evening!" Ada exclaimed. "We, too, have not lacked for drama!" She cast a significant glance at the two maids. "Come on! We must get in position." She glanced at the foyer clock. "People will start to arrive in five minutes."

The two maids brought up the rear. Gemma pointed toward the carriage and said to Mam'selle, "There's your chance."

For a moment the woman seemed about to maintain her resistance but then a cunning light crept into her eyes and she said, "Yes! I 'ave ze laughs for me!"

"What the devil!" de Vivian cried out when he became aware of Mam'selle's departure. "Stop, I say!"

The driver stopped halfway through reversing to face in the opposite direction, blocking the street.

"It's for the best — don't you think, ma'am?" Gemma said.

After a momentary uncertainty Ada said, "Yes, perhaps it is. Miss Penhallow can easily pass for a French maid — as we have only just discovered!" She signalled the driver to continue and added, "I told you — we have had our drama here, too."

There was no time to argue or explain. De Vivian raised his hands in a gesture of despair and led them within. Gemma plucked at Peter's sleeve and said quietly, "Go and telephone Trewithen in St James's Square. Tell him to go at once to my room and take out the drawers in my chest of drawers, one by one, until he finds the one with an envelope glued *behind* the back bit of wood. It holds my pass book and papers. Ask him to take them out and look after them for me." As Peter moved away she added, "And tell him Mam'selle is leaving tonight and he should watch the silver and help her to Victoria." And when he was halfway to the manager's office, she called after him, "Also tell him to write *Bon Voyage!* on a slip of paper and stick it in the envelope!"

35 At around ten o'clock the dancing stopped and people were invited to help demolish the magnificent buffet that had been arranged in one of the smaller halls. Beatrice, whose programme had, naturally, been full, seized this her first chance to tell her brother what had happened on her way to the Empire Rooms with their father.

They had, as she had started to tell him, been stuck in traffic in Mayfair when a gentleman in the next carriage had recognized their father. He lowered his window and gestured to the pater to do the same. In the ensuing conversation it transpired that he was the chairman of the National Provincial Bank and ...

Peter needed no further explanation. Indeed, he now supplied it to her. She had not entirely believed the man's story and was astonished to have it confirmed. "You must have been mad," she said. "Why did you not simply bank it under a false name?"

He explained about wanting Gemma to have the money, without any fuss, if anything should happen to him.

She tried to think of other ways in which he might have achieved the same purpose but, on the spur of the moment, could not.

"Did the old man give out any hint of what he intends doing?" he asked.

"I should have thought the explosion when we arrived was hint enough!"

"I'm surprised I haven't seen him before now. I haven't exactly been hiding."

"He's been closeted in a council of war with the mater; she'll tell him what to do."

"In that case I hope she gets him to send me home tomorrow — ahead of the rest of you. I've got arrangements to make down there. You could help, actually, sis."

"Me? But I don't want to be sent home before ..."

"No! You could find some way of hinting to the mater that my one dread at the moment is of being sent home at once — leaving poor little Gemma to their tender mercies."

"Poor little Gemma!" she echoed sarcastically. "Materkins won't believe that!"

"I must go and look for her now. D'you know what all that business was — why Mam'selle left in such a hurry?"

Beatrice shook her head. "She tried to gabble some explanation to me but there wasn't time — and it didn't make sense, anyway. Why? D'you know what happened?"

"I wasn't actually there but it seems that Mam'selle tried to poison the mater against Gemma in some way. And it obviously didn't work."

"Didn't work? That's putting it mildly. I'd say it blew up in her face by the look of things."

A rather breathless Tabitha found him at that moment and warned Peter that his father was searching for him — and looking rather grim.

Peter thanked her and slipped away, making for the upstairs rooms where the lady's maids were waiting to be needed.

"I thought you'd never come!" Gemma said as she walked halfway down the passage to meet him.

"Let's go out for a stroll," he suggested. "I was trying to find out why my father was so angry. Now I know."

"He discovered about you and that money," she said.

"You've heard?"

"No, but what else could it be? Shall we take a hansom and close the blind — there's less chance of being noticed."

He took her arm. "And more chance of kissing."

"That, too." She patted his hand as they strolled out into the alley behind the building.

Still arm in arm they walked slowly up the street to Pembridge Square, where most of the carriages were parked. Groups of drivers had gathered here and there around the square, gossiping, smoking, taking nips from hipflasks, looking for some sort of amusement. They found it, of course, in the sight of a young toff in earnest conversation with a lady's maid. And they were not shy in coming forward with advice on both the keeping and the taking of a girl's honour.

Among them, however, was a hansom cabby who could sniff a fare almost before it came in sight. "Trip round the park, sir?" he cried out. "Nice and slow, eh? Luvverly evening!"

To more ribald laughter they accepted his offer, and the loafing drivers almost collapsed in hysterics when the man solemnly explained how the blinds could be lowered and secured.

"Oh, England! England!" Peter exclaimed as they set off — with the blinds open. "If I were in footman's livery or if you were in lady's evening dress, we wouldn't be worth a single raised eyebrow. But put a swell and a maidservant together and they fall about like baboons." He smiled at her. "Shall we close the blinds — since the man was so kind as to …"

"Not just yet," she said. "Business first. It's darker than I thought out here, anyway. What d'you think your father will do now? He must guess it can only come from gambling. He'll try and get the money back off you, surely?"

He shook his head. "I think he must already know it has all been put in your name."

"Oh, my gidge!"

"You can pass it all on to Carteret, if you like. He'd look after it for us. I've got to know him quite well since Derby Day. Or give it to Sapphire, of course."

Gemma sat several inches taller. "No," she said. "It doesn't matter whether they know I've got it or not. I've already decided to give in my notice. I'll let your mother know about it tomorrow."

Excitement and alarm mingled within him. "Isn't that a bit sudden? Why not wait until we're back home?"

She told him what had happened that evening on their way to the Empire Rooms and why Mam'selle had departed in such unseemly haste.

When he had finished laughing he fell silent rather swiftly and hung his head. "I, too, did not know you speak French."

"Why should you?" she responded. "I'd have told you if you'd asked. I wasn't deliberately keeping it from you — not from *you*. It's just that we've had so few opportunities to get to know each other. But that'll change now. That's why I'm giving in my notice. I'll leave at once, as soon as we're in Falmouth."

"You'll forgo your wages," he warned her solemnly.

"Ten shillings! I shall just have to grin and bear it."

"And then? No doubt you have something nice planned for the pair of us?"

"Oh, don't worry about me," she replied, reaching up and tugging at the bows that held the blinds. "I'll easily get a place somewhere else — perhaps even with Mrs Roanoke. Sally Kelynack has fallen for a valet who says he's as good as certain he can get her a place at …"

"No!" he exclaimed. "Absolutely not!"

She smiled to herself in the dark and said, "What, then?"

"I have a better idea. You remember the question I asked you at the Derby — the one you said you wouldn't answer?"

"Yes."

"Well, I think I know it, anyway. Stop me the moment I say something that's not true. I think you've loved me almost as long as I've loved you, which was pretty much from the very first day." He paused for her to contradict; all she did was squeeze his arm. "What held you back, though, was ... well, two things. First, you were afraid it was just a flash in the pan with me — maybe Roger Deveril was equally convinced he was in love with Sapphire, or Ruby as she then was, in the beginning. And, second, when you realized it wasn't a flash in the pan for me, you became afraid of marrying me and becoming the next Mrs de Vivian. You heard my parents' sneers about the tooth-puller's daughter and you were afraid of even worse sneers behind *your* back." He paused. "Still no contradiction?"

"Still no contradiction," she replied. "I suppose you think I'm just being stupid!"

"Well, to be quite honest with you, Gemma — and I hope we always will be quite honest with each other — I have to answer yes. I *do* think it's stupid. You devalue your own character by thinking that way. Your spirit, your backbone, is ... is ... I mean, in sheer character you *tower* over those moral pygmies who might sneer at you. Their sneers would tell the world everything about them and nothing whatsoever about you — so there! That's my humble opinion, doctor — what's yours?"

She drew breath sharply, no doubt to argue that, even if what he said were true, those 'pygmies' still ruled the roost. To prevent the argument from deteriorating into a squabble of that kind, he added, hastily, "However — I know better than to try to talk you out of a conviction like that. I realize that only time can show you how much you're really worth. So — if you won't join me on the bridge, I'll come down and join you on the lower decks!"

"Really?" she asked. "Oh, Peter! Do you really mean it?"

For a moment he was too astonished to answer; he had expected some argument from her at the very least; most of all he had expected blank incomprehension.

"You don't really mean it," she concluded from his silence.

"Of course I do," he answered hastily. "That's what I'm going to arrange if I can provoke my father into rusticating me tomorrow. If not, it must wait until next week. Either way, I'm going to rent some old boathouse or sail-loft where I can transfer the *Gem* and all my tools. I'll build her and sail her and win every race against much superior craft ... and so pile up the orders. And meanwhile I'll live at home to keep them sweet, and I'll pretend I've got over my silly infatuation with you, at least until October the twelfth."

"And then?"

"The twelfth is a Sunday this year, so, if you're still agreeable at that time — after getting to know me a great deal better, I hope — we'll call the banns that very morning and get married four weeks later, in November. And you can be Mrs de Vivian, the boatbuilder's wife — and let who dare look down on you!"

Utter silence greeted this suggestion.

"Well?" he asked.

She sniffed heavily.

"I say!" He gave an embarrassed laugh and slipped his arm about her. "Nothing to cry about, old girl!"

But his faltering voice belied his own words as he choked on the last of them.

Tears mingled as they caressed each other, cheek to cheek. "You'd do that for me?" she asked in a whisper.

"Oh, God, Gemma, sometimes I feel so much love for you inside me that I think I'm going to burst with it."

"I know! I know!" she said, breaking down and crying as if her heart had, indeed, already broken.

"Don't be silly!" He giggled and cried at the same time, fishing out his handkerchief and mixing their tears in its fibres. "I'm never going to wash this hanky," he said.

It was the one most bathetic, domestic touch that could have saved her from a fit of almost unquenchable weeping; instead she burst out laughing, choked, coughed, and so calmed down at last.

"I doubt I shall ever deserve you," she sighed, settling her head against his shoulder.

He thought of telling her the rest of his dream — how the boatbuilding thing was only to fill the time until no one could stop their marriage. Then, as man and wife, they would travel the world together, just as he had described it to Jenny that morning. But he held it back for some future occasion, of which he hoped there would be plenty over the coming summer.

"I have never done the slightest thing to deserve you," he replied as he stuck a finger beneath her chin and lifted her face to his again.

Her lips were so soft and warm and vital that they seemed to assume an independent life, especially there in the dark; they had a hunger all their own; they devoured his mouth with a passion that would have astonished anyone who knew her rather prim, controlled, everyday self. Her whole body shuddered against him. And then, somehow, her hand was inside his tail-coat and her nails were scratching his back like cat's talons. He wanted to unbutton her bodice, to scratch her back in the same ecstatic way but, fearing she would misinterpret the action, he took her head between his hands and ran his fingers through her hair, raking his nails gently across the taut skin of her scalp above and behind her ears.

She removed her lips from his long enough to gasp for breath and cry out in ecstasy. Then she fell on him again, this time with open mouth. Her tongue touched his lips and retreated again. Cautiously he followed after it with his own. The moment she felt it there her lips closed around it and she sucked at it like a starveling. The symbolism was not lost on him — nor, he suspected, on her. Neither of them mentioned it, however, when, having kissed and sighed to exhaustion, they collapsed against the worn upholstery, panting in a happy stupor.

Somewhere nearby a clock chimed the half-hour. "Crikey!" he exclaimed suddenly. "It's almost time for my dance with Mrs Roanoke!"

He found his cane and tapped the roof. When the cabby opened the trap he told the man to get back to the Empire Rooms as soon as he could.

"That won't be difficult, sir," the fellow replied with a laugh. "I assume you'll be wanting to walk the last part yourselves?"

They opened the blinds to discover they were still in Pembridge Square — and had, indeed, been going round and round it all this while. A cheer went up from the loafers, who had been enjoying the spectacle.

"No!" Peter said grandly. "Drive us up to the front. Stop directly in front of the foyer, if you please."

"You're the boss, squire," the man replied dubiously.

"Are you sure, Peter?" Gemma asked.

"Let's nail our colours to the mast, eh?"

But, as sometimes happens when people try to make grand gestures, there was no one there to observe their arrival — except a lone commissionaire. And he had seen everything in his time.

36 Guinevere was waiting for Peter, alone, at the edge of the dance floor; he reached her side just as the violins were retuning. "You cut it fine, I must say!" she exclaimed. "Hiding from your father?"

"Something like that," he replied as they glided out on to the floor. "You're looking radiant tonight."

"I'll come to that," she said, smiling mysteriously. "First tell me what's been going on among the de Vivians this evening. No Mam'selle. And your father and mother closeted together like a pair of Balkan anarchists. Something's afoot."

She listened in rapt silence as he outlined that evening's dramas. Her first comment surprised him. "Didn't you know that Gemma speaks French?" she asked.

"Did you?" he replied.

"Well, all right — I can't claim I'd *generally* know such things. I had Miss Isco-Visco to tea just before we came away. She's Gemma's teacher. She told me. All the same, I'm surprised *you* didn't know."

"To my shame. I said as much to her. Anyway, we are about to have as many opportunities as we could wish for — to get to know each other." And he went on to outline his and Gemma's plans for the next few months; he also told her about his dream of travelling the world at random with her once they were man and wife.

Guinevere was amused — and slightly jealous. "Suppose you get to know each other so well between now and October that you decide not to get married after all?" she asked archly.

"Well, Guinevere," he replied, "at the risk of giving you a hurtful reply — wouldn't it still be much better to find out such things *before* tying the knot?"

"Touché," she said bleakly. Then, brightening suddenly, she added, "But I haven't told you *my* good news."

He waited, but she said no more.

"Well?" he prompted.

"When we reach those twin pillars," she replied. "If there's no one beyond them, I'll tell you there."

There was no one beyond them. "You remarked just now that I'm looking radiant," she said. "Well, there's a very good reason. You will, I hope, be delighted to hear that I am in what is called 'an interesting condition'." She grinned from ear to ear.

He understood her at once but it took a moment or two longer for the understanding to sink in, to mean something. "You're pleased," he said, slightly dazed still. "Well then — so am I, of course."

"Of *course* you are!" She laughed at the implication that it could be otherwise.

He blanched. "You mean ... *I?* ... That I ..."

"Who else?" She looked at him accusingly. "What sort of woman d'you think I am?"

"Well ..." He almost choked on his embarrassment. "Of course, I didn't think *that!*"

"Liar!" She grinned and pressed his nose like a bell-button. "That's exactly what you thought! But I'm so happy I'll forgive you just this once."

"Well, that's the main thing, isn't it," he said. "To be happy. How will Roanoke take it?"

Her grin took on a savage colour. "He'll fume and fret and gnash his teeth — but he won't be able to do a thing about it."

Peter felt a sudden chill in his stomach. "What d'you mean?"

"What I say. The last thing he'll be able to do — publicly — is admit it's not his!"

"But surely you'll ... er, I mean ... you know ... when you get back home, you'll ... you and him ... as soon as possible ..."

She let him flounder around the unsayable suggestion awhile before she rescued him with a laugh — a compassionless, vengeful laugh that made his blood run cold. "I would fly a hundred miles before I let him get within six feet of me!"

He took a step back from her. "You mean to say we ... I mean, just that one time?" he asked.

"One *occasion!*" she corrected him. "We lost count of the number of *times,* if you remember? Even so, once is enough — as many a ruin'd maid can confirm."

A further thought struck him. "It's only been ... what? Two months? I don't know much about these things, but can you be absolutely certain?"

"Oh, don't you worry about that! I am certain."

"You just *used* me," he complained.

"Diddums!" she replied. "Don't try and claim all the virtues, my dear. We used each other. You'll make Gemma a better husband for having spent that night with me — and you know it!" Her voice trailed off and a distant look came into her eyes!

"What now?" he asked suspiciously.

"I've just had a thought. Your parents can't possibly keep Gemma on after what happened tonight. And Sally Kelynack has given me her notice. She's fallen in love and has the offer of a place in London as a married maid with a chauffeur-valet husband. So ... what if ..."

"No!" he said.

"Don't you think that's for Gemma to decide? Or are you going to be one of those husbands whose word is law and whose fist enforces it?" Guinevere was remembering that Gemma had seen Peter going into the old governess's room with her that night; it would be an exquisite tease to make the girl her lady's maid and then watch her response as she slowly became aware of her, Guinevere's, 'interesting condition'! In fact, whose condition would be the more interesting then!

"Well," she said vaguely, "it was just a thought."

Any further thoughts along those lines came to a halt at that moment. With a cry of "Gotcha, at last!" his father pounced on him from behind one of the twin pillars. Fortunately it was the one on the open, or ballroom, side, so Peter knew he could not have been hiding there all this while.

"Where have you *been,* Pater?" he asked, as if it were his father who had been avoiding him all evening.

"Oh," his father jeered, "you must think you're the smartest man in town, my boy. But while you've been skulking around this place ..."

"Need Mrs Roanoke be bored by this homily?"

His father turned and apologized to Guinevere, saying she might stay or go as she pleased. The whole world would know soon enough, anyway.

Guinevere said that, in that case, she'd stay.

He turned back to his son. "While you've been skulking around here, trying to avoid us, we have been busy, your mother and I. There is a cab outside, waiting to take us to Paddington, where you'll take the eleven-fifteen stopping train to Cornwall."

"The sleeper leaves at midnight," Peter said, hiding his glee.

"You are not going on the sleeper. You will travel in the second class, sitting up all night. It will give you time to reflect on your transgressions."

"You have no right to interfere with my life like this!" Peter said angrily.

Several people around turned to stare. His father pushed him behind the pillar. "Don't you dare raise your voice to me like that! Until you are twenty-one we have *every* right to control and discipline you. And you would do well to remember it.

Peter was so happy he almost forgot to make his nostrils flare and to breathe like a fighting bull and to glower in angry, impotent silence.

"That's better," the old man said. "Now I want you to control yourself like a gentleman while you cross the ballroom floor with me. You will smile to right and left until we are in the cab. And then I shall give you further instructions. Come on!"

"My hat and coat ..." Peter started to say.

"They're already in the cab," his father called back to him.

"Call of nature," Peter tried as they reached the staircase.

"We'll be at Paddington inside ten minutes," replied his implacable father.

The cab was the same one he and Gemma had ridden in earlier; he recognized the driver. "You should enter the yo-yo championships," he told the fellow — who responded with a hearty laugh.

"What's that about?" his father asked suspiciously.

"It's the same cab as brought me from the Wilkeses' place," he explained, winking at the driver with the eye his father couldn't see. He was glad he'd tipped the fellow generously earlier. It was important to have the man's cooperation.

His father's tone moderated once they were in the cab. "Look, young chap," he said, "we don't mean to be hard on you. Some parents would punish you for punishment's sake but we aren't like that, your mother and I. This is for your own good. I know you won't see it like that at the moment, but in the fullness of time — believe me — you'll come to bless us."

Peter let the words wash over him. They would, after all, form the basis for his 'conversion' to their point of view over the next few months — until the twelfth of October, in fact. He began to sit up and take more notice, however, when his father started talking about his 'infatuation' for Miss Penhallow.

"We've all felt such stirrings in our loins, my boy," he said. "A pretty girl is a pretty girl no matter *what* class she comes from."

"Or ends up in," Peter added.

"It never works, you know. A servant girl could marry a chief cashier or a teacher or someone of that class. These things aren't absolutely rigid, thank heavens. We're not Hindoos. But for a servant girl to leap all the way up to *our* class is ..."

"Whores have become duchesses before now, Pater."

"Yes, but they were the *king's* whores. Don't quibble! However, I'm glad you've mentioned whores. *There's* your answer! These urges you feel are only natural in a fit, healthy young fellow. And it's also natural to mistake them for sacred love. But that's what whores are for — in your case, anyway. They're the safety valve on a young man's boiler. I'm prepared to guarantee to you that, if you'll just engage the services of a pretty little *fille de joie* — 'whore' is such an ugly word, don't you think? — I guarantee that all this pent-up steam which is driving you toward thoughts of sacred love and Miss Penhallow will entirely dissipate ..."

"Dissipate is the *mot juste,* I think," Peter said coldly.

"Yes," his father sighed. "There is an undoubted danger that you will become addicted to such debauchery. But you're a sensible, level-headed fellow, so I believe it's a very small danger. Far better to run that risk than the certain life of misery you'd endure in a marriage across the yawning chasm of class — a marriage that can *never* prosper."

He drew out his change-purse and emptied it dramatically into his hand — quite a pile of silver and gold. "Here's all I have," he said as he tipped it into Peter's pocket. "When you get to Falmouth and have thoroughly rested from the strains of tonight's uncomfortable journey, I want you to go to Vernon Place — you know where that is?"

"It rings a bell," Peter said vaguely. "Somewhere beyond the Roanokes' house?"

"You'll find it anyway. I'm told that every house in that whole terrace is a *maison de plaisir*. Go there and pick the prettiest filly you see and get her to lower your temperature a bit. Don't part with more than ten shillings, mind — or twenty-five if you stay all night. And a half-crown tip if she's *very* good. *Then* we'll see how keen you are to ruin the life of a bright, intelligent, and above all virtuous servant girl — not to mention your own. Promise me, now?"

"If you command it, Pater!" He sighed — and told himself it was not exactly a promise.

"There's a good fellow. I envy you in a way. But we'll say no more about it. You'll find that Society is wise in the arrangements it decrees for dealing with these unfortunate impulses."

When they arrived at Paddington, de Vivian went to pay the cabby — and then remembered that his purse was empty. Smiling, Peter leaped up on the step to pay the man, instead — taking the opportunity to murmur, "Say nothing for the moment but go directly to Royal Oak and wait for me there!"

The man bade him a cheery goodnight and said he definitely would enter that yo-yo competition. Peter then had the exquisite pleasure of offering his father a couple of half-crowns for the cab fare back to the Empire Rooms; but the old man declined, saying he'd probably be able to rustle up some loose change when he got there.

There were ten pretty sticky minutes until the stopping train departed. His father insisted on staying there not simply until the train pulled away but until it had gathered enough speed to make it impossible for Peter to jump out again. What he could not prevent, however, was a pull on the communication cord, like the one that brought the train to an unscheduled halt at Royal Oak, a mile out from Paddington. Peter dropped the five-shilling fine 'for improper use' into the hand of an exasperated guard and went out into the Harrow Road.

"Good man!" he cried to the cabby, who was waiting, as instructed. "Back to Paddington, please — in time for the midnight sleeper!"

37 Gemma waited all that week for some kind of axe to fall. The de Vivians knew that Peter had opened a bank account in her name and had paid six hundred pounds into it; they also knew that she had connived at it by supplying specimen signatures. And, in case they sought final proof, she left the pass book and other papers in − not behind − the drawer Mam'selle had told Mrs de Vivian to investigate. She laid a small handkerchief diagonally across its corner and, when next she looked, it was still diagonal but the pass book had been carelessly tucked in between the folds rather than beneath the whole thing.

What further proof did they need?

But still nothing was said. In fact, Mrs de Vivian now behaved as if Mam'selle had never existed. Gemma asked Beatrice to discover if her terminal salary had been sent after her − and had there been a generous *bonne bouche?*

Beatrice said she very much doubted it. The salary would no doubt be sent in due course, but why should the creature get a penny extra?

Gemma begged her to ask, nonetheless.

Beatrice returned with the slightly mysterious message that it would all be dealt with as the family's best interests dictated − and that Gemma would certainly be informed of it at the right and proper moment.

The right and proper moment came at last when they were on the train back to Cornwall. When they alighted to stretch their legs at Exeter, Gemma was surprised to see Mrs de Vivian making a beeline for her; she was even more surprised when the woman issued an invitation to take tea with her in the restaurant car, once the train set off again.

After Exeter, the GWR mainline runs southward, down the western bank of the Exe, through Starcross and Dawlish Warren, where the river's broad estuary opens into the English Channel. Nervously Gemma picked her way along the corridors of the intervening coaches, arriving just after the train thundered over the Exe bridge. Her mistress was already seated and waiting.

"I think we'll have everything, don't you?" she said. "Toasted teacakes, scones with strawberry jam and clotted cream, fruit cake, and tea. Darjeeling? Or do you prefer China?"

Gemma, who had kept her eyes and ears open during her time in London, said that if they had Lapsang Souchong, she would prefer it. She took her seat as daintily as she knew how and hoped her nervousness did not show. She was in no doubt but that she was on some kind of trial here; she did not dare hope it was to assess her suitability as a de Vivian (in *their* terms), though, naturally, she could not entirely suppress the thought, either.

Mrs de Vivian ordered China tea for both and smiled at Gemma as if she had passed a small initial test. "First of all, Miss Penhallow," she said when the waiter had gone, "I gather you are worried that Mam'selle should be well 'looked after,' as the saying is?"

"I think a French maid can do a great deal of harm with her tongue, ma'am," Gemma replied. "And there is one time-honoured way of ensuring that she doesn't — that's all."

Her mistress thought this over and said, "You're right. I shall take care of it tomorrow. What, in your opinion, would be an adequate *bonne bouche?*"

Gemma demurred. "D'you think that's for me to say?"

"In ordinary circumstances, no, of course not. But these are not ordinary circumstances, are they?"

Gemma stared out of the window. The receding tide had revealed the gaunt skeletons of half a dozen beached ships in varying stages of decay. Some flew seaweed like pennants; others were perches for evil-eyed seagulls, the rats of the foreshore. "I suppose twenty guineas would seem quite adequate to her."

"That's what you would send, is it — in my place?"

"No, ma'am." Gemma looked the woman in the face. "I'd send ten, and, in the accompanying letter, I'd somehow let her know I wouldn't be mentioning her little trick with the distress-letter from her sister to any other lady."

Mrs de Vivian smiled, rather grimly, Gemma thought; these answers were not entirely to her liking. Suddenly all her nervousness was cured; she discovered she did not care what the woman thought of her — not even as a mother-in-law. She doubted Peter would ever communicate with her — or even be allowed to — once the banns were read. Roll on, November!

A station flashed by.

"Starcross!" Mrs de Vivian murmured. "How appropriate! That is what I really wish to talk to you about, Miss Penhallow. Star-crossed lovers and all that. Ah, here comes our tea." With a little flick of her finger she indicated that the waiter was to serve Gemma first.

"Shall I be mother?" Gemma picked up the teapot while the waiter helped them to the teacakes.

Mrs de V looked daggers at her and Gemma knew she was longing to say, 'Not if *I* have anything to do with it!' Suddenly she was weary of all this delicate shadow boxing.

"I'll bring your scones directly, ladies," the waiter said.

The moment he had gone, Gemma said, "I think it only fair to tell you, Mrs de Vivian, that your son, Peter, has asked for my hand in marriage."

"And?" Her face could have been carved in stone for all the life there was in it.

"I told him I have no intention of being sneered at behind my back by all the high-quarter folk in Cornwall."

And now, indeed, there was animation in that basilisk mask! Ada's face was suddenly garlanded with smiles. "Oh, Miss Penhallow!" she exclaimed. "I should have known! From the moment I met you I have always regarded you as sensible and level-headed far beyond your years. Indeed, far beyond your station in life. And once again you prove me right in my judgement. But then I am so rarely wrong — though I say it myself, and I shouldn't. God knows I am no snob. I am probably the least snobbish lady of my class that you could possibly meet. But even I, admiring you as I do, and loving my own son as I do … even I had to snigger at the notion that you and he might marry. Well!" She rubbed her hands gleefully as the waiter again approached them, this time with a plate of scones, strawberry jam, and clotted Cornish cream. "Let us enjoy this royal repast!" she went on. "Your eminent good sense has spared me what I was dreading, namely a painful and melancholy interview at the end of which I should have been forced to behave in an utterly uncharacteristic fashion — by putting my foot down and absolutely forbidding such a marriage."

Gemma, who was wearing lace mittens, delicately wiped the butter from her teacake off her fingertips and said mildly, "So he has decided to join the working classes instead." She craned her neck to peer back along the line and added, "Starcross is out of sight already!"

And, indeed, they had reached the point where the line curves sharply westward to follow the Channel coast — quite literally, for the rails there lie on an elevated road between the bright red cliffs of Devonian sandstone and the tidal sands; and, where rocky headlands jut into the sea, it leads straight through their heart in a series of short, surprising tunnels.

Mrs de Vivian's exclamation of shocked surprise coincided with the first of these tunnels; she had to put her hand to her mouth to stop a bit of teacake from falling out. It left a buttery stain on her glove, which annoyed her doubly. "That's your fault!" she snapped. "Well, you'll have to get it clean again."

"I doubt if I will," Gemma said. "Be required to get it clean, I mean. I see no future for myself at Alma Terrace."

The woman swallowed her mouthful so precipitately that it made her eyes water. "You mean ..." she squeaked before pausing to take a sip of tea. "You mean you are *not* intending to hand over this sum of money he has given you? But I naturally assumed that would be part of your ..."

Gemma stopped trying to smile politely. The temperature dropped several degrees. "I think you had better make up your mind as to what — exactly — your objections are, Mrs de Vivian. My marriage to your son? My possession of our money? His freely expressed desire to engage in honest toil?"

"All of it!" She raised her voice to such an extent that she began to attract attention. "Now look what you've made me do," she added more quietly. "I object to all of it, of course. That money is *not* yours to keep."

"I think the law will say otherwise."

"And as for this preposterous idea of his becoming a common labourer ..."

"I did not say that. I agree. The idea *would* be preposterous."

"What, then? I distinctly heard you say ..."

"Honest toil. He will design and build racing boats for his rich friends. I think we shall be quite comfortably off once we get properly established."

Mrs de Vivian's expression was blank again but her thoughts were racing. Why had she never thought of this? It was so obvious once the girl had said it. Peter could, indeed, make a living as a designer and builder of racing yachts. *And* he had enough rich friends to keep him in clover. What a fool she had been to ignore something so obvious! However, it called for a completely different approach to this formidable young lady if she was to prevent her marriage to Peter.

She smiled. "But why didn't you tell me that at once?" she asked in a jovially accusing manner. "Why has Peter never said a word about it?"

She was glad to see that this new approach had Gemma rattled. "You mean you wouldn't mind?" the girl asked.

"Mind? Why, it would be the crowning of him, as my Irish ... er, nanny used to say. The crowning of him. He's so good at it — well, you hardly need me to tell you that. And it's the one thing he's really interested in."

Gemma stared out of the window. Were those children down there with their buckets and spades real? Or was this just a dream? Could the sea really carve these rocks into such phantasmagorical shapes? Could any sort of stone in nature be quite so red?

"Did you truly think we'd object?" Mrs de Vivian said.

"You don't? Honestly?"

The woman wanted to skirt around questions of honesty, however. "Listen!" she said. "I quite agree with you about your continuing as lady's maid — a most unsuitable position for a future daughter-in-law. Let me see ... suppose I were to make you my companion, instead? That way, you may accompany me on all my social calls in Falmouth and I shall be saying, in effect, to the Foxes, the Stantons, the Trevartons, and the Dicks — and all the other high-and-mighty ladies of the district — that I regard you as deserving acceptance among them. It would be a sort of halfway house, you see. Although ..." She fell silent and her eyes clouded.

"Although what?" Gemma asked.

"Nothing!" Whatever troubled her, she brushed it aside. "Think it over," she concluded.

"I believe I know what you were going to say," Gemma told her. "You were thinking that there might not be much point in it, anyway — trying to get me accepted — because as long as Peter was going to be working with mallet and chisel, and glue and nails, neither of us would be acceptable, anyway." She smiled as if to say: 'Tell me I'm wrong!'

"Oh, but you're wrong there," the woman assured her. "He's still a de Vivian. If he designs the best racing yachts afloat, people will think of him as a designer first and a craftsman second — like Lutyens or Sir George Gilbert Scott in architecture. Lutyens will get a knighthood before long — you'll see. Peter could, too, if he designs yachts that win the big international prizes for England!" She smiled conspiratorially at Gemma. "You would become *Lady* de Vivian, eh! *Then* let them sneer behind your back!"

She pretended to believe that no one would jeer at Gemma then but she was glad to see, from the girl's glum response, that she did not believe it.

"You don't seem too happy at the prospect?" Ada said after a while. "Hadn't it occurred to you?"

Gemma shook her head.

"But that's not like you, Miss Penhallow." She was concerned now. "What else has not occurred to you, I wonder? I suppose you and my son have spent many clandestine hours together ... discussing these plans from every possible angle?" She laughed to show she did not really mind — considering how happily it had all turned out.

"No," Gemma murmured. "We hardly had the chance."

"Oh, dear!" Mrs de Vivian bit her lip and gazed out of the window in mild embarrassment.

"What?" Gemma asked anxiously.

"Well, if you haven't discussed it very much ..." she began. Then, apparently thinking better of it, she started a different sentence: "He *is* rather given to sudden wild enthusiasms, you know. He is a most impetuous boy — and in many ways he *is* still a boy. Well — he gave you proof of that the very moment he set eyes on you!" She laughed. "Wasn't that an embarrassing day!"

"What are you suggesting?"

"Far be it from me to suggest *anything,* my dear. You, as I say, are the most sensible, level-headed young woman I have ever known, and Peter — well, he will come of age quite soon, God help us all! There comes a time when we grown-ups must sit back and keep our mouths shut." She smiled. "Speak only when spoken to! As in childhood. They call it 'second childhood,' don't they!"

"And if I speak to you now, Mrs de Vivian? If ask you what you think I should do …?"

"In your place? My — that's twice we've changed places already — it must not become a habit! But seriously, my dear. I think, if I were in your shoes, I'd go away somewhere quiet and have a good long think about it. You've got enough money …"

"Think about what?"

"Well, for instance, are you quite sure about Peter's staying power? He is such a *young* man."

"I'm not the one who made him decide about boatbuilding. He offered that of his own free choice."

"After what? I mean, did it just come out of the blue? Had he mentioned marriage to you before that?"

"*Had* he?" Gemma asked sarcastically.

"So he had asked you to marry him! And what did you reply? Not if it meant living in Society?"

"That sort of thing," she agreed uncomfortably.

"And *then* he came up with this idea of … how did you put it? Joining the toiling classes?"

"I suppose so, yes."

"So he did it to please *you,* mainly. You more-or-less made it a condition of accepting his proposal?"

Gemma nodded unhappily for she could clearly see what Mrs de V was driving at. "In effect, yes."

"Well, these are the things I'd ponder if I were you. Since it's not really *his* idea, but rather one you've as good as forced upon him, how long d'you think he'll stick it? Suppose the orders *don't* come pouring in? Nothing in the larder … maybe a little de Vivian on the way …"

"You wouldn't help?"

"Of *course* we would! The very idea! You *must* think we're monsters. But he's a proud young man and it would be a bitter pill to him to have to accept our charity for *your* sake. Are you sure he wouldn't then start recalling that it was *you* who insisted on this failed way of life?" She shook her head at the general sadness of things. "I'd also like to make sure that my own conscience was quite clear — again, putting myself in your place. Do I really have the right to insist that Peter should make such a sacrifice ..."

"But it's the one thing he truly wants to do!"

"That's what he says — *now* — in the first flush of his love for you. But listen!" She grinned conspiratorially. "I'll tell you how you may test him."

"How?" Gemma was ready to clutch at any straw by now.

"Tell him you've withdrawn your objections. He can stay at home and go on building boats just as a hobby. You'll still marry him — and just learn to put up with all those sneers, somehow. Tell him that and see if he's still quite so keen on this idea, which you claim is his and his alone!"

Gemma said nothing, pretending she was momentarily busy with spreading the clotted cream.

"You're not so sure now, are you!" her tormentor said. "Mind you, I'm not suggesting I'm right. And I'm certainly not trying to put answers into your head. All I'm saying is that you should think these things over — and be absolutely sure about your answers — before you tie that irrevocable knot."

"You're right," Gemma said glumly. She tried to take a bite of her scone and found her appetite had quite disappeared.

"You have plenty of money now," Mrs de Vivian pointed out. "You could take rooms somewhere — in Penzance, say, or Newquay — and not communicate with him until you're sure."

"Not communicate with him?" Gemma was horrified.

"It's your decision, of course, my dear. But you know what an *enthusiast* he is. Even if you communicate with him by some roundabout means, through a third party, or even through several parties, he'd drop everything and give nobody any rest until he'd wormed your whereabouts out of them."

By now Gemma felt herself boxed in from every angle; but the woman was right. Peter was, indeed, given to sudden enthusiasms. He might very well repent of the whole thing if life played its usual trick of kicking them in the teeth. She had to be sure of him before she made those irrevocable promises.

"If I tell *you* where I am," she said, "will you call me back if anything happens?"

"What d'you mean?"

"You know — if Peter falls ill or gets hurt or something. God forbid — but just in case it does?"

"Yes, my dear! Of *course,* I will. Where will you be?"

"In Penzance. I'll find a boarding house there somewhere. I've got a cousin there — a second-cousin to my mother — James Collett. He has the photographer's studio there. You can always send a message to him."

"James Collett, photography studios, Penzance! Market Jew Street, I believe?" Mrs de Vivian tapped her brow. "It's as good as written in indelible ink."

"And you will tell Peter I've gone away to think it over?"

"I won't say where."

"But you will tell him — promise?"

"Promise," Ada replied, making a mental note that no precise time was stated for its fulfilment. Nineteen-sixty-seven would do nicely, she thought — on her hundredth birthday.

38 The de Vivians alighted at Truro for the branch line to Falmouth; Gemma stayed aboard to complete her journey to the western terminus at Penzance. She did not entirely trust Mrs de Vivian, though it went against the grain of her upbringing to doubt the word of a lady. So she also told Trewithen of her plans for the immediate future. She also wrote a note for him to deliver to Peter, explaining what she was doing — and why. To reinforce its message she also told Trewithen that he was to beg Peter not to come and visit her except in the most extraordinary circumstances.

Trewithen, who had undertaken some researches of his own during his days off in London, had a suspicion that 'the most extraordinary circumstances' might not be too long in arriving; but first he needed to cover himself, secure his own escape routes, and make a little intelligent provision for his old age. So he said nothing about it to Gemma before they parted at Truro.

Peter had meanwhile slaved away at his racing dinghy, burning the midnight oil and the pre-dawn oil as well. By the afternoon of the Friday on which Gemma was to return (together with the rest of the family, to be sure), he had removed the cellar window, hauled out the hull, shaped the mast, stepped it, rigged it, demounted it again, and hauled it on a flat dray to a mooring at Custom House Quay. His plan was to meet Gemma off the train and take her directly to the little harbour for a quick sail along the waterfront and back. On his way to the station he passed Billy Trevaskis, a local handyman who had agreed to replace the cellar window and repaint it for a pound.

"Trevaskis!" he cried.

The man started guiltily, recognized him, broke into a cheerful smile, and called back, "I'm on my way up your place this very minute, boss!" — which, considering he was trundling his little handcart in the opposite direction, and that the said handcart was laden with panes of glass and a tin of putty, was rather hard for Peter to swallow. "Immediately after I done this li'l-ole job, o'course," he added.

Peter was too excited at the thought of seeing Gemma again, after four year-long days and nights of separation, to argue. He arrived at the station with almost half an hour to spare. He walked up and down the empty platform for five minutes, went back outside, checked his pony and dogcart, let the creature have its nosebag, and walked over the hill to the seashore between Pendennis Castle and the Falmouth Hôtel.

The horizon was never free from sail or smoke. Even the big passenger liners from Southampton stayed within a few miles of the Cornish coast, ready to turn at the Scillies for Queenstown or New York. One day soon he and Gemma would be on one of them ... or no. They'd be on one of those sailing ships, slow cargo carriers with a few cheap cabins at the stern for economy-minded passengers. He leaned against the railings of the clifftop path and imagined they were the taffrail of just such a vessel and that Gemma was at his side ... with no turbines thundering away, shaking the decks beneath them, just the swirl and gurgle of the water beneath them and the soughing of the wind in the rigging above and the creaking of her planks and masts. And all the time in the world before them.

The whistle of the train as it came through the cutting at Spernen Wyn brought him sharply back to the here-and-now; he had to run all the way back to the station, arriving just in time to see it round the final bend. The platform, which had been deserted when he first arrived, was now quite bustling, for this was the connection to the London express and the holiday season was at its height.

At a snail's pace the little branch-line saddle-tank engine puffed and wheezed into the station on skirts of steam. But its very slowness allowed him to pick out the second-class carriages and to move toward the point where they would finally grind to a halt. He waved to his sister and parents as their first-class carriage trundled by but he held his ground and kept an unblinking gaze on the eight doors of the leading second-class coach, one of which, he prayed, would open and release — no, it would *radiate* — the rarest, sweetest, most wonderful girl in all the world.

Every door along the full length of the train seemed to open at once. Ladies and gentlemen of fashion descended from the first class and looked back along the platform, hoping to see that those hand-picked servants they had brought along were already diligently sorting out the luggage, snapping up porters, and generally smoothing their paths on this, the most tedious part of any holiday. Peter, in the thick of all that activity, sought with increasing desperation among the milling valets and lady's maids for the only one among them who mattered.

His heart skipped several beats when, at last, he spied Trewithen. Heedless of whom he bumped into or forced to swerve from the line of duty, he ran toward him, crying out, "Trewithen! I say, Trewithen! Where is Miss Penhallow?"

The man avoided a surreptitious glance toward the first class but he inclined his head in that direction and said quietly, "Try not to appear concerned, sir. We'll sort out our luggage, you and I, and I'll explain while we do so. D'you understand?"

"She's all right?"

Trewithen spoke over his shoulder as he led the way to the luggage vans. "She was smiling when last I saw her, sir."

"In London?"

"No. In Truro, about forty-five minutes ago. Do try not to look so agitated, sir. I have a note from her, which I will pass to you when it is safe to do so."

That moment arrived a short while later, when he and Peter had shouldered their way into the van that held the de Vivian luggage. "I should wait until you know you're alone before you open it, sir. Miss Penhallow was most insistent that your parents should know nothing of it." He cleared his throat. "Also there is the danger to my own position to consider."

Reluctantly, Peter stuffed the envelope into his pocket and set about helping Trewithen with the luggage before going up the platform to join his parents. "If I may advise you, sir?" the man commented as they parted, "I should make no very strong comment on Miss Penhallow's absence — nor seem particularly agitated about it, which is what your parents will expect and what you plainly are."

He saw that Henry Roanoke had joined his parents on the platform. Since Guinevere was not expected before Monday, he must have come down with the express purpose of meeting them — no doubt in response to a telegram from his wife. Dear Guinevere! Such a *nice* sense of humour! At that very moment she was probably smirking to herself at the thought of this enforced confrontation between her husband and the father of her child-to-be.

Peter also noticed that Beatrice was looking at him in a rather agitated manner. It was something to do with Gemma's absence, no doubt.

"Hallo, Peter," Roanoke said cheerily. "I hear you returned last Tuesday. I wondered why I'd seen nothing of you — but did my eyes fall on the explanation of the mystery, tied up at Custom House Quay?"

"They did, sir." Peter hoped his awkwardness did not show. He wondered if he would ever feel easy with the poor man again. "It's awfully good of you to come and meet us. I brought my own trap. I suppose I could take Beatrice?"

"Does this mean you've finished your dinghy?" his mother asked, half annoyed, but also half proud, since Roanoke was obviously impressed by what he had seen of it.

"Does this mean you still have a lot of loose change in your pockets?" his father added sternly.

"'Fraid so, Pater," he replied.

"Have you sailed her yet?" Roanoke asked.

"All of twenty yards!" Peter laughed. "Just from the launching ramp to her moorings inside the little harbour. Care to go for a spin in her this evening?"

"You're on!" he replied eagerly. Then, turning to the older de Vivians, "Shall we be off? Your man seems to have your luggage under control."

"Peter!" Beatrice exclaimed suddenly. "Haven't you noticed?"

"Be quiet!" her mother snapped.

"What?" Peter asked.

"Someone's missing."

He frowned.

She nodded toward the second class.

"Oh!" He laughed. "Miss Penhallow's not here, you mean? But that's by arrangement." He turned to his mother. "Surely she let you know?"

He still had no idea what had happened, of course, but he was sure his parents were behind it, whatever it might be. He just said that to rattle them.

And he succeeded.

"What d'you mean?" his mother asked sharply — and then immediately added, "Yes, of course she told me!"

"Good!" he responded, rubbing his hands cheerfully. "I'm glad you seem to have accepted it so calmly, then. Come on, Bea! I'll take you home via the Custom House Quay. You won't believe your eyes." When they were a little way off he turned and told Roanoke he could join him for a spin around seven-thirty, down at the quay.

The look of consternation on his mother's face was almost an adequate compensation for Gemma's absence.

"*What* was all that about?" Beatrice asked as he helped her into the trap.

"Wait till we're out of their sight," he replied as he went forward to remove the nosebag again.

As they drew out of the forecourt he added, "I just wanted to wipe that smug grin off the mater's face."

"Well, you certainly managed that! She's behind Gemma's disappearance, I'm sure of it. She invited her to tea in the first class, you know."

"What else d'you know?" Peter longed to hand her the reins and tear open the envelope of Gemma's letter, but he reluctantly decided to wait until he knew more about what had happened.

They drove under the railway bridge, where the view opens to give a panorama of the entire harbour, with Roseland away to the east and Trefusis Point dead ahead.

"Oh, dear old Cornwall!" Beatrice exclaimed, opening her arms as if to embrace it all. "Isn't London just beastly? And isn't it nice to be home?"

"I have to admit," he said, "that one's first view of all those little pocket-handkerchief fields and twisty lanes and tucked-away cottages, after one crosses Brunel's bridge and the Tamar, does bring a tiny lump to the throat."

Beatrice laughed in disbelief. "Here's a change of tune!" she exclaimed. "Still, I suppose one love recruits another. I'm head over heels in love with Radnorshire — and I've never even seen it yet."

"Eh?" He stared at her in bewilderment.

"Radnor Castle," she said. "Carteret's seat."

"Oh, lord!" he said wearily. "You can't mean it!"

"It's not serious, you know. Passionate, yes, but not serious."

"This is some nonsense the Wilkes girls have put into your head. Anyway, tell me what you know about Gemma. Why isn't she here? She obviously started the journey with you."

"Why weren't you surprised not to see her? *Was* it pre-arranged between you and her?"

"No. Trewithen warned me. He said he last saw her at Truro. Did she stay behind there or what?"

"She certainly didn't get *off* at Truro, so if he's sure he saw her there, she must have stayed on the train. I noticed she wasn't on the platform as the train was pulling out again. Then the mater told me she'd left our employment by mutual consent. That's all she'd say."

"That's all? Was there an argument? She invited her to tea, you said?"

"Yes, but we weren't there. She made the pater and me wait until the second serving. Sorry I can't be more help."

He handed her the reins then and took out Gemma's letter. "Maybe this will explain it," he said.

My darling,
Forgive this scrawl, which I'm trying to write in haste on the train. I expect your sister will tell you I've just had tea with your mother, on the train, and it will not surprise you to learn she did her best to put every obstacle in the way of our love and specially of our marriage. I let her think fondly she succeeded, but I can tell you this — there is nothing, neither threat nor argument as will ever reconcile her to a marriage between us. She wriggled like a fish on a hook when we

talked but she never yielded on that point. So I thought any idea of us both staying in Falmouth until 12 Oct is just out of the question. It will be best to lull her instead. Reculons pour mieux sauter!

I wish we could have met just once more for a nice talk and a cuddle like that wonderful evening in London but we must behave sensibly now. Your mother wanted to know what I intended doing with the money and I said nothing. She has offered to go on paying my wages as long as I stay away from Falmouth and do not communicate with you. I was not easy in my mind about accepting but I could see no other way to stop her interfering between us and doing far worse. Also en amour la ruse est de bonne guerre! So I accepted. And here I am breaking my word already as I intend to continue doing so. I told her where I am going and said I would not let you know, which I fully intended keeping from you when I said as much. But now I have decided I will tell you, after all, because otherwise it's like saying I don't trust you to behave responsibly, by which I mean you are to make no effort to visit me until we are beyond harming by your mother.

If I may advise you, dearest, I believe you should mope and be angry at my disappearance for a few weeks and then slowly appear to recover from your disappointment, as if you were beginning to suspect it was all calf-love and you're now getting over it. Do anything and everything to make your parents believe there is nothing more between you and me, for if they suspect there is, they will move heaven and earth to wreck it.

I will dip into our money as little as possible. Your mother's offer with the wages will help. I will stay in Penzance and look up a second-cousin once removed on my mother's side. His name is James Collett and he has a photography studio in Market Jew St. He's married to a Helston woman, who has some connection with the Falmouth Trevartons. Mam told me once but I've forgotten. I don't know if they're old or young but, seeing as they're once removed backwards from me, they should be around 40ish.

You can find their directions in Kelly's or the telephone book and you may write to me c/o them. I will write to you c/o Martha's father on Fish Strand Quay and we can also arrange occasions to talk by telephone. I'll work for them unpaid, any sort of dogsbody job, which I'm sure they'll be glad of and, in return, I'll get Mrs Collett to teach me what she knows about managing a business and keeping books and things. I know she does all that for their business so, you see, I shall be much more useful to you, or to us, when we join our destinies together in November.

I hope you think I've made the wise decision, I had so little time. You may think I exaggerate the danger of your mother to us but I believe I do not. Let us play for safety anyway, it's not for long and then we'll have all our lives together. Meanwhile I should also tell you that some of the things your mother said were quite wise, which is not to be wondered at since, apart from her unreasonable attitude to us, she is a quite wise woman. You should think about some of the things she said to me. Like would you still be quite so happy about giving up your rank and allowance if the boat-design and building did not prosper? With no food in the larder and maybe a baby on the way (her words), would you not feel the least bit resentful toward me for insisting on not trying to make a society lady of me?

She also made me realize that my refusal to try to be of your class is a kind of upside-down pride. I even thought of swallowing my pride and braving the sneers of the grandes dames of Falmouth, which would no doubt please you greatly. But suppose it then turned out I couldn't tolerate it. Suppose you came home one day and found me in tears. What would your opinion of me be then?

We have to think of these things, my darling. Darling, darling, darling … I love writing that word and looking at it and knowing it's really you. These next three months are going to be very hard for both of us but we do have our love, our wonderful, wondrous love, to help us endure it. I shall go to the library and copy out bits of poetry that say all these things better than what I can.

Here we are now going through Polperro Tunnel. Buckshead Tunnel next and then it's Truro and I must seal this (with the wettest kiss ever!) and give it to Trewithen for you. By the way, he knows something. Every now and then you see this funny smirk on his face. I thought it was about us but now I'm not so sure. He's up to something, though I can't guess what. Keep an eye on him.

    All my love my dearest darling man,
    your ever loving Gemma.

P.S. If you need money, of course, you know who's banking it for you!

39   Gemma followed the directions the girl at the station buffet had given her — along Chyandour Cliff to the house with the bright blue door and then up the hill to a house on the right near the top called *Mulberry.* Also on the same girl's advice, she had deposited her bags in the left-luggage office. "That Jim Collett's a gert big lump," she said. "He can come down for them later."

Mulberry, said the shingle on the gate. A well-loved house by the look of it, with roses halfway up to the auvis, and the door and all the windows freshly painted. A girl of about fourteen was setting out some bedding plants by the path alongside the house. She rose and wiped her hands in her pinny when she saw Gemma hesitate.

"May I help you, miss?" She came down the path.

"I was wondering — do Mister and Mrs James Collett live here, by any chance?"

The girl assured her they did, adding that she was their daughter, Rosalind. And that they were at home, but if it was about taking a portrait …

At that point the front door opened and a tall, blonde woman in her mid-thirties — and strikingly handsome — put a foot across its threshold. "Who is it, Rosalind?" she asked.

"I'm Gemma Penhallow," she called from the gate. "I'm a second cousin to your husband."

"Not on the Wilkinson side? Are you from Redruth?"

"No, Mrs Collett. From Penryn."

"And originally from Penhale Jakes in Roseland, I believe?" exclaimed a male voice from the dark passageway behind her.

Mrs Collett opened the door wide as her husband stepped out past her. "Gemma, did you say?" he asked as he tripped lightly down the steps. "Gemma Penhallow — Tom's daughter?" He advanced up the path to meet her.

The girl in the buffet had been half right — he was a well-built man but much too lithe to be called a 'gert big lump.'

"Come in, come in!" he cried, opening the gate for her. "Crissy! This is Tom's daughter, Gemma. My wife, Christobel. Do come in."

"How d'you do, Mrs Collett?" Gemma shook hands.

"None of that," her husband cajoled. "We're cousins. We're Crissy and Jim to you. You won't remember this but I took your portraits when you were about three or four. Remember that day, Crissy? Over Penryn?"

"Two dear little twins. What was the other one ... Ruby!"

No sooner was the name out than the pair of them froze — remembering suddenly. They both stared at Gemma, who laughed to put them at their ease. "Ruby's landed on her feet," she said. "Don't worry. I'll tell you about it later, maybe."

"Is she also in Penzance?" Crissy asked as she led the way into the parlour. "Don't say she was afraid to come with you!"

"No. She's in London."

"You'll have a sherry?" Jim asked, opening the sideboard.

Gemma looked about her. It was obviously a prosperous household — though not an ostentatious one. "Thank you," she replied. "Dry for preference."

"It's an amazing coincidence, really," he said. "We are negotiating to open a branch of our business in Falmouth."

"Now that Stanton's are closing down?" Gemma guessed.

"Yes. I was once apprenticed to Stanton's. So when I went out on my own there was a restriction on my setting up in Falmouth — which, of course, no longer applies. But, in fact, I'm going to Falmouth next Wednesday and I had already decided to call on your people in Penryn and catch up on all your news. Isn't that extraordinary!" He passed her a generous sherry in a cut-crystal glass. "It's not as much as it looks," he added with a wink. "There's a lens-effect with the glass."

Rosalind joined them, having washed her hands, and asked if she could have a sip — only a sip. Her father just stared at her, and her mother, when appealed to, simply looked away.

"I'm staying in Penzance for the next few months," Gemma told them. "So I thought I'd make myself known to you."

Crissy asked whereabouts.

"Well, that's the thing, you see. I've actually just arrived. I came down from London this morning. It's quite a story. When I left Paddington, I was quite convinced I'd be returning to Falmouth, where I'm a lady's maid to the de Vivian family in Alma Terrace ..."

"The de Vivians?" Jim looked at Crissy, who said, "I don't know them but the address is one of the best."

"They're from Plymouth, really. Anyway ... how can I put it? Events on the train made it necessary for me *not* to return to Falmouth. Oh, dear! Where do I begin?"

"Are you in some kind of trouble, Gemma?" Crissy asked.

"No!" Gemma glanced nervously toward the girl. "Not that kind, anyway."

"That must mean you haven't eaten," Jim said, having silently worked out the timing of her day.

She said she'd had a very filling tea, but he rose and took the glass from her. "Come on! I'm sure we've got some cold mutton in the larder?" He questioned Crissy with his eyes.

"If you don't mind eating in the kitchen," she said as she rose to accompany them out. "Rosalind, darling, you could wash some salad."

"Oh, please! I didn't mean to ..." Gemma protested to their departing backs.

Over the impromptu meal she told them her story, beginning with that by now unforgettable moment when the de Vivians arrived at their new home.

"He sounds like a thoroughly nice young man, your Peter," Crissy said when she'd finished. "Why d'you laugh?"

"I was just thinking of all the times people said 'your Master Peter' to me and I'd snarl back at them, 'not *my* Master Peter'! But he's much more than just a thoroughly nice young man, Crissy. And — I must keep reminding myself — he's not mine yet, either."

"I wonder if he's met Tony Fox?" Jim said to Crissy. "He used to be Mark's sailing partner." To Gemma he added, "Mark Trevarton is Crissy's uncle and a partner in our business. They live next door."

"Ah. I don't know. I never heard him mention the name. Talking of living next door, I'd better be making tracks for wherever I'm going to be staying ..."

"You're there already, Gemma," Crissy said as she scraped the gristly bits off the plate for the dog, who suddenly woke up at the clatter and came wheezing across the kitchen. "He's called True," she added, giving him a gentle tickle behind the ear. "He'll be fifteen years old next month. We got him as a weaned puppy the year we moved in. I don't think he'll be with us much longer."

"Don't say that, Mummy!" Rosalind screamed, stuffing her fingers in her ears.

Crissy grinned and mussed her hair, mouthing silent words, pretending to say something extremely pleasant. The girl realized it rather late and pulled her fingers out to catch what she could. Crissy at once said, "It's what you've always wanted, isn't it — but you'll only get it if you're very good."

"What? What?" the poor girl pleaded. "I didn't hear."

"Well, darling — if you will go stuffing your fingers in your ears, what else can you expect?" It was all the reply her mother would give.

"You're teasing — and I hate you!" Rosalind flew at her mother and flailed away with feather-light punches, then hugged her and laughed.

Watching this happiest of scenes, Gemma, after all the emotional twists and turns of her day, felt the pressure of tears in the corners of her eyes. She experienced a sudden yearning to have a daughter like Rosalind and to enjoy just such a friendship with her, too. Crissy, perhaps guessing what was going through her mind, smiled encouragingly and said, "Are your things at the station? Jim'll go down and get them. You go with him. We'll air your bed meanwhile — you must be exhausted. I know what those long train journeys are."

The sun was dipping down in a cloudless sky over Land's End as she and Jim set off down the hill. A two-day-old moon was following it down, a pale silver crescent in a flood of gory gold. It was going to be a dark night. Indeed, the darkness had already invaded the sea, whose inky ripples flashed here and there with echoes of the sunset that served only to emphasize the deep colour of the water.

"Look at that!" Jim stopped and waved a hand across the scene. The whole of the western end of Mount's Bay was spread out before them, calm and serene. Far out on the never-empty sea, masthead lights and portholes were twinkling in the dusk. On this near-windless evening you could easily tell the fast-moving steamers from the sailing ships. "Will there ever be an emulsion to capture colours like those?" he asked.

Gemma laughed.

Surprised, he asked why.

"What you said — it was just the sort of thing Peter might say. All that beauty out there, all that wildness, and to both of you it's just a sort of page on which to write some new invention."

"Not *just* an empty page," he protested. "But *also* an empty page." He glanced sidelong at her. "D'you sometimes wonder if it's *ever* going to work out for you and Peter?"

"Why?"

"Just the way you told your story. You sounded a bit pessimistic at times."

For a man he was very sensitive, she realized. She wondered if Peter would have noticed such a thing; he was always so insanely optimistic — which was why, although she was not *cheerful* at being parted from him for the next three months, she had no qualms. "If it does eventually end happily," she replied, "it'll be more thanks to Peter than to me. He's the one who can't see any difficulties and will never take no for an answer."

They walked on in silence for a while.

"He is," she insisted, as if he had disagreed aloud.

"I wonder ..." he mused. "I got a sample of pitchblende once, to do some photographic experiments with. It gives out x-rays, you know. You're supposed to keep it wrapped up in lead sheet but I was careless with it once and left it in a drawer. And it completely fogged a box of unexposed plates two drawers down. It was quite uncanny. The stuff didn't move. It didn't change. It didn't *do* anything — apparently. Yet, two drawers down, a box of plates was ruined! I thought at the time — there are *people* like that. They don't appear to move — at least, they don't *start* things moving. They just are. And they radiate this ... this absolute determination. And ... things happen. They have their effect far beyond the sphere in which you'd think they had any influence. I know — I'm married to just such a person!"

"Well!" Gemma was amazed at his frankness, thinking he was implying that Crissy ruined people without meaning to.

He caught the implication in her tone and laughed. "I don't mean she ruins people's lives, the way the pitchblende ruined the negs — although, mind you, she does quietly ruin the plans of people who oppose her! D'you know her story — how she and I met? It has curious parallels with yours, in fact."

"My father told me something about her being related to the Trevartons who own the mills in Penryn."

"Her mother was of that family — Selina Trevarton. But she fell for the coachman — a fellow called Barry Moore ..."

"I see what you mean by parallels!"

"Yes, well, let's hope your tale has a happier ending. All this happened about forty years ago, and times have changed. It went well for them at the beginning. Moore started a haulier's business in Helston and did all right. They had six children. Crissy was the second. Then the father took to drink and the business went downhill ... they moved to a hovel in Porthleven and Selina took in washing ..."

"Did the Trevartons have any part in ruining them?" Gemma asked, thinking of Mrs de Vivian and how she would behave in like circumstances.

"I'm sure there was a bit of that, but it was also in his character. Anyway, they both died in the same week — about twenty years ago — and then old Grandmother Trevarton really showed her true colours. Crissy went over to Falmouth, looking for their help. She was the *doer* in that family, not Marion, the eldest. But by the time she got back to Porthleven, her five brothers and sisters had been taken away and split up."

"No! Just in that short time?"

"Indeed, yes! Marion was in Little Sinns, the home for wayward girls; the oldest boy was in an agricultural reform school near Saint Austell; the two younger boys in an orphanage in Plymouth; and Teresa, the little girl, who had tuberculosis of the hip, was in a convent here in Penzance and was later adopted by a couple who went to India."

"Oh!" Gemma stopped dead. "I would have *died!*"

He chuckled. "Somehow, I don't think so, Gemma. I know you're related to me, not to Crissy, but there's something of her spirit in you, nonetheless."

He led her straight past the station entrance — which Gemma was just about to point out when he explained: "I don't wish to go past the buffet. The girl who works there had her portrait taken last month and then her father fell ill and now she can't pay for it. Some people get apologetic when that sort of thing happens. Others get abusive. Best to avoid them, eh?"

They went in via the goods door and collected her cases and gladstone bag. "We'll take a taxi," she said, embarrassed at the combined weight of them and the thought of the hill ahead.

"We will not!" he rejoined, picking up the two cases and making them look no heavier than feather pillows. "Unless that bag's too much for you."

"I was thinking of you," she said, picking it up. "Did Crissy ever get her family together again?"

"*Did* she!" He laughed. "Within eighteen months! She even got Teresa back from India. We got married during that time so I had a ringside seat. You can just imagine the celebration dinner we had at Mulberry that night! But she achieved most of it the way that pitchblende fogged the plates — quietly, secretly, making no *apparent* moves. And all from within the very heart of the Trevarton family, because — and here's another parallel with you — she became lady's maid to her own grandmother!"

"No!" Gemma laughed with delight. "Didn't the old woman know they were related?"

"Oh, she knew, all right. She realized Crissy was the awkward one, the trouble-maker. So she thought it best to have her where she could keep an eye on her. Little did she realize! The Trojan Horse wasn't a patch on my Crissy!"

"Oh, you must tell my father about this when you see him next week. I'm sure he doesn't know."

"I will," he promised. "But the reason I'm telling *you* is to wipe away that pessimistic streak I detected. You'll get your Peter just as Crissy got back her brothers and sisters. You both have the same quietly insistent character — and, come to think of it, you're both fighting the same enemy."

This last statement puzzled Gemma.

"Class!" he said. "Will the English ever rise above it! And why do we Cornish ape them? But we do. If the Trevartons had welcomed Barry Moore into the family and helped him, instead of sniping, he might be still alive and running the biggest haulage business in the West. Even without their help he was on his way to it before he took to drinking the profits. But they couldn't bring themselves to do it, all because of class. And it's exactly the same with you and Peter."

"The de Vivians came over with the Conqueror," Gemma said. "That's what Mrs de Vivian loves to point out. And in the very next breath she'll tell you she's the least snobbish person on earth!"

"There you are!" He set the cases down and exercised his cramped fingers.

"I said we should've taken a cab," she remarked.

"Not at all!" He picked them up again and set off as jauntily as ever.

"Listen, Cousin Jim," she said, changing the subject. "I can well afford to pay for my keep while I'm with you. I hope you'll let me."

He said nothing.

"Please?" she prompted him.

"Shh!" he replied. "I'm trying hard to pretend I didn't hear."

"But ..."

"You're not going to persist in insulting us, are you?"

Gemma gave up. "At least let me contribute my labour. I can do most things with a needle and thread. You've never seen goffering like mine. I can add pounds, shillings, and pence all at the same time. And ..."

"Stop! You just said some magic words — at least, Crissy will think they're magic. You could help her do the books and manage the bills and stocks."

"Very well." Gemma let out a big sigh of satisfaction. "Come to think of it, it'll do me no harm to learn as much as I can about running a small family business."

She stepped ahead of him to open the gate. Behind her, he smiled to himself, for, quite unconsciously, she had just proved he was right in everything he had said about her quietly insistent character and the way it somehow induced the world to cooperate. Mind you, he had watched Crissy do the same thing for the past twenty years, so it required no supernatural insight on his part. All the same ... two of them under the one roof ... there were some interesting times ahead.

40 Peter allowed his cheerfulness to decline over the days following his family's return — and Gemma's failure to accompany them. Finally he judged it time to indulge in another brooding session out on the lawn, as if to suggest he had just received some bad news. He chose a spot close to where his mother lay in her bamboo lounger, reading her latest new novel from Hatchard's — *The History of Mr Polly*.

"Not sailing today, darling?" she asked when his sighs finally penetrated her concentration. "I should have thought this wind was perfect for you."

"I'm just not in the mood." He sighed yet again.

"You're not missing Miss Penhallow, by any chance?" she asked brutally. "No, of course you're not!"

"Ha!"

When she did not follow up her question, he added, "You knew, didn't you!"

"Me, dear?" she asked innocently. "I knew nothing about the matter. I still don't, come to that."

"You have no idea where she's gone?"

"No, dear. I thought you were quite sure about that."

It was his turn for silence.

She repeated the jibe more insistently: "I thought *you* were quite sure about that."

"Yes! All right!" he snapped.

She was delighted. "You mean you don't know, after all?"

He sighed again. "It would seem not." After a huge internal struggle he forced himself to add, "I don't suppose she told *you* where she was going?"

"Newquay," Ada replied at once. "Or so she said. She has an uncle there. But perhaps she changed her mind. To go to Newquay, she ought to have got off at Truro with us and gone back up the line to Bodmin Road." As an afterthought she added, "Perhaps she said it deliberately. To throw us off." She closed her book. "Poor darling! It certainly looks as if she's thrown *you* off!"

Peter continued to brood, wondering how far she would stretch her web of deceit without any prompting from him.

"I hate to see you glowering like this, darling," she said. "And even though I hope you never find her and that we never see her again ... well, if you must, you must. Go to Newquay, I mean. That's where I'd start looking — Newquay."

It was a clever choice of decoy-town, he thought. Not impossibly far away but far enough to fatigue him in getting there and back by train, for it would involve two branch lines and one stretch of main line. And, above all, it was opposite in direction to Penzance.

"It has been an expensive lesson." She eyed him cautiously.

"In what way?" he asked.

"Well ... putting six hundred pounds in her name like that. What an unfair temptation to offer a poor girl who's probably never handled *ten* pounds in her life — not all at the one time." Then, seeing how the suggestion angered him, she added, "Still, she's a moral girl at heart. I'm sure she'll think better of it and return the money at least. I'd *hate* to think she wouldn't."

The following day she added a twist to this fantasy. After breakfast she took him into the morning room, sat him down — as if preparing him for a shock — and told him that his father had made discreet inquiries through his friends in the National Provincial Bank and had learned that Gemma's account had been transferred from Falmouth to Newquay and then cleared out. "So it does look as if she's in Newquay somewhere, after all," she said. "Or was there a few days ago."

A week or so later, when Peter still had not started looking for Gemma in Newquay — even though he was obviously brooding about her and her apparent treachery — a fat letter came through the post, bearing a Newquay postmark. The address was typewritten, so the exterior gave no clue as to the sender. It was also, by a curious coincidence, one of those rare days on which his mother came down to breakfast, rather than have it sent up to her room.

She stabbed the letter open with only the most casual interest but crowed with delight as soon as she saw its contents. "She did!" she exclaimed, drawing forth a bundle of notes. "Good girl! I *knew* there was no real evil in her."

There was a total of £600, all in fivers and all bundled in National Provincial tape. His parents did things thoroughly; he had to allow them that.

"She must have drawn it out and sent it directly from the bank without unwrapping it," his mother said. "Well? Isn't it a relief to know it's all over, darling? She's done the honourable thing. She's cleared out of your life, leaving no trace. I don't think there'd be much point in scouring the streets and boarding houses of Newquay, now — do you? Though, knowing you, you probably will!"

She started to slip one of the binders.

"No!" he cried. "Leave it — just as it is. Put it all back in the envelope and lock it in the safe. Please? She'll come back to me — I know she will. And the first thing I'll do is give it to her all over again."

Still Ada hesitated.

"Please?" he begged.

"Oh, very well! For one month! I'll humour you that long. By then, we must hope your good old common sense will have returned to you."

"Never!" he responded.

"Well, we shall see," she said patiently. "Now! Mister Roanoke has invited us to sail on the *Guinevere* to Devoran House, where we're all to take luncheon and stay for tea with the Wilkeses. I suppose you're in the crew?"

Peter sighed. "I was. But I don't honestly feel up to it. I'll go round and cry off. I'm sure he'll understand. I'll make my own way there in *Gem.*"

"Oh!" She raised her hands in exasperation. "I wish you'd change that name!"

"Bad luck, Mater," he replied as he left. "I'll go and tell the cap'n now."

He had to stop himself from skipping as he walked out into Alma Terrace — which was just as well because, if he had been skipping when he reached its corner with Wood Lane, he would almost certainly have fallen over in surprise.

"Jenny?" he called out incredulously as he crossed the road to join her.

She advanced one of her nether limbs so that the toe of her boot peeped out below the hem of her skirt, which swept the ground. "Don't you think these extra six inches in the length of my dress entitle me to a 'Miss Divett'? 'Jenny' was the one whose ankles you *could* see."

"The difference is already engraved on my heart, Miss Divett," he replied solemnly as he raised her hand for a formal kiss. "But where is your chaperon?"

"I am a 'single business lady' now."

He remembered the placard. "Then I think you are staying at the Roseland View Teetotal Hôtel — Annexe for Single Business Ladies. Am I right?"

"Sharp!" she said admiringly.

"I'm learning. Were you on your way to see me?"

"I was trying to pluck up the courage."

He offered her his arm, pointed along Wood Lane, and raised his eyebrows. She accepted the unspoken invitation.

"Pluck up the courage?" he echoed. "That doesn't sound like you, Miss Divett."

"Come! Once is enough. Jenny will do thereafter. No, but you're right. I thought it was hard enough making the transition from angel to fallen angel. The first time I stood on the pavement with my ankles exposed and my knees giving away and my heart hammering fit to burst ...! I thought that was the worst. But now I feel a fraud *everywhere* I go. I didn't expect that. Half a mo! I don't want to go back to the hôtel."

"I just want to call on a friend and tell him I can't crew in his boat today. It won't take a minute."

"Not because of meeting me?"

"No. I'll explain as we go."

They started to retrace her steps along Wodehouse Terrace, heading now for the Roanokes'.

"But we were talking about your difficulties in making the leap back to pure angel again," he said.

"Not pure — whited."

"You got used to being despised, I suppose. Every time you sallied forth into Shepherd's Market you steeled yourself against those looks of contempt from other women — and now it's hard to break the habit."

"That's right." She gave a dry laugh. "I might have known *you'd* understand."

"Are you being sarcastic?"

"Not at all. I mean it — every word. I hope your Gemma realizes what a lucky woman she is. How is that business progressing by the way?"

He told her — in outline, anyway. It occupied the entire stroll to the Roanokes'.

Only Guinevere was at home. Peter tried to deliver his message to the maid who answered his knock but, the moment her mistress heard his voice, she came to invite him in. Then she had no choice but to invite Jenny in, too, though it clearly displeased her. In the circumstances the interview did not last long.

"At the risk of seeming indelicate," Jenny said when they were on their way again, "that woman is *enceinte*. I'd almost stake my life on it."

"You'd be in no danger," he assured her.

"You know?" Jenny was surprised. "She told *you?*"

An older, more experienced man would not have hesitated. But Peter left it too late and his stumbling explanation that Guinevere had told Beatrice and she had told him failed to convince. Jenny looked all about her and said, "Why, it's not so different from London, after all! I suppose it went on in Durham, too, but I was so innocent then."

"By the way, why were you coming to see me this morning?" he asked, to change the subject. "D'you think I can cure your nerves, somehow?"

She became serious at once. "In a way, yes." She drew breath to speak but the words seemed to get stuck in her throat.

"Go on," he urged. "I'll help if I can."

"Why?" she asked, more puzzled than aggressive.

"I don't know. I must like you. There aren't many girls one can talk to so easily." He grinned. "Don't make me say how much I admire your spirit and all that rot again. So, what can I do to help? Not much, I'm sure."

"It may not seem much to you but it'll make all the difference to me, Peter, honestly. There's an estate agent down the bottom of Smithick Hill and, according to his advertisement in the *Falmouth Packet*, he's got two empty shops on his books. One of them I'm very interested in — Stanton's, the old photographer's studios ..."

"On the corner just above Fish Strand Quay! I pass it almost every day — when I go to the ship's chandler down there."

"That's the one. It already has a certain social *cachet*, you see. Falmouth's upper crust are already accustomed to going there. It would be ideal for my little fashion establishment."

"And what am I to do to help? I can't lend you money. Gemma's got it all."

"No, no — nothing like that. If you'll just accompany me there — as if you have some financial interest in my establishment ...? No?"

He pulled a dubious face. "If that's what you want, of course I will. But d'you think it wise?"

"You don't?"

"People will take you less seriously if they think the money is mine and you're just some glorified manageress."

She bit her lip. "What d'you suggest, then? Actually, shouldn't we go down these steps?"

He remembered that the only other way down, from where they now stood in Clare Terrace, was through the infamous Vernon Place — hardly the most tactful way to choose! They descended by the flight of steps she had indicated, though, for someone in long skirts like hers they were both steep and hazardous. They continued on down Gyllyng Sreet, which turned into Smithick Hill after the lower end of Vernon Place. From there on it was impassable to any vehicle.

"What d'you suggest, then?" she repeated when they reached the bottom of the steps.

"I'm just a friend who's squiring you around. I'll hover in the background, look at the pictures on the walls, act bored ... you know — that sort of thing. It'll leave them in no doubt who holds the pursestrings."

"Perfect!" She took his arm again and gave him a friendly squeeze. "Suddenly I feel all confident again. D'you know what the real difficulty was?"

"What?"

"You won't laugh? Promise?"

"Promise."

"There are two lady typewriters in the office. And the way they looked at me when I collected the details ..." She shuddered. "It's the look in other women's eyes. I feel sure they *know.*"

"It'll pass," he assured her. "And I'm certainly not laughing. D'you know what would help?"

"What?"

"Just let it drop casually that you're the daughter of the bishop of Durham."

"Not the bishop — the rural dean, remember?"

"Oh, yes." He thought about it for a moment. "I'd still *say* bishop, though."

"Why? I'd only get caught out in the lie, sooner or later."

"You'd be caught out in *that* lie. Then people would imagine they know the full, ghastly truth about you and they wouldn't delve any further. Like the man who went to Harrow but told everyone he went to Eton. They found him out soon enough but no one ever dug deeper. They never learned he was actually kicked out of Harrow!"

When they had finished laughing he went on, "Actually, the bishop is really the *prince*-bishop, isn't he? Wouldn't that make you a princess?"

"Not any more." She laughed but soon became serious again. "I don't think I'd dare do that. My parents ..."

"The daring would all be on *their* side," he said. "Let them explain why they're disowning a daughter who is engaged in a respectable and socially esteemed business!"

She wavered. "Well ... maybe," she said.

"This is the place, isn't it?"

They went indoors and Peter did exactly as he'd promised, except that he also flirted with the two lady typewriters, who, once they heard his name was de Vivian, felt sure their employer would not mind. He was amused to hear Jenny casually letting it drop that she was a daughter of the prince-bishop of Durham. The most believable lies are the big ones.

After a while, she rejoined him. Her face was as long as three sermons. "Someone else has put in a bid since I was here yesterday," she said out of hearing of the two ladies. "You'll never guess who!"

"Tell me."

"Who did you say Miss Penhallow was staying with?"

"Jim Collett, the photographer in ... oh, my God!"

"Apparently he was apprenticed in the old firm there. You can understand why he wants the place. You don't think your Gemma could talk him out of it?"

He shook his head. "I wouldn't want to put her in such an embarrassing position. How much is his offer?"

"Eight hundred and fifty."

"You could go to nine."

"And be left with no working capital! Six hundred and fifty was the most I was prepared to bid."

He smiled all round; every eye in the office was on them. "We can't get any further here. Go back to him as if I've just encouraged you to bid higher. Don't *actually* bid, of course! Just say you have to formalize a new arrangement or some jargon like that. Buy a bit of time, that's all."

Outside again, they started off up Market Street, one of the main shopping thoroughfares. Stanton's, the former photographer's, was at its farther end, where a slight bend marked the change of name to Church Street.

"It is an absolutely splendid location," he said. "We must come up with the money somehow. I wonder if Wilkes has another hot tip?"

But Jenny was now quite sure she had lost her chance. "Let's see if there's another suitable place," she said.

There was — but it was at the farther end of Church Street, directly facing the church itself, and that was more than Jenny thought she could take, day after day.

"Something'll turn up," Peter said cheerfully. "It always does — often when you least expect it. Meanwhile, come and see the *Gem,* my little dinghy — she's only round the corner."

But they had hardly taken a dozen paces along Arwennack Street when Peter got the second shock of the morning, for there, at the corner of Hill Quay, which leads down to the Custom House harbour, stood Gemma and Trewithen!

Or was it Ruby? It was certainly not Sapphire — not dressed in those quiet, modest clothes. It couldn't be Gemma, either, he thought. She would never break their arrangement and risk everything — certainly not to stand where she could be seen by dozens, if not hundreds, of people who knew her. Therefore it must be Ruby. But why was she dressed like that? Because she wanted people to think she was Gemma, of course! She knew nothing of what had happened and she wanted to see Falmouth again, so she had chosen the obvious disguise.

It was clever, he had to admit. But it was also potentially disastrous to him and her twin. He had to do something to get her out of sight before she did any more damage.

Take her sailing! Up to Penryn? To the pier by the railway station? Anywhere!

This jumble of thoughts raced through his mind in a flash. All Jenny noticed was a few seconds' hesitation, as if he were trying to remember something. But after a while she had to ask if anything was wrong.

"I'm sure that's Gemma's twin sister ahead. She's come back to Falmouth and she obviously doesn't know she's wrecking our plan. Come on — we've got to spirit her away somewhere!"

Their haste drew Trewithen's attention and, a moment later, they were both waving at him like grass in a gale.

"Ruby?" Peter called out as they drew near.

She turned to Trewithen with a laugh. "See! I told you *he* wouldn't be fooled — not even from a distance."

"Listen!" He took her arm and turned her back toward the quay. "There's no time to explain now, but your very presence here is jeopardizing a carefully constructed plan of Gemma's. And mine. If you stay here, you'll ruin *everything*. Just take my word for it, all right?"

"Yes, yes! I'm sorry — honestly. I had no idea …"

"Never mind. Maybe no harm's been done as yet. But every second counts."

They had arrived at the quayside by now and he began to relax once again.

"Peter?" Jenny said, coming up behind, with Trewithen hard on her heels.

"Sorry, old thing!" he said. "I just *have* to get Ruby here away from Falmouth. You go back to the hotel and …"

"Surely your mother *knows* Gemma has a twin?" Jenny interrupted.

He stared at her blankly for a moment and then murmured, "I don't think she does, now you mention it." He turned to Trewithen. "D'you think the Walkers ever told her? I know Bea and I never did."

"I'm quite sure they didn't, sir. The word 'twin' having such melancholy meaning for her …"

"Not to mention the stain on Gemma's character!" Ruby said heavily — causing Jenny to look at her with new interest.

"Even so …" Peter waved a hand to dismiss the point. "She'd only be the more convinced that Gemma had broken her agreement and returned secretly to Falmouth. If I then tried telling her Gemma has an identical twin … ha! They'd hear her laughter in Roseland. So — it makes it even more urgent to get you away at once." He nodded at Ruby.

"Begging your pardon, sir," Trewithen put in. "But I think there's something you ought to know."

"Not now," Peter said. "What are you doing here, anyway?"

"I brought Miss Ruby down here, thinking you were tinkering at your boat and might not have left just yet. I mean, it was our only hope."

Peter shook his head at this 'explanation' and said, "I'm sure Ruby knows her own way to the Custom House harbour! However, I don't have time to question you further ..."

"I think you have time to hear what Mister Trewithen has to say, Peter," Ruby said quietly.

He stared at her uncertainly. "You know what it is?"

She nodded. "He was telling me on the way down. It may be the answer to all your problems — yours and Gemma's."

"Especially Gemma's," Trewithen added.

Peter clenched his fists in frustration. "Very well," he said at last. "But it had better be good. And you, Ruby, get out of sight. Please!" He pointed to the boatbuilder's yard beside Upton Slip and said, "Go and hide just inside the gate there."

"I'll keep you company," Jenny said tactfully.

"Now what is it?" Peter asked impatiently as soon as they were alone. "Make it as brief as you can."

But Trewithen was in no mood for brevity. He began a leisurely monologue on the uncertainties of a servant's life and the necessity to provide for his old age ...

... which was at least forty years away, Peter pointed out.

Unruffled, the man continued. Masters had been known to promise the earth to their servants, only to renege when the time came to deliver.

"How much?" Peter snapped.

It was not a simple question of money. He, Trewithen, had a great respect for Master Peter — always had done. Indeed, there was a feeling of personal warmth, insofar as such a thing was possible between two men so far apart in rank. Besides, he was too diffident to name an actual price himself. He would prefer the young master to say how much it would be worth to him to have all obstacles to his union with Miss Gemma cleared away, this very day.

Peter laughed in disbelief. How could Trewithen have found the answer that had eluded the nimble brains of the two people most closely involved? It was absurd.

But Trewithen patted his breast pocket with a confidence that shook Peter into saying, "You're sure?"

"I can't think of anything *more* sure — knowing all the parties as I do, sir."

"The greatest obstacle is my mother, of course."

"Of course." He agreed.

By now Peter was beginning to experience an absurd hope that Trewithen had, indeed, found the answer that had eluded him all these weeks.

"Six hundred pounds," he said. "That's all I have — all *we* have. But I'm sure Gemma won't grudge it you, *if* you really have found the magic bullet."

Trewithen shook his head. "I wouldn't take a penny from you *now*, sir. That's not my intention."

"What, then?" Peter was baffled all over again.

"I'm a patient man, sir."

"You certainly *are*, Trewithen!" He laughed. Then the penny dropped. "You mean you can wait until my twenty-eighth birthday comes around!"

"Nineteen-seventeen, sir." He smiled. "I can wait until then."

"A thousand pounds on my twenty-eighth birthday. All right? Done! Now what's this magic bullet of yours?"

"Shall we join the ladies, sir? It's not that I distrust you — perish the thought — but even the nimblest get trampled by runaway horses. So I have prepared a bill of exchange dated the thirteenth of October, nineteen-seventeen — the day *after* your twenty-eighth birthday, I believe?"

"How did you know the actual date?"

The man laughed. "From the records in Somerset House, sir. It's amazing what you can discover there — if you know where to look and the sort of thing to look for. So I thought — if you were to sign the bill of exchange and Miss Ruby were to hold it as a neutral in the matter until you have seen the documents I will then pass over to you — and not hand it to me until you are satisfied they are worth it ...? Would that be acceptable?"

Peter hesitated. "You must be pretty sure of their value to me — these documents."

"I was never more sure of anything in my life, sir."

Peter laughed. "By God! You've talked me round to it, man. Let's sign this bill and be done!"

"With the ladies as witnesses, sir," he replied as he led Peter to the boatbuilder's yard.

They surprised Jenny and Ruby, who were deep in animated conversation; Peter wondered if they had revealed their histories to each other. Jenny's sudden interest when Ruby had hinted at her own disgrace had not gone unnoticed by him. What did two such girls talk about once they had leaped the barriers of their inhibitions? Men? He decided he'd rather not know.

"Make a back, one of you," he said jovially.

"No — me, sir," Trewithen said as he handed him the bill and turned about. "They may sign as witnesses."

Peter took out his fountain pen and signed with a flourish, handing it to Jenny to add her autograph, followed by Ruby.

Trewithen managed the procedure with formal dignity, handing the bill into Ruby's safe keeping before he delved in his breast pocket and withdrew a brown manila envelope and passed it to Peter.

It was disappointingly thin, though he made no remark as to that. In fact, it contained only two pieces of paper — a certified copy of his mother's birth certificate and a certified copy of *her* parents' marriage lines.

Peter read them through and saw nothing of the slightest value to him and Gemma. He stared in disappointed puzzlement at Trewithen.

"Your mother's birth certificate ties her to one Concepta Darbyshire, née Kelly, sir," he explained patiently.

"My grandmother, yes. But that's not news, man. We've always known it."

"And you'll see the same Concepta Kelly's name on the marriage lines, sir?"

"Yes! Goodness, what a surprise! So she was lawfully married to my grandfather!"

"And the date, sir?"

Peter looked at the dates and burst into laughter. "Born in wedlock but conceived out of it! Well, well, well!"

His laughter soon died, however. "But see here, Trewithen, that's hardly worth a cool thou', is it?"

"That is but the sugar icing, sir. You have yet to discover the cake. What is beneath your grandmother's name, sir?"

"Spinster?"

"And beneath that?"

"General — in brackets."

"Technically called parentheses, sir."

"Never mind that, man. What does it mean? Was her father a general or something?"

Trewithen smiled. "Ah! Now I see your difficulty, sir. In Ireland they use the term 'general' to describe what we call a 'tweeny'! Your mother's mother was an in-between maid, sir. A maid-of-all-work."

"A skivvy!" Peter's delighted cry echoed all around the boatyard, bringing all work to a halt for a few seconds. "A bloody skivvy ... pardon my French, ladies." He began a wild dance in the dust and shavings. "My granny was a skivvy! My granny was a skivvy!" he shouted to the well-known rhythm of the school-playground taunt.

When he had calmed down again, Trewithen cleared his throat delicately.

"Oh, yes!" Peter exclaimed. "For God's sake, give it to him, Ruby, before I alter it to *ten* thousand!"

41 With half the morning gone, Peter realized it was too late to try to get to the Wilkeses' garden party at Devoran House by dinghy — even though the *Gem* had already shown herself to be the fastest thing in the harbour. And besides, both Ruby and Jenny had their reasons for wanting to accompany him. Jenny wanted to ask Conrad Wilkes, who made ladies' hats as well as men's, if he'd come in as a partner in her establishment; and Ruby wanted to speak rather urgently to Lord Carteret, who also had an invitation to the party. But the *Gem* had room for one passenger at most — and one who didn't mind a possible soaking, at that. So he rented a steam launch from the boatyard and, while they were getting her in steam, he took the ladies up to the Arwennack Hôtel for a swift morning coffee. Just before they entered, Jenny told him they each knew about the other's 'shame.'

"That was quick," he replied.

"You get an eye for it," Ruby added.

"Even when you're both dressed so modestly?" He ushered them into the lounge, which overlooked the harbour. "No wonder you're walking on eggshells, Jenny."

As soon as they were seated, Ruby asked why her appearance in Falmouth had jeopardized her sister's plans.

Peter explained.

"So she's with the Colletts in Penzance! I wonder how they received her?"

"She says they're getting on famously. How long is it since *you* last saw them?"

"I can just dimly remember him coming to Penryn and taking our portraits, when we were about four. His wife's tall and blonde. I remember that — although everyone's tall when you're only four. He had an egg that split in two when he secretly pressed a rubber bulb and a baby chicken popped out. That's how he got us to laugh. And so!" She turned to Jenny. "They're the ones who are also after Stanton's old shop and studios! Have you got the details of the property?"

Jenny rummaged in her bag and produced a sheaf of papers.

While Ruby read through them — rather thoroughly — Jenny said to Peter, "As to meeting Conrad, I obviously won't be able to come up to the house from the jetty, but if the tide's right, and you can …"

He interrupted to say it would be high tide just after luncheon so they should be all right as far as that went.

"So you could moor a little way down the bank, behind some shrubs or something, and perhaps talk Conrad into coming down to see me?"

"I'll do my best," he promised. "Would you like me to put the general idea to him first? Otherwise he might imagine there's some tremendous mystery — if I'm not allowed to tell him what it's about."

Jenny said she'd think it over.

Ruby had a thoughtful look as she handed the papers back.

Peter asked her why she was dressed so modestly; was it to pass as Gemma and avoid embarrassment?

Ruby grinned like a child caught red-handed at some mischief. "I didn't think she'd mind," she explained. "Of course, I didn't know about all this brouhaha, or I wouldn't have dreamed of doing it."

"Did you go up to the house?"

"No — why?"

"If you had, and my mother had seen you … whew!" He blew on his fingertips as if he had scalded them. Then a thoughtful look crept into his eyes as he actually pictured the scene and the sort of things his mother might say. Or scream.

The maid brought their coffee and a selection of mouth-watering cakes on a four-tiered tray.

"Are you good sailors?" he asked. "Otherwise avoid the ones with the garish colours!"

They looked at him in disgust, trying not to laugh.

"Experience speaks," he told them.

Boldly they went for the neapolitan slices and the ones with the bright green or yellow icing.

"How did you meet with Trewithen, then?" Peter asked next.

Ruby looked for sympathy from Jenny. "Is this an inquisition?" she asked.

"No — I just want to know how many people might have seen you. That's all."

"Well, I know Trewithen always tries to slip out around half-past ten …"

"To collect and winnings and place new bets?" Peter guessed.

"Ah, you know about that, do you?"

He grinned. "And so do you, obviously. But Gemma didn't. That's interesting."

Ruby shrugged. "She was always more strait-laced than me. And Trewithen's sensitive to things like that. He'd try to keep it from her if he felt she'd disapprove. Anyway, I know he's always at the Oddfellows around ten-thirty. So I went there."

"Ah! So you've only been in Swanpool Street, New Street, and Quay Hill — where we met you just now? That's not so bad."

"And from the station to the Oddfellows. Why is this so important, Peter?"

Jenny interrupted: "He probably keeps all his chisels lined up parallel and exactly the same distance apart."

"I do, actually," he admitted, smiling at both of them. "Sorry. I'm being a bore. It's of no importance."

"You're plotting something!" Ruby accused him.

"Not at all. Let's talk of more interesting things. For example — how can Jenny raise the wind?"

"Or alternatively," Ruby said, "you could tell me how much Carteret has been seeing of your sister lately?"

From Peter's expression she inferred that he thought her rude for still hogging their attention. "It's actually got something to do with Jenny and the need for capital," she added. "If you'll just bear with me. Has he been seeing her a lot?"

"Quite a bit," he admitted awkwardly.

"Every chance he gets?"

He was even more awkward. "I suppose so."

"And you never wondered about me?"

He hung his head by way of apology.

"They never do," Jenny told her. "We get paid, don't we — what more do we expect?"

"He told me you were taking a holiday," Peter said. "He seems quite a different fellow from the languid, tired-of-life wet rag I met at Ascot."

"Tired of life!" Ruby echoed glumly. "That just about sums it up. He's tired of *that* sort of life, anyway — idleness in London. When he heard you were building your racing dinghy, he was absolutely green with envy. He wants to go back to Radnor Castle and create a whole lot of little canals and water gardens in the grounds there."

"Back to his wife?" Peter said.

"He hasn't got a wife."

"She's called Gwendolen." Peter laughed like one who knew better. "It's there in *Debrett.*"

Ruby looked pityingly at him. "If a sixth-generation peer of the realm tells the editor of *Debrett* he's got a wife, then that's what they'll print!" To Jenny she explained: "He invented this wife so that she could have what he called 'tactical relapses into invalidism' whenever his debts exceeded his income from rents. After each quarter-day his wife recovered miraculously and he appeared in London again to discharge his debts and start acquiring fresh ones."

"I'm not surprised he's tired of life — *that* sort of life," Jenny replied. "And what about you?"

Ruby raised her eyes to the ceiling. "I tired of it inside two months," she replied. "But the pay was excellent and the duties enjoyable — and Carteret's good company. No one can deny that. I just wonder how generous he's going to be when he pays me off — which I can feel coming any day now. Should I create a big fuss? Or be terribly sweet and trust to his good nature?"

She looked toward Jenny for an answer but Peter cut in. "What's turning over in that devious mind of yours?"

Ruby continued staring at Jenny as she replied: "Oddly enough, I've always thought of opening a little shop of my own someday — not in Falmouth, I admit. But why not, I say now? And I was just wondering if this young lady had thought of taking a partner — since *she* hasn't enough money to do it properly, and I *probably* won't have enough, either ... perhaps we could manage it between us?"

"There's a thought!" Jenny said cautiously.

"At least you don't say an outright no."

"Certainly not!"

"Can I ask a few things about the premises?" Ruby went on at once. "For instance, will you be living in the two top floors?"

"They are living quarters," Jenny pointed out.

"But they could be turned into storerooms and workrooms — and then you might not need the floor immediately above the shop, which is presently equipped as photographic studios."

The penny began to drop with Jenny. "Go on," she said.

"And a big double window like that is really more suitable for a general *shop* — a milliner's or a haberdasher's — than for the sort of exclusive establishment you were telling me about on the quay just now. You've seen those places in the Burlington Arcade? And there's a couple in New Bond Street, too. We *demimondaines"* — she spoke the word with fastidious irony — "used to shop in those establishments all the time, of course. Nothing reach-me-down for us! But they all have *tiny* windows, you'll find. And they just put one or two items in them — dramatic, eyecatching things, of course. And costly! And lots of velvet spilling around the place, or gold lamé cloth, as if money was no object — which it isn't to their clientèle, of course. So nobody could *possibly* mistake it for a shop where you might stroll in and ask for half a yard of bias binding and a penny packet of pins!"

The accuracy of this analysis made Jenny laugh in a sort of helpless amazement.

"Did you only just think of this?" she asked.

Ruby shook her head. "I realized it when I first saw those shops with the tiny windows in the Burlington Arcade, and I thought of it again when I read that Stanton's old place has two front windows of about a hundred square feet each. If my cousin, Jim Collett, would be happy with all of one window and all the existing studios on the first floor up, you might have the rest for half his present bid. Or you might let him buy the lot and just take a twenty-one-year lease, pay rent out of income, and use *all* your savings for working capital."

"And now you've just talked yourself out of a partnership!" Peter said.

Ruby shrugged. "Very likely. But I couldn't keep it to myself, could I. It wouldn't have been right."

"And yet they do say that two heads are better than one," Peter mused, watching Jenny closely.

"And Ruby has both of them!" Jenny replied. "Let's first see how generous Lord Carteret is going to be, eh?"

"Then," continued the indefatigable Ruby, "we could return to London for a few days and go round the more exclusive houses, telling each other what we like and what we dislike, because if our tastes are *too* different, there's no point in making any other plans."

"I say!" Peter exclaimed admiringly. "You are taking it all very seriously, aren't you!"

"What about *your* future boatbuilding business?" Ruby asked. "Don't you take that seriously?"

"Nope!" he replied cheerfully, and went on to outline his plan to marry Gemma and travel light before they settled down.

"What does she think of the idea?" Ruby asked. "I'll bet she took some persuading!"

"Why?" he responded nervously.

"Because it's something she'd *enjoy*. Whereas marrying and setting up a home is a sort of social duty. And Gemma always has to be talked out of duty and into enjoyment. You mean you haven't even told her yet?"

He shook his head.

"More fool you! Come on — let us hie us hither to Devoran House! Suddenly I can't wait to see how generous Carteret's going to be!"

42 While Peter was advising the two young ladies on the colour of the cakes they should eat before embarking, Gemma was adding up figures in the office of Collett & Trevarton, photographic artists of Market Jew Sreet, Penzance. Her boast that she could add up all three columns — pounds, shillings, and pence — at the same time had not been idle. Crissy, who was watching her surreptitiously from across the partners' desk while pretending to read the day's correspondence, was eventually moved to admire her skill out loud. She waited until the girl had jotted the total in the carry-forward box at the top of the next page and said, "There'll never be a machine to add as quick as a human — unless they can teach machines to read, of course. How you do it, I don't know. Sometimes, if it's just a few figures, I can add shillings and pence at the same time, but never all three."

Gemma pointed to the current total in the pounds column — fifty-six. "It gets more difficult now. I think the human brain can handle figures under twenty without any trouble. Twenty to fifty gets more and more difficult. After fifty I have to concentrate on that one column alone. I once had an argument with Miss Isco-Visco about it, because, of course, all things French are superior and all things English are barbarous, in her eyes. So we took a grocery bill and translated the figures into francs and centimes and she added up according to her system and we added up ours and she was last by a good few seconds. The pennies column never goes above twelve, you see, and the shillings total is always under twenty — so of course it's quicker."

Crissy laughed. "What did she say to that?"

"She just pretended she was hopeless at sums. And anyway, she said the French were more logical. So I asked her to divide ten francs equally among three people. What sort of logic is it that makes it impossible to divide by three? It's the same with temperatures. In our system, we know the thirties are freezing, the forties are cold, the fifties are cool, the sixties are mild, the seventies are warm, the eighties are hot, the nineties are sweltering, and anything over a hundred is unbearable. Name any temperature and you know exactly what clothes to put up.

But with their *centigrade* degrees you don't know where you are. She just keeps saying that decimals are logical. If you can divide it by three, it has to be barbarous."

"Actually," Crissy pointed out, "you can't divide a mile into three. One thousand, seven hundred and sixty yards won't ..."

"You can if you work in inches."

"Oh ... yes."

"You can't divide a gallon into three, though — not even in fluid ounces. That's our only failure."

"You're still mentally in Falmouth half the time, aren't you," Crissy said fondly. "You say Miss Isco-Visco *says* this and *does* that — not said and did, which is what you would say if it really were all behind you. I suppose it's the effect of these daily letters between you and Peter?"

Gemma gave up trying to total the next page. "That's part of it," she admitted. "But also I keep thinking ..." She hesitated.

"What?"

"I keep wondering if it isn't Peter who's right and I'm wrong. When you work as a lady's maid in an upper-class house like that, you get sort of hypnotized to their way of thinking. You're not like the other people they might employ. You're not like the man who comes to mend a leaky pipe or put in a new pane of glass ..."

"Not to mention the man they pay to take their photographs!" Crissy added.

"That's my point. A lady's maid is *inside* their class-system. She's part of it — *I* was part of it whether I wanted to be or not. In fact, it didn't even cross my mind to ask whether I wanted it or not. Of *course* I wanted it! It was a big step up from being a parlourmaid, wasn't it! More money. Being called *Miss* Penhallow instead of just Penhallow. Hearing a few secrets. Being asked for advice. Of course I wanted it! But now, since coming here ... I mean, I thought I could help you out in the house or the studio and in return I'd learn some of the tricks and pitfalls of running a family business. But actually, I think the best thing I've learned while I've been here is to step *outside* that system of theirs and see how little it really matters."

"But we are still part of a class-system," Crissy objected. "Not the same part, of course, but Jim and I don't have too many friends who dig ditches or unload fishing catches!"

"That's quite a different matter. I'm not talking about that sort of thing."

"Ah," Crissy said. "Then I don't understand. What *are* you referring to?"

Gemma stared at her a moment and then said, "Perhaps you've forgotten what it's like. I mean, you've got a real *position* in Penzance now. But when you were lady's maid to old Mrs Trevarton ... didn't you hear her and her friends giggle and sneer behind the back of any lady who stuck her little finger in the air when she sipped her tea?"

Crissy nodded.

"And if one of them forgot to turn the corner of her visiting card down on the proper occasion — or turned it down when she shouldn't have — didn't they sneer then, too?"

"Yes," Crissy admitted.

"Well, that's what I'm saying. I was *part* of that way of thinking. When I was up in London for the Season, the great ladies spent half their time sniping at each other like that behind their backs. 'Did you see, my dear — diamond earrings at luncheon! And she called it 'lunch' — eeurgh!' That sort of thing. If you asked for someone's 'address' instead of their 'directions' or called a 'Fri-to-Mon' a 'weekend' or cut fish with a knife or if a so-called gentleman left his cane and gloves in the hall when calling on a lady 'At Home' ... we hugged ourselves with glee for hours, talking about it afterwards."

"And now, of course, you see how absurd it is. Why d'you think they do it?"

"I used to talk about that with Trewithen, the valet. His hobby is heraldry and genealogy. *Kelly's Handbook to the Upper Ten Thousand* is his favourite bedtime reading! As Bridget Condron says — she's the Irish skivvy at Alma Terrace — she says he'd tell you 'the seed, breed, and generation' of just about anybody. And I remember one evening, when we gave our big ball at the Empire Rooms in Bayswater, Trewithen and I were up in the gallery, watching them all having fun below, and he said, 'It's a remarkable thing, Miss Penhallow, but nine out of ten people here are struggling to forget that their grandparents were lucky if they had one good pair of boots to their name!' It's funny, isn't it, how some casual remarks can almost change your life for ever! I suddenly realized why they're looking over their shoulders all the time, sniping at each other and sneering at us 'lower' classes. It's to hide their uncertainty! They're only two generations away from the farmyard and factory bench themselves — most of them."

"I've often noticed that," Crissy agreed. "The loudest, angriest preacher is the one who feels he might fall prey to temptation at any hour of the day or night. If a man has to sew up his flies, how can any woman feel safe near him!"

"One of the few people I met who isn't like that," Gemma went on, "is Lord Carteret — Ruby's ... you know."

"'Protector' is the word, I believe?"

"Yes. He's the sixth baron in the line, so there's no uncertainty there. He'll talk to a ditch-digger just like he'd talk to a king. So that bears out my theory, doesn't it — no uncertainty." She fell into a reverie — until Crissy glanced at the clock and said, "It's time to go and meet the ten-thirty. D'you want to come and help? You haven't done that yet, have you — handing out our leaflets on the platform?"

Gemma sprang up eagerly. Crissy — or someone from Collett & Trevarton — met every train that brought summer trippers to Penzance and handed out leaflets advising them to keep an eye out for the firm's strolling photographers on the beaches and esplanade; the same leaflet also offered prints at a discount if they presented it at collection time. The films were snapped between ten in the morning and two in the afternoon and the prints were available at the kiosk on the station forecourt from midday onwards. Crissy was especially proud of the system, which she had invented back in 1891; it had kept the firm afloat through good times and bad ever since.

"That's the second time you've gone all thoughtful when you were speaking about Lord Carteret," Crissy said when they reached the street. "Is there something else about him you haven't told me?"

Gemma chuckled. "You don't miss much!"

"Not that I wish to pry, mind."

"It's just something Ruby said last time we met. She told me she thought her association with Carteret might soon end." She gave out a brief, ironic laugh. "It seems that he's turned quite serious about Beatrice."

"I see! And what does Beatrice think about that?"

"Oh! She couldn't be happier. Even before we went up to London ... I mean, she wasn't the least bit interested in getting a husband, but she told Peter he was to find a wicked lord for her. The sort of man who would make the parents and guardians of marriageable daughters throw up their hands in horror if he wasn't a lord." Gemma laughed. "She said it would drive her mother mad with indecision. She meant it as a joke but she's been proved absolutely right. A man with a dubious reputation but an undoubted title — an ancient one, too. Which way is poor Mrs de Vivian to jump!"

"She knows his reputation, then," Crissy mused. "Does that mean she knows specifically about Ruby?"

"Heavens, no! If she had, I wouldn't have lasted a single day. She doesn't even know I have a sister — much less a twin. Anyway, the word 'twin' gives her the vapours." Gemma went on to explain why.

Crissy's mind raced ahead, canvassing various possibilities, as was her habit. "So, if Carteret brings Ruby down to Cornwall with him ... and your mother happens to see them together ... what's she going to think? She'll think it's you! She'll assume you were so outraged by your dismissal that you went straight to Carteret and tried to steal away his affections!" She laughed with delight.

Gemma thought it amusing, too — but quite impossible. Not only would Ruby never come back to her home town on Carteret's arm, but his lordship himself was much too serious about Beatrice to bring Ruby with him. As Ruby herself said, their days together were probably over.

"Or ..." Crissy went on excitedly "... you could have the sort-of situation they love in grand opera. You know — where Mrs de Vivian locks Ruby up, thinking she's you, while you make good your escape with Peter. Then you elope to Gretna Green! The possibilities are endless. You *must* use your likeness to each other in some way."

Again, Gemma thought it no more than amusing to indulge in these fantasies. But she had a serious point to make, too. "I don't think there'll be any runaway marriage 'over the anvil' at Gretna Green — not for Peter and me, anyway. As I was about to say before we came away just now ... since I've had my eyes opened as to how stupid and petty-minded the sneers of upper-class women are about those they consider their inferiors, I've lost my own fear of being ridiculed if Peter and I were to marry. He can have his boatbuilding as a hobby and I'll settle down very happily as the next Mrs de Vivian."

"And how will you live?" Crissy opened the door to the ticket hall — the door Jim had passed by on that first evening. A draft of warm air, laden with the mingled aromas of tar-oil, fish-glue, soot, and steam, assailed their nostrils.

"D'you go in by that door?" Gemma asked.

"Why ever not?"

"Doesn't that way lead past the buffet?"

"Yes. That's actually why I'm coming this way. I want a quiet word with the manageress. One of her assistants has been saying rude things about us to the passengers, and I intend to put a stop to it."

When they reached the buffet, Gemma stayed outside and watched through the window. One look at Crissy's face as she issued what looked like threats or ultimatums to the manageress was enough to fill her with pity for the waitress in question.

"We'll hear no more of *that!*" Crissy said decisively as she regained the platform. She peered up the line. "That's its smoke now, see? It's now coming in through Long Rock. We'll go and stand there, just this side of the ticket collector. Don't waste a leaflet on anybody with luggage. You didn't tell me what you and Peter are going to live on, if boatbuilding is to be no more than his hobby?"

Gemma smiled sweetly. "When one becomes a *lady,*" she said, "one no longer bothers one's pretty little head about such things. It's for the gentleman to worry about, don't you know. If Peter is so keen for me to become a lady, then it's his problem, not mine! Isn't that the way of it?"

"Come, now — surely you don't mean it!" Crissy was prepared either to laugh or be genuinely shocked, depending on how serious Gemma was.

Gemma grinned. "What I'm saying is that I really don't mind being a lady *or* the wife of a yacht-designer and boatbuilder — or both, if that's possible nowadays. The only thing I really want, with all my heart and soul, is to be Mrs Peter de Vivian — and as for the rest, well … let the world think and do whatever it likes."

43 The only queasy part of the three-mile voyage, as far as Ruby's and Jenny's stomachs were concerned, came when the launch rounded Trefusis Point. There the dying remnants of the open-sea swell came northward up Carrick Roads and criss-crossed the smaller, wind-driven wavelets running eastward from the long fetch between there and Penryn. Once they were round the point, however, they gathered speed and were soon cutting their way through the swell on a more even keel.

To distract the women from this temporary choppiness, Peter pointed out a creek on the Roseland peninsula opposite, especially to Ruby.

"What about it?" she asked.

"Run your eye up the valley," he replied. "What's that on the skyline at the top?"

A smile spread slowly across her face. "Oh, my gidge!" she exclaimed. "So it is!"

"What?" Jenny asked.

"A farm called Penhale Jakes," Peter told her, and went on to explain its tragic history and its significance for Ruby and Gemma. By the time he'd finished, a headland had closed off their view of the valley. "When we've spoken to Carteret and Wilkes," Peter added, "we might come back here and see if there's a mooring near enough to let us walk up for a close look at the place. Have you ever been there?"

Ruby shook her head.

"Nor has Gemma. I don't suppose she'd mind my taking you there first. Ah — there's Devoran House!" He opened up the steam valve, making the engine shudder and strain. "Let's see if we can get up enough knots to ram our way clear out of the water and halfway up the lawns! It's only a hired boat, after all."

For one wild, terrifying moment, they actually believed him.

Meanwhile, on those same lawns before Devoran House, a furious Ada de Vivian, standing a little apart from the gathering, was telling Martha Unwin she was just about the most useless bag of bones that ever lived. Though she was careful to speak under her breath, there was no doubting her anger. She, Martha, couldn't perform the simplest task without making the most dreadful mess of it. All she'd had to do was go back to the *Guinevere* and hunt for some lorgnettes which she, Ada, was sure she'd left there. And she hadn't even been able to do that much properly! She was about as useful as a lighthouse in Leicestershire.

Martha endured as much of this as she could take before drawing a deep breath and speaking her own mind. She was not a lady's maid, never had been a lady's maid, never would be a lady's maid, did not want to be a lady's maid in the first place, had warned her and Mrs Walker about it, and was just about fed up to her back teeth with Mrs de Vivian's endless complaints. So if it was all the same to Mrs de Vivian, she'd give in her notice with immediate effect — as an earnest of which she started removing her pinafore, there and then.

"But you can't!" Ada snapped. "In the middle of a day ... and just when I need you ... you simply can't."

"Whether I can or I can't, don't matter. It's what I'm going to do," Martha replied.

"But my lorgnettes! What am I to do without them?"

"You found your way up here without even noticing they'd gone," Martha pointed out calmly. "Also, since they've only got plain glass in them, I can't see what good they do you anyway."

"How d'you know that?"

"'Cos I looked. Who shall I give this pinny to?"

"You won't get any sort of character from me, you know," Ada threatened.

Martha replied that the Unwins had been in Falmouth for centuries; their good reputation was widely acknowledged and she thought she might survive the blow.

"Well, at least stay until the end of the day — *please?*"

An unrelenting Martha said it was a bit late to turn on the waterworks; she'd drop the pinny off at Alma Terrace as soon as convenient and would collect the wages due then as well — less one week for the notice she wasn't working out, of course. And she'd be obliged if Mrs de Vivian would have them ready.

"But who is going to find my lorgnettes?" Ada asked finally. If she survived an entire afternoon without their assistance, the whole world would know she did not actually need them.

Martha said the the *Guinevere* was moored on this nearer bank of the river, so Mrs de Vivian wouldn't even need the faith of Saint Peter to walk across the water. And with that she left her employment, and her employer, high and dry.

Understandably, then, Ada de Vivian was not in the most joyful humour as she made her own way down to the jetty where the *Guinevere* was moored, to conduct her own hunt for her socially, if not optically, necessary lorgnettes.

The grounds of Devoran House were landscaped on the lines laid down by Capability Brown a century and a half earlier, with sweeping vistas and strategically placed groves of trees, sometimes providing the focal point for a small classical temple or a ruined folly. One such grove, however, would never have gained the great landscaper's approval, for it obliterated the best view of Mylor Creek, the prettiest of the many river creeks around the Fal estuary. This particular grove owed its existence to a feud, fifty years earlier, between the owners of Devoran House and those of Mylor Villa, directly across the water; quite simply, the then owner of Devoran House had planted mature willows and poplars at precisely that part of the bank which would obliterate the view of Mylor Villa from the terrace in front of his home. He had then moved the jetties, which he had considered to be an unsightly clutter, to the farther side of this new grove; and, to make it look a little more intentional, he had built a new classical pavilion a little way inland, surrounded by ornamental shrubs and wild roses. It was here that Peter decided to conceal Ruby and Jenny while he went to bring Lord Carteret and Conrad Wilkes, respectively, to them. He got no more than half a dozen paces from the pavilion, however, when he saw his mother approaching. One glance at her, at the pugnacious tilt of her head and the jackboot planting of each foot, was enough to tell him all he needed to know about her mood and he retreated at once.

"What now?" Jenny asked.

He put a finger to his lips and motioned to them to crouch down low, behind a waist-high solid wall that enclosed most of the pavilion floor.

"Who was *that?*" Ruby asked in a hushed whisper when Ada had disappeared among the trees.

"My mater," he told them.

"Ha!" came the cry from down on the jetty. "The girl's an idiot! Didn't I say it!"

A moment later she appeared among the trees again, tossing her head and practising sundry contemptuous movements of her lorgnettes — during one of which she found herself staring directly into Peter's eyes, which were just visible above the sill of the low pavilion wall.

"Mater!" He rose, laughing awkwardly. "I didn't know it was you." He stepped out of the pavilion. "Did you see the launch I hired? She's a beauty, don't you think?"

He hastened toward her, trying to turn her away from the pavilion, toward the house.

If he had been less eager, she might have been less suspicious. She stood her ground and said, "How long have you been skulking here?"

"Just arrived." He took her arm. "Why did you come down here? And what girl is an idiot? Martha Unwin, I suppose. You should never have dismissed that other lady's maid ... you know the one — Miss Whatsername."

She was not even listening. "There's somebody in there," she said sharply. *"That's* why you were hiding. Who is it?"

She broke free from his grip and took a step toward the pavilion. But he leaped nimbly ahead of her and spread wide his arms. "No, Mater!" he cried. "I beg you — please go no farther. If you value the unity of our family, turn about now and ..."

She was still not listening. Staring over his shoulder, she suddenly raised her lorgnettes and shrieked, "Jezebel!" To Peter she cried, "Miss Whatsername, indeed!"

Peter spun round to see Ruby standing there, calm and silent, just staring back at his mother.

"You are a traitor to your very core!" Ada shrieked at her. "I suppose this has been going on behind my back all these weeks — and all the while, I have been paying you to stay away from my son!"

"What?" Peter pretended to be scandalized, though Gemma had told him of the arrangement in her first letter.

"Oh!" His mother rounded on him. "Don't try to pretend you knew nothing about it! You're every bit as bad as she is — worse, in fact, for you've been brought up to the very *highest* standards of honesty. Unlike some!"

"Honesty!" Peter raised his hands high and walked in a small circle, exasperated, carefully keeping between her and the building. "Honesty!" He let his hands fall again. "I suppose it was honesty drove you to tell me Gemma was in Newquay when you know very well she's in Penzance! And it was 'the very highest standards of honesty' that *forced* you to tell me she had cleaned out our bank account?"

"It was for your own good. This ... this *creature* here ..."

"She has a name, you know."

"It shall never pass my lips — that I can promise you."

"Ah!" He pretended the penny had dropped. "I see your trouble, Materkins!" He laughed. "You are suffering under the delusion that this young lady is Gemma!"

"Miss Penhallow, if you please! Yes, of course she is. Anyone can see it. What nonsense is this?"

"No nonsense, Mater. Allow me to present Miss ..."

"You will do no such thing! How dare you presume like that? You will *not* present this ... this traitress to me!"

"Then at least allow me to inform you that the young lady you think is Gemma Penhallow is, in fact, her sister Ruby. You might as well stand up, too, Jenny. This is Miss Jennifer Divett, daughter of the prince-bishop of Durham and a friend of the Wilkeses. May I present *her* to you at least?"

It threw Ada completely off her stride. "I don't believe you!" she snapped. Then, in the same breath but a more emollient tone to Jenny, "Is this true, Miss Divett?"

"Every word of it, Mrs de Vivian — including what your son told you about Miss Ruby Penhallow here. She is Gemma's twin. So your mistake is quite ..." Her voice trailed off as she saw Peter rushing to support his mother.

He had assumed that the dreaded word would bring about its usual consequences; but this time his mother was too beside herself with fury to faint or have a fit of the hysterics. "How *could* you!" she shouted at him, spittle flying around her trembling head. "Of all the cruellest deceptions you might have dreamed up to practise upon me ..."

"It is no deception, Mater!" he tried to assure her.

"Be quiet! You could less easily persuade me that this ... this *person* is her own sister than that you have truly been your own brother Paul all these years — and that would take more lifetimes than anyone could number. You are everything he was not. You are disloyal, idle, shallow, a wastrel ..." The words choked her at last.

"Oh yes!" Peter sneered. "You've rammed him down my throat from the day he died. Every time I've disappointed you in the slightest degree ..."

"You have never done anything *but* disappoint me, Peter. You have been one unending disappointment almost from the day you were born." She raised her eyes to the heavens. "Why dids't Thou not take *this* one? Why dids't Thou not spare my darling boy, my true and only son?"

"Yes, why not!" Peter pretended to join in her blasphemy while the two young women watched in silent horror. "Paul would have been prime-minister by now — *and* archbishop of Canterbury — *and* admiral of the fleet — *and* field marshal!" A new thought struck him and he gave out a bitter laugh. "At least he'd have been a *general* — and why not? His grandmother was a general before him!"

This time he truly thought his mother was going to faint; he had never seen her face lose colour so quickly. Her jaw dropped. Her lorgnettes fell to the ground and she paid them not the slightest heed. "What did you say?" she whispered.

Peter had no chance to repeat the damning words for at that moment Lord Carteret called from somewhere beyond the shrubbery, "Mrs de Vivian? Are you there?"

"Is everything all right?" Beatrice added.

Ada, showing that presence of mind which had saved her in awkward situations all her life (though none had ever been so awkward as this!), recovered at once from her threatened apoplexy. "Here!" she called out. "All's well!" Meanwhile she held an accusing finger an inch or two from Peter's nose and murmured, "One word of this and I shall not answer for myself. I don't know what you may think you have discovered, but ..."

"I have discovered 'General' Concepta Kelly's name on a certain document," he said calmly.

"I see. Well, we shall accept your disgraceful fictions about these persons while Carteret and your sister are here."

Ruby stooped and retrieved the lorgnettes, which she had to thrust into Ada's hand — without the slightest acknowledgement, of course.

"You were gone such a long time ..." Beatrice was saying as she rounded the bend in the path. Then, catching her breath, she exclaimed, "Gemma?"

Ada was about to crow but Beatrice, noticing Peter's grin, looked again at the girl and said, "Or is it Ruby? It is! It's Ruby!"

"Not you, too!" Ada cried.

"Ruby!" Carteret said, taking his cue from Beatrice. "What are you doing here?" Though he tried his best to smile, he was clearly displeased.

She took a deep breath and said, "I bring you bad news from Radnor Castle, my lord. May I have a word in private?"

A by now thoroughly bemused Ada watched them go down to the riverbank. "Is it true?" she asked her daughter.

"Is what true?"

Ada waved a hand after the retreating pair. "That she is *not* Miss Penhallow?"

"But she is! She's Miss *Ruby* Penhallow."

"Why did nobody tell me!" It was more of an accusation than a question. All her fire had died. Peter and Beatrice suspected she was close to tears — genuine ones, this time.

"I felt sure Mrs Walker would have mentioned it — even before we moved from Plymouth. You mean she didn't?"

"Of course she didn't," Peter said.

They both stared at him.

"Well, for one thing," he went on, "Ruby left Falmouth under a slight cloud — to put it mildly. And for another thing, Pater went all round the servants telling them never to say the word 'twin' in *your* hearing, Mater."

"Peter!" Beatrice watched her mother in alarm.

"It's all right, dear!" Ada waved a dismissive hand. "I've had so many shocks in the last ten minutes, I'm past all feeling." She turned to Peter. "So ... it truly is not" — she steeled herself to say the name — "Gemma!"

"No," he agreed coldly. "And therefore you needn't have revealed your lies and treachery."

"Peter!" Beatrice exclaimed yet again.

He rounded on her bitterly. "Oh, you've no idea what we've been treated to down here. Still, it's out now. It's said and it can't be unsaid."

"It was for your own good," Ada repeated.

"No it wasn't," he replied with the calm of contempt in his voice. "It was to protect *you* from your own sense of insecurity."

Beatrice laughed. "The mater? Insecure?"

Jenny, who had remained in the background during all this, accidentally crunched some gravel underfoot — which recalled Peter to his duty. "Forgive me," she said. "Beatrice, may I present you to Miss Jenny Divett, daughter of the prince-bishop of Durham. Miss Beatrice de Vivian."

The two young women bowed and smiled at each other. "May I ask how it is you came to know my brother, Miss Divett?" Bea asked.

"We met in London during the Season," Jenny replied easily. "I mentioned that I was thinking of opening a little *boîte* or *boutique* — as the French call it. And ..."

"A *shop?* You — a bishop's daughter?" Ada's social habits were rapidly reasserting themselves.

"A fashion establishment." Jenny spoke the words as if they were a correction. "Highly select. Nothing under ten guineas, you know. And plenty for two hundred and more."

"Really?" Ada was interested now, almost despite herself.

"Yes. And your son mentioned Falmouth as a possibility and I thought, why not ..."

The talk drifted on to questions of fashion, where Ada had always felt safe.

Meanwhile, Ruby was saying to Carteret, "I can either pretend to be bringing news of your alleged wife's grave illness or of her actual death. It's got to be one or the other, so you decide."

"In that case," he said after an uncomfortable pause, "we'd better make it her illness."

"Why? You're still shillyshallying, John. Surely it's time to kill her off once and for all?"

"I simply don't feel ready," he replied awkwardly.

"Nonsense!" Her peremptory tone could have been borrowed from Ada de Vivian at her best. "You just want to eat your cake and keep it whole. The only reason you haven't paid me off is that you still think, somewhere in the back of that devious, scheming mind of yours, that I'll go on being your missy *after* you've got a genuine wife in Beatrice. Look me in the eye and deny it!"

He looked her in the eye and swiftly turned away.

"So which is it to be?" she went on relentlessly. "Is she dead or is she dying?"

"Oh, very well!" he said crossly. "Let's kill her off."

"Consider it done." Ruby giggled. "And now let's talk about paying me off."

"Do we have to?" he wheedled. "I'm very fond of you. And Bea has got this art-disease pretty badly. I love her dearly but I can foresee times when I'll want a bit of a breather from it all. A bit of that comfort you're so good at giving!"

"And meanwhile, I suppose I just languish in my gilded cage, waiting and waiting for you to get the itch? Thank you for doing me the honour, John, but I must regretfully decline. Let us talk about putting me into a partnership in Miss Jennifer Divett's exclusive fashion establishment."

"Not now. Tomorrow, perhaps."

"*Now,* John."

44 The following Monday, Crissy asked Gemma if she wouldn't mind doing the most boring job of all in the entire business; the girl who usually did it was at a funeral and she herself had to go to the hairdresser. The most boring job of all proved to be standing in the kiosk, selling prints of the snaps taken by the wandering photographers on the beaches and esplanade — and taking orders and money in advance for any reprints people might wish to order.

"I don't think it will be boring at all," Gemma said. "Not the first time, anyway."

The photographers started down on the esplanade and beaches at ten. From half-past onward, a messenger boy ferried their exposed film up to the studios, where they were developed and printed at once; the same boy then carried the prints down to the kiosk in the station forecourt before doing another round of the photographers to collect the next batches of exposures. The first lot of prints, however, were collected and carried down to the kiosk by the seller on duty for that day — usually, of course, by the girl who was away to a funeral on that particular Monday. So Crissy collected them, instead, and took Gemma down to the kiosk to show her the system.

"Each print has a serial number and today's date on the back," she explained. "You only need that if they want to re-order. We keep the negatives exactly a month. After that it's too late because we send them to the silver recoverers. We keep the prints a month and then they go the same way. We get back five percent of our costs that way, so it's worthwhile. Anyway, you arrange the prints in these numbered slots, see? Beginning here with number one — big surprise! One to sixty on this board ... sixty-one to a hundred and twenty on the next ... and so on, right the way round to number three hundred and sixty ..."

"D'you ever reach that high?" Gemma asked.

"Only on the hottest bank holidays."

"And then?"

"It doesn't matter. You won't get anywhere near it today. Oh, I see! You want to know how to cope back home in your *own* business — when Peter suddenly gets orders for three hundred and sixty *racing dinghies* all on the one day! Well, we've got a spare set of boards we can hinge like shutters on top of the fixed ones round the kiosk. Happy?"

"Planning is the cure for panic," Gemma said.

"You think so? I *planned* to be at the hairdresser by quarter to eleven and now I'm starting to panic. There's your float — four pounds in silver. There's the book where you take down reprint orders. Get a card if they carry them."

"Call of nature?" Gemma asked.

"Lock up. Hang up this notice — 'Back in five minutes' — and use the ladies' in the station. We give the girl fifteen minutes for lunch — oops, *luncheon!* — but she watches over the kiosk from that window in the station buffet. However, I'll be back at lunchtime so that needn't bother you. Any questions? I must fly!"

Gemma looked at each serial number and dropped the prints into their numbered slots. Then she went outside to admire the result. So many people! Some caught by surprise. Some posing frightfully. She actually saw a man she knew — a clerk at the mills in Penryn, where her father worked. He had his arm around a young lady who, Gemma felt sure, was not his wife. However, the wife was there in the next picture, with a whole group of youngsters, so it must be a family outing. Still, it showed how easily you could get caught out, if you took a day off with someone you shouldn't. Suppose your boss came along and saw your picture there! He could buy it and use it as proof to sack you! She began to weave a mystery story around such a sequence of events.

By one o'clock, when Crissy returned to relieve her, she had grown tired of looking at the front of each print and just stuck them into the appropriate slots and then surveyed them for a general check that they were the right way up.

"Jim told me to ask you if you'd seen print number seventy-one?" Crissy asked as she approached. She had a strange smile on her lips.

"I've stopped looking at them — just the serial numbers," Gemma replied. "Why?"

"Come out here and look. It's the second one down and second one in on the number-two board."

Gemma had to look twice to believe it for it was a snapshot of Peter, standing in Market Jew Street and holding up a placard on which he had written in huge letters: YES GEMMA IT IS ME.

She turned to look at Crissy, thinking this was some sort of photographer's prank, when she saw Peter himself, standing in the goods entrance to the station, holding his arms out toward her. "And about time, too!" he roared. "I thought you must have gone blind."

She flew across the forecourt, straight into his arms, and for the next minute or so she was oblivious to all but the touch and taste of his lips and tongue. The touch was magic but the taste — cheese and onions — forced her to break contact at last. "You've had your lunch already!" she accused him.

"Only one sandwich." He laughed. "I was about to order a second when Crissy rescued me."

"Crissy? You mean you've met?"

"I've been in that buffet, watching you and dying of love, for more than half an hour."

"But what … how … I don't understand. It doesn't matter, anyway. I'm starving."

But she neither let go of him nor made the slightest move toward the buffet.

"It's easily explained," he said. "I arrived at noon, saw you in the kiosk, thought of playing this little trick, went up to the studios, introduced myself, explained … they laughed … and the rest you can imagine. The only hitch was that you went blind in the meanwhile."

"Oh, Peter, Peter, Peter …!" She laughed and kissed him at each repetition of his name — and thus passed another minute or two.

But at last hunger — and Crissy's shout of, "When you've quite finished!" — brought them back to the world. Gemma ran back to her, dragging Peter by the hand. "I'm sorry, Crissy!" she said. "Could I go and have lunch now? Your hair looks lovely, by the way. You and Peter have already met, he says."

"Yes. Why did you never tell me he's such a *nice* young man!"

Gemma's only reply to that was a heavenward glance and an expostulating rasp of her lips.

"You can take more than lunch, actually," Crissy went on. "You can take the rest of the day off. In fact, why not take the rest of the year! Or the rest of your life — it sounds as if Peter has plans for it."

These words had the effect of sobering Gemma up. "Really?" she asked, turning to him again. "You've not done anything foolish by coming here? Does your mother know?"

He smiled. "My mother, you will be delighted to hear, is no longer an obstacle. I've come here to get your permission to start calling the banns — *if* you haven't found someone else you'd sooner marry in the meantime?"

She dug him with her elbow and started to lead him toward the station buffet. But he held back. "We can afford better than that," he said. "Let's stroll along to the esplanade and have a decent lunch at the Queen's."

"For that I can wait another ten minutes," she said, turning smartly on her heel. "Oh, God, I have missed you!"

"Same here. Letters just aren't the same, are they. Just to hold your hand again is magical."

Billing and cooing of that sort kept them happy and occupied all the way along the harbour front, past the old lifeboat station and the swing bridge to the inner harbour. But as the euphoria settled, the nagging questions began to creep back at the edges.

"Are you going to explain to me," Gemma asked at last, "why your mother is no longer an obstacle?"

"All thanks to Trewithen," he replied.

"Eh?" She stopped dead. "How on earth …?"

"You know he's always been keen on genealogy and heraldry and things? This is strictly between you and me, of course. As far as everyone else is concerned, it was *I* who did all the sleuthing — during the time we were up in London, when I was actually mooning around the West End, reading love poetry in all the bookshops. Anyway, he discovered my grandmother's wedding lines — my mother's mother, that is. Granny Concepta. I can barely remember her. She had a bristling moustache — that I do remember. But on the marriage lines it gave her occupation as *general!*"

He expected her to ask what that meant, but, it seemed, she already knew. She burst into laughter and, the more she thought about it — and all the times Mrs de Vivian had boasted of coming over with the Conqueror, and all the snobbish remarks she had passed — the louder and wilder her laughter grew.

Peter waited until it died down and then said, "You obviously know what 'general' means."

"Only because of little Bridget Condron," Gemma said, dabbing the tears from her cheeks. "She once said she wanted to go back to Ireland and be a general. She couldn't understand why we thought it so funny."

They rounded the corner, past the Trinity House dock with its collection of gigantic marker buoys, which lay sprawled on their sides like vast chessmen, painted in strident patterns and colours. Then Gemma became serious again. "We're not blackmailing her, are we, Peter? I wouldn't like that."

"Really?"

"No. Much as I dislike her — or her attitude — I'd hate her to think we're the sort of people who would stoop so low."

"She'd stoop far lower than that, my darling — indeed, she *did* stoop far lower. She told me you'd as good as stolen our money and disappeared. She'd have been quite happy if I'd gone to my grave thinking you were a thief."

"Even so, I'd hate her to think we are like that, too."

"Anyway, she couldn't care less about us. She told me Paul was her only real son."

"No!"

"She did. All her thoughts are now directed toward Beatrice and Lord Carteret, which looks set to become quite serious. We can do what we like — or else!" He laughed.

Gemma did not join in. "Did you actually confront her with this discovery, darling? How did it come out?"

He started to tell her how he'd taken Ruby and Miss Divett out to Devoran House ... but she interrupted him to ask more about this Miss Divett. He explained her away, using more or less the same words as Jenny herself had used in accounting to Beatrice for their association — that they had met 'during the London Season.'

My first lie to Gemma, he thought wryly — not an out-and-out lie, just a lie by omission. It did have the virtue, however, of protecting Jenny's future reputation.

He went on to describe how his mother had mistaken Ruby for her — and what awful truths had come out into the open following it. All her vitriolic comparisons between him and Paul ... and how he had been stung into replying ... and how that had led to his savage joke about their grandmother being a general before him ... "So, yes," he concluded, "it's blackmail if she wants to look at it that way. Otherwise, it's just a secret that can remain a secret for ever — as long as she behaves sensibly."

"As long as she doesn't stand in our way, you mean."

"Just so."

Her silence compelled him to speak. "Surely you don't mind? There's little love lost between you."

"But we'd still have to live in Falmouth. We'd be bound to meet, and quite often, too, I should think."

"Ah!" He grinned. "That's the next thing I was coming to."

But Gemma thought they had not finished with the present matter. "Does she know about us setting up in the boatbuilding business?" she asked.

"Well, that's the other thing I wanted to talk about ..."

"I knew it!" she cried triumphantly. "You weren't serious, were you! You were just humouring me — giving me time to see sense, as you would no doubt put it. Well, let me tell you this, Peter de Vivian ..."

"No!" he interrupted her. "Let me tell you this! What about kissing Falmouth goodbye for a few years — before we settle down? In fact, let's kiss England goodbye, too. Go out and see a bit of the world. No master plan. Just follow our noses. Travel cheap. Slow cargo boats rather than big ocean liners. And we won't stay in the big hotels, either. Just ordinary pensions and boarding houses for people of limited means ... so that we get closer to the real life of the country."

He sensed that the idea attracted her so he pressed it a little farther. "And we could go picking grapes in California, perhaps. Or the Cape. And we could do other things in other places. Teach English in Japan, for instance. Be butler and housekeeper in Argentina ..."

"You?" She hooted with laughter.

"Yes." He was hurt. "D'you think I couldn't do it?"

The laughter died. "No. I'm sure you could."

"And pretty well, too."

"Yes, yes! The more I listen to you, Peter, and the more I think about it, the more I realize that you have a vast number of talents that qualify you for the lower rungs of society's ladder!"

"You mean the idea doesn't appeal to you?"

"I didn't say that. I like the idea of travelling and seeing the world. Who wouldn't! And I like the idea of avoiding the posh hôtels and country clubs. But it's the singing-for-our-supper part that doesn't appeal quite so much — maybe because I've never really done anything else."

"Yes." He was chastened. "I should have thought of that."

They went into the Queen's, where a variety of delicious lunchtime aromas drew them infallibly to the dining room, a mock-Tudor chamber with high ceilings, modern lights, a minstrel gallery that would not bear the weight of a child, and the very latest in Arts-and-Crafts furniture. They went straight to the carver's buffet, where the roast pork looked too succulent, and the crackling too crackly, to refuse.

As they took their seats, Gemma said, "It's often struck me that those who are most keen on the virtues of manual labour are those who could sit and watch it happen before their very eyes all day."

"All right!" He held up his hands in surrender. "You win. I take your point."

"But we could reverse our positions," she went on. "You could pick grapes in the Cape while I lay back in my deck chair and admired you. Then you can have your dream come true and I can have mine."

"Gemma!" He reached across the table and squeezed her hand rather hard. "Enough!"

The waiter brought their meat and the waitress followed him to serve their vegetables.

With the edge taken off their hunger they became more relaxed, less eager to tease.

"You've changed your tune a bit, haven't you?" he asked. "Now you actually *want* to become a lady of leisure."

She nodded, unable to deny it. "I was telling Crissy ... being here ... not being part of the hierarchy in the de Vivian household ... has given me a different view of things. I think I could do what your Granny Concepta obviously did — take my place as Mrs Peter de Vivian, with all that entails, and *force* people to accept me."

"But only *after* we come back here from all our travels," he put in anxiously.

"Yes, that will help. But all I'm saying is that the idea no longer terrifies me ... what does that smile mean?"

He gazed at her a moment, wondering if he ought to explain. "Why not?" he said aloud. "D'you recall a conversation with Gwynneth Jones — Tabitha Wilkes's maid? You were ironing something, I think."

Her eyes narrowed. "Vaguely. We were goffering frills, actually. It's a bit more skilled than mere ironing. Why?"

"Afterwards, she told Tabitha not only that you were undoubtedly in love with me but that if I waited long enough you'd lose your fear of moving in society."

"Oh, really!"

"You're not annoyed, are you?"

"Oh, no. I'm ecstatic to discover I've been spied on and reported on at every turn!"

"Delicious pork!" he commented.

She chewed in silence.

"Tabitha was intrigued at the thought of our illicit love affair. If you know a way of stopping a wayward, sixteen-year-old girl whose head is full of romance from meddling in such a situation, I'd be forever grateful to hear of it."

Gemma tried her hardest not to smile but at last gave up the unequal struggle.

After that their conversation turned to third parties. He told her of Beatrice's plans to study art in London. Carteret had a friend at the Slade School, who was on a painting holiday in

St Ives. He had looked at Beatrice's paintings and told her she'd have no difficulty getting a place; all she needed to do was turn up on the first day of term, in September, and he'd make all the arrangements. She was going to live with the Wilkeses and become officially engaged to Carteret, who was going to study the history of architecture at the Bartlett School, which was next door to the Slade — both schools being part of University College London. He'd use his knowledge to guide him in the improvements he wanted to make at Radnor Castle.

And Carteret had meanwhile decided to part with Ruby — 'Sapphire' no more — giving her a generous settlement — enough, anyway, to go into partnership with Miss Divett ... which brought Peter to his *other* reason for coming to Penzance that day: He had been deputed to talk with the Colletts about the possibility of renting the ground-floor shop and one of the upper-floors to use as stores and workrooms. And what did Gemma think they'd say?

45 Gemma did not actually believe the old Cornish superstition that a marriage on the full moon was especially blessed but she thought one might as well go along with it unless there were pressing reasons not to. The October full moon fell on Tuesday the eighteenth and so that was the date she and Peter set for their wedding. In every way it was planned without the slightest cooperation from anyone at Alma Terrace. Indeed, Peter no longer spoke of 'my parents'; they were now 'the opposition.'

Ada de Vivian soon discovered that her ill-tempered treatment of Martha Unwin has been ill-advised, as well. As Martha herself had warned her at the time, her family had a long history and a high reputation locally, so there was no hesitation in choosing between competing explanations for her sudden departure. The word went out among the domestic classes that that-there Mrs de Vivian was an employer to avoid. Martha, as parlourmaid, had been paid £20 a year plus uniforms and 'the run of her teeth,' as Bridget Condron put it; but to replace her, the de Vivians suddenly found they had to offer, £21, then £22, and finally £22 10*s*. — an increase which, the Walkers advised, should be reflected all round among the other eight servants or it would lead to bad blood among them. And so an annual wage bill of around £250 a year was raised closer to £280 — all because of a missing pair of lorgnettes! And when other employers in Falmouth got to hear of it (which, thanks to their own servants, they did within days), the de Vivians were not the most popular members of Falmouth's Upper Hundred.

Gemma lodged at home with her parents in Penryn. They would not, however, forgive Ruby the disgrace she had brought upon them; so she joined Jenny at the Roseland View. Together, they almost wore out their fingers, working on Gemma's wedding dress, which was to be displayed during the week before the ceremony in the window of *A la Mode,* their new establishment on the ground floor of the former Stanton's photography studios. And in the week after the wedding, the photographs commemorating the event were to be displayed in the *other* window, now belonging to the new Falmouth branch of Collett & Trevarton, photographic artists.

Everyone — even those most closely involved — said it was ridiculous to be working in such haste, but, as Guinevere Roanoke had once remarked to Peter, some things have to be done immediately or they get put off for years.

The banns were read at St Gluvias, the parish church of Penryn, which had been rebuilt, somewhat barbarously, less than thirty years earlier; only the ancient granite west tower had been preserved. Peter worshipped there with Gemma on the three Sundays preceding their wedding. They sat beneath a brass memorial to Thomas Kyllgrave and his wives. He died in 1487, according to the inscription, which testified to nothing beyond his piety and worthiness. Gemma knew every line of the text and the images by the time the vicar said, "This is for the third time of asking."

"It's like that bit on the railway line just this side of Exeter," she said to Peter afterwards.

"What is?" he asked.

"Hearing the last of the three banns called. It's like that bit where the line goes through three tunnels — or maybe it's more than three. Anyway, it's where you come out into the sunlight at last and you know there's a clear line ahead, all the way home."

"No it isn't. There are two short tunnels just before Truro."

"Oh, don't be so fussy! You know what I mean. They're more like wide bridges than short tunnels, anyway." She gripped his arm tight. "Two more days and we'll be man and wife! I still can't believe it. Can you?"

"D'you want a quick outing in the *Gem?* Just half an hour? I came up the river in her this morning. She's below the bridge."

Gemma told her mother what they intended and then they went directly to the mooring.

"I've always thought of you as my wife," he said, answering her earlier question. "Certainly ever since that evening at the Empire Rooms."

He handed her into the boat, raised the main sail, and cast off; a shiver of a breeze through the arches of the bridge pulled them out into a lazy current. "The tide'll help us back," he said. "It's just on the turn now."

She stared out at the gleaming mudbanks all about them and said, "We live in different worlds, really, you and me. I'll bet if you woke up at three in the morning and someone asked you what was the state of the tide at Custom House Quay, you could say it to within an inch. It's there in the back of your mind all the time, isn't it — what the sea is up to."

"I suppose so. You mean you couldn't?"

She shook her head. "If I happen to notice high tide on one day, I could probably tell you what state it was if you asked me the next day, and maybe the next after that. But then I'd lose the feel of it. What is it? Forty minutes later each day?"

"Roughly. But why does that mean we live in different worlds?"

They were clear of the waterside buildings now and the breeze filled the sail. The fleet little boat leaped eagerly ahead, with the ripples beating a silvery tattoo beneath her bow; they had to sit, facing each other, right against the port gunwhale, to keep her on an even keel.

"When you say I've been your wife ever since that evening, what d'you mean? What does 'being your wife' mean?"

He stared at her in bewilderment. "The same as it means to any man — that you're the most special woman in the world. That I want to live alongside you — and only you. That if anyone harmed you, I'd kill them. That if it was your life or mine, I wouldn't even need to think about the choice. You know! All that sort of thing. Why? What did you think I meant?"

She sniffed, blinked rapidly, many times, and shrugged; her lips were trembling.

He pretended to busy himself with rearranging the sails.

"I can't think why I ever doubted you — now," she said at last. "You haven't changed a bit, have you — not since that very first day we met."

"I have! I was frantic until I knew you felt the same about me. I must have been an absolute pain in the neck to you."

"Well ..." she replied in a dubious tone, hugging herself into herself. "It was rather nice, actually — being pursued and *not* giving out any encouragement in return! I don't think women are very nice creatures when it comes to love, do you? We *want* to make it difficult. We want to be given the most for yielding the least."

"But do we fellows complain? That's the real test. I don't. By turning up your nose at me all those long *years,* you made that moment when you finally said, 'I love you,' a thousand times more precious."

"I do love you, Peter. So much. I think I must be the luckiest girl in the world."

"In your own small way," he replied loftily. "But when it comes to luck, you're not in the same league as me."

They were passing the old cemetery on the left bank, just below Bissom.

"I wonder if pious old Thomas Kyllgrave is buried there?" she mused, "And his wives. Or are they up there with their memorial in the church, somewhere?"

"Did you notice what they did with the other memorials when they rebuilt the nave?" he asked.

"What?"

"They kept the little statues of Samuel and William Pendarves in the main bit of the church when they restored it, but they moved their wives round the corner. I'll bet the Pendarves children thought, when they put up those memorials, that their parents would be there, facing each other, to the end of recorded time. But what were the restorers thinking of when they separated them like that? It's like saying, 'Give the church your money, by all means, but don't rely on us to carry out your wishes!' Mad!"

"Vanity!" Gemma sighed.

He had the impression that other things were on her mind.

"Everyone's talking about your dress in the window," he said.
"Mmnh."

"Getting butterflies in the tummy?"

She smiled. "Sort of."

"Want to call it off?"

She drew breath to reply but then merely stared at him, as if seeking help.

"Gemma!" he laughed. "That's one question you absolutely *have* to answer!"

"It's not about the wedding," she said. "It's about the other ... you know."

"Going away after."

"Yes. Everybody looking at me — and you know what they're thinking. All those jokes."

"I don't know what we're going to do about you, Gemma! No sooner do you put one fear behind you than you start encouraging another! And it's always about what other people will think. What does it matter *what* they think?"

She just lowered her eyes and stared at the keelson.

He sighed. "Isn't there someone you can talk to about it? Your mother?"

"Ha!" was all she replied to that.

"Crissy Collett, then?"

She looked into his eyes at last, and smiled as if he'd just said something wise.

"You mean you already have?"

She swallowed heavily and nodded, not taking her gaze off him. Those magical pale green eyes still had the power to transfix him.

"And?"

"She said she felt just the same as me before her wedding with Jim, which was back in eighteen and ninety-one — on the first day of June."

"But it all magically evaporated the moment she said 'I do'?"

"No. It all magically evaporated three days *before* the wedding."

For a moment he was genuinely puzzled; then he did not dare believe he knew what she was talking about.

"She didn't plan anything," Gemma said. "Nor did he. She just couldn't bear the thought of everybody knowing and sniggering behind her back, so she thought she'd like to be able to say to herself, 'Snigger away, you fools. I know something you don't!' And then, when Jim collected his severance wages at Stanton's and took her to luncheon at the Falmouth Hôtel and they went for a walk at Gyllyngvase afterwards ... and it suddenly struck her that Fenton Lodge at Swanpool was empty and she had the keys and ... and so ..."

"They jumped the starter's gun!"

"If you want to put it that way. She said she was never more glad of any action in her whole life — especially during their honeymoon on the Scillies." She gestured toward her right. "There's a jetty over there."

"It's ... private," he pointed out, having to clear his throat between the two words.

"Good!" she said. "So is the bit of woodland beside it, I hope. Happy birthday, darling!"

46 On the great day itself, Ruby brought the wedding dress over to Penryn just before nine; she thought that if there was to be one day in her life on which her mother might forgive her — or at least deign to speak to her — it was this one. What her mother actually said was, "You were gone some time. I was beginning to get worried."

"No more than fourteen months, Mother," she managed to reply before her voice gave out. She would have loved to say more but her heart was beating all over the place. She laid the box carefully down on the table. Her head was spinning.

"Ruby?" Her mother was aghast. She had barely glanced at the girl when she entered; now she stood and stared.

Ruby could not utter a word. She flew to her mother and flung her arms about her, sobbing her eyes out and saying, "Please ... please ..." over and over again.

For a long while her mother just stood there as if carved in stone — stiff and unrelenting. But eventually something snapped within her and Ruby, peeping over her mother's shoulder, watched her in the mirror. The reflection shivered through her tears but she could see the woman engaged in a battle of wills with her own arms; it was as if the arms wished to hug her, while her mother fought to keep them off her. Eventually the arms won and Ruby had the sort of homecoming welcome that, in biblical times, went along with feasting on fatted calves.

"Where's that Gemma gone and got herself to, then?" her mother asked eventually. Her attitude was severe, as if to atone for her sentimental weakness in forgiving Ruby and welcoming her home like this.

"I passed her on the bus coming in," Ruby replied. "She was up the banks by the rope works, picking white campion and things for her hair and bouquet."

"My dear soul!" Mrs Penhallow exclaimed. "What is she thinking of? She'll be late."

"Guss-on! Church isn't but five minutes' walk from here. And it won't take ten minutes to dress her."

"We aren't walking. We got the loan of Fox's carriage!" The proud smile faded and Mrs Penhallow grew worried again. "But I can't make that Gemma out these days. Ever since she come home from Penzance she's been so nurley as a bee butt. You couldn't say a thing. But these two days now past, since Sunday, after they called the last banns, she's been so docible as a breeze. Singing like a linnet all day. There's no 'counting for her, at all."

"Don't you want to see the dress?"

"I shall see it soon enough, I daresay." Her voice was indifferent but her hand plucked impatiently at the lid of the box.

"Let me!" Ruby lifted it off carefully and pulled out the tissue paper covering the gown.

"White, eh?" her mother commented. "That's one *you'll* never wear, then!"

"It never suited me, anyroad."

"What you went and did — that was wrong, Ruby."

"I'll never strive you down there, Mother. I know that, so I shan't try."

"Nor you won't, neither. Still — it could have turned out worse. That's a proper dress. A beauty."

"Will Father still not speak to me? Aren't these pretty? Jenny and I nearly ruined our eyesight on these little petals."

"How a bishop's daughter can take a Fallen Woman into partnership, I don't know. She's a saint, that's all I can say. And you lead a charmed life, little worm! I hope you're properly grateful to her, that's all."

"I fall on my knees and bless her daily! If I was a papisher, she'd have beads all to herself. Where is Father, anyroad?"

"He went to polish up the harness. He'll be late, too, if he's not careful."

Gemma came in by the front door at that moment. Her arms were full of wild flowers and greenery. She took in the scene at once and her eyes darted anxiously between mother and daughter. "Well?" she inquired of her twin.

" 'Tis all right, little cooze," her mother said. "The tears is come and gone."

"Look what I got!" Gemma spilled her armful on the table beside the dress. "Autumn saffron." She held the pale rosy-mauve flower to the embroidered collar of her wedding dress. "See! I knew it would go. White mullein, calamint, water forget-me-not — that's for something blue — lady's bedstraw — though I think I shall lie on something a bit more comfortable than that tonight! Comfort*ing,* anyway!"

"Gemma!" Her mother tutted and blushed. Then she turned to Ruby. "See?"

"See what?" Gemma asked.

"Never you mind," her mother said. "You'd best bunch they flowers now. Did you get lucky white heather?"

"From up the top, yes. That field used to be one carpet of wildflowers when we were giglets, but I had to search all over to find these."

"Yes," her mother said grimly. "But that was in the middle of the great agricultural depression. Us don't want that back."

Ruby slipped an arm about her mother's waist and hugged her sideways. "I missed you," she said softly.

"Guss-on!" Her mother shouldered her away crossly. "Silly great hake."

"You missed her, too, Mother. Tell her."

"I did not. How d'you know I did? I never said."

"You never needed to. Not in so many words, anyway. You dusted her photo every week, along of mine. I saw! You never turned it to the wall."

"Did you?" Ruby asked excitedly, bending down to peer into her mother's averted face.

"And if I did?" she admitted grudgingly. "I didn't want people noticing and axing questions — that's all."

"Really?" Gemma was relentless. "And so what, I wonder, was the *silent* prayer you said *after* you'd named all the other people out loud?"

"Well, it worked, didn't it? She come to no real harm."

"So why can't you just tell her you're glad she's back home — specially today?"

"And specially so's I needn't keep looking over my shoulder when I have to face Father?" Ruby added.

"Yes!" the old woman said severely. "And don't you deceive yourself he's easy. He's not soft, like what I am."

"There he is now." Gemma ducked her head and peered out of the low window. "He must have left the horse and carriage behind. Say it to Ruby, Mother — go on."

"Barney Coleman will bring the horse and carriage round to the door when it's time."

"Say it!"

The sound of their father's boots could be heard on the flagstone path outside.

"I'm ever so glad you'm back home, our Ruby," she mumbled.

"I hope I sound a bit more glad than that tonight!" Gemma said softly, for Ruby's ears alone.

Which explains why their father was confronted by both his daughters, where he expected but one — and both of them with their hands before their mouths, trying to cover up smiles. Smiles! Was anything less suited to the occasion?

For what seemed an age the four of them stood thus, frozen in the attitudes of discovery. Then Gemma said, "Mother tells us you're a hard man, Father, and even if you were pleased to let bygones be bygones with Ruby, today of all days, you'd never admit it."

If Thomas Penhallow disliked anything more than a wayward daughter who turned up uninvited on one of the great days in his life, it was being told by any female in his family what sort of man he was and how he would inevitably conduct himself. "Oh, she says that, does she?" he replied, bristling all over. "Come here, girl!"

Nervously Ruby went round the table toward him. He raised his arm when she came within reach but she stopped at the full length of it and lifted his hand to her cheek. "Strike, if you will," she said.

He reached a little farther, crooked his hand around her neck, and pulled her into a bear-hug that almost squeezed her insensible. He sniffed violently, several times, and swallowed with such violence she thought he must surely do harm to his throat. Then he pushed her away and said gruffly, "Come-us on! We dursn't squander the day like this. How isn't she in her wedding dress yet, then? And where's they bridesmaids?"

He meant Beatrice and Rosalind Collett, who were both still in Falmouth.

"Miss Divett is dressing them," Ruby told him, speaking over her shoulder as she and Gemma went upstairs. "She'll bring them on in the livery carriage in good time. Mother and I will go on with them and you and Gemma can follow in your own time in Fox's carriage."

Half an hour later, when there was less than thirty minutes to go before the appointed time to leave, they returned down the stairway and paused three steps from the foot of it — at the point where their heads, including Gemma's bonnet and veil, came into view.

"Oh, my gidge!" Their mother burst into tears and stuffed a handkerchief into her mouth.

"Well, Father?" Gemma asked, for he seemed to have lost his voice entirely.

"Why, you'm so pretty as a mabyer, cheel-vean," he said quietly. "The pair of 'ee," he added, noticing that Ruby, too, was dressed in a most stunning creation — a living advertisement for their new establishment, of course. He was not to know that Gemma had smuggled it home yesterday, ready for her to put up now. Then, recovering something of his more customary robustness, he added, "I don't think I shall be able to give 'ee away, after all, maid. You'm too damn pretty!"

Their mother cleared her throat impatiently.

"What?" he cried, rounding on her. "Can't a man use a bit of strong language on the day he gives a daughter away?"

"He can o' course," she replied. "And not just strong language, neither." She tilted her head significantly toward the sideboard.

"Ooh, ah!" he said, remembering suddenly. "Now this is a little bottle o' something washed up by the Lord on Ponsharden foreshore. I dunno what 'tis, rightly, but I had the feeling when I saw it that 'twas to be spared for an occasion like this."

Ruby turned the bottle round and peered at the dark, sea-battered label. "Maybe the letters p-o-r-t could be some sort of clue?" she suggested.

"Could be," he said, as if the thought had never crossed his mind. "What? Think it fell over that pertickler side of the boat, do 'ee?"

"That must be it," Ruby agreed. "Here! You'll break the cork if you push like that. It's clear to me the Lord never washed up too many bottles like this at your feet before."

"I should think not!" their mother cried. "We're Band of Hope in this family."

"Or you were yesterday and you will be again tomorrow!" Gemma said.

By dint of careful twisting and pushing, Ruby extracted the cork without breaking it. Her mother meanwhile brought four small glasses from the china cabinet in the front parlour — the room they hardly ever used.

"Tawny," Ruby said as she poured out four small measures. "It has an excellent colour, too — which it should be, seeing Who sent it!"

When each had a glass ready, the old man lifted his and said, "To Gemma's marriage — may it be as happy as our'n!"

Four glasses clinked; four lips puckered and sucked at the sweetness; four throats let out a grateful gasp of fiery satisfaction at the liquor's afterburn.

"May her family be as united as ours," Ruby added. "By which I mean, may that Ada de Vivian come to her senses and realize what a pearl her son has chosen."

They drank to that, too.

"May all Gemma's troubles be small," their mother put in; she looked about as if she expected the others to chuckle at this conventional shaft of wit.

"Little ones!" Ruby hissed by way of correction. "May all her troubles be little ones!"

"That's what I said."

"No, you didn't. You said, 'May all her troubles be *small*' — which isn't so funny. Little ones ... you know?" She mimed holding a baby with her one unencumbered arm.

"Weel!" Their mother burst into self-deprecating laughter. "I heard people say that scats o' times — and I never understood why folk laughed. Weel! May all your troubles be little ones, Gemma, my lover!"

"In the fullness of time!" Gemma added to the toast.

Crissy had told her all about that, too — which she would also never have learned from this dear, sweet, innocent-minded lady; a box from Nurse Rendell's postal marketing service was already packed in her going-away valise — minus the one lozenge, which had almost melted in church last Sunday.

They drained the glasses hastily, without the excuse of a toast, when they heard the livery carriage with Jenny and the brides-maids draw up outside. And they whisked them out to the scullery before a hand went to the latch.

Jenny, too, was in an outfit to take the breath away — though perfectly calculated to complement the wedding dress itself.

Ruby saw her mother's face fall — though the smile was fixed again as soon as she realized that eyes were upon her.

"What's the matter?" she asked quietly as they filed outside, leaving the bride alone with her father. "You're not feeling unwell, I hope?"

"No, cooze. Nothing like that. I just realized you'm all grown up. Look at 'ee! Standing there so pretty as a mabyer — and then starting a business ... making fine fashions for grand, high-quarter ladies. There's nothing in the way of life's wisdom I can teach 'ee, no more."

"'Course there is!" Ruby replied impatiently. "Maybe not about fashion, but about all the important things — like rearing a family ... loving ... forgiving ..."

"Guss-on!" Her mother pushed her away again. "You'll make me ruin my eyes afore it's time to ruin them!"

Peter was there in his place, with Carteret, his best man, at his side. There was the merest handful of people in the church — and if they had not taken seats on both sides of the aisle, Peter's side would have been almost empty; only a radiant Guinevere and an uncomfortable Henry Roanoke were there from the high-quarter side. Peter smiled at them gratefully, fiddled with his collar-stud, his cuff-links, his cravat-pin, then went back to smiling at the Roanokes again — as if they might all vanish if he did not constantly verify their presence.

There was a minor stir among the congregation when people became aware that Ruby was back in the fold. The fact that she and her mother walked down the aisle arm-in-arm left no room for doubt.

Peter smiled at her and nodded approvingly.

"No trouble?" he asked when they drew near.

"They're close behind," she replied. "Rosalind and Beatrice had better go up to the porch now."

The two bridesmaids arrived at the porch just in time to take their places, holding up Gemma's train. The organ broke out with the *Wedding March,* heads turned, gloved hands went to gaping mouths, gasps of wonder rose from unguarded throats, almost drowning out the sonorous chords. Peter alone, suddenly superstitious, did not turn to stare in wonder at his bride.

But he could have charted her approach to the inch, even without help from the swishing of silks. His flesh had lost none of its sensitivity to the magic of her presence; it tingled with the special warmth he always felt when he knew she was near.

"Dearly beloved brethren, we are gathered together before Almighty God and in the sight of this congregation to witness ..." the vicar began as soon as Gemma came swishing to a halt at Peter's side.

And so the ceremony rolled on in its old, stately majesty to the climax of their vows and the wonderful, mystical, life-altering words: "I now pronounce you man and wife."

But the moment the service was over, he informed them jovially that, if they wanted the *state* to recognize their marriage, they now had to retire to the vestry to complete the civil part of the ceremony, have their signatures witnessed, and collect the appropriate certificate.

Then they all piled into the two waiting charabancs — all except Peter and Gemma, who had their own beribboned Armstrong-Siddeley to travel in — and set off for the wedding breakfast at the Falmouth Hôtel.

Carteret made a witty speech — though his remark about Peter learning the ropes while serving on the *Guinevere* and then winning the race in the *Gem* did not go down too well on one of the tables. Thomas Penhallow made a dignified speech that managed to stop just short of turning into a sermon. Peter remembered to thank every single person who ought to be thanked and ended with sentiments that put a lump in many a throat and a dainty handkerchief into many a hand.

And then it was time to pose for the last series of the photographs that would be printed in the *Falmouth Packet* and displayed in pride of place in Collett & Trevarton's window over the following days.

"Where's Bea?" Peter asked as they began to shuffle toward their positions on the terrace steps outside the hôtel.

"She said something about going across the valley to get your mother and father," Jenny said.

He was on the point of retorting that she might as well have saved her legs the walk when the girl herself appeared — with not only her parents but the entire staff of Number One, Alma Terrace, too. Then, what with all the hugging and handshaking and backslapping, it required a further fifteen minutes before they were all assembled again. Peter's parents were at his side, Gemma's were at hers. But, after a couple of plates had been exposed, she suggested that she and Peter should change places — to show it was amity all round.

"I hope this means we are reconciled, Mother-in-law," she murmured to Mrs de Vivian as she took her place beside the woman. "And that we can now start to bury the hatchet?"

"To a degree," she admitted coolly. "But wholehearted warmth may take some time to develop. I hope you understand?"

"Perfectly!" Gemma assured her. "Actually, you've been on my mind a great deal lately."

"Really?" the woman responded petulantly, annoyed to notice that Jim Collett had decided to move the camera to a slightly different position for the next few exposures.

"The Irish connection, you know?" Gemma went on brightly, smiling at the sudden alarm in the other's eyes.

"I hope you are not going to ..." she began to splutter.

"Not to the smallest degree," Gemma interrupted. "But listen! The way Bridget Condron tells it ... the Normans conquered Ireland shortly after they subdued England. But it didn't work. So the English conquered them again under the Tudors — several times. And none of them worked either. So they did it again under Cromwell. And it still didn't work. They almost managed it under King Billy but they had to conquer the people all over again in the 'Ninety-Eight rising ..."

"Is there a point in this history lesson, Daughter-in-law?" she asked coldly.

"Oh! I felt sure you'd see it already — no? My point is that Englishmen have had more goes at being conquerors than any other nation on earth. They've surely earned the name! So, when your mother married an Englishman and *came over here* with him — what's the one certain-sure thing you can claim about her?"

The open O of Ada de Vivian's mouth elongated slightly; little pointed corners formed at its outer edges until it was more diamond-shaped than oval; the diamond stretched wider; the eyes started to twinkle despite all her efforts to prevent it ... the head went up and a rhythmic, tinkling sort of exclamation rose from her throat, to be repeated at an accelerating pace ...

And thus it was that, when the flash powder detonated, to fill in the shadows cast by the sun, it caught the mother-in-law and her new daughter-in-law 'sharing a hearty joke' — as the caption in the *Falmouth Packet* expressed it.